PENGUIN BOOKS

INSPECTING THE VAULTS

Eric McCormack came from Scotland to Canada
in 1966 and has been teaching at St. Jerome's
College, University of Waterloo, since 1970. His
areas of specialty are 17th century and contemporary literature.

INSPECTING THE VAULTS

BY ERIC McCORMACK

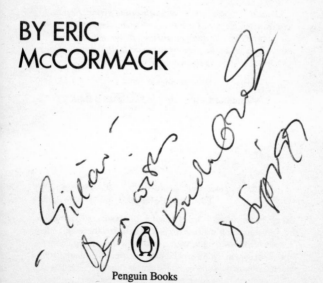

Penguin Books

PENGUIN BOOKS
Published by the Penguin Group
Penguin Books Canada Ltd, 10 Alcorn Avenue, Toronto, Ontario,
Canada M4V 3B2
Penguin Books Ltd, 27 Wrights Lane, London W8 5TZ, England
Penguin Books USA Inc., 375 Hudson Street, New York,
New York 10014, U.S.A.
Penguin Books Australia Ltd, Ringwood, Victoria, Australia
Penguin Books (NZ) Ltd, 182-190 Wairau Road,
Auckland 10, New Zealand

Penguin Books Ltd, Registered Offices:
Harmondsworth, Middlesex, England

Inspecting the Vaults first published in Viking by Penguin Books
Canada Limited, 1987
Copyright © Eric McCormack, 1987

The Paradise Motel first published in Viking by Penguin Books
Canada Limited, 1989
Copyright © Eric McCormack, 1989

Published in this combined edition by Penguin Books, 1993

1 3 5 7 9 10 8 6 4 2

*Publisher's note: This book is a work of fiction. Names,
characters, places and incidents either are the product of the
author's imagination or are used fictitiously, and any
resemblance to actual persons living or dead, events, or locales
is entirely coincidental.*

Manufactured in Canada

Canadian Cataloguing in Publication Data

McCormack, Eric P.
Inspecting the vaults

ISBN 0-14-017473-7

I. Title

PS8575.C38I68 1993   C813'.54   C93-093903-4
PR9199.3.M33I68 1993

Acknowledgements

The following stories first appeared in the following publications: "The Fragment," "Edward and Georgina," "Captain Joe," "Inspecting The Vaults," *New Quarterly;* "The One-Legged Men," *Interstate;* "No Country for Old Men," "Knox Abroad," *Prism International;* "The Swath," "The Hobby," "A Train of Gardens," Parts I & II, *Gamut;* "Twins," *Malahat Review;* "The Fugue," *West Coast Review;* "Sad Stories in Patagonia," *Magic Realism and Canadian Literature: Essays and Stories,* University of Waterloo Press.

Contents

Introduction

I heard recently about an elderly man in some gulag. He had endured solitary confinement for many years, for a forgotten political crime. The only light that ever brightened his cold cell would occur briefly at midnight every night. The guard on duty would pull a switch to turn on the recessed ceiling bulbs in all of the cells, then he would stroll along the stone corridor to check the prisoners. The elderly man was always ready. As soon as the light came on, even though the glare stung his eyes, he would force them to focus on the page of a book he was holding, and try to read a sentence or two. The guard would peer in through the grill, slide it back shut, and move on to the next cell. The entire process would take about two minutes. Then darkness again for another twenty-four hours.

For those who enjoy reading, the idea is nightmarish. To be deprived in this way of one of the major pleasures in life seems an unendurable torment. The elderly man is a heroic lover of books, his fate pathetic. What book, we wonder, is he reading? How many years will it take him to get through, say, *Crime and Punishment* (that's the one I think he has), or *Being and Nothingness* (God forbid) at such a rate?

The story of the prisoner in the gulag is testimony

to the power of the written word. In the Scottish village where I was born, I had my first experience of that same power. The people were workers without much education (a neighbour asked my mother what "definitely" meant, in a War Office telegram that said her husband was "definitely missing in action"), and they admired the ability to use words well. When I was about five or six, a letter arrived for my father from an uncle in London. After our family had read it over a hundred times — learnt it by heart almost — I got hold of it, fairly tattered by this time, and kept it with me for weeks, reading choice parts to anyone who'd listen. When that thrill wore off, I traded the letter to Phil Duffy, a schoolmate, for something I had never owned — a penknife (it had a fine bone handle, but the blades were broken). It was a fair exchange. No one in his family had ever received a private letter, and they were grateful for even a vicarious one at last.

That was my first literary transaction, a fairly mercenary one.

Till I was twenty-six, Canada was a fantasy known to me only through films, TV and books. When I arrived here, I could hardly believe the beauty of the place. Were these real trees, squirrels, cars, buses, houses? Were these people real? I couldn't keep my eyes off them, the way they moved, smiled. The men were manly, the women absurdly beautiful. Their voices were soothing to the soul and the ear of a man who'd spent a lifetime amidst the chain-saw burr and the violent glottal stops of Scottish speech. And the size of the place: on the train west from Montreal, I was convinced that one lake after another must be Lake Superior, they seemed so huge after the "great lakes" of Scotland — Loch Lomond and Loch Ness.

Eventually, in the Winnipeg winter of 1966, less pleasant realities struck. For the first time, my bare eyeballs felt the pain caused by freezing cold air. The hairs in my nose turned into wire. And that winter, my good Scottish overcoat, with its foam rubber lining, actually split in halves, right down the join at the back, when I took it off. It lay there on the floor like the broken shell of dead sea-creature. I think now I was shedding more than just a Scottish coat that day.

I've lived and worked in Canada for more than twenty years now. I'm taken by surprise when someone comments on my accent. I can't hear it any more. But perhaps my writing still has it. Many of my stories, I think, dabble in the marginal, slightly alien areas of everyday experience — such as that of the elderly man in the gulag. The need to write about them is probably like the need to drink whisky, or to take drugs, or to do all three at the same time. And the reasons for the need are as complex. The writer may be in love, or in love with words. He may be in despair at the state of the world, or at his own state. Or he may be, in a roundabout way, just celebrating, having a great time. Perhaps it's his way of shouting his hurrahs for being, at last, by the purest of luck, in a good place. For many of us who are travellers, in mind or in body, that's what Canada is — one of the last of the good places.

INSPECTING THE VAULTS

20 Short Stories

To those who cared

Inspecting the Vaults

I

The founders of this settlement have built it near the fjord, on the edge of a ravine whose sides are crumbling like stale cake. But the buildings are solid. They squat upon spacious "vaults," as they like to call them here, not "basements," and especially not "dungeons" — a most unsuitable word. The housekeepers, in particular, who live in the upper, visible parts of the buildings, stress their pride in conditions below ground. I would not deny that these vaults are "well-appointed," fitted with "most mod cons." I have inspected them all and can testify that certain comforts — a wooden frame, say, with a straw mattress; a cold water spigot, low in the cement wall; even the occasional roughly made book-case or table — are ungrudgingly supplied. Yet there are times when, no matter how generous the efforts made at muffling sound — twelve-inch-thick layers of insulation, for example, or cheerful military marches played non-stop over the PA system — the anguish of one of the vault-dwellers, as they like to call them here, penetrates all barriers, the howling insinuates itself into the ears of the passer-by. It should be physically impossible for the other vault-dwellers, underground, to hear the cry, yet invariably they all take it up. Yes, they all take up the cry, so that it mingles with the wind's constant whine down the ravine, along the great slit of the fjord, and it exposes, beyond all dispute, the fact of their unhappiness.

This, then, is the settlement, a place of many zones, built all along the ravine on land that once was forest. Each zone consists of six buildings, each with a vault, and one other house where the inspector lives. For each zone has its official inspector who lives in a seventh building that looks similar to the others but lacks a vault. The name-plate "INSPECTOR" is nailed to its front door.

The buildings of my zone (I am the inspector) rim the jagged edge of the ravine like sutures on a wound. My task is suitable for a man of retiring disposition. I inspect the vaults of the six houses once a month, then write a report which is picked up by the official courier at the end of each month, assuring the administration that the housekeepers are efficient, the vault-dwellers well looked after. The rest of the time I spend in my own house, reading, or writing my journal, for the administration discourages all outdoor activities, all movement between zones. No social gatherings of the housekeepers take place —

none, at least, to which I have ever been invited.

Inspections are necessary. Experience has shown that we cannot always trust the housekeepers. They never fail to smile, to reassure me when I inquire about the vault-dwellers. They shake their heads disarmingly at my concern, they are quick with appropriate phrases: ". . . quite happy . . .," ". . . turn for the better . . .," even ". . . soon be on the mend. . . ." If I stare long enough into their friendly eyes, however, I begin to feel uncomfortable.

The houses are a uniform brown in accordance with administration guidelines — last year the prescribed colour was dark blue. These houses have no windows, no eavestroughing. Gardens are forbidden. As a result, the untrained eye would have difficulty distinguishing one house from the other. The housekeepers, therefore, take pride in the *names* they have given their houses. They have named each house individually, burning the letters into wooden shingles they hang above their front doors. In this way, each house achieves some uniqueness in a landscape whose identifying features have been minimized. The great forest and the earth around the houses have been levelled. High brown canvas backdrops curtain the zones from the ravine and from each other. No effort has been made to tamper with the distant roar of the sea battering the cliffs of the fjord, for though that sound is irregular, it embraces all of the buildings without distinction.

On inspection days, I always begin my round of visitations during a period when no wailing has erupted for some time — "a quiet spell," they like to call it. On some days, if the wailing is incessant, I cancel the inspection. "Timing is all," was the final advice my predecessor, a man with a sure touch in such matters, passed on. "No inspector can survive if his visits coincide with the wailing. No matter how strong-willed he may be, the wailing will undermine him."

I knock, as always, first on the brown painted door of *Trade Winds* — a peculiar name for a house that sits within a hundred miles of the tundra.

The door swings open. A rather heavy, round-faced, middle-aged woman welcomes me. She tries to look surprised, although I am expected — mine are the only visits she will receive in the year. Always, I encounter the same ritual: a plain woman or a fresh-faced, wiry man, both honest-looking, both accustomed to looking honest. Always they beckon me into the dim interior with its dark mahogany furniture, its absence of mirrors. Always they press me to sit in the overstuffed armchair. Always they insist I share the pot of tea they have just, by coincidence, brewed. Always I refuse.

I remember how, on my first inspection of the zone, I expressed to the housekeepers of *Trade Winds* my surprise at the name of their house. I asked them how they came to choose such a name in such a place. The plain woman, or the wiry man, I cannot now remember which, laughed heartily, and assured me the name was the most natural thing in the world, absolutely the most natural thing in all the world. I have not asked about house names since.

The formalities, at this point, always begin to flounder, and I am aware of the anxiety in their smiles, their chatter. I tell them I must now see the vault-dweller. As expected, they demur feebly for a while, mumbling about his condition without much conviction: ". . . getting over it . . .," ". . . quiet today . . .," ". . . such a pleasant chap. . . ." All too clearly, their eyes show how, at this moment, they loathe me.

Yet I must insist. I unhook the heavy red-enamel storm lantern which, by regulation, must hang near the entrance to the vault — the stairs have no electric light. I place the lantern on the dark mahogany table and light it, holding the match steady, for they are alert to any weakness on my part. The man then peels back the worn carpet in the corner of the living room to reveal the trap door. He swings the door over heavily against the wall. Without hesitation, I step down into the darkness.

The light gradually spills over the stairs, and I follow it down till I stand in a pool of brightness on a flagstone floor. The leaden door of the vault in front of me glistens with damp. I put the lantern on the floor beside me and slide back the viewing-grille.

The stink immediately seeps out, offending my nose, the smell of dampness and decay. The man himself lies there, on his bunk, withdrawn as ever. His arm across his face wards off the glare from the caged bulb in the ceiling. He is blubbering softly, rhythmically. There is an indefinable, shapeless quality about him. His protecting arm looks like a fallen log in an undergrowth of wild grey hair and matted beard.

I do not speak to him. I never speak to these vault-dwellers even when they wish to speak to me. For my function is clearly defined: I am to inspect, to have visual association only with them. Nor am I at all sure I could survive any other way.

This vault-dweller, like all the others, is not identified by name even in our files. But though their names have been taken away, an inspector is required to be familiar with their case histories so that he may record any behaviour that might be of interest to the administration. I am not certain yet what kind of behaviour this might be, and so, acting on the advice of my predecessor, I report everything.

This man I observe through the grille is the last survivor of a great family from the North. Over a period of several hundred years his ancestors erected a man-made forest around their manor house. From the mid-sixteenth century, the family devoted itself to removing carefully each natural tree, each shrub surrounding the house, and to shaping instead copies of them — the details were not precise, but the general outlines were persuasive — made from a kind of papier mâché strengthened in the early days with wire, and, as time passed, with plastic and synthetic supports. They made hop hornbeams and dwarf chinquapins; they made bebb willows and panicled dogwoods; they made balms of Gilead and tacamahacs; they made shagbarks and bracted balsams; they made trees-of-heaven and madronas; they made arbor vitaes and witherods; they made Judas-trees. They copied even the root systems, and by ingenious engineering techniques, inserted them into the holes left by their natural predecessors.

The results were quite remarkable — a private facsimile forest of a thousand acres, utterly convincing at a distance. No seasons violated its constancy. In the fall, there were no deaths.

When our administration came to power, it denounced all such aberrations. A regiment of the élite Blue Guards, like beetles in their sleek blue fatigues and flame-throwing antennae, was sent in with orders to scorch the forest to ashes.

The incineration began, great clouds of black smoke and sparks erupting into the air, visible as far away as the capital. The forest was doomed.

What no one was prepared for was the animals. As the fire rolled towards the outer edges of the forest, like water tilted on a table, the forest animals in their thousands ran blundering right into our men. It was not the eyes of these animals, shining with unnatural understanding, that frightened the Blue Guards, soldiers chosen for their fearlessness; it was not their *polyphonic howling* (I use the report's exact phrase). No, observers say it was the shapes of the animals themselves — no one had ever seen such creatures before. They *resembled*, in a general way, all the animals one would expect to find in a forest — rabbits, squirrels, bears, deer — but they ran in a stiff, disjointed manner, and their shapes were not clearly defined. Their strangely wise and multicoloured eyes of different sizes were irregularly placed around the amorphous lumps that suggested heads. Mouths were gaping caverns situated anywhere on the body, rimmed with jagged bone that served as teeth. Legs were awkwardly located, some dangling uselessly from the backs or bellies of the animals. When these animals stumbled too near the flames, they would suddenly melt into pools of liquid, or explode like living shrapnel with a bang. The Blue Guards were ordered to remain calm and to kill every one of them.

This man lying here, when he saw what our soldiers were doing, came rushing towards them, screaming at them, "Murderers! Murderers!" They pushed him to one side, and he wept, begging them to spare at least some of the animals. The men ignored him, and after a few minutes he was at them again, this time slashing with a machete, so that they were obliged to defend themselves and club him to the ground.

The morning after the incineration, when that forest had become a vast cemetery of smouldering stalagmites, they transported him here. And here he lies, in his odd, shapeless way. He is one of those who, over the years, has never made any effort to speak, as though he thinks that by saying nothing he will disappear. Our administration hopes that one day he will speak, say something about the birds that lived in the forest — the birds that vanished during the fire, but are still seen from time to time throughout the country, startling our children as they hurtle clumsily overhead more like flying clumps of earth than birds.

The man never speaks, however, though he often weeps soundlessly, as now, and can be relied upon to join in the general wailing.

I close the grille and climb the steep stairs. I thank the housekeepers (their relief is patent, mine hidden), and step out into the chilly air before the stifling fumes of the doused lantern upset my stomach. The first of my visits is over.

The rituals will be repeated with minor variations at the remaining houses: the same rehearsed surprise of the good-hearted, untrustworthy housekeepers, the same damp descents into the damp vaults, the same heartfelt relief on all sides at the end of the visit. We all share one great hope: that the wailing will not begin. We cannot be sure what starts it, for whilst we, the inspector and the housekeepers, understand each other, we do not, as yet, understand the vault-dwellers. Perhaps it is the secret of the wailing the administration hopes to uncover.

Six vault-dwellers live in this zone. I know them all yet I do not know them. They will always be familiar strangers.

II

The second vault-dweller lives under the brown house called *Chez Nous*. He, according to his file, is an inventor, a natural genius without formal education. He can see right into the heart of machines, this small, bent man with the wheezing in his chest, looking up now from where he lies on his bunk towards the grille. Looking up, but not moving.

He is the inventor of a compact throwing machine that keeps throwing a ball for a dog to chase *interminably*. The dog fetches the ball, returns it to an open container on the machine, which instantly throws it away for the dog to fetch again. And so on, *interminably*. No, not *interminably*, only for a limited period of time, a modification brought about after one of his prototypes ran his wife's pet Irish wolfhound to death by exhaustion.

He is the inventor of a machine that feeds horses measured quantities of oats whilst the owners are away from home on weekends. One of his prototypes kept feeding the horses till they overate. The shocked owners, friends of his wife, returned to find the horses swollen and feverish. They tried to make the horses walk off the fermenting oats, but it was too late: the animals ballooned into elephants and burst. The inventor learnt from this disaster, made some adjustments and perfected the machine.

He is the inventor of a machine that rolls through meadows in the dawn light and collects exotic mushrooms. An earlier model, made for a friend of his wife, gathered, by accident, a lethal variety of toadstools. The consequences were too unpleasant to consider.

In the capital, he was renowned as a machine doctor, a man able to heal the indispositions of machines of any sort. Members of our own administration relied on him to repair their presentation antique watches.

His wife turned him in. She began to notice an excess of bloodstains on his white working overalls whose pockets bulged with wrenches and screwdrivers. One day she saw, horrified, a thick trickle of blood seeping under the door of the backyard shed where he developed his inventions in seclusion. Our agents answered her plea, coming to the house whilst he was away on business. They smashed open his shed door and fell over the raggedly decapitated bodies of a dozen German shepherd dogs and an assortment of alley-cats piled on the floor beside his latest invention, a device that looked like a guillotine, three feet tall.

His guillotine operated in a unique way: after the button was pressed, a set of double blades with saw teeth began to sink very slowly to the wooden chopping-block below. The teeth moved back and forth, back and forth, in a sawing motion. Our agents realized that when the blades — which were still congested with fur and flesh — came into contact with a victim's neck, they would very deliberately sever the head from the body, like a slice from a roast of beef.

Our agents never did find the two human heads: only the headless bodies of two of his wife's friends lay under the heap of animal corpses.

The inventor was arrested in the city and brought to the settlement — our administration feels his skills may yet be valuable to us. He lies on his back on the bunk, wheezing heavily, and smiles as the sliding grille rasps into its slot.

The third vault-dweller lives under the brown house called *Hill Top* (there is no hill). She is still young, astonishingly beautiful, with brown hair to the waist.

I slide back the grating and she looks up towards me from where she sits on her bunk. She is unsmiling as she rises, as she loosens the buttons of her dress, exposing her full breasts and her dark sex to me. She whispers words I cannot quite make out, as though she is speaking to me from under several inches of water, and fixes me with her eyes, knowing I am watching her, though she cannot see me in the darkness outside the door.

The administration ordered her to this place after one of our most respected magistrates visited, on his annual circuit, the country village where she lived. The villagers dragged her before him — according to our files — accusing her of being a mouth-sorceress, a manipulator of spells. Two village policemen held her at a safe distance by ropes, avoiding looking directly into her eyes, avoiding contact with her body for fear that their clothing would burst into flames.

The magistrate began to question her but she screamed and cursed so much she started to vomit. According to our files she vomited up: four Moray eels, each one a foot-and-a-half long: seven hanks of wool, all the colours of the rainbow, braided together like intertwined snakes; a bone-handled carving knife; a loaded .44 automatic pistol; a dozen compacted balls of cat and dog hair, mainly ginger and black; three engraved granite rocks, each six inches in diameter (she heaved them up, they say, like a snake regurgitating eggs); an unknown quantity of dung of such animals as cows, horses, and rabbits; countless pints of blood, not her own type, according to our pathologists; a book written in a language experts have not yet been able to identify; and a parchment that contained a detailed description of this very encounter with the elderly magistrate — had he chosen to pick it up and read it as soon as she vomited it up, tragedy might have been averted. He chose not to, which the parchment had foretold.

This fit of vomiting lasted for four hours. The old magistrate himself, shocked, begged her to stop, but did not know how to help her. The spectators were too terrified to touch her.

Eventually, she could vomit no more, and knelt moaning hollowly, like an animal that has given birth to a steaming litter, her eyes empty, her face lined with exhaustion.

There is no confusion over what happened next. Eye-witnesses record that, after a while, she raised her head and said in a soft voice to the elderly magistrate, "You have sucked me dry." Then she picked up the pistol from the glistening heap in front of her, and fired the full barrel point-blank at the man's stomach before anyone had the power to stop her. And she fell into a coma. All of this happened exactly as the parchment predicted.

She has lived under *Hill Top* for seven years, and the administration has made it clear she will never go free. Now she is sitting quite still on the bunk. Now she shakes her long brown hair back over her shoulder and catches it in her hand, and looks up towards me. Her eyes are smiling. She is usually the one who starts the howling. Her voice seems able to penetrate any barrier.

Always when I visit her, I hold my breath, hoping she will not begin. All that I have ever heard from her during the inspections are her seductive whispers. If I ever understood the words, would I have the power to walk away?

The fourth vault-dweller lives under the brown house called *Home Sweet Home.* Through the grille, I see him as usual, this bald-headed, benevolent-looking man in wire glasses, studying, as always, one of his frayed charts, spread out on the table under the dim bulb, his big, farmer's hands fingering lightly the fragile parallel rulers as though they were the first leaves of some spring plant.

For twenty-eight years, according to his file, in a clearing in a pine forest known for its strange sighing and groaning sounds, not far from his fieldstone house, this farmer, this kind father and husband, devoted all his spare hours to a secret task. Using only children's construction sets consisting of small pieces of plastic less than one inch in size, he built a replica, exact in all its measurements (150ft L.O.A., 40ft beam), of the *Santa Cruz,* the galleon of an admiral of the fleet in the Spanish Armada. He fitted together, without any kind of glue, according to our records, sixty billion pieces. The masts and the booms were built in this way, only the ropes and the rigging, the Manilla sheets and the chains were made from any other material.

Our soldiers discovered the galleon by accident in the dark wood during the early days of our administration when all woods, even this one fifty miles from any body of water, were being searched for precisely such objects. They spread out and hid themselves in the undergrowth in the hope of capturing the unknown shipwright.

Just before dusk, they heard someone stumbling along the path (he was a clumsy walker) without any attempt to be silent. He hummed to himself as he climbed aboard the galleon by its dangling rope-ladder. He mounted the quarter deck and entered the Admiral's state-room at the stern. Our men slinked aboard after him. They could not help marvelling at the strength and the precision of the structure. The rigging creaked soothingly in the night breeze and the smell of salt air hung about the ship as though it had just put into port after a long voyage.

They thought they heard voices from the direction of the state-room, laughing and debating good-humouredly in what sounded like Spanish. They crept up to the door, and with their guns at the ready, burst into the cabin. They found the farmer seated at a wide chart-table, poring over ancient charts, plotting out courses with parallel rulers and hand compass. He looked up at them without any show of surprise. He was completely alone.

They carefully searched the rest of the ship but found no one, not in the cramped crew's quarters before the mast, nor in the cargo hold, even though provisions of dried beef and biscuits enough to last fifty men for six months were stored there. They did disturb several large ships' rats, which scuttled overboard and disappeared into the forest. The farmer was placed under close arrest.

Our administration was uncertain about this man, feeling that perhaps he was not irretrievably lost. They did something rare, they gave him a second chance, appointing him under-watchman at the northern, sunless gate of the capital. He would be both watcher and watched.

Unfortunately, he began acting in a disturbing manner almost immediately. Each morning, as the sun laid a withered arm on the eastern horizon, he would climb the watch turret of the great wall that surrounds the city, a wall built in some forgotten fashion without mortar or machinery — we are gradually replacing it — by our forgotten ancestors. Once up there, he would screech, at the top of his lungs, "Light! Light!". The other guards would seize him and drag him away, watched fearfully by all the people who lived near the gate.

After a while, there was no option but to bring him here. The housekeepers have claimed from time to time that they hear other voices in his cell speaking to him in strange languages, but that when they open the grille, he is, of course, alone. Our administration has warned the housekeepers that there can be no other voices.

I myself will not admit to having heard anything. I know this: on some occasions at the end of a visitation, I have watched him working anxiously over his charts at some projected odyssey he alone knows about. Sometimes, after I have slid the grille shut and started up the stairs, I hear a babble of what seem to be voices coming from his vault. I never go back to check, I avoid the knowing looks of the housekeepers at the top of the stairs, and I move on to my next visit without delay.

The fifth vault-dweller lives under the brown house called *The Nest*. Through the grille I see him dangling by the finger tips of his right hand from a tiny crack in the brickwork near the angle of the wall and ceiling of the vault, whilst with his left hand he hammers a piton into the concrete. He has climbed over every inch of the vault, marking the route over particularly danger-ous pitches, fixing ropes to impossible overhangs. The vault looks like the home of a giant spider.

He pays no attention to me.

He is thin like an ascetic bird, he is an albino with a red beak. His hair is long, straight and fair. His mother, according to our file, was a West African princess, his father a Scottish ship's engineer who brought her back with him to the North-western Islands. Too alien to survive on the bleak islands, she died of pneumonia after giving birth to a boy. The father died in a storm on his next voyage, and a maiden aunt was left with the responsibility of the child.

A useless task. After a few years, the pimpled and surly boy wanted only to be alone, to clamber over the sea cliffs pounded by that northern ocean, clinging to treacherous rock-faces with the limpets and the cold barnacles.

In time, he made his name as a climber. By the age of twenty-one, he had climbed all the fearsome rock faces of the world. There are photographs of him in our files, standing high against killing blue skies.

He became a philosopher of mountains. He began to talk of "climbing beyond the peak." He came to feel that no earthly mountain could challenge him. Yet he still had ambitions. "I must make my own mountain," he told his small circle of mountain-climbing friends. He found a collaborator, an engineer who loved ingenious projects, and together they planned to build, on an island by the northern ocean, a man-made mountain that would dwarf any natural mountain. They were beginning to move in the first shiploads of granite when the plan fell into the hands of our administration. They sensed the danger and immediately transported the climber here.

Yet though he has scaled heights inaccessible to all other men, he shows no dismay at being locked in this vault. He never stops climbing. Even when he sleeps, he lies face down, his arms and legs moving incessantly, like a man groping for holds on some steep rock face. When I slide back the grille, I never know where to look for him. Yes, I see him now, hanging upside down in the corner, calculating all possible angles before he makes his next move. I am happy to leave him dangling there.

The sixth vault-dweller lives under the brown house called *Cozy Corner.* She is the dignified one, the little mayoress, sitting upright on her bunk as though ready to preside over a council meeting, her mayor's chain still around her neck, her mayor's robes a little shabby after so many years. The sound of the grille opening elicits a trained smile in my direction, but the eyes are lifeless. For many years, she was mayoress of a small

town in the western wilderness. She it was who introduced monthly festivals in which she encouraged all
her townspeople to exchange their clothing with their
neighbours and adopt each other's lives for twenty-four
hours (black face-masks, she suggested, would give the
necessary anonymity).

The festivals flourished, according to our files. For
one day a month, the lives of her people were transformed. The newly created day-long marriages were
filled with love and excitement. Men who had been
lifelong enemies often became firm friends for a day,
not recognizing each other. Parents for a day, children
for a day, found fresh delight in each other. The townspeople even adopted the occupations of their neighbours for a day: no job that lasted only one day seemed
to them intolerable.

After a year of this, the mayoress and her council,
delighted by the results, decreed that the practice
should become permanent: the townspeople need
never return to their original selves, but might forever
disguise themselves as someone else, changing roles
whenever they became bored.

Time passed. The townspeople began to forget who
they once had been, often inadvertently returning to
their original roles. In the end, all problems seemed
minor, even when the bread from the baker's would
occasionally be burnt to a cinder, or the plumber would
be unable to fix a leak. The doctor's surgery was always
deserted.

When our administration came to power, it moved
rapidly to remedy the situation. The mayoress was

arrested by a squadron of our soldiers, and an interim military tribunal ordered the townspeople to resume their former selves — so far as they could be established (our files hint that a significant number of sex changes had occurred).

The little mayoress was sent here, and so she sits, looking sad, though as dignified as ever. She sits here, without question, but is she the mayoress? Because of the confusion brought about by the festival, our administration can never be sure we have arrested the right person. Our policy is, therefore, to replace her periodically with another of the townspeople, just in case. In this way we are certain we will eventually have her.

III

Six vault-dwellers live in this zone, twelve housekeepers, and one inspector. It is not always easy for a man like myself to understand how our administration decides who should be the vault-dwellers, who the inspectors.

When I first came to the capital, with its strange walls and its watch-towers, I registered with the police, as was required. I gave them the name of the place I had lived all my life, a remote fishing village by the northern sea. They looked at me suspiciously as they copied down the information from my creased papers.

Late that night, two of their black-coated agents quietly forced the room door of the seedy hotel I had booked into, and placed me, quite discreetly under arrest. On the way back to the city jail in their limousine, with its black windows, they accused me of falsifying my papers, and said that there was no such place as the village named there. I laughed: although the village might be too small to appear on their maps, it had existed for centuries, and had a population of three hundred people of whom every single one knew me.

They did not argue. They locked me up for the night in the city jail, in a small, brick-walled private cell — quite unlike these vaults. I lay there soothed by the chirruping of the cicadas. In the middle of the night their singing suddenly stopped, and I was afraid.

Next morning the guards brought me, worn out with anxiety, to the hearing room where the jail commandant, a spruce, fat man, a retired officer of the Blue Guard, presided. His face showed no sympathy for me. I was made to stand to attention behind a worn wooden railing whilst he addressed me briefly:

"We have checked your story with all of our agencies in the northern area. They have assured us there is no such village as you claim. Your name does not occur in any of our files. You will remain in custody and will appear in court again within a few days." He rose abruptly and left the room.

I was returned to my cell where a lawyer appointed to help me was waiting, a small man with a brown

mole on his left cheek and a tired voice. I repeated
everything I had already said about my village, remembering clearly how it had looked on the morning I left,
somehow aware, even then, that it would be my last
look. I told him about the little granite buildings
running down either side of the cobbled street with
its post office, its commercial hotel, its general store,
its steepled church, towards the harbour gleaming in
the sun at low tide, the pilings erect and dry as match-
sticks, the scissor-tailed birds crashing into the calm
water, the work-boats (one of them skippered by my
own father) nosing towards their tasks like anxious
dogs swimming out of their depth, the debris of old
ships exposed on the oily sand like fossils from some
distant era.

I gave him names, unhesitating, the names of a
hundred villagers to testify on my behalf. The lawyer,
the mole on his left cheek twitching as though inde-
pendent of him, seemed persuaded and said he would
try to do something.

Two days later, they awoke me early, ordered me
to wash and shave myself, and brought me before
the commandant again. He was more spruce, more
grim than ever. Administration agents had, he said, at
the insistence of my lawyer (I could see him standing in the corner of the hearing room avoiding my
eyes, I could see his mole pulsing rapidly), gone to
the area where I had indicated my village was
located. They had not found any village, but they had
found, there by the edge of the ocean, the ruins of
what might not long ago have been a village — the

outline of a street, charred pieces of wood, fragments of brick and mortar.

More alarmingly, they had found in a nearby meadow a massive mound of freshly bulldozed earth which they feared might cover something unthinkable.

The commandant now spoke, in a controlled voice, about the house, the only intact house the agents had found, down among the jack-pines by the shore.

The house was empty, the agents had reported; but in the backyard, with its trim privet hedge and its blossoming flowers, they again found the signs of a burial on the otherwise smooth lawn. Carefully, with the long-handled shovel lying nearby, they dug till they struck what was buried. At first it seemed like a large brown leather bag, but as they uncovered more of it and tried to pull it out of the hole, they saw to their horror that it was in fact the tanned hide, completely empty of bones and organs, of a young woman. It was completely intact, in texture like the deflated rubber inner tube of a car. The insides had been removed without any sign of a scar.

As they wiped some of the mud from the area of the face, they saw that it was covered with tiny tatoo marks. One of the agents cleaned the mud from other parts of the body and they realized it was completely tattooed from head to toe with columns of words, so that it looked like the remnants of an old newspaper left in a damp cellar.

The agents rolled up the body and carried it with them in a suitcase to the capital where experts could examine it.

The commandant's distaste for me shone plainly in his eyes:

"Until our inquiries have been completed, therefore, you will be held here in the capital indefinitely. Dismissed."

A year ago, on a sparkling summer day, I was brought to this settlement in a military jeep escorted by a motorcycle platoon of armed Blue Guards. When I arrived here, I was informed I had been appointed inspector of this zone, and that I was to take up my duties immediately. I was installed in the inspector's house, handed the final report of my predecessor, and the files of the vault-dwellers.

These are dark times, I do not sleep well. I think constantly about that buried girl, I wonder why the administration has told me nothing more about its findings. I try to keep up appearances, for fear of being reported by the housekeepers because of some imagined grievance. I avoid (an easy matter here) any form of intimacy. At all costs, I suppress the temptation to join in the wailing. Do you hear it? Listen carefully. There it is now — difficult for the untrained ear to pick out at first. Yes, that's it, that high-pitched lament rising above the distant base of the sea's percussion, drifting steadily down the fjord, converging, at last, with the endless moaning of the northern winds.

The Fragment

Of all the odd things, it was a phrase from Robert Burton's *Anatomy of Melancholy* that caused my return to Scotland in the summer of 1972. A reluctant return. I prefer more exotic places and sunnier climes. After all, I put in the first twenty-four years of my life in the vicinity of Glasgow's murk — paid my dues. Some Presbyterian deity must have been tickled pink to see me slink back to that rejected birthplace to resolve a problem that stemmed from my research in a godless, new-fangled New World.

Burton's encyclopedic seventeenth-century treatise has been the focal point of my studies for some years. In particular, I have been attempting to disentangle the section of the *Anatomy* dealing with "Religious Melancholy" — an amalgam of esoteric information on the disorders that afflict the soul in crisis. Burton drew his insights on the subject from all quarters, thereby showing, for an Anglican divine, an astonishing boldness: cabbalistic and necromantic sources abound, most of which modern scholarship has traced.[1] However, a few references remain tantalizingly obscure. One of these was the bait, if I may call it so, that lured me, a rather unwilling prey, to Glasgow.

In Partition Two, Section Four, Member One, Subsection Four of the first edition of the *Anatomy*[2] (this is Burton's own idiosyncratic way of dividing his book), the author asks rhetorically:

> Could any folly exceede that of those Caledonian Eremites who must ever remayne as *Jacobus Scotus* has it, *casti, muti, et caeci*; chaste, silent, blind?

The passage is typical of Burton: the macaronic mingling of Latin and English; the arbitrary spelling and capitalization; and the rather vague attribution. Yet one might feel he supplies information enough to allow the assiduous scholar to track down the source.

Unfortunately, *Jacobus Scotus*, James the Scot, had baffled the researches of generations of scholars. Such well-known Scottish literary Jameses as King James, and James of Kelso had been scrutinized in vain for allusions to the Scottish hermits Burton

---

[1] Cf. *Bibliographia Burtoniana*, ed. James Brown, Edinburgh, 1968.

[2] Burton scholars will be aware that I quote from the original 1621 edition to avoid the many errors in the so-called definitive edition of A.R. Shilleto, 1893.

mentions.[3] The many ecclesiastical histories[4] of a devoutly religious age reveal nothing of the existence of a sect which adhered in any outstanding way to the principles *Jacobus Scotus* notes. I even began to suspect, at times, that Burton had invented the quotation and the source — as he had done on other occasions in the *Anatomy*.

Still, I felt I ought to make one last, prolonged effort to trace the reference, and so it was that for several weeks in that notably bleak Scottish summer I sat in the reading room of the draughty archives of Glasgow Cathedral. The Cathedral is an impressive, Calvinistic pile, the spiritual equivalent of the great Victorian business houses that stand nearby. Together, they carry the twin banners of the Elect.

For several weeks, I made no progress in my research, merely eliminating false trails. Then, one memorable afternoon, as I was leafing quite inattentively through a motley heap of uncatalogued sixteenth-century manuscripts, I came across an untitled fragment which I was about to shuffle aside when a phrase near the bottom of the page thrust itself at me: *casti, muti, et caeci* — and I knew the search was over. I read the creased manuscript with elation. It was a remarkable document. I present the entire fragment here, roughly translated from its stark Latin:

[3] R. Macduff, "Burton's 'Caledonian Eremites': Possible Sources," *Cult. Celt.* IV, 1947.
[4] *Compendium Historiarum Ecclesiae Caledoniae: 1200-1700*, Edinburgh, 1902.

. . . They took us in a sailboat across the Mull on
a Tuesday, seven of us, all sworn to serve the
Brethren. There was no sun that day, and the
strong wind drove us to the island in three hours.
Some wept to think they might never return to
their families. A hut stood by the jetty where the
steward met us and conducted us up to the
monastery by a cobble-stone path. There was
little vegetation. The building was made of
granite, square and strong, hewn, I think, out of
the island's own rocks. The only sound was of the
sea and the wind.

The steward led us to our living-quarters and
assigned our tasks. I was to fill the place of a personal servant who had died, to lead my master
from his cell to the chapel, the refectory, and the
lavatories. My master's name was Thomas, and he
was a young man, scarcely older than I. Yet the
empty eye sockets made him seem pitiful to me.
In the refectory I found my task repulsive, as I
helped him to eat, for the stump of his tongue
had been clumsily cauterized, and he choked over
his food. It was a common difficulty amongst
them. My master had received his castration, as
had they all, before taking his final vows. For these
Brethren had vowed to be *celibate, silent, and
blind.* I thanked God that I was not one of those
appointed to aid the barber-surgeon.

I stayed on that island for only four months
before bribing the boatman to transport me to the
mainland. I decided this on a day I found my

master on the floor of his cell, convulsed like one weeping. He heard me enter, and with a piece of rock, scratched on the tiles in a blind man's scrawl, "KILL ME." All the while, he clutched my robe and uttered piteous grunts. I could not console him. And so I made plans to leave at the first opportunity, for it was more than I could bear. Nothing will ever make me return. May God's mercy preserve me.

James

An astounding document. How Burton came to read it remains a mystery; perhaps it was more widely circulated in his day than we can now ascertain. Be that as it may, we at last know the implications of the reference.

Clearly, in that age of widespread religious fanaticism and radical ecclesiastical reform, a group emerged which felt that words alone were facile and inadequate testimony to faith. The flesh itself must bear witness. The Brethren willingly severed their manhood to ensure purity, they cut out their tongues to make easier the silent meditation of the spirit, they plucked out their very eyes that they might no longer offend. They tried to make themselves the perfect embodiments of spiritual self-sufficiency, worlds to themselves. Yet though these blind, mute eunuchs isolated themselves from the temptations of the flesh on that rocky island, the body continued to exist, more painfully, more insistently than before. They now needed servants to help the stubborn organism perform its basic functions.

James (without doubt Burton's *Jacobus Scotus*) says little, implies much. His master was a young man (so were most of the Brethren, I imagine), one who had abandoned half measures, the circumspect compromises of an ancient church, preferring the act to the word. He and his brothers, the truly strong, would make commitments from which there would be no retreat.

But then, the doubts, the doubts. Burton the ironist, reveller in the vagaries of human behaviour, must have relished the paradox: the more a man, in his search for God, strips himself of his humanity, the more pathetically human he renders himself.

Well, I won't labour the point any more. Another piece of minor scholarly detective work, you will say. Yet the image of those Brethren will stay with me always. I am a man of books, but no book has affected me more deeply than the scrap of paper that fell into my hands that day through four centuries of darkness.

Sad Stories in Patagonia

The stony Patagonian wilderness south of the Rio Negro has always been renowned as a dinosaur graveyard. But nowadays several reported sightings of a *live* Mylodon (ancestor of the South American sloth) have led to a number of expeditions from various countries bent upon capturing this last survivor of the Age of Dinosaurs.

P. Hudwin, *Monsters of Patagonia*, Edinburgh, 1903

When the members of the expedition squatted round the campfire on that first summer night ashore in Patagonia, the hiss of the fine drizzle on the logs reminded us, sitting on the wet grass, of damp summer nights in our own country, and the telling of sad stories began. The leader of the expedition, the distant gloom of the Andes behind him, spoke first. He was commander of our great endeavour to find the last mylodon alive, this cautious man, his balding skull pimpled with rain, this admirer of whisky, a man who wept, if anything, too easily.

"I am no authority myself on sadness" (we did not disagree, though his misfortunes were legendary — the aristocratic wife whose affairs scandalized society; the pistol-cleaning "accident" which perforated his left ear; the addiction to cards that led to the dissipation of an inheritance one warm night in Monte Carlo), "but I do remember seeing something pitiful when I was heading an expedition to the Mparna range in Lower Borneo.

"While we were provisioning to ascend the Central Massif, we were living in a village in the foothills. In the centre of the village a large bamboo cage stood, curtained with coconut matting. The villagers told us that a young boy, or what was *once* a young boy, was in that cage. We could all hear frightening snorts and hisses coming from it all day and all night.

"The boy was being trained as Guardian of the shrine of Rimso, the spider-god of the region. They always keep a few apprentices in training in case the official Guardian should die suddenly.

"The witch-doctors acquire these apprentices by raiding villages out in the bush where male infants have been newly born. The witch-doctors in their devil-masks descend on a village in the dawn mists. It must be an eerie sight. The wailing of the mothers is a waste of time. No one dares to defy the witch-doctors. If a baby looks strong, fit to withstand the training, they tear him away from his mother and bring him to a cage like the one we saw in that village.

"All of his bodily training takes place here for seven years. The training is aimed at completely reversing many of the child's natural physical instincts.

"They know a way of restructuring the body. It is the same method they use to train the branches of the banyan tree. In the first months of the child's captivity, they twist his upper body a little at the waist, so that the shoulders are turned slightly out of alignment with the hips and feet. Then they clamp it in position with vines and an ironwood frame, until, after a few months, the child becomes used to that posture. Then they twist him a little further, using the same clamping method for another few months, and then a little further, and so on. They do this again and again until the torso is turned one-hundred-and-eighty degrees around, and the boy's face is directly over his buttocks. So, when he bows his head, he is looking directly down at his own heels, his right arm dangles beside his left hip, and his left arm by his right hip. His spinal column is permanently coiled, like a spring, or like a plastic doll twisted out of shape by an angry child. The process takes about five years in a normal boy.

"The villagers often hear howls of anguish from the apprentice Guardian in the middle of the night. This is caused by the operations the witch-doctors perform upon him at each full moon to give him the walk of a spider, in the image of the god. They have a method of grafting four thick membranes of human flesh (no one dares ask where they find the material) onto his arms and legs. The membranes form a webbing at the angles of his knees and armpits, so that he cannot ever straighten out his limbs. He is forced to crouch, on all fours, like a monstrous spider, with his genitalia exposed to the skies, his chest and haunted face to the ground.

"I saw this apprentice only once, on the morning he left the cage. It was, as usual, misty in the jungle dawn. All of the villagers and the expedition-members were watching from the safety of the compounds, for we knew that by now the apprentice's teeth had been replaced with bamboo fangs full of spider venom.

"Through my binoculars, I saw four witch-doctors in spider-masks come up to the cage armed with long goads. They unfastened the gate and poked through the bars at whatever was in there, driving it towards the opening. Something tumbled out. A huge form, entirely covered in matted hair, lay there quivering for a moment, then shook itself and scuttled quickly into the fringes of the bush, grunting inhumanly, the four witch-doctors jogging behind it, jabbing it with their goads. I never wanted to see such a creature again, and I was glad that our expedition would soon be setting out into the mountains.

"In this way the witch-doctors train the body of an apprentice Guardian in public, to frighten the people. How they train the boy's mind I do not know. That part of the training takes another three years: no outsider may witness it and live.

"But these apprentices do not disappear from public view completely. After the final three years of training, they are often seen again. Some of the men on the Mparna expedition swear that while we were setting up camp one night in the rain forest under the mountain, a monster unlike anything they had ever come across shuffled out of the undergrowth towards them, grunting brutally, cowing the hunting dogs, silencing

all the jungle creatures. They could see insane red eyes
under a wilderness of hair. For some reason, it suddenly
stopped and slithered back into the bush. If what they
saw really was an apprentice, they were lucky, for,
according to the villagers, its appetite for inflicting
pain, either on itself or on others who stumble onto it
in jungle paths, is insatiable. Its only food is living flesh."

That was the end of the leader's story. Darkness was
eliminating the world around us, the Andes had vanished, even the nearby bushes were barely clutching
shreds of their reality. We could see quite large bats
wheeling on the edges of extinction. The leader
squinted rapidly at us, tears flooding the outer deltas
of his eyes. He slid a Mickey of whisky from the pea-
jacket under his sou'wester, unscrewing the cap with
unerring left hand whilst lifting the bottle to his open
mouth with his right.

In spite of his own popularity, the leader's narrative
did not please all of those assembled in their dripping
oilskins around that roaring Patagonian fire. Some of
these men who would rise next morning to pursue the
last living mylodon criticized the story for its lack of
relevance to their situation in Patagonia. They
demanded realism, not the kind of primitivist fantasy
they detected all too often for their tastes, they said, in
the leader's stories. Not the cook, however, with his
scraggy red beard and flaking skin. He praised the
story's "organic structure, its thematic integrity, and its
attention to the unities of time and place." No one else
was willing to go that far, but there was general
acknowledgement of the requisite element of sadness

in the story. The discussion was all very revealing, all very useful.

Johnny Chips, ship's carpenter and expedition handyman, had a sad story to tell. He rocked back and forth on a small barrel, which, because of his weight (he was a heavy man) had already hollowed a smooth indentation in the wet, reddish earth beneath him. For all his drooping moustache and long face, Chips had seen us through hard times — many a lifelike female miniature he had carved for the comfort of the lonely men before the mast on a long voyage.

He himself, however, was above everything a scholar, his cabin stowed to the gunwales with books that took precedence over his carpenter's tools. He always kept his nose covered with a little black leather cone tied behind his head with black shoelaces. When he was telling a story, his eyes would become unstable, strobing wildly in time with his words. The rasp of the wood file was in his voice:

"Thomas à Kempis was a medieval Dutchman who never went to sea, who never knew of Patagonia's existence. He was the man who wrote *Imitatio Christi*, known to us as *The Imitation of Christ*.

"He lived out his long life and died in due course, everyone agreeing that he was the holiest man of the age. Soon, miracles began happening around his grave: missing legs and arms sprouted back, eyesight and hearing were restored. He was especially good with piles and syphilis — decayed noses would grow on again."

The men around the fire did not doubt that the plight of Chips's own nose was the result of a carpentry accident long ago, as he had often assured them.

"Because of the miracles, the Church set out to make Thomas à Kempis a saint, they didn't begrudge him that. They delegated a team of specialists led by a cardinal to see to the exhumation of his body six months after his death as part of the canonizing procedure. The body would have to be completely uncorrupted to satisfy them. Even better if it had a very nice smell coming from it, a sure sign that the man buried there was a saint.

"On the day of the exhumation, a wet wintry day, a big crowd gathered, it being a Saturday afternoon, and not much else going on. Some of the people who claimed Thomas à Kempis had cured them (along with the usual quota of phonies) took the occasion to show off their shiny new eyes, or lily-white legs (no one seems to have received teeth, the most frequently requested and most rarely granted miracle in those days and since, according to researchers). The grave-diggers started shovelling the heavy earth, and after they had penetrated the topsoil, the most aromatic of smells filled all the air of that graveyard, sweeter than any rose, or even any tulip they had ever smelt.

"Then, Bump! The long-handled shovels clanged against the coffin! The diggers looped ropes around it and a gang of workmen jerked it up to the surface, all sheathed in lead, the damp clay sticking to it. It had been in that hole, by then, almost seven months.

"The cardinal ordered the soldiers to keep the crowd back. The coffin was laid out on trestles, and one of the team began to jimmy off the lid. The people were hushed now, though some of them were already praying quietly to Thomas à Kempis, hoping to impress the saint-to-be with their confidence.

"The lid squealed ajar. The cardinal and his team moved closer to have a good look at the disinterred saint. 'Oh Christ!' shouted the cardinal, cowering back at what he saw inside that half-open coffin.

"He saw that the interior of the lid of the coffin was grooved with deep scratches. That Thomas à Kempis's dead face was indeed perfectly preserved, but his eyes were bulged open. That his fingers were curled like the claws of a vulture and his fingernails were all broken with wooden splinters to the quick. That his winding sheet was stained around his middle with urine and excrement.

"Poor Thomas à Kempis. The cardinal who had witnessed the opening of the coffins of hundreds of candidates for sainthood understood. The body had not been fully dead when they buried him, but had been in a deep coma. Who could know when he woke up out of it and into his nightmare? One of the men who had been at the funeral half a year before said he was sure he had heard noises from the coffin on that day, but was afraid it was the devil's work.

"Well. That was it for Thomas à Kempis. The cardinal ordered the coffin closed and put back in the earth. No one needed to be told that Thomas couldn't be made a saint, for what curses might he not have howled in that narrow coffin? The scratches told everything. Wouldn't a real saint have been content with his fate, even if he had been buried a little too early?

"No. That was it for Thomas à Kempis. His book was marvellous, the whole world agreed. But the author was only human after all."

Chips rocked gently on his barrel, his eyes resuming their usual orbits. His story was over.

The rain fell a little more heavily now in Patagonia, and even the bushes near the fire had lost their battle with the night.

Debate immediately began over Chips's story. Some of the men were indignant over the way Thomas à Kempis had been treated, and insisted that anyone in their right minds would try to get out of a coffin if they'd been buried alive. The case only reconfirmed their worst suspicions about institutions and regulations generally. Chips rocked gently on his barrel.

One of the men objected to the *way* in which Chips told the story. He charged that, in deliberately delaying the final revelation for so long, Chips had indulged in the most hackneyed of attention-holding devices. The leader himself came to life at this point. He disengaged himself a moment from his bottle to argue that Chips ought to have begun with the ending, rather than toying with their feelings in what the leader, now weeping helplessly, considered to be a heartless fashion, and one that he himself would never have used. Chips refused to be baited.

Some men quibbled over the historical factuality of the story: in their minds, Chips ought to have made it

clear right from the start that he was dealing in speculation, at best, and certainly not in history. This criti-
cism startled one of the little cabin-boys, a great
favourite of Chips, who had been allowed to stay up
late. He said that Chips was always telling him such
stories about historical figures, and that he'd never
doubted their truth. On hearing this, a few of the men
reckoned Chips ought to be ashamed of himself.

The cook, however, had been biding his time. His
red beard challenged all opposition. He congratulated
Chips on "his refusal to be intimidated by history," and
praised him for "the intransigent penetration of his
metaphor."

This comment effectively ended the discussion.

Chips rocked backwards and forwards on his barrel,
backwards into the flickering darkness, forwards into
the light of the blazing fire, and said nothing, nothing
at all. Just smiling, in that damp Patagonian night, the
tense smile of a man not given to smiling.

Hundreds of bats, it seemed, were now swooping in
and out of the firelight above us. The leader pulled out
his pocket-watch and dangled it in the light. He
yawned.

"Time for one more," he said.

We all turned towards the chief engineer. He was a
man from the islands, who would occasionally take
over medical duties when the ship's doctor was ill (an
illness brought on by whisky). The chief's hands were
familiar with bunker oil and heavy steel piping, yet he
had the elegant fingers of a pianist or a surgeon, the
milky blue eyes of a dreamer. He spoke into the silence:

"A thing happened in my home town when I was a young boy. A new doctor with a strong foreign accent came up to practice at our end of the island, bringing his wife and four children, two boys and two girls all under ten years of age. The man was thin with a head like a snake. The wife was beautiful.

"After only a month, the thing happened. On a sunny September morning, this new doctor stumbled through the door of the police station looking very upset, and said that his wife was missing, having gone for her daily walk the day before and not come back. He had looked everywhere.

"The police made sure she had not boarded the ferry for the mainland, then organized a search for her. They searched day and night for two days, but there was no sign of her.

"The children showed up at school as usual. They did not look well, they were all pale and washed out as though they had been crying. What was most noticeable was the way they walked. All of them walked the stiff walk of an old man.

"The island children did not know them well, and were shy about asking what was the matter, thinking it must have something to do with their mother's disappearance.

"But on their second day back at school, one of the little girls, who was six years old, turned very sick and fell over from her desk onto the floor in convulsions, holding her stomach.

"The old schoolmistress made her comfortable in the staff room with blankets and a pillow and phoned her father, the doctor, to come right away.

"The little girl kept on groaning in agony, and the schoolmistress tried to coax her to show where the pain was. The little girl was not willing at first, but she was in pain and saw the schoolmistress wanted to help. So she began to unbutton her dress. But her father, the doctor, came rushing into the staff room shouting, 'No! No!' and lifted her away in his arms out into his car. He then came back for the other three children, and took them all away with him.

"But the old schoolmistress had seen enough, and phoned the police station.

"Without any delay, the sergeant and his constable drove to the doctor's house on the cliffs overlooking the ocean. They knocked, and had to wait a few minutes before the doctor, looking nervous, came to the door. The sergeant said he'd like to look at the children. The doctor at first said they were too sick to be disturbed, but had to let them in.

"All the children were lying in their beds in one large room on the ocean side of the house and anyone could see how sick they were. The sergeant knew what he had to do. He asked them to open up their clothing for him. They all did so, with groans and gasps of pain.

"He understood the reason for their suffering.

"The sergeant saw that each of those four children had a large incision along the centre of their abdomens, the sutures fresh, the wounds inflamed.

"Their father, the doctor, stood watching all of this, sobbing loudly. When the sergeant asked him why the children had been operated upon, he would say nothing.

"The sergeant took all four children to the hospital at the other end of the island.

"The resident surgeon there, a kind man, saw the sergeant's concern, and ordered the little girl who had been in the greatest pain to be taken into the operating theatre where he was about to conduct a class in pathology for some nurses. The little girl was anaesthetized, and the resident showed the nurses how pus mixed with the blood was oozing from the wound. No wonder she had been in agony.

"The resident then cut the sutures and lifted them away. He slid his fingers into the wound and groped around. He said he could feel a lump of some sort. He managed to grip part of it with his calipers, and carefully fished it out, holding it up in the air.

"All of those assembled round that table saw something they would never forget. The resident had snared in the calipers a severed human hand, dripping blood and pus. He was holding it by its thumb, and they could all see, quite clearly, the gold wedding ring on its middle finger, and the scarlet polish on the long fingernails."

No one stirred around that camp-fire in Patagonia. The night had turned chilly, the members of the expedition crouched nearer to the fire's heat. The chief engineer continued:

"That was how they found out that the new doctor had killed his wife. He had cut off parts of her and buried them inside the children. Each of the four children contained a foot or a hand. Later, the family pets, a Highland collie and a big ginger cat, were found lying in the house cellar, half alive. They too had abdominal incisions. The local veterinarian discovered the woman's eyes in the dog and her ears in the cat.

"The resident testified later that he hoped never to perform such a salvage operation again. He was sure that if the man had had enough children and pets, he'd have managed to conceal every part of her. As it was they found the rest of her body under some rocks by the shore.

"The resident said the father's workmanship was a marvel, he had never seen such skill. The murderer himself was silent. He was later sentenced to death, though his children pleaded for his life. The islanders would never allow hangings on the island for fear of bad luck. They did not object, however, to his being hanged on the mainland."

The chief engineer's story was ended. The Patagonian darkness silenced the men for a while. Then Chips, rocking smoothly on his barrel, said in his grating voice that he thought the story was well enough done, but that it was disgusting rather than sad, and therefore not really suitable to the occasion.

The cook rarely liked the chief's stories. He could hardly wait, his scraggy beard bristling, to denounce this one as "another rather boring instance of the meta-physical/erotic struggle for authenticity and freedom in daily life, and of the problems of coping with the dichotomy of the Word/word, its abstract and concrete dimensions in experience and language."

No one seemed enthusiastic about pursuing this particular line of analysis.

One of the men, a friend of the chief, tried to be diplomatic, suggesting that perhaps the story should be understood symbolically rather than literally. He doubted, anyway, that the human body could be used as a repository of dead limbs.

The chief engineer answered this last objection, and all objections in a very simple manner. He rose to his feet in the Patagonian night before the smouldering fire, and pulled the front of his shirt up from his waist. There, just above the waistline, we could all see a long horizontal scar, a white corrugation about nine inches long dissecting his pale, northern skin.

That seemed to settle everything. The leader, a man of habit, never commented on the final story of an evening. Yet his tearful eyes told all. A man of habit, he yawned, nevertheless, his ritual last yawn, his mouth bracketed by flowing tears, and he stood up.

"Time to turn in," he said. "Tomorrow morning bright and early it will be our task to ensnare the last mylodon on this earth."

Without reluctance, we all arose now, drowsy with pleasure at the sadness of the world, anticipating the warmth of sleeping bags, the shelter of canvas against the rain which whispered noisily to the failing logs. Soon the fire would be dead, and the darkness would extinguish us all, here in Patagonia.

Eckhardt at a Window

The dusty wooden frame of the window holds nine double-glazed panes of glass, three levels of three panes on top of each other. If Inspector Eckhardt stands on tiptoe on the threadbare carpet, the top panes are at his eye level. The middle row is comfortably situated for him, for he is a man of medium height. He has to stoop slightly, however, his chin on the sill, to look through the bottom row. If he stands a few feet away, the window is all one greater window, the panes look symmetrical, crystalline, even identical. But from close up, at nose distance, which he prefers, each pane is individual, unique, each discloses new worlds to Inspector Eckhardt's eye. A bevel in the double glass here, a warp there, reveal the reflections of twin, overlapping grotesque faces in two grotesque rooms, Chinese boxes that do not quite fit. As for what he sees on the outside — a warp in the pane, a bubble, a bevel, invent a city he can scarcely recognize of monstrous trees and night-mare houses reshaping themselves constantly as he moves his grey head, a landscape of plastic writhing forever in an inferno.

Inspector Eckhardt is thinking about the deaths, one year ago, of a woman and a man. He remembers the tall, beautiful, fair-haired woman he first met on that dull, November day, in this northern city. She was shivering, wearing a thin dress under a short coat. Her face was oval, a noticeable nose, green, green eyes. The lower lids were convex, half-eclipsing those two green worlds.

Inspector Eckhardt, a widower without children, a meditative man, liked the look of her right away, her voice, an innocence about her. She was long-legged, long-striding in spite of her grief — she had come to the old police station to report a death. In her deep, surprising voice, she wanted to tell him about the ludicrous accident that had happened less than an hour before. Her strange eyelids could not stop the tears from spilling out.

She was apologetic, but not about her grief. She was sorry for this: that in her confusion, she hadn't paid much attention to the location of the house where the accident had happened. It had no telephone, so she ran outside, along the street till she found a taxi, and asked for the nearest police station. And now, where was the house with the dead body? She was sure of one thing only: it was on a tree-lined street, maybe a mile or two away.

The Inspector smiled at her insistence on this fact. He did not tell her that the entire district for miles around the station was full of tree-lined streets, that it was a forest masquerading as a city. People who had lived here a long time knew their way around, knew how to see the differences between one street of trees and another. His new men often lost their way the first few times out.

Darkness was sinking in as she talked, sitting in the wooden chair in front of his desk. Through the window behind her, Inspector Eckhardt could see those very streets beginning to fade into night. It was a cold November darkness, and the lamps would hardly illumine those streets, making it useless to go looking for the house. She didn't know, in fact she said she'd never known, even the number of the house, or the name of the street. He told her, as kindly as he could, that it didn't matter much. Her friend, being dead, would be content to wait till the morning.

She shuddered. Yet she wanted to talk, and he wanted to listen to her, to watch the movement of those strange eyes, as much because of the pleasure it gave him as to help her ease herself of her burden of sorrow. He told her a formal statement could wait till the morning, but that he'd like to hear all about her friend. She should just relax and say whatever came to mind.

"A little spout of blood." She used that phrase several times. She said this little spout of blood, just a drop or two, used to spurt from her friend's forehead right between his eyebrows at least once a day. Surely that would be remarkable in anyone. The blood would trickle down his face, and he'd wipe it with a Kleenex, nervously, a horse flicking at flies. She wasn't long up from the country, and had been sitting in a bar, when he picked her up a month ago. She liked the look of him, and said nothing even when she first saw the blood spout. It used to frighten her, and it would fill him with a devastating sadness. But she said nothing.

She found out, eventually, why the blood made him so sad. One day they were sitting, talking. He was stroking, as usual, the crystal of his digital watch as he talked, intent on the nervous transformations of the little figures under the glass. He looked up and stared into her eyes. He was afraid, he said, that the blood that spouted out of his forehead wasn't his own. It was the blood of all the people he'd killed gushing back out of him.

Killings. He saw how shocked she was, and so he began telling her about them.

When he used to kill, he said, he felt as though he was watching someone else do it, a creature who looked like him, but who was on the other side of a two-way mirror. Years ago, when he was a child, he used to think it must be some other child who looked like him burying cats alive or setting them alight with gasoline, watching them try to leap out of their pain, living Catherine wheels. Then, years later, surely that was some other young boy who just happened to look like him, pushing another lonely boy into a disused canal, standing there, fascinated by the muddy gurgles, and the eventual brown calm. Or shoulder-charging an old man, light as a feather, down the dark stairwell of an apartment building and watching him crumple silently at the bottom, a broken butterfly with blood at the mouth. And even now, he could hardly admit that this killer was no one else but himself, this brown-bearded man who killed for hire and showed no pity for any of those he destroyed with his gun, his knife, his car, by fire, by water, or by other necessary means.

But one night as he was getting ready for bed, the blood gushed, for the first time, out of his head. He was undressing in front of the mirror, trying to comprehend the man on the other side of the glass, when it erupted. He quickly wiped it away, already fearful, and saw that there was no sign of a cut, not even a burst pimple, only the smooth forehead of a killer.

It wasn't long after, one night in a bar, that he met her, and they became lovers, he loving someone, and that, too, for the first time in his life.

He told her he felt he was divided once more into separate parts by meeting her. She'd somehow built a transparent wall around him, so that now his past life was someone else's, an unloved man he hardly knew.

He wanted to dedicate himself now to loving, the way he had before to killing. He wondered if love could cancel out, somehow, all of the deaths. So he began taking her to the places where he'd done his murders over the years, and they made love standing up in alleys and hallways, lying down in city parks and seedy basements, in daytime and in the night. Always, in spite of everything, the blood came.

Then, just that day, they went to a house in a tree-lined street. He'd phoned her early in the afternoon, and they'd taken a taxi to the house.

They went straight upstairs, she hardly noticing the

creaky stairs, the faded prints in their cracked frames
on the walls, to a dusty room with some shabby chairs
and a rusted wall-mirror. In the middle of the bare floor
stood a metal-framed coffee-table with a glass top.

They made love in front of the mirror. She watched
his hands move under her clothing in the reflection:
the image of the two lovers in the mirror before her,
and the feel of his hands on her flesh doubled her
pleasure.

After the love-making, he'd sent her downstairs to
the kitchen to make coffee. She was standing by the
stove when she heard a crash upstairs. She called up
to him from the hall to ask if anything was wrong. She
thought he called back that it was okay, so she went
into the kitchen again.

After a few minutes, a drip fell past her head onto
the chipped white stove, a reddish splotch. And
another. For a moment she didn't understand. She
looked up at the ceiling where a reddish-brown drip
was gathering. She knew then what it was.

Terrified, she ran out of the kitchen and up the stairs,
her feet hollow on the worn linoleum, hardly noticing
the faded prints of hunting scenes behind broken glass.
She reached the landing and looked through the open
living-room door.

The bearded man is spread-eagled across the frame of
a low coffee-table whose glass top has collapsed. He
himself is impaled upon a sliver of green glass about
eighteen inches long. It has pierced his back, travelling
on through his body inside the left shoulder-blade,

driven by his weight, slicing through his heart like a butcher's knife.

The point of the glass protrudes through his chest without tearing his green silk shirt, but far enough to make an obscene bosom. His eyes are open and he looks surprised. In the middle of his forehead, a little ruby of wet blood is forming.

She runs to him, sobbing. He is quite, quite dead.

He must have sat right down on the glass-topped table, making it cave in, explode at the weight of him. It was meant to take a vase of flowers, or a glossy picture book, never a man's weight. He must have fallen backward into the empty frame, crucifying himself, skewered by a long sliver wedged against the floor, his body making new lips to suck in the glass.

Inspector Eckhardt felt sorry for her. Her green eyes were full of tears, this tall, fair-haired woman, occasionally touching his arm as she talked. She still couldn't believe what had happened. For so long she too had been alone, sad. Then she met the bearded man and her life was full of meaning, love became a barricade against an unbearable past. And now the barrier had been demolished.

She looked tired now. The Inspector nodded in sympathy. He didn't even know her name, but that could wait. Nor did she call the bearded man any name at all. Always it was "he," with a little emphasis. Inspector Eckhardt wondered if she even knew the man's name, but he didn't ask. He'd enjoyed listening to her, and he could get all the details from her tomorrow morning.

He told her she could go home now and come back in the morning early to make a statement and help them find the house. Again, her strange green eyes filled. She said she'd no place to go, she'd given up her apartment just that day, so that she could move in with the bearded man.

Inspector Eckhardt looked at her, liking the looks of her, tall and warm. He liked the way she would reach out across the desk and touch his arm quite unself-consciously, trusting him.

It was no problem, he said. She could stay in the station's little night-shift room. He'd ask the duty sergeant to get her a cup of coffee and a sandwich. She should try to sleep, even though it was early, because next morning she'd have to help them find the house with the body of her dead lover.

After she left with the sergeant, the Inspector sat for a while, thinking about her, and the strange accident she'd come to report. He thought, too, about his own mood of contentment, that he'd be seeing her again in the morning. He couldn't help feeling that in some way he wasn't yet sure of, this was a remarkable day for him.

Inspector Eckhardt did indeed see her very early the next morning. The fair-haired woman must have slipped out of the station during the night, and when he saw her in the early morning, there was a great change in her condition.

Dawn is just breaking, a frosty November dawn in the city. The sky is a heavy sheet of opaque glass with fissures prised apart by wedges of sunlight.

On a piece of waste ground stands a huddle of men, their breath silently trumpeting in front of them. A car pulls up on the nearby street, the engine throbbing, and a grey-haired, older man in a heavy winter coat picks his way through the sparkling weeds towards the men.

"Over here, Inspector Eckhardt."

The Inspector nods to the men, and leans forwards to look at the shape lying on the iron ground. He can see that it is the frozen body of a long-legged young woman in a skimpy dress, her clothes, her fair hair sculpted in hoar-frost, a sparkling Christmas bundle. She sprawled on her back. Her eyes are the eyes of a statue, completely whitened in the frost of this November morning.

Inspector Eckhardt also sees, glittering in the occasional sunshine, the long splinter of frosted glass protruding from her belly, a lethal banner which she grips in her two frozen hands.

Inspector Eckhardt was too shocked by this death, too saddened by the thought that he'd never see the woman again. He knew he must work, and work, and work. The investigation of her death wasn't in his hands; it was his job to find the body of the bearded man, and he'd waste no time that day in getting on with it.

He and his team knocked on door after door, peered through dozens of dusty windows, examined every house that seemed unoccupied in those tree-lined streets. In vain. Some of Inspector Eckhardt's men wondered out loud whether, perhaps, her story was just a bit far-fetched. Late in the afternoon, he himself began to probe the fringes of that possibility: that there was no body, that she had made up an insane lie.

Then, just before dusk, news came in that the body had been found.

The house is on one of those tree-lined streets in the maze of tree-lined streets surrounding the station. The streets are mirror images of each other. Only a bump on the road here, an oddity in architecture there makes the difference to those who know.

The grey-haired man steps out of the cruiser and walks up the pathway of a small, run-down house. The door opens, and staleness makes a brief raid on the sharp, colder outside air. He notes the creaky stairs, the faded prints on the wall, the worn linoleum. On the dim landing, he glimpses three rooms: a bathroom with a chipped sink, an empty bedroom with a cracked mirror on the wall. Then the living-room, with another smell, one he knows only too well.

"Right in here, Inspector Eckhardt."

Through the parasitic fuss of photographers and detectives, the Inspector sees, by the light of a bare ceiling bulb, the dead man, crucified on a rectangular metal frame, broken glass all around him, his eyes wide open. His face is bearded, a thin brown beard on a thin face, his hairline receding. It is the face of a young man who has never been young. His cheeks are lined with experience and sadness.

But two things are ominously wrong. No gush of blood stains the dead forehead, one of the last things she had told him. The bearded man's brow is smooth and unmarked. But more disturbing still, he has not been pierced through his back. Instead, Inspector Eckhardt can see, as can all the others, the broad end of a long sliver of glass protruding sickly from between his legs, an obscene phallus coated in blood and excrement.

That was all a year ago, a year in which no resolution to the mystery of the deaths had appeared. Inspector Eckhardt had made sure the investigation of the fair-haired woman's death was pursued without slacking. But no witness could be found, no motive appeared. Her past was a blank, no one claimed her or identified her. The investigators dealt with her death as a murder, but they did concede that it was just possible she might have stabbed herself with the shard of glass — a very unpleasant way to commit suicide.

As for the bearded man impaled on the glass, nothing could be discovered about him except that he had just recently paid a year's rent on the old house on the tree-lined street.

Inspector Eckhardt remembered how she said they'd always make love on the scene of former killings. So, day after day he wearied his eyes with the dust and faded type of old files. He even began having nightmares about seedy crimes camouflaged by the trees of those streets. But he could find no record of a killing in that house. It belonged to an old couple who had retired and migrated to the South.

Soon the entire case of the fair-haired woman and the bearded man was interred, in its turn, in a filing cabinet. Inspector Eckhardt's superiors told him plainly that the two deaths, no matter how strange, of an apprentice hooker and a presumed lover-cum-hired-killer were of minor importance in the general scheme of things.

But Inspector Eckhardt did not forget, could not forget. For him, he didn't quite know why, the case was of major importance in his "general scheme of things." He'd stand for hours looking out of his window, a juggler with too many rubber balls, trying just once to put it all together. He was beginning to consider that his career up to that point had been a time of innocence, a novitiate. He felt that he too had walked right through a mirror, and everything was changed.

The case, he had to admit to himself, delighted him as much as it puzzled him with its possibilities, its enigmas. Yes, she was dead. But now he was high priest of his own private religion, and must create a theology around the mysteries. Part of his ritual was to meditate daily upon the fair-haired woman, at times his goddess, at times a demon. Why had the description she'd given of the death of the bearded man been so accurate yet so wrong? How could the dead man have answered her call from the kitchen? Why had she left the police station during the night? What had made her go to the waste ground to die?

Daily, he invents ingenious resolutions to the mystery.

For example, he theorizes, keeping the details sketchy, that it could be a murder-suicide. The essence is this: the fair-haired woman must murder the bearded man by somehow (this is one of the very vague parts) forcing him to sit on the fragment of glass in the old house, then she must slip away to the waste ground to stab herself in the stomach.

Or, in another version, it is the bearded man who must be the murderer. He must go to the waste ground to meet the fair-haired woman, stab her in the stomach with the piece of glass, then return to that musty house and sit down, quite deliberately, on the sliver of glass.

Naturally, in this second version of the murder-suicide theory, the order of the deaths is reversed. But then, neither first nor second version accounts for her visit to the police-station, nor for her determination to tell her story. Yet the Inspector finds something satisfying in both versions, maybe the suggestion of a doomed, perverted love, maybe the symbolism of the glass. Or maybe, it's just the enigma of which of the two is the murderer, which the suicide.

Inspector Eckhardt is also gently nursing a double-murder theory. It goes like this: someone wants to kill the fair-haired woman and the bearded man, perhaps to avenge one of his paid killings — the motive is unclear. The murderer somehow forces the bearded man to sit on the sliver of glass (again, the Inspector is unhappy with this part), somehow terrifies the fair-haired woman into lying convincingly to the police (slightly less difficult for the Inspector to imagine), and then into leaving the station in the middle of the night for the waste ground, to meet her own murderer (tricky, this part too, the Inspector admits).

Sometimes the Inspector even proposes two separate murderers, one for the bearded man, one for the girl, perhaps acting in collusion, perhaps not, although the use of the glass is so unusual it suggests a conspiracy. The flexibility of the two-murderer theory, however, is its main appeal: the permutations of which-killer-kills-whom-and-why are expanded marvellously by this simple ploy.

Inspector Eckhardt likes all variations of the double-murder theory for another reason. They exonerate the fair-haired woman, making her perhaps the tragic victim of her love for a felon. Besides, the slaying of the bearded man, an admitted assassin, is reassuring for the Inspector: justice, no matter how rough, still prowls the streets of the city.

But one thing always bothers him. Why, he constantly asks himself, did the fair-haired woman come to the station and lie? That, he still finds hardest of all to take.

For a year, Inspector Eckhardt speculated and speculated, enjoyed speculating, standing there by his window. He never lost patience at the incompleteness of his theories, for he felt confident that, in time, the whorls, the distortions, the bumps would disappear, and the clear, inevitable truth would stand forth.

Then, just that morning, almost a year to the day after the deaths, he was obliged to look at the whole matter differently. Not a mile from the station, a crew of

hydro-company men had been making routine inspections of the lines. They had been checking out an old
house when they found something grisly.

The grey-haired man, stocky in his winter coat, swings
his legs out of the cruiser. He walks along the path to
the door of the house where some men in hard hats
stand smoking and talking. It's a small house, paint
peeling from the clapboard. This house would be hard
to distinguish from most of the others in the tree-lined
street.

He pushes open the creaky door, ducking past a brief
ambush by the stale air, and walks along the hallway
to the staircase — he can hear the sound of voices
upstairs. He climbs the creaking staircase with its worn
linoleum, his shoes echoing. He notes the faded prints
on the walls. He stops on the landing, where the smell
is even mustier. In a room with an open door, a few
men are scuttling around, maggots in uniform.

"Come in, Inspector Eckhardt," one of them says,
without turning. And he sees what occupies their
attention.

The fully-clothed body of a man lies on its back in
the metal frame of a glass-topped coffee-table surrounded by broken glass. The body has lain there a long
time. The Inspector can see that the face and the
exposed parts of the flesh have turned a mottled blue.
The cheeks have partly decomposed, exposing the
bone. The eyes have dried up to raisins. The clothing
and the floor beneath the skeletal frame of the table
are heavily stained by the leakage of body fluids.

The cause of death is very clear: the body has been pierced through the back by a long sliver of glass, wedged against the floor. The glass has penetrated so deeply that the point, a deadly nipple, sticks out of the chest through the material of what was once a light green shirt.

Lying on the button band of the shirt, a rag of brown hair has peeled away from the chin. A scalp of long brown hair hangs from the back of the lolling head like a trophy. The ends of the fingers have decomposed, exposing bone, but on the mottled blue left wrist, a digital watch dangles. The angular numbers are still prowling agitatedly under their glass cover.

Inspector Eckhardt, back in his office in the station, stands by his window, late in the afternoon. He is thinking of the fair-haired girl, the bearded men, and the possibility of faceless, shadowy avengers. In the window panes, he fancies he sees them, playing a variety of parts, here stabbing themselves, there stabbing each other, or each being stabbed by all the others in a frenzy of glass.

The Inspector sighs. The darkness outside is deepening, and soon he will see with cockroach eyes the multiple images of himself reflected more distinctly in the window. Vaguely, through the double glaze, the nightscape of the city will emerge on this November afternoon, creating itself in light, the beginnings of a miraculous painting-by-numbers.

Inspector Eckhardt, standing by his window, is not discontented with the way things have worked out. He knows now that he has no wish ever to solve his mystery (he feels sure that it *is* his, meant for him alone), only to contemplate it, to delight in its complexities.

He walks slowly back to his desk marvelling again at the discovery of the second bearded man's body. Behind him, nine, or is it eighteen, other misshapen Inspector Eckhardts slide, hobble, somersault back to their separate desks. They sit down in unison. After a moment's pause, as on a signal given, all of them, with the most convoluted motions, reach for pencils, find them with an impossible accuracy, and begin to write.

The One-Legged Men

You're on their ground now. Don't be fooled by their looks. Watch out for the following: abnormal frequency of stumbling over kerbs and doorsteps, studied balance in walking, reliance upon arm-strength in getting up out of chairs, stiffness in lower limbs, hesitancy in picking up dropped things. A sure sign is one sharp crease and one dull in a pair of trousers. You can often go by shoes: in a suspect pair, each will seem well used, but one of them not by any natural foot. Remember this: whenever you note great animation and expressiveness in conversation by the use of hands and upper body, you're probably on to something.

From "A Description of Muirton," James R. Ross, Ayrshire Today (Glasgow, 1950)
Muirton, East Ayrshire, nestles in a treeless valley beyond which the Lead Hills stutter towards the Border with England. It is one of those villages that cluster around a coal-mine. The mine itself

looks, to the visitor, like a suppuration from the bare, but otherwise healthy flesh of the timeless moorlands. Yet, in the usual paradoxical way, the huge slag-heaps of these ugly mines that abound in this part of Ayrshire may also be likened to breasts that nourish a breed of men and women capable of great physical tenacity and intellectual vigour. Like the scrawny heather that grows all around, these people have their seasons of beauty.

The boys of Muirton don't like school. The boys of Muirton don't like poetry. The boys of Muirton do like: playing soccer; trout fishing; pitch-and-toss. So far as talking goes, they like: talking about girls; talking about getting a job in the mine when they're fifteen. The six-times-a-day hoot of the mine's siren is like the Pied Piper's tune to them. It calls, coaxes, cajoles them into an exclusive abyss.

From Annals of the Modern Ayrshire Parish, *Rev. James O'Connell (Dumfries, 1979)*
The day that brought Muirton fame for its excess of one-legged inhabitants occurred during my first year as minister there. It was a day not blessed in its beginnings so far as weather was concerned. A murky morning carried the threat of rain — the Lead Hills, so appropriately named, in my view, were hidden in mist —even though summer had ostensibly begun. June in Muirton, I was to learn, is only slightly warmer than January. The day-shift

workers, many of whom were my parishioners, set out along the shrub-lined roadway to the mine at about six o'clock. There were fathers, sons, uncles, nephews, cousins, in truth "by the dozens." On their way, they passed the homeward-bound night-shift workers, all black-faced, even the young boys — God bless them — bound for dinner and bed, their world topsy-turvy. No one, of course, had any premonition of the trial some of them were to undergo that very day in fulfilling the mysterious will of their Maker.

The men and boys of Muirton. They stand in clusters at the gates of the mine elevator. The gloomy tower creaks eerily above them. A giant Ferris wheel. They await the daily, commonplace, infernal descent.

From Coalminer to Honourable Member, *Tom Kennedy, MP (Glasgow, 1946)*
The first few times you went down in the cage it scared the wits out of you. Your stomach never seemed to get back to its usual place. Some of the new boys used to wet their trousers and everybody would make wisecracks about the poor lads for many weeks afterwards. But we all got used to the cage eventually, and most of the time it never crossed your mind how far down you were going —1,000 or 10,000 feet, it didn't make any difference. As you went deeper, the air used to get warmer. Even in the middle of winter, the sweat would be lashing off you.

What I miss now — I wish we had some of it
here in the House of Commons — is the great spirit
we used to have in those days.

This one jokes, this one laughs, this one yawns, this
one spits, this one whistles, this one day-dreams, this
one scratches his neck, this one turns his head and
looks up to the shroud of hills. The final squad enter-
ing the cage.

From The Ayr Daily News, *July 4*
MUIRTON HORROR UPDATE

No one knows yet for sure how the disaster happened that shook this little Ayrshire town yesterday morning. One thing is certain, hardly a family
has been spared.

Experts from the National Coal Board are examining at this very instant the wrecked elevator cage
at the bottom of the shaft to determine why the
braking mechanism failed. They expect to have a
report ready for next month's Inquiry. However,
they reconstruct the tragedy as follows:

At approximately 6:40 A.M., forty men and boys,
the final day-shift squad, entered the cage for their
descent to the coal face. Some time in the next
few minutes as the cage descended to the 4,000
feet level, they would hear the alarm bell and see
the flashing red light, warning them that the cage
was out of control.

At this point they would take the normal pre-
cautionary measures. Inspector David McCann,

54, of the Miners' Safety Board, describes these: "The miners are drilled once a week in safety procedures. In the case of a cage going out of control they all know what to do. They have to reach up and grasp firmly one of the leather hand-straps attached to the roof of the cage. Then they lift one leg off the floor.

"In this way, with any luck, depending on how far the cage has to fall, they might save one leg when they hit the bottom even though the cage comes down quite hard."

This afternoon I met two of the rescue team who were present when the smashed cage was opened. They were, Orderly John McCallum, 43, and Orderly Tom McLeary, 29. McLeary had no comment to make, but McCallum gave me this brief reaction:

"It's the worst thing I've seen in years at this job. It's hard to believe anybody survived it. The cage was all twisted so we had a very hard time with the acetylene torches getting inside it. We could hear noises so we knew some of them were still alive. When we got the front off, it wasn't easy to know what to do, it was such a sight."

It is now established that there were thirteen survivors out of the forty, so it seems that the safety measures worked in part. At the point of impact, the leather handstraps absorbed some of the shock, but then snapped — that was to be expected. The rest of the body-weight was then transferred completely to the supporting leg. That leg was smashed immediately to pulp.

The Jury is Out. The Jury is In. Boards of Inquiry, Commissions of Inquiry, Industrial Tribunals, Insurance Adjustments, Compensation Committees, Medical Examinations, Burdens of Proof, Amendments to Safety Subsections, Revised Regulations, Compulsory Hard Hats.

From "Your Letters," The Edinburgh Times, *November 6*
Sir,
I would like to add some pertinent data to your recent correspondence on the issue of the physiological appearance of any part of the human anatomy upon its being smashed to a pulp.

As one of the physicians who examined the victims of the recent Muirton disaster, I feel qualified to comment with some authority upon the effects on the lower limbs of what is now called "the pulping phenomenon."

I would like, first, to dispel the speculative notion that pulped limbs after a massive fall look, as one of your correspondents hypothesised, "like minced beef à la Sweeney Todd." Nonsense. Aside from the inordinate amount of blood on the cage floor at Muirton, the signs were much less obvious.

Let us consider for example the pulped limbs of the thirteen survivors. It appears that at the moment of impact, the femur, patella, tibia, and fibula disintegrated, though, in one case, the femur was pushed up into the lower intestinal tract causing severe, but not fatal injury.

But, after the disintegration of the bones, the limbs appear to have sprung back into their accustomed positions with skin and muscle seemingly intact. At first glance, therefore, it was impossible to assess the damage. It was when the Orderlies tried to move the bodies they discovered that they were attempting to lift limbs that were completely gelid. Immediate amputation was, of course, absolutely necessary.

I might add that, in the cases of the dead miners, one or both legs of each had been similarly traumatised. Why death resulted instantly in their cases, even though their upper bodies remained quite functional, is worth, surely, of some research.

I trust these remarks will be of help in settling the issue,

Sincerely,
J. Blair, MD

Tell me, do you know? can you say? would you mind? could you try? got the message? get the picture? walking on four feet, and two feet, and one foot, and three feet, the fearful, fearful beast.

Bits and Pieces, Odds and Ends
1. A survivor, one year later: "I'm going to carry on living in Muirton. At least when I'm here, people don't look at me as if I'm a freak."

2. A Muirton children's skipping song:
> Skip me one,
> Skip me two,
> Tell me what does your daddy do?
> He lies in his bed,
> And eats fried egg,
> Because he's only got one leg.

3. Stephen Neil, Headmaster of Muirton Primary School: "I know the families of most of the survivors. I get the impression that some of the men and boys have never recovered: they're under psychiatric care for constant nightmares and depression. And impotence."

4. A survivor, one year later: "Did you ever hear tell that a drowning man is supposed to see his whole life passing before him? I often say to the wife that's what happened to me as we went down. I even saw my grandmother, and she's been dead for twenty years now."

5. A survivor, one year later: "I never thought I'd have to do it. Even when we practised the leg-drill, we all used to laugh, because we thought, 'if we ever have to rely on this we'll know we're dead men.' Big Jock McCutcheon used to say, 'Do they think we're all daft? Standing on one leg like a chicken is no way to die.' "

6. A survivor, one year later: "I couldn't make up my mind which leg to give up."

7. A member of the rescue team: "I think they all hoped they were dead."

Knox Abroad

The voyage is over. John Knox stands, sways a little, with Clootie, his cat, on the forest-ragged banks of the river (more like the shore of the ocean), on land at last. It is October, and this is an alien place. He looks around and smiles. Nothing has changed, even after a wilderness of sea. His shoes touch dead leaves, the discreet vomit of the trees. He observes the paralysis of the rocks. The winds still blast down from directly above, threatening to hammer him, like a stake, into the ground, drive him under, bury him alive. Every night of the voyage, he saw (he has seen the same thing for twenty years of nights) the planets and the stars desert, rush centrifugally away into the outer universe, as though fleeing a plague. In the mornings, as always, the sun searched him out, singed his ever-so-delicate grey skin. Again he smiles. Even amongst the trees there is no refuge. He bends over and lightly strokes Clootie's black coat. Together they turn and walk along the beaten path, fade into the forest gloom.

"An etymological footnote on the name *Canada*.
John Knox, the founder of Scottish Presbyterian-
ism, was apprehended in 1547 by the French and
sentenced to serve as a galley-slave in the French
navy. After eighteen months, he escaped. A
Breton legend, however, suggests that before
escaping, he served some months on an exploration ship to New France. This is not impossible.
A less reliable tradition supplies the information
that, many years later, after his return to Scotland,
one of his disciples asked him for his opinion of
the New World, which had now become a refuge
for the persecuted. Knox is said to have replied,
'I *canna dae* wi' it, I *canna dae* wi' it,' thus, albeit
inadvertently, giving the country its name."

> M. Gobert, *Mémoires des Ecossais,*
> (Geneva, 1897)

In the galleys he was supposed to be the slave, but he
was master, he knew it and they knew it. The same on
the expedition ship. The mate lacked the nerve to make
him holystone the decks alongside the others, for fear
of his tongue. No ears could endure the monstrous
words (predestination! election! reprobation!) he
would hurl against them. Still, he was no burden: when
the barber-surgeon drowned in a storm, two weeks out
of St Malo, Knox took his place — no one else had the
stomach for the job. Though he loathed the unbearable closeness of other living bodies on the ship. Give
him solitary confinement, a narrow dungeon, and he
would have been more content.

The captain, knowing his prowess as a controversialist, tried often, on this tedious journey, to entice him to his cabin for dinner, to dispute on matters theological. Knox spat at him as an idolator like all the others, and refused the bait.

Knox jettisoned the statue of the Virgin. It was on a Sunday, and the crew assembled for the weekly statue-kissing, a good-luck ritual. Knox grabbed the statue from its perch by the mainmast and hurled it, head over tail, halo of stars over serpent's head, out into the ocean. Where it sank like a stone. The sacrilege horrified the French sailors, but they kept their hands off him. He joked to his cat: "The Queen of the Sea cannae swim, Clootie." But they kept their hands off him.

Physically, Knox was scrawny. He was an aggressive talker, except to his cat, Clootie, a black creature, sleek, with wicked eyes. The cat was a growler, a hisser, and in the minds of the sailors, was Knox's familiar demon. Knox, too, was a growler, but never growled at Clootie:

"Well, Clootie, my wee man, did you ever see a country so naked of churches? It won't do. I can already imagine a forest of steeples along this river-bank. Churches could make this obscene river a lovely thing." (Knox could speak perfectly good English, ungnarled by "ach's" and "dinnae's," whenever he felt like it.)

The cat would purr its admiration of his voice, winding itself around his narrow shins. The man would squint about. If they were alone, he would allow the rubbing to continue, melting into it. If someone was watching, Knox would boot the cat out of his way, its tail swishing angrily.

Thank Christ I am off the ship at last. That fat pig-wife of the captain's spying on me everywhere with her pig eyes. The only favour I ever did for her was to tear the dead baby out of her by the feet. Now she wants me. The black sows farrowing on my father's farm sickened me less. And thank Christ to be out of that stinking fo'c's'le. Filth and corruption everywhere. Men opening their breeches to show off the size of their organs. Ship's boys acting as their fancy-women.

But during the storms, the truth flared up in them. Fear bulged in their eyes, and I taunted them all, every single one of them, with the burning fires of hell. I was on deck during the great storm in mid-ocean, admiring the fury of the waters. They were trying to lower sail when a boom snapped, the sail ripped, and sheets flogged everywhere. A young sailor, the worst balls-strutter of the lot, caught his arm in the grip of a ratchet. The bone was half-broken, like a sappy branch, and all the flesh torn, the muscles severed. I took the surgeon's saw and sawed the arm away from his jerking body, then I carried him below and dipped the stump in boiling tar. For days, I was the one to bite off his rotten flesh and suck out the pus. I even swallowed it if they were watching. They couldn't match me. As long as I can remember, death and sickness, sickness and death have been my allies.

Now the voyage is over. This was a good place to land. All around me, beautiful sites for churches, plain churches, with plain cemeteries, no flowers if I can help it. I have planted already the men nobody else would touch, who died of cholera on the voyage. I've

manured the soil with corpses the way we did with the
dead cattle on the farm. I buried their sad priest, sick
since we left France. Only Clootie and I attended his
funeral. We commended his body to the devil. Back on
the ship, I cleaned the shit and the vomit of the sick
from the decks. It gives me an advantage over them all,
they are so concerned about staying alive.

The sailors presented the natives with pieces of
coloured broken glass, brown wooden beads, pieces
of rope, and scraps of cloth. The natives seemed
uninterested. One gift only, an iron knife, they all
admired. The captain insisted it go to the chief,
Quheesquheenay, to win his favour. They offered the
natives pieces of Breton cheese, quite rank after the
voyage, which the natives, in turn, gave to their dogs;
fried chicken legs (chickens had been kept aboard),
which the natives relished; boiled chicken eggs, which
they spat out. Wine they treated as contaminated water,
and could not understand why the sailors drank it when
there was so much fresh water around. They munched
cautiously on some lumps of black bread from the
captain's pantry.

The natives gave little in return, no gold or silver,
which was really what the sailors hoped for. They did
give them amulets full of rats' giblets and bones. The
sailors objected to the smell and threw the amulets into
the river while the natives looked on. They invited the
crew to eat a sort of stewed beef that smelt very appe-
tizing, but the sailors were afraid it was made of human
meat. Some of them vomited spontaneously at the very

sight of it. The natives watched all this impassively.

Finally the chief's council offered, as a special treat to the captain, a bowl full of fresh assorted testicles of forest creatures, from the huge rubbery testes of the moose and the bear to the tiny soft beads of rats and rabbits. The captain hid his nausea and diplomatically accepted the gift. He took it back with him aboard ship, and after dark, flung the testes overboard. They caught in an eddy, and floated around the ship for days, swelling grotesquely till they burst and sank.

The male natives were tall, for the most part, well muscled, dressed in neatly stitched animal skins. Sickness was unusual amongst them. There were no wens, no leprosy, no bloody flux, no stopping of the stomach, no gout, no strangury, no fistulas, no tissicks, no spotted fever, no headmould, no shingles, no rickets, no scurvy, no griping in the guts. There were no congenital deformities. There were no pest-houses.

The skin of the warriors was bronze and clear, except for battle scars. They had flashing dark eyes, and they all seemed to be superb athletes, capable of feats the puny Bretons could only envy. They could lope with ease along tangled forest paths, hurl their spears gracefully, paddle their bark canoes at amazing speeds. They wrestled with ferocity, not hesitating to break on opponent's limb if the opportunity offered.

The natives had heard about the French from neighbouring tribes who had been visited by earlier ships, but this was the first time they themselves had seen the strangers. Clearly they were disappointed, for they found it impossible to respect men whose physical prowess was so defective. But they did respect the power of the arquebuses and the ship's canon, which the Frenchmen quickly demonstrated.

The French sailors learnt to be careful in their approaches to the native women. A warrior's wives were private property and it was death for a stranger to tamper with them. All the other women were available to all the tribe, and were quite free with their sexual favours, even widows and grandmothers. Which was as well for the Frenchmen, since the young women, golden-skinned and lithe, would have nothing to do with them. They had the bodies of dancers. Their clothing was provocative, their breasts dangling loose, their nipples erect when excited, which was often. Their skirts were split to the waist. When they ran, their hairless crotches were visible. Often, while they were relaxing, or were just sitting down, they would finger their groins unconsciously, or sometimes consciously if they saw the Frenchmen squinting at them.

At night the warriors would flit around their bonfires, whooping fearsomely. Or they would stretch on beds of skins moodily sucking on their tobacco pipes with glassy eyes. If the visitors were present, there would be an air of tension. The chief of the tribe, Quheesquheenay, would sit there on his deerskin mat, making no effort to communicate, staring intently at the Frenchmen. The solemn beat of drums would resound, echoed by other drums great distances away across the river.

"Oomhowoomareoomtheoomaliensoom?"

"Oomtheyoomstinkoomouroomvillageoomoutoom."

"Oomkilloomthemoom."

"Oomweoomunlikeoomyouoomonlyoomkilloomwor-
thyoomenemiesoom."

"Oomcutoomthemoomupoominoompiecesoom."

"Oomevenoomifoomweoomcutoomthem
oomupoominoompiecesoomandoomsewedoomall
oomtheoombestoompartsoomtogetheroomweoom-
stilloomwouldoomnotoomhaveoomaoomrealoom-
enemyoomforoomtheiroompenisesoomareoom
likeoom wormsoom."

"Oomuseoomtheiroompenisesoomtooomcatchoom-
fishoom."

"Oomtheoomfishoominoomouroomriveroomareoom-
toooomsmartoomtheyoomknowoomwormsoomare-
oomnotoomthatoomsmalloom."

I have the heathen under control. They despise the
others but they fear me. I notice the young braves,
showing off to each other throwing their spears at
targets, grow silent even when Clootie appears
amongst them. Their shaman is terrified of the cat. I
am sure he has tried all his curses against me and
Clootie in vain, since the time when the daughter of
the chief, Quheesquheenay, developed a terrible fever
and was clearly going to die. The shaman couldn't cure
her, he could only make things worse. The chief was
desperate and asked if I could do anything. They
believe that those who are indifferent to death have
great power over life.

What makes John Knox tick? A question he sometimes asks himself. He tells himself this story:

Once upon a time early in the sixteenth century, a little Scottish boy lived on a farm near Edinburgh. He was a quick-witted little boy, too smart by half for his school-fellows, who hated his guts. He possessed certain time-honoured schoolboy traits: he liked to pluck the legs and wings from insects to see their reactions. He possessed, too, certain other traits not so time-honoured: with an axe, he enjoyed cutting the legs off live rabbits and chickens. From time to time, he would take pleasure in dropping a dead mouse into his mother's stew. On such occasions, he would play sick, and reap the double benefit of watching the others eat the stew, and of being himself considered rather delicate. This gained him additional attention. In short, that was the kind of boy he was. A practical joker.

He had many sisters, some of them quite attractive, and no brothers. His attitude towards his sisters was somewhat ambivalent. He hated their guts and would steal their make-up and pinch their arms quite cruelly. But, he liked to peep at them before bedtime, through a crack in his bedroom wall, admiring the breasts and pudenda in their various stages of development. Yes, he found that rather a stimulating part of his day.

His mother and father, it should be noted, were honest-to-goodness farmers, and regular church-goers.

(John Knox always likes the story to this point.)

One of the practical jokes the boy liked to play concerned rats. He would capture rats in a wooden box.

Then, when no one was around, he would head on
over to the pigsty, and call out the pigs. There was a
small round hole through the wall beside the feed-
troughs. The boy would chase the rats out of the box,
into this hole, and right into the mouths of the pigs.
The pigs had grown fond of such a regular treat. This
was one prank the boy really enjoyed.

One thing leads to another. It happened that he was
looking after his littlest sister, three months old, while
his parents were making jams inside the house. As he
wandered past the pigsty, carrying the baby, he wondered how the pigs would deal with a tiny pink infant,
rather than tiny pink rats. He gently laid the baby on
the muddy floor of the sty, and called out the pigs. Well,
who knows what goes through a pig's mind? Did they
even notice the different proportions, the different
texture? Four huge porkers seized the baby limbs, and
ripped her to pieces, regardless of her screams, and
swallowed her in great slobbering gobbets.

The howls of the baby and the snorting of the pigs
attracted the attention of the honest father and mother,
and they came running down from the farmhouse to
see what was going on. What they saw horrified them.
They saw the bloody mess on the sty floor. They saw
their little boy looking at them apprehensively.

At that very moment, just then, quite as if by design,
the boy found religion. As soon as he saw the genuine
anguish on his parents' honest faces, he began to shout,
as if by instinct, "O Jesus, O Jesus," and, jumping in
amongst the pigs, kicked and slapped at their snouts,
shouting, "Begone, Satan, begone," an expression he

had often heard from the preachers at the church to which his honest parents took him each Sunday. His father grabbed him by the coat and pulled him out of that sty. The boy said, "I was takin' the babby doon for a walk, when a great hairy black beastie wi' fire comin' oot o' its mooth and its ears pulled the bairnie oot o' ma airms and threw it over the wa' to the piggies."

He could see that his parents already half-believed him, certain that no human child would be capable of feeding his baby sister to pigs. The boy understood then that all the quirks in himself he had misguidedly thought to be unnatural and perverse were really, if properly perceived, signs of a religious disposition. And so he decided that, as soon as he grew up, he would become a Reformer. And he did. His parents became, in due course, very proud of his achievements, though he sometimes thought he could see a sceptical glint in their eyes. But they all lived happily ever after.

Such is the tale John Knox tells himself: he knows it doesn't cover all the bases, but it is generally quite pleasing. One thing still surprises him after all these years: when alone, religious matters never enter his head. He wonders if the other Reformers are the same, but hesitates to ask.

With my pussy-cat, Clootie, I went to her tepee. As we entered, a sweaty young man left, hitching up his loin-cloth. The tepee was all shadows and foul smells, the shaman's smoke. The girl lay on a frame bed of stretched skins, staring at the roof. She was naked, and

she too was covered in sweat. Her legs were parted
and her hand was at her crotch, fingers stroking. The
chief, two of his councillors, and the shaman, stood
beside the bed. He is a mouth-shaman, and was leaning
over her spitting some green mixture into her mouth.
I saw her spit most of it right back in his face, and vomit
up the rest. The shaman looked fierce with his red and
white stripes, but his eyes were anxious. He shook his
rattles and howled, but they all knew, and he knew, he
had failed. The girl looked over at me and smiled, the
shreds of vomit around her mouth. She lifted her hand
from her crotch, and stretched it out to me, her fingers
glistening.

She had sweated out her disease, her *furor uterinus*
for days, and she would die soon, for they did not know
how to save her. All they could think of was to supply
her with men to satisfy her deadly appetite and to trust
in the shaman's superstitious mumbo-jumbo.

"That hill, over there by the sacrificial stakes, would
be a good spot for a church."

"Ah, yes."

"The long-house would be all right as a temporary
church, but they'd have to strip away those ornamental scalps and skulls."

"Indeed."

"If we burnt down the whole forest on the penin-
sula and ripped up the weeds and the flowers, and anything else alive, we could build a whole set of churches,
one for every day of the week. Nothing fancy, no orna-
ments or any of that kind of thing, just plain seats and

a stool for the preacher. Cats would be welcome. We'd have plain cemeteries with picket fences for each church.

"Interesting."

"How about a church under that waterfall? Made of fieldstone, very plain. You'd have to carry an umbrella for going in and out. A nice effect."

"Quite so."

I told them I must have absolute freedom in the treatment of the girl or I would do nothing. I ordered the shaman out with his barbarous cures. He mumbled at me, cursing me, no doubt, in his heathen way. I wouldn't let him away with that, but I replied moderately, damning him only according to the Scriptures. Clootie, as ever, snarling at him with hunched back, terrified him, and he hurried out of the tepee, along with the chief and the others. I called in two of the older sailors to help me begin this holy work.

First we forced her hands away from her groin. We lashed her hands and her feet to the sides of the crib to stop her thrashing about. She sweated even more and began screaming. I opened my Bible in my left hand and, from under my coat, I unsheathed my whip, which I had brought with me on purpose.

Everything was ready. I ordered the sailors to stand outside the entrance of the tepee, and allow no one to enter. I began to read from the Book of Psalms in a loud voice, uncoiling my whip slowly before the patient's eyes. Clootie jumped onto the bed and rubbed himself against her.

My wounds stink and are corrupt because of my
foolishness.
For my loins are filled with a loathsome disease:
and there is no soundness in my flesh.
Thou shalt break them with a rod of iron.
The heathen are sunk down in the pit that they
made.
Upon the wicked thou shalt rain snares, fire and
brimstone, and an horrible tempest: this shall be
the portion of their cup.
Then did I beat them small as the dust before the
wind.
And I smote his enemies in the lower parts:
I put them to a perpetual reproach.

I began to read the verses a second time, more loudly.
But this time, after each verse, I lashed her naked body.
She screamed as the skin lifted, the welts rose across
her breasts. Then I aimed lower on her body, across
the thighs and the open vulva. She stopped screaming.
She gave great gasps and whimpers, and it was my turn
to roar. I shouted the verses and lashed harder and
harder. Her body convulsed, and, at last, the demon
rushed out between her legs in a liquid gurgle. Clootie,
who had been rubbing himself against her all through
this, howled, and his hair stood on end. I myself was
roused by that evil in her. To ensure it was completely
gone, I lashed her several more times. Then I put my
hand cautiously towards her groin, fearful of the bite
of the beast. With my fingers I could feel nothing at the
entrance, so I slid them into the round, moist cavern.

Still nothing to be afraid of. Unsatisfied, I inserted the long sweaty handle of my whip, turning it, moving it in and out, in and out, the sure way to scrape any remnants of the demon away. Her eyes glazed as she looked up at me, thankful for my precautions. I jerked the handle up and down rapidly, she convulsed again, sighed, and immediately fell asleep. I too was drained by my exorcism, but satisfied. I knew that all was well.

I sat for a moment to catch my breath, then I opened the tepee flap and let the chief and his men back in. I sensed their revulsion as they saw on her body the stripes of the lash. Yet she was in a deep, untroubled sleep and her fever was broken. I expected no thanks and received none. The shaman untied the ropes, and covered her sleeping body with skins. I told the chief that somebody must administer the same cure to her each time she fell into that fever. I told him, though I am not sure he understood, that he must build churches, churches, churches, in memory of her cure.

"You tell us we should not eat our enemies, yet the captain says that in France, he and his men eat Jehovah daily. Explain this."

"Filthy heathen, spare me your quibbles."

"Before original sin, did men still fart and shit after they ate?"

"Filthy Heathen, you do not understand."

"What good is heaven if all our tribe do not go to heaven? What good is heaven if my wives and my sons and my dogs are not in heaven with me? What good is heaven if my enemies are not there so that we can all reminisce together in heaven about old battles?"

"Filthy heathen, cease your blasphemy."

"How can you hate the women and yet desire them so much at the same time?"

"Filthy, lying heathen. You are one of the damned."

How ugly the aliens are, their skin is wormy white and marred by scabs. Boils sprout on them overnight like forest toadstools. Their clothing is clumsy and heavy. Their minds are a mystery. They adore their Book, a collection of dead words. We would have annihilated them long ago, but for their guns. We have never before faced enemies who were contemptible as men, yet could defeat us in battle because of their weapons.

Their shaman, the little man, Knox, is the living death. He has made a few converts amongst our people, even my own daughter. Pain was his gift to her. The captain, a simple man, admits that many like Knox will come to our hunting grounds in the future. Our own shaman has dreamed, for three nights, the end of the world.

"I am curious about the function of your shamans across the ocean. Here, our shaman prays for good luck, curses bad luck, sings songs and tells good stories at our feasts, blesses the penis and vagina of the newly-weds, teaches the children how to bind arrows well, how to be brave in battle. He defies the demons of darkness; in times of famine, he fasts and moves his tepee to the forest so that the rest of us may eat well and live in company in the village. He weeps for all the dead, he rejoices at births. He loves the river, the trout, the moose, the eagle, the pack-wolves, the musk-rats, the morning sun, the snow in winter. He is the friend of our friends, he admires the ferocity of our enemies. Nothing that exists disgusts him."

"He is a filthy heathen fiend and is already damned."

Their stay amongst us has lasted only two moons. They must sail away before the winter storms. They have wiped out all game within six miles of the village — we will now face a hard winter. Some of our children have died of a cough we have never known. As a final gesture, the aliens say they will kill for us, with their guns, our enemies in a neighbouring village. I have thanked them and refused their offer. Our shaman is glad they are leaving, but he still whispers to me that he sees only death in his omens.

One night around midnight, while the village fires were still flickering, two huge marauding bears came barging out of the forest. Knox's cat, Clootie, fur on end, charged at them screeching from deep in his throat. The bears, startled, turned and ran. For days afterwards, Knox would wheeze with laughter at the memory. "Ach, Clootie," he would say, "ane wee Scottish cratur is mair than a match for a' the beasties in the New Warld."

Some thoughts on a brief code of behaviour to be followed by converts after I am gone
A. *Sexual Matters* Strict monogamy is a must, even

bestiality is a lesser offence than adultery; sexual inter-
course only for breeding; cover the flesh: shirts and
trousers for men, underwear and breast-bindings for
women; absolutely no kissing, cuddling, or touching
of the body of the other sex before marriage; the men-
strual abomination to be dealt with in complete
secrecy by the women.
B. *Other* Hunting needs to be organized on a less sea-
sonal basis to keep the men from being idle for lengthy
spells; rites of passage for the boys should not be dis-
couraged, the pain being a valuable discipline; likewise
the practice of torturing enemies: it teaches contempt
of the flesh (much of these heathens' behaviour may
be turned to good account).
C. *Build churches, churches.*

The French captain (his wife was party to it) coaxed
one of the older native women to be his mistress. She
would then gossip with the other women about his fat
paunch and his stinking breath. And about how, with
his wife looking on, he always made love to her from
behind like a dog. Whenever the captain appeared in
the village afterwards, Knox would trot in front of him,
barking as loudly as he could. All the village dogs would
join the chorus. Some of the native women, inspired
by this, would squat on the ground and urinate, as the
captain passed, their tongues dangling like those of
hounds.

We will root out the shaman Knox's followers after he
has gone. Even my own daughter. We will saw off their

heads with the iron knife they gave me, then we will throw the bodies and the knife into the river. Nothing of him will remain. He longs to return to his homeland where his enemies are more like him. We are too innocent for his liking. This alone is certain: we are our only friends.

The day before they were due to sail, a native guide led a group of sailors through the forest and showed them a mound of earth in a clearing. Knox and his cat Clootie went with them, as always, when there was the prospect of some hunting. The sailors began digging in the mound, hoping to find some of that elusive treasure. Instead, skulls. Hundreds upon hundreds of human skulls. They presumed they were in some kind of traditional tribal burial place. But the skulls, belonging to men, women and children, all seemed recent. Perhaps some disease was responsible. Then they noted that many of the skulls had been split, pierced with sharp objects. They saw too, that the bone had not been picked clean by worms and ants. The guide told them the mound was the top of a shaft, hundreds of feet deep, and that it was the place where they had, for generations, buried the heads of enemies who had been decapitated. Their heads were boiled, he said, their brains eaten. In the last three moons before the sailors arrived, he said, Quheesquheenay's people had beheaded in this way at least one thousand enemies, and had filled the pit to overflowing. On the basis of that good omen, the arrival of the aliens had been welcomed. Some of the men were appalled, but Knox laughed heartily. They lacked faith, he said: it was clear from the Bible that Providence frequently operated by means of a timely massacre or two. Knox secretly suspected that Quheesqueenay had arranged the "discovery" to deter the Frenchmen from ever returning to the New World.

The coastline of France looms in the distance. Knox alone, of those on deck, does not need to be there. He relishes the ferocious cold, the thin snow falling in a gusty wind. The coastal hills are dappled with it, like leprosy. Or is it, he smiles, heaven's vomit? Clootie would have purred at the idea. Clootie who is not with him. Clootie who had to be left behind, prowling, he imagines, those forest thickets, terrifying man and beast for years yet, especially that old heathen shaman. Reminding them of something they would not easily destroy. He thinks of Clootie with fondness but with no regret. The New World was child's play. Now the battle will be amongst professionals, like himself. He breathes deeply, fills his lungs with the chill air sweeping over the water from all the chill regions of the Old World. His home.

Edward and Georgina

There is no shortage of rumours about the Byfields. The Byfields, Edward and Georgina, brother and sister. Edward the meek, Georgina the strong. They live among the down-and-outs and the still-hopefuls in a building of clapboard that buckles from age and neglect. Edward has a steady job, but lacks ambition. He is content to remain here, in his shabby apartment in this octoplex spawned by an opulent mansion from a dead age.

If he is a middle-sized, middle-aged man (he is about fifty), she is of imposing height for a woman of similar age. He is heavy and pale. She is thick-set but always ruddy-faced. Though the colour must be the product of make-up, for she doesn't go out much. When she does emerge, her neighbours hear the spiking of her semi-high heels on the brown linoleum of the stairway, less hollow in the hall, resonant again on the sidewalk. She walks upright, her black wig leaking wisps of grey.

The neighbours believe that, silent though she is,

she is in charge. They say Georgina and Edward are a combination of opposites. The empress and her eunuch.

Rumours cling to them. Unrefined rumours, because no one really cares much about them. For the Byfields are remote, grotesque as circus clowns. Of their past, all anyone knows for sure is that they came from England years ago. For the present, it is enough that they share, with all the tenants of the octoplex, a communal smell of ragouts, pastas, goulashes, curries and fricassees that mingle without much acrimony in the hallways. Is there in it too a tinge of mothballs? Or of decay?

Edward shows no interest in women. At his job with the Parks Department (in summer he operates a lawnmower, in winter a mini snow-plough) the young men tease him:

"You're not past it yet, Ed. You come with us tonight and we'll fix you up."

Edward invariable refuses, unsmiling. He may say, in his flat North-of-England accent:

"Georgina wouldn't like that at all."

They are certain that he is touched, and queer. Occasionally, stifling laughter, they'll plead with him for a date with Georgina. Edward is always indignant and suggests they've no chance with her. He never tells them why. They suspect he is jealous.

The lives of Edward and Georgina seem to dovetail perfectly. Neighbours note that on weekday mornings and afternoons the TV blares in their apartment.

Georgina accepts no callers. Newspaper boys and Jehovah's Witnesses have long ago recognized the futility of trying to get her attention during the daytime.

Then at five o'clock, Edward returns from work. Promptly Georgina emerges, freshly made-up, revitalized. She descends upon the corner store to garner odds and ends for dinner. Or visits the laundromat where she ostentatiously washes Edward's soiled uniform. Meantime, no doubt, he relaxes at home, weary after another day of toil with the Parks Department.

On summer weekends, other families, to escape the city, endure the windblown confinement of overloaded cars and head for the lake. Edward and Georgina, car-less, prefer to stay at home. Georgina, who rarely speaks, is reported to have said to a neighbour in her sonorous voice:

"It's so quiet when everyone goes away in the summer. Just right for Edward."

But every two years, nevertheless, they do spend a week at the lake together. Edward talks about it in advance at work, vague as to destination, but firm as to purpose:

"It'll be good for Georgina, you know."

Implying that he himself would rather not. He asks a neighbour to keep an eye on the apartment while they're away. He does not hand over the key, however, for he says he dislikes the thought of anyone prying around amongst Georgina's intimate possessions. The neighbours are used to his candour.

Then they're gone. No one sees them leave, early in
the morning, though one or two people could swear
they heard them go. From their apartment, no rasping
of floorboards, no clanking of dishes, no insistent TV
laughter, no gargling of pipes, no penetrating whispers.
During the next week, now Edward, furtive and unnatural, now Georgina, self-possessed, may be glimpsed
at far Wasaga Beach, or maybe Port Elgin, amongst the
genuine holiday-makers. They will send a card to their
neighbour: "Having a lovely time. Home soon." It will
be variously signed, "Edward and Georgina," "Georgina
and Edward," or, "The Byfields." The hand is unmistakable, lurching to the left or to the right in an erratic
scrawl.

Seven days pass and they're home again. Early in the
morning, the sounds of their presence permeate the
apartment. Neighbours look out for them. Georgina
appears at the corner store, glad to be back. Their
absence was a hastily corrected wobble in the constant
orbit of their lives.

Rumours. That they are not really brother and sister,
but lovers, fugitives from some long-forgotten romantic disgrace. (No one wishes to envy them, so that
rumour dies.) That they are indeed brother and sister,
living incestuously. That they fled from England to be
free to pursue their illicit love. (Some of the women
are convinced that Georgina has too knowing a look,
and wonder how she got it.) That he is an IRA informer,
living incognito; a convicted strangler out on proba-
tion. That she is a countess who married beneath

herself; a defrocked nun; a prostitute who knows Edward's guilty secret.

Life may end, rumour lives on. In an unusually cool September, Edward falls sick. He takes a few days off work, feels no better, and goes at last to see a doctor. The diagnosis is not good. Edward ought to slow down or there will be dire consequences.

He returns to his job and tells his co-workers that he must be careful:

"I've to stop burning the candle at both ends."

They do not laugh for they see in his eyes that he is unwell. He is worried about Georgina, and they urge him to be careful for her sake:

"She'd be lost without you."

He agrees with them.

The neighbours note that Georgina herself seems out of sorts, worried over Edward. She is careless about her make-up, even more careless about her clothes. Sickness brings out the family resemblance between the two. To inquiries about Edward's health, she shakes her head miserably and will say nothing.

On a cold morning in December, Edward collapses near his snow-plough. In the freshly fallen snow, his body duplicates itself in intaglio, with angel wings. A passer-by finds him, a taxi rushes him to Emergency. He is grey, grim. The nurse asks him about next of kin and he gives Georgina's name; he mutters:

"Don't send for her, leave her alone, I'm all right."

But he isn't all right. Before his own doctor arrives, Edward is dead.

Georgina can't be reached. It is impossible to phone, for Edward refused to have a phone in their apartment; it caused too much unwanted disturbance. A police sergeant is sent to break the bad news to her and find out what she wants done with her brother's body. No one answers his knock though he can hear the sound of the TV quite clearly through the door. The neighbours say they haven't seen much of Georgina lately at the store or the laundromat. That decides the sergeant. With the help of a fellow-officer, he forces the door of the apartment.

The smell seems stronger inside. The entranceway is tidy enough, some coats draped over wall hooks. Then a living-room with a brown rug, stuffed couch, and chair: a still life with black-and-white TV. One of the policemen switches it off. Silence. Faint noises from the street penetrate the window in the niche of the kitchen. The open bedroom door reveals a disordered double bed, a brown varnished dresser with an android plaster head, on which sits Georgina's black wig. The last door, shut, leads to the bathroom. The smell in the apartment is oppressive as the sergeant slowly turns the knob.

The door swings back, clangs heavily against the rim of a chipped enamel bath tub. "Empty," "No one Here," it gongs. The policemen are relieved. They can do no more. They leave a note for Georgina and ask the neighbours to watch out for her return.

Three days pass. Still no sign of Georgina. Edward's funeral takes place, only a single representative of the

Parks Department in attendance, bringing a wreath of imported narcissus. The clergyman on duty did not know Edward. He murmurs appropriate prayers as the coffin discreetly slides through the curtain to test the efficiency of the Cremato-Gas Furnace.

Where is Georgina? She is needed to accept the offerings of the insurance company, to receive the other official relics of Edward's life. For the sake of tidiness, Georgina must be found. Georgina must be found.

But there never was a Georgina. There never was a Georgina to find. The insurance detective sensed that immediately. A reliable man, near retirement age, he loved his daughters and his grandchildren above everything. He understood at once why so few of Georgina's things remained. The shabby black coat, yes; the old fashioned high-heeled shoes, the florid dress, the patched blue underclothes in need of cleaning. But where were the purse, the photographs? What about the jewel-box, the fading letters, the Harlequin romances, the tokens of a past that should have cluttered the case? His instincts, alert to every kind of seedy deception, let him straight to the truth. Georgina did not exist.

No, she did not exist. Edward had never had a sister. Was it the wig on its androgynous skull that gave the game away? The detective was not fooled by the female paraphernalia, the plastic bag full of lipsticks and rouges left lying in the bathroom that led the police (so mechanical in these matters) to deduce that Georgina had packed her suitcase and left town in a hurry.

He introduced himself to the neighbours and coaxed them (he had an air of dependability — it was, with his white hair, his strong point) to tell him about the Byfields. Everything they said made him more certain. Always, in all seasons, Georgina had worn the shiny black coat, the florid dress protruding obscenely, the black shoes clumping. They had often seen the fringe of phoney black hair (a plain woman's conceit, they thought) under a multicoloured headscarf with scenes from Niagara Falls. He had found the scarf, still tucked inside her coat sleeve. Sometimes she seemed to them like a witch in all that make-up, unseemly in an elderly woman.

But none of them remembered, no, not once, ever seeing Georgina and Edward together over the years.

During a last, reluctant search of the apartment — the smell offended him — the detective found, as he knew he would, the final evidence: a letter, recently written. It lay under the brown-paper lining of the dresser's bottom drawer. He recognized the crude handwriting he had seen on the holiday post-cards:

Dearest Georgina, my ever-loving sister,

I hope this finds you well. My old "ticker" (ha! ha!) is not so good now as you already know, but you're not to worry about what will happen to you when your Edward is gone away. What I want to say is "Chin Up!!" I'm sure you'll be "hunky dory" without me to worry about. Just keep "a stiff upper lip!!" as they used to say, and remember me and then I won't really be gone at all!!

We've had some lovely cries together, haven't we, dearest Georgina? But I hope this letter isn't making you cry. Before I had you, my lovely sister, I didn't want to live any more! Can you believe that?? I must have been going "off my rocker!!" as they say. But then I had the loving friendship of a dear, sweet, lovely sister (this is very "luvvy-duvvy!!"). I had someone to "have a chat with" at last. Now when I feel so ill I know you're always with me. No real brother and sister could have been happier than us, and I know our lovely lovely "secret" (three guesses!!) will last forever and forever. Never never forget me and rest assured I am,

> Your "best friend,"
> Sincerely,
>> Edward Byfield.
>> XXXXXXX Love and Kisses!!

The detective folded the letter carefully and put it in his briefcase. He closed the apartment door quietly behind him as though not to disturb sleepers.

He was not a callous man. His daughters' happy marriages, his affection for his grandchildren filled his life. He felt only pity for Edward Byfield and all the other subterranean lives his work obliged him to wrestle out into the light. This investigation was almost complete: it would do no harm, it would be a kindness to Edward's memory to leave the neighbours to their illusions. For them, Georgina had existed even more concretely than her anaemic creator. Even if Edward had invented

Georgina for some other, fraudulent end, his own death had, ironically, thwarted it. So he would report the whole truth only to headquarters, and assure his employers that the case could be discreetly closed.

But now rumours have begun again. The detective hears reports daily of her movements: Georgina disappearing into a crowd of shoppers in Market Square; Georgina's unmistakable back receding along King Street on a busy Saturday morning; the sound of Georgina's shoes ricocheting at night down the alley towards the corner store; Georgina glimpsed on a passing bus, her wig askew, her make-up vivid as always.

There is a rumour that Georgina, less reticent than before, has told some neighbourhood children she'll be back one of these days to collect Edward's things. These rumours are hard to pin down, and the detective is disturbed by them. One particular rumour fills him with dread. It is said that Georgina has been spotted walking in the park, accompanied by Edward, pale and heavy as ever. This is the first time Edward and Georgina have ever been seen together. The detective has asked to be taken off the case. He spends all his spare time with his daughters and his grandchildren and waits with growing impatience for his retirement.

Captain Joe

That's Captain Joe on the right. There he stands,
caught in the sepia print on page two of this album,
its pages in tatters, reliquary of a family heritage.
Notice how in these old pictures they'd look straight
at the camera and smile. Except for Captain Joe. The
Grandfather smiles there beside him. Does anyone,
aside from me, remember these men from another
time, a distant world? See how they're dressed:
trousers bag, boots curl. But the Grandfather wears
a shirt with long sleeves, no collar. The Captain, it
seems, prefers wool, the black sweater of a fisherman.
He wears a sailor's skipped cap, his left hand grips
something — a pipe, maybe. He looks just like a
captain. But he does not smile, he looks intently at
the mechanical eye as it transfixes him in time.

In 1940 he arrived in that village in Central Scotland. Because of the sailor's cap, they called him
Captain. A man of about sixty, he looked his age. But
he had never been a sailor though he had lived near
the sea. The villagers thought him a curiosity — a

Perth man, at least a hundred miles from home, who wanted to live with them. It was a village of Irish immigrants who worked in the only industry, the iron foundry. And it was wartime, but their job exempted them from conscription into the army.

The Captain found things to do around the village. He sickled the grass that choked the cinder paths and he cleaned the soot from out-of-the-way windows. At length he became the village's alarm clock. In the mornings at six he would knock on the doors of the day-shift workers, shocking them out of dreams or embraces into the bitterness of the dawn. So he made enough to pay the rent of a small row house, buy his food and tobacco. The older men took to him, yet wondered why this quiet Scotsman had chosen their village.

The Grandfather hit it off with the Captain from the first, and the boy liked to be with them. Those were the only times the Captain laughed: the boy felt his laugh hadn't grown as old as the rest of him because it hadn't had much use. They would play draughts together. The boy enjoyed a game with Captain Joe, for he didn't play with the guile of the Grandfather or any of the other men, so the boy could beat him. After school he often went over to the Captain's little house for a cup of tea. They'd play draughts till his brother's shout of "Dinner's ready!" signalled last moves.

Nothing lasts forever. During the Captain's second winter in the village he began to die. He would sometimes be so sick, creases in his face, that draughts would cease for weeks on end. The Grandfather used to sit by his bed most of the time: two quiet men, they might exchange an odd word, or the Grandfather might read him pieces from the newspaper, or they might doze like two old friends.

A district nurse called in to see the Captain daily. She and the Grandfather between them made sure he ate something, that he was not too uncomfortable, for he did not complain. The boy visited him some evenings so that the Grandfather could go to his daughter's for a decent meal. Captain Joe's bed had been removed from the cell of a bedroom into the living-room. A coal-fire's glow fended off the night chills.

One evening when the boy came in, the Captain looked much better (that was the way the sickness now affected him). He was up out of bed, his sailor's cap on, looking as though he was waiting just for the boy. The cup of tea was ready, but he did not want to play draughts.

"No draughts tonight. I want to say some things while I'm in the mood."

The boy was taken aback: he wasn't used to having grown-ups confide in him. He'd rather have played draughts. On went the Captain:

"A while back, I told the Grandfather about my life before I came here. I was going to tell you too, but I didn't want to frighten you. The Grandfather thinks there's no harm in it now. I know what they say about me: Isn't it queer for a man my age to come and settle here? — Surely there's something wrong with a man who leaves his family and friends in wartime when nobody knows what'll happen next? They're right. I came from Perth, up in the Highlands where it's clean and fresh, not like down here. I was a grocer there. In the mornings when I arrived at the shop, I used to cut myself a slice of hot bread, plaster the yellow butter on it, and wash it down with a glass of cold milk. I can still taste it. I think that was what I liked most about a grocer's job."

The Captain breathed deeply. Then he told how, when he was eighteen, he met a girl called Laura. They went out together for a year, then, like everybody else in those days, they got married. That was in 1900. He was young and healthy — on Sundays he used to climb for miles up into the hills to catch the big brown spotted trout for dinner. Laura liked to fry them. He said he used to call her his "Fair Maid of Perth. . . ."

The memories hurt. Captain Joe's eyes spouted tears. The boy was full of embarrassment for him. He had never seen a man cry. He watched the bowed head of the Captain, the fingers that made a cage over his face, tips buried in his grey hair.

The Captain wiped his eyes with a rag, made no excuses:

"One night that November I worked late and walked home after dark. There was a chill in the air, there were no stars out and nobody in the streets. When I got home, I felt tired but good. I ate some supper and sat for a bit by the fire. I went to bed around midnight, cuddled in against Laura in the cold sheets, and slept."

What a sleep it was.

"I never slept like that before. When I woke my head was full of a dream about an old man. I couldn't remember his face, but the dream was about all the things he'd done in his life. I was glad the dream was over, for I felt like a peeping Tom.

"But the memory wouldn't go away. I turned to Laura for comfort. My God! The face beside me was the face of a grey-haired old woman. I pulled back from her. I must still be asleep, for my bones were all aching like an old man's, and there was an awful taste in my mouth. The skin on the back of my hand was wrinkled like an old man's skin. This was a nightmare, and I just wanted to be out of it. There was something about that man in the dream that upset me. It was like recognizing parts of a book I knew I'd read a long time ago. Then I remembered the man's face clearly, just for a split second. It was an old man's face, but it was in some ways very like my own. I began to sweat. I slid out of the bed and shuffled across the linoleum to a mirror on a dark wardrobe by the fireplace. A face stared back at me. It was the face in the dream, and it was my own face, the way it would look when I was old. It was my own reflection I saw in that mirror."

The Captain and the boy were silent. The Captain looked like a sick man again, his face like chalk, so that the boy was worried about him and rose to go for help.

"It's all right. Just wait a minute. Hand me that glass of water."

The boy was afraid, not only because the Captain looked so ill, but because the story scared him. But he wanted to hear it out and the Captain wanted to finish.

"I went to sleep on a November night in 1900. When I woke and looked in that wardrobe mirror, it was a morning of November in 1940, and I was sixty years old. I mean what I'm saying. I was a boy when I went to bed, an old man when I woke. If I did wake. At the time they thought I was mad and confined me to bed because I kept saying it was all a bad dream. It would have been better to say nothing. How could I ever prove to them that it was a mistake? I even knew their names and faces — I'd seen them in the dream. They laughed at me for saying I was only a twenty-year-old boy. They seemed so sure of themselves I sometimes caved in. I felt I'd been cheated out of a life. Then I would cry in front of that old woman, Laura. She didn't like that — a man of sixty should have more self-control. But she had had years to learn to be old, and I was a newcomer to it."

One morning, the Captain said, when he was by himself in the house, he opened the wardrobe and found clothes and a seaman's cap. He was surprised they fitted so well. He went to the desk where the old woman kept her purse. He took a few pound notes and slipped out the side door. He never went back.

He'd been on the move ever since. He lived for a week here, a week there, Aberdeen, Stirling, Glasgow.

When he would feel bad, he'd try to tell someone what had happened to him. It was a sure way to lose friends. He had learnt one thing: there was no help for a man like him. It was better to suffer in silence.

"After I left Glasgow, I came here. I liked it that the people were all immigrants. They're all lost too. It's a good place to wait and see how things work out. The Grandfather knew there was something wrong right away: he coaxed it out of me, I think he believes me. Maybe you'll believe me too. One thing. There's no reason for me to be afraid of death. Everybody knows you can't die in a dream, you can only wake up. I love to go to sleep at night. I always hope that in the morning I'll open my eyes and I'll be back in Perth, only it'll be forty years ago, the sun at the bedroom window, Laura there, and our whole lives ahead. We'll laugh about this weird dream. If those forty years can disappear so easily, surely they can come back the same way?"

Captain Joe looked tired, but he had told his story. He thought he'd go to bed now. So the boy went out into the night air and hurried the few yards home.

The Grandfather was waiting for him at the door. He had his cap on, a scarf around his mouth to protect him from the cold, so that only his eyes were visible. He asked how the Captain was, for he was going over to sit with him for a while. He looked at the boy, and the boy had to ask:

"Do you think what he says could have happened?"

"Do you think the Captain's a liar?"

"No, no! but what an awful thing. How could someone young have a dream and wake up an old man?"

The boy could no longer see the Grandfather's eyes.

"That would be very sad, you're right."

And then:

"Would it be less sad if an old man had a dream, and woke up believing he was really only a young man, even though everybody thought he was mad?"

That was what he said. Then he put his hand on the boy's shoulder as he always did to bid him goodnight, and went off into the dark.

Well, of course, I was that boy. I was that boy and I made up my mind, right then, to find out the truth. I would ask the Captain next time I saw him all about his life in Perth, about Laura and that old woman, about his travels before he reached the village. I would ask him (for this troubled me) how, if it was all a dream, the Grandfather and I fitted in.

I did not get a chance to ask my questions. Three days later, Captain Joe died in his sleep with the Grandfather beside his bed. They sent news of his death to Perth, but no word ever came back. The village arranged a funeral for him. The Grandfather took me into the little house where some people were gathered for a last look at the Captain in his coffin (they didn't use to mind exposing children to the dead). Over the body of his friend he whispered to me:

"I wonder if he's finally awake?"

I had no answer for him. I looked down at the face of Captain Joe. On it there was, as usual, no smile. Yet it had about it something strangely youthful in its final, absolute repose.

The Swath

This is its first anniversary. It began (I am one of those not afraid to remember it) on this very day a year ago, as dawn was breaking over the prairies. Though it disturbed at first only the monotonous chorales of crickets and bullfrogs, seismographs all over the world immediately started to scrawl out their alerts. Richter Scales registered an unwavering "8". The phenomenon lasted for precisely twenty-four hours, then, with precision, stopped. Those are the facts. Whether the acknowledgement of them will help prepare us for a recurrence is questionable, though, for all I know, elaborate systems of alarms are by now in place. Nor can I say with any assurance what lesson we are supposed to have learnt.

The time, as I said, was dawn, 6 A.M. on the morning of Sunday, July 7th, near the town of Trempe, Saskatchewan, Canada, 52 degrees latitude, 108 degrees longitude. Such details are important. As the sun started to colour the eastern sky, a fissure began to open on the misty surface of the prairie. A fissure with a remarkable property. It streaked towards the west, moving at a constant speed of one thousand miles an hour, leaving in its wake a chasm three hundred feet in width, one hundred feet in depth, with walls and bottom smooth as marble. As though, while the first rays of sunlight mingled with the dawn mist, the first strip of an endless pink lawn was being mowed, the first swath of the earth itself.

The human being who first observed the swath lived not far from Trempe. The swath lifted his clap-board prairie farmhouse. George Ferguson was his name, a sensible man, forty years a rancher. It was his usual time for waking. In his half-sleep he heard a pleasant swishing sound, like a prairie morning wind. He did not hear, because it made no sound, the anni-hilation of part of his house: the part with the bedroom in which his son, George Jr, nineteen, slept, the part with the bedroom in which his son, Peter, seventeen, slept, and the part with the kitchen in which his wife, Martha, following her early morning custom of many years, sat sharing honeyed toast with Robbie, the black farm-dog, before making George's breakfast. So it was that in an instant, whilst George Jr was snoring loudly, Peter was dreaming one of his strange erotic dreams, Martha was patting Robbie's black head, Robbie was licking his black lips with his long pink tongue, they all vanished.

A surprise, then, awaits George Ferguson this prairie summer morning. He awakes as usual, yawns, slithers out of bed and shuffles towards the bathroom door. He fumbles it ajar. Sees everything. This practical man is the first man to open his eyes on the miracle. His bathroom, once bounded by walls and window, equipped with bath, hand-basin, toilet, adorned with shaving mirror, comb, brush, glass for dentures, and wall cabinet, is transformed. The outside half of the room has been removed with absolute neatness and precision, like the hinged section of a bizarre doll's house. The window, for example, is cut down the middle, as are the bath, the hand-basin and the mirror. Only half of the tumbler in which his dentures have soaked nightly for twenty years remains. With passing interest (he may still be dreaming) he notes that half of the water that was once in the glass and half of the dentures are still there — as though in a trick glass. Through the gaping wall, he can see the vast expanse of the swath itself, and on the far precipice, through the morning mist, he can make out faintly the shapes of his herd of black and white Holsteins, he can hear their distant lowing as they crane perplexedly towards the house.

After a quick survey of the rest of the house, George Ferguson acknowledges everything: the swath, the evaporation of the two bedrooms, two boys, kitchen, wife and dog. But, ever a practical man, he has to chuckle at the neatness of the swath. There are no frayed ends of pipes, wires, walls. The steep sides of the swath itself are smooth, no untidy roots or rocks protruding, the geological strata well defined as in a sandwich. The swath is as clean as any groove made by router or chisel, clean as any joint which must accommodate some other piece. There is no debris alongside the swath, no rubble on top, no edgeworks. Everything is as clean, George Ferguson tells himself, as a whistle.

He begins to laugh. He laughs, and he laughs, surprising himself. He laughs at the fate of his two loyal sons, he laughs at the disappearance of his good old wife, and he laughs at the loss of his affectionate dog. Still laughing, this practical man turns his attention to the problem of reaching the cattle moaning to him across that great abyss.

The swath, all this while, swept on west, neatly cleaving the highway in front of twenty-three pick-up trucks and seventy-nine private cars leaving (according to the box-office clerk) the all-night quadruple-feature at the *Rodeo* drive-in movie theatre. The occupants of the vehicles, their minds still conditioned to accept the marvellous, strolled to the edge of the abyss, and stared in good-humoured amazement into the gulf left by the swath. There is a report that, nearby, a house was on fire. Its owner, an elderly lady, the relative of an English duchess, sat on the manicured lawn in front of the house playing her accordion. The swath swept away house, lady, and lawn minutes before the Fire Department could reach the scene.

The swath's progress was a wonder to see. Gently it peeled away a strip of the foothills of the Rockies. It made an incision through Jasper National Park. Mount Robson received that neck shave that was so fetching to all who saw it. Campers tell of a beautiful young woman, quite naked, in the woods around the mountain at that time. In the dawn mist she stood breast-feeding a handsome Clydesdale horse. The swath took them to itself.

The swath now approaches the Fraser River. For the first time, its remarkable effect on rivers, lakes and oceans becomes evident. The swath charges right into the Fraser, excising a path through the river bed and out the other side. Even though there is now a three-hundred-foot gap in it, the river seems to flow on as usual. The water reaches the point where the swath bisects it, disappears completely for three hundred feet, then reappears, flowing just as strongly. The two ends of the interrupted river are smooth as walls of glass, the river itself visible in cross-section through them. As though in some trick with mirrors. Salmon, trout and all the other fish discover, however, that there is no water in the gap — they fall out of the two walls of water into the damp furrow. This phenomenon is not to be explained lightly.

The swath then began descending the seaboard side of the Rockies in a more southerly direction, thrusting eagerly toward the Pacific. Moving at the same speed as the earth itself, it plunged into the cool waters of the Hecate Strait and struck the Queen Charlotte Islands, grooving them as neatly as with a chain-saw. Zoologists regret to report that the rarely seen eight-legged moose was grazing in its path. It has not been sighted since. Nor have the remnants of the once-glorious Shabana tribe of Coastal Indians, whose village was in the way. They, at least, were used to the idea of annihilation, and for years their shamans had predicted the imminence of the final swish of the Raven's wings. In the dawn light, the swath rushed at last into the open sea.

In July, the North Pacific bustles with business and pleasure, pleasure and business, fishing vessels and cruise boats, freighters and sailboats. The swath's journey could not pass unobserved. The coal-freighter, the *S.S. Hamilton,* reported it. Her radar operator picked up something impossible, and unde-viating line not far ahead, moving at one thousand miles an hour across the water, leaving a permanent trace on his screen. The ship at once hove to.

As the dawn light strengthened, the ship steamed cautiously ahead. The watch, from high on the mast, reported to the deck that, dead ahead, the water was furrowed by a deep, seemingly boundless chasm, three hundred feet or more wide, with frothy edges. Nearer, with his binoculars focused on the far face, he could scarcely contain his laughter as he described disoriented schools of herring, surprised-looking dolphins, one round-eyed killer whale pop out of the vertical face and plunge into what seemed to be a flat, calm canal some one hundred feet below. The skipper of the *S.S. Hamilton* sent a radio message immediately to his owners in Seattle, where it was disregarded.

The small ketch *Blighty* out of Vancouver, crew of

two, had no radio. It sailed before a gentle east wind.
The owner, John Jones, dozing at the wheel, was disturbed by a gurgling noise twenty yards off the starboard bow. In the clear moonlight he saw the water
frothing ahead, perhaps from the wake of a whale.

Of course, it was the brink of the swath. The
Blighty half-slithered, plummetted, bow first in a
seemingly endless plunge, as though thrown by a
rogue wave, or sucked down into a maelstrom. The
boat struck the level canal far below and was completely immersed for endless seconds before rising
slowly to the calm surface like a half-filled bottle. The
mast had snapped, the sails burst.

John Jones was tangled in his lifeline. His shipmate
emerged, choking, from the waterlogged cabin
where she had been asleep. They looked around
themselves. They were becalmed in an endless
trough between two sheer walls of water. A fish now
and then plopped out of the wall near them and
plunged into the level trough. The crew of the
Blighty took it all in, and could only laugh at their
predicament. Their laughter resounded through the
silence of that eerie channel.

The swath entered the coast of Japan with the
breaking of the dawn. Scientists from the University
of Tokyo had been observing the strange behaviour
of their machines, mystified by the permanence of
the shock pattern. On their computers, they
observed the swath track on a gentle south-west
curve towards Mount Fuji. They watched from their
observation towers as it gently made its mark on the

Holy Mountain like the brush stroke of a Zen Master, and headed full tilt towards the city of Kyoto.

The effects of the swath on the city with its great Shinto Temples, its marvellous gardens, might be called devastating. A three-hundred-feet-wide gouge was made through the middle of the city. One hundred thousand people were simply vacuumed away.

The only inhabitants spared in its path were early morning commuters more than one hundred feet below ground in the metro subway. They ascended decapitated escalators to find themselves on the smooth bottom of the swath. Around them they could see the walls of the swath, fringed by the tidy remains of the city's skyscrapers. One of the commuters, according to news reports, a survivor of Hiroshima who had been taking his pet pig on its first train ride, laughed so infectiously at the sight of the swath that all the others joined in, the pig oinked loudly, and the sounds of their merriment filled that misty canyon.

That was the way of the swath. Despite the terrible decimation of human life, as in Kyoto, it aroused no apparent hostility. Indeed, early theorists presumed its benevolence. The truth is that the swath did not mutilate any living organism, animal or vegetable. No records exist of severe injuries, of amputations of limbs, as might have been expected, of terrible dissections. So far as living things were concerned, the swath took all or nothing. As for inanimate objects, it proceeded inexorably, following an undeviating path, dividing, obliterating, without partiality.

The swath sucked its way along the coast of South Korea, neatly eliminating two boatloads of drowsy fishermen, but leaving intact their bulging seine-nets in the Cheju Strait. Still maintaining its distance ahead of the rising sun, it hissed across the Yellow Sea, and onto the mainland of the People's Republic of China. Reports, as always, are rather erratic from that part of the world, but it appears that in the provinces of Shensu, Szechwan, and Tsunghai, dawn workers in paddy-fields of collective farms noticed the frenzied chirruping of crickets trained to warn of earthquakes. Government agencies did, however, pass on, with their official blessing, the information that collective farm workers in their blue dungarees heard an unfamiliar sizzle — the swath passing near, efficiently meting out oblivion, without regard to class background.

This swath was no respecter of national boundaries. Chinese border guards, with a great deal of good humour it seems, challenged it, and even fired upon its dark shadow as it eviscerated its three-hundred-feet-wide strip from the remote territory of Tibet, furrowing towards the walls of the forbidden city of Lhasa. The swath, at that point, seemed to be rushing at the Himalayas and the great breast of the world, Mount Everest.

Then, it changed course. The swath began to swing further west in a gentle but resolute manner.

This change of course has caused much speculation. Had the swath "achieved its goal"? (such terms are used by contemporary philosophers who study the phenomenon). Or did the invocation of certain cryptic Tibetan mystical powers divert it from its path—the screech of ten thousand prayer-wheels and monotonous chanting from the *Tibetan Book of the Dead* by innumerable devotees greet its arrival? Was the power that moved the swath deflected by the great mineral residues of the Himalayas and bent protesting in a different direction? It is, in hindsight, surprising that no one seemed to consider the swath as the other side's secret weapon. There was always difficulty in perceiving it as any kind of threat at all.

The westward wheel of the swath brought it to Tamarat in Northern India where the warrior hill-tribes were fasting for the great penitential feast of Rabakhan. In the cool dawn light, the brahmins squatted nervously on a high podium before half-a-million followers in the city square. The ritual of brahmin-hurling, an ancient rite in which the most powerful of the warriors competed in throwing a priest from the podium as far into the assembled crowds as they could, had just begun. Everyone heard the hissing sound as the swath arrived. It bored past them, removing podium and brahmins (except for one who was revolving in mid-air at the time), leaving only the tell-tale cavity behind. For a moment there was silence, then a few of the disciples began to smile, then shudders of massive laughter rocked the warrior assembly.

Who knows how the town of Darafi in Afghanistan responded to the swath's passing? The town, with its five thousand inhabitants, was sprawled along one narrow street in the swath's path. It completely vanished, leaving a few bewildered mongrel dogs and some tardy racing pigeons to investigate the canyon left behind.

Twelve hours had now passed since the swath began. There is general agreement that this was a momentous hour in its journey. After startling Iranian nomads at the oasis of Dasht-i-Lut during their dawn prayer (they thought it was an approaching sandstorm), the swath entered the land of Israel. It crossed the River Jordan, disposing, according to eyewitnesses, of two camels in a rowing boat in the middle of the river, swished across the Gaza Strip and plunged into the Mediterranean Sea.

Was the swath's impartial embrace of all the desert lands a miraculous symbol of Arab unification, as has been suggested by certain Muslim fundamentalists? Or was that Jewish cult (the swath spawned cults wherever it passed — even in California where it did not pass — Zoroastrian Swathists, Soka Gakkai Buddhist Swathists, Dakshincharin Hindu Swathists, Mirza Ali Swathists, and a vast selection of antinomian, homoiousian, and latitudinarian Christian millenial Swathists) right to concentrate rather on the swath's linkage of Israel and the Gaza Strip, and its complete neglect of Egypt?

Did the swath, tired and thirsty after the desert, emit

a great sigh as it dipped into the Middle Sea? So certain observers with hagiographic intent have implied. At all events, for the next thousand miles the swath bored its way across that blue sea, disturbing only occasional hashish smugglers, the ghosts of Odysseus and the nymph Calypso, the long-drowned armies of a thousand internecine wars. On the small island of Pellas, however (so reliable authorities report), three naked sisters were playing a six-handed Mozart piano sonata piece on their patio in the early dawn light. Sisters, piano and island disappeared into the swath.

The swath approached the Pillars of Hercules, the gateposts of limitless ocean. Gibraltar had been evacuated, leaving only the baboons to enjoy, at last, the pristine union of rock and sea. A squadron of fighter planes was sent to reconnoitre. The boyish pilots, through the plastic hatches of their aluminum machines, were the first human beings to observe from the air, through the mellow dawn light, the swath's implacable progress as it gouged its aquatic channel. As it passed over shallows of that ancient sea, they reported that they could see seaweed-covered Atlantean columns and unbroken wine vats in wrecks of Carthaginian quinqueremes.

From a height of two thousand feet, the young pilots watched with amazement as the swath, like an archer, seemed to take careful aim, then shot right through the narrow strait into the green depths of the North Atlantic on a gentle north-westerly bearing. Their good-humoured commentary crackled over the air-waves, till they were ordered back to base.

In that dawn, the swath funnelled through the ocean just north of the mountainous Azores. By now, all the world was aware of the swath. Thousands of English and German tourists had assembled, irreverent of official cautions, on the slopes of the northern Azorean islands hoping to catch a glimpse of the wonder.

One particular group, from an international nannies' convention, chartered some local wooden whaling boats which had often faced the more orthodox perils of the deep. They rowed out towards the swath's path. All were in high spirits. They displayed, it now seems clear, that universally felt intuition that the swath "meant no harm." The swath, accordingly, swallowed the nannies to the unanimous approval of those watchers on the hills.

The great military powers, less susceptible, did not cease investigating, dispatching U2 reconnaissance planes, anti-submarine rockets, B52 bombers fitted with H-bombs, MIG 15s, photoscrutiny balloons, multiple-headed inter-continental ballistic missiles, earth-orbiting satellites, and undetectable hydrosensitive deep-sea probes.

We should not complain. Without their paranoid probings, we would lack the only visual records we have of the swath's sea passage, those fascinating, grainy films of the event. At first, in the dim light of the dawn, the camera reveals only the wrinkled face of the ocean far below. Then you become aware of something unnatural, a moving straight line bisecting the natural body of water as though drawn with a ruler.

The camera descends and the line broadens. You notice that it has depth, is actually a spectacular geometrically angled furrow through the fluid ocean. Lower still, a slight foam is perceptible at the edge of each bank. The flat calm of the "canal" itself reflects the low-flying plane like a mirror's face.

The plane containing the camera now descends below the level of the swath's banks and hurtles along between the shining sides at frightening speed. The sensation, even on film, is uncanny, as though one were travelling at enormous speed between parallel and interminable fish tanks. The walls are glassy, transparent. From close up, you see the heads of huge groupers protruding from the bank. In vain the fish try to twist themselves back: invariably they fall, writhing, into the canal below to disappear with a flick of the tail.

One particular segment of film caused much comment. The quality is imperfect, the image less than clear. It shows a great sperm whale sticking its head out of the bank and opening its vast jaws wide in astonishment. Analysts of the film are certain they can see, in the recesses of the throat of the whale, a man with a long beard and flowing robes, looking out with some curiosity at the passing plane. No explanation of this phenomenon has yet been proposed.

One of the planes arrives at the front end of the swath. At last, we can see plainly how the trough is formed in the water: it simply *appears,* full-blown, perfectly shaped, with no sensation of effort or power, no displacing of water. It is three hundred feet wide, one hundred feet deep, geometrically cornered, as though a great scoop, a great plough, a great vacuum cleaner. . . . No, there is no analogy, all analogies collapse beside the reality of the swath. The swath is simply there, moving relentlessly on its north-west swing. It contradicts physics and the basic laws of nature. It defies scientific understanding. It is completely convincing. The planes bear away.

The swath hissed on towards the North American coastline, in spite of a hastily organized effort to divert it by a group of psychics internationally famous for their ability to bend spoons by the powers of their minds alone. All of them testified that they could sense the aura of the swath but were quite overwhelmed (one very sensitive lady psychic swooned) by its power.

The swath seemed much more deliberate now in its progress. The whole continent awaited it. Those who were in its projected path, people who would have fled at the first warning of a hurricane, were reluctant to believe they were in any peril. They would not evacuate their houses, boats, wigwams. In fact, they showed every sign of welcoming the swath. Eyewitnesses speak of their good humour, their curiosity: "I'm really looking forward to it," was the comment on everyone's lips, as they awaited the swath's annihilating passage. Analysts have suggested that those who would not take evasive action were akin to lemmings. There were innumerable reports of suicides caused by leaping into the canyon left by the swath, or, especially, by running directly into the swath's path — as one source said, "as if to embrace a lover."

The swath penetrated the fogs off the Grand Banks and glided smoothly into the Gulf of the St Lawrence. In the dawn light, it mounted the Quebec coastline. Thousands had driven out from the little towns of the North Shore to welcome it, to watch its passing. TV cameras, microphones, photographers and newsmen from every corner of the earth assembled. Roars of approval went up, as the swath appeared, gently dissecting, calmly obliterating all before it. It *seemed* slower, but scientists say this was an illusion: the swath always kept pace with the advancing dawn. Huge flocks of sea-birds that had fed on the fish falling out of the two walls of the swath were now joined by land-birds dipping playfully in and out of the symmetrical gorge.

The swath's passage was now more like a triumphal march, a royal procession, evoking a carnival spirit, a sense of general goodwill. Its progress was stately, inexorable, a thing of beauty.

Scientists around the world had made a prediction: if the swath continued on its present course, it would arrive back at exactly the place where it began — in Trempe, Saskatchewan, twenty-four hours after it began. So it was that on a misty prairie dawn, with the sun's beams just beginning to penetrate from the east, more people than the town of Trempe had ever seen gathered to watch the swath complete its circumnavigation. They lined up on either side of its

projected path as though to watch a parade. Mothers
sat in lawn chairs, fathers carried babies on their
shoulders so that they would have the best possible
view. The excitement can only be described as
intense. Helicopters warned of the swath's approach.
With only a mile to go, it had definitely slowed down,
so that children were able to run alongside it, and
throw their candy-wrappers in its path to watch them
disappear. Young men were able to play chicken by
dashing in front of the swath, jumping back out of its
way at the last minute. Great gales of laughter arose
from the crowd when any of them would slip and disappear in its path.

At 6 A.M. exactly, as the cameras whirred, the
flashes blinked, the crowd whistled and roared, the
forward edge of the swath dissolved the final wafer of
solid earth separating it from where it had set out
twenty-four hours before. The swath was over.

A great moan arose simultaneously, recorded on
innumerable recording devices. Did the sound come
from the assembly of spectators who, till then, had
been filled with good humour and laughter? Was it
caused by the realization of some collective sense of
loss? Was it the death-rattle of whatever force drove
the swath itself? (Some eyewitnesses swear the sound
came from *above* them.)

These questions, like all others on the nature of the
swath, may never be answered. For, before we could
comprehend the phenomenon we had witnessed, it
reversed itself. At exactly one minute after six, whilst
the sun was still rising over the eastern horizon, the

great gash that scarred half the globe, instantly healed itself, the swath was erased. Buildings were reconstructed exactly as before, the land returned to its former levels, mountains had their scalps restored, rivers and oceans reverted to their previous condition (the dismasted *Blighty* found itself tossed helpless once again on the great expanse of ocean). Everything that had vanished reappeared.

Everything reappeared — except for the living things. George Ferguson, who had been trying all day to find some way of reaching his cattle across the swath, ran back to his house when he saw the restoration. He opened the door and called to his wife and sons, whistled to his dog. No response. Yet he smiled. All along the path of the swath, widows and widowers, bereaved parents and children, dog and cat owners were calling out to their lost loved ones and receiving no responses. Yet they were smiling. We used to call the missing "the victims of the swath." That was a misnomer, for we did not really regret their passing. The bereaved would smile shyly, they would sound more as if they were boasting than mourning as they recollected, "I lost my wife" (or mother or father, or son, or daughter, etc.) "in the swath, you know."

Of course, the swath encouraged speculations as to its cause: early on people wondered if it was all a trick with mirrors that somehow went amiss. On the other hand, romantics theorized that the divine mind had fallen asleep for a moment and thus cancelled out a part of the Creation. A group that favoured inter-galactic co-operation suggested that the missing peel of earth was a kind of skin sample taken by exploring aliens, who had then returned it minus the life-forms. The theory that gained most currency, however, amongst secular humanists, was that the swath came about owing to a certain distribution of people, objects, climates (religions and races are sometimes included in the formula) which gave the impression of deliberateness to a purely mechanical occurrence. Laboratory experiments have not so far succeeded in reproducing the swath-effect. Yet there are scientists who maintain that such a distribution of ingredients is no doubt organizing again. They have been feeding every imaginable combination of data into their computers in the hope of being able to predict the next occurrence.

The situation has changed. A year has passed and the very fact of the swath's appearance is in dispute. Witnesses are nowhere to be found, or disappear under mysterious circumstances. It is whispered that more people have gone missing since the swath than during it. I myself have received threatening phone-calls, the Office of Taxation has audited my returns for no apparent reason, and the bank has called in my loan. Many of my colleagues have been discredited, their careers in ruins. Researchers into the swath suddenly find that government records are unavailable; more and more, officialdom refers to the event as "mass hysteria."

As for us, Rowena my dear, the swath brought us together. We met, sponsored by our various universities, during that last geological dig permitted by the government, in the Rocky Mountain segment. We made love for the first unforgettable time where the swath began its annihilating descent towards the Pacific. You smile. You insinuate *I* caused the swath for this purpose. I smile. I disclaim any such power, I merely celebrate the miracle.

Festival

Two of us went to the festival, one came back. We took the night plane, but we didn't sleep, neither of us being great sleepers at any time, never mind on planes. Coming in over the coastline at dawn, I thought to myself, what a beautiful place, the black headlands, the long aprons of beach round green northern water, the grass and the trees greener than was possible.

"Are you all right? Are you sure you want to go through with it?"

"I'm fine."

We took a taxi from the airport. It was ancient, and so was the driver, a man who wanted to talk. Neither of us obliged. I was tired. I wasn't in the mood for small talk, and I may have been sharp with him, or at least he stopped trying, and left us to ourselves.

We came down from the high moorland through a gap in the hills into the outskirts of the town (we still considered it a town, though it was more of a village,

a small village). The graveyard looked as though it had
no new graves, just the old ghosts. We passed the first
buildings on the edge of the town, run-down looking,
as though no one lived in them. Then we drove past
small fieldstone houses, along deserted streets with
wisps of early morning fog still lying across the lawns.

We arrived at the bigger grey granite buildings at the
centre of the town, one of them the hotel. The provost
had made no reservations for us (did he think we would
change our minds and not come in the end?), and we
were not able to find separate rooms. Even though the
festival was a local affair, enough people came from the
surrounding countryside to make accommodation
scarce.

We slept, or tried to sleep, making the possible
rigours of the festival our excuse for lying down
together and not touching.

About six in the evening, we rose, ate briefly, and
joined the crowds in the street walking towards the
school gymnasium. The night was foggy, but not
unpleasant. The children seemed impatient, but the
townspeople did not hurry. They chatted to each other,
and made special efforts to be polite to us. Some of
them seemed to recognize us. But their avoidance of
direct questions was, for me, a sure sign they knew
why we were here. I thought at times I saw a glitter in
their eyes, but we ourselves were excited and perhaps
every one of us looked unusual.

The school gymnasium smelt like a school gymnasium. Benches on risers had been set up along the
two side walls, as though we had come to watch a

basketball game. Faded pennants hung from the
rafters, the corners were webbed with ropes. Just
inside the main doors, I could see the provost,
smiling as always, a bald man with a chain of office
and steel-rimmed glasses. Beside him, the school's
headmaster, a youngish man who seemed a little over-
awed by the occasion. They greeted everyone, the
headmaster paying special attention to the children,
all dressed in their best clothes, unable to hide their
excitement.

The provost smiled with delight when he saw us,
and he shook us warmly by the hand, saying he was so
glad we'd been able to accept his invitation. He knew
we'd want to sit together (we didn't contradict him),
and took us by our elbows to the only two wooden
chairs in the entire gymnasium. As he walked us along
the front of the audience, some of the crowd who were
already there applauded us courteously. We sat down
and he went back to his post.

"We still have time to change our minds."
   "Yes. But we won't."

At seven-thirty, the seats were filled. The lights began
to dim, the audience quieted down. A cluster of spotlights shone down on a circular area of the floor
covered in rope mats. A small door in the wall to our
right opened and a figure, hard to make out at first,
moved slowly into the circle of light. She had her back
to us, a young woman with waist-length jet-black hair,
wearing a white house-coat tied with a cloth belt. She

walked in a very self-possessed way, in spite of occasional nervous coughs amongst the audience.

In the middle of the circle, she stopped, loosened the belt and allowed her house-coat to slip from her shoulders to the mats.

She still had her back to us as she stood there, quite naked, her shoulders heaving from deep breathing. She began to turn around slowly, allowing the audience on our side to inspect her. To see her pale face. To see that her belly, dazzling white in the glare, was swollen, that her breasts bulged.

The audience was alert. The woman lowered herself gently to the mats, letting out a gasp as she lay down.

Now her breathing became loud, deep breaths, expelled noisily from her throat. "Ahh! Ahh!" For a few minutes, very regularly. "Ahh! Ahh!" Then I heard additional sounds, coming this time from the audience. "Ahh! Ahh!" All round the gymnasium, voices, soft at first, perhaps the children's, then gradually louder as the adults joined in, all of them taking up the sound. "Ahh! Ahh!" Much louder now, basses, baritones, tenors, contraltos, the fluting voices of sopranos and altos, all breathing rhythmically in time with her. "Ahh! Ahh!" Her stomach convulsing in the harsh light, deflating, puffing up. "Ahh! Ahh!" In the glare, I thought that at times the shape of her belly became geometrical, rhomboid, angular. So that I wondered, I suppose we all did, what thing was struggling inside her to be born.

The heavy breathing stopped. Now she bent her knees, opening her legs wide. From where we were sitting we could see quite clearly the pressure on her cervix. She was making a new noise now, a kind of grunting. "Uugh! Uugh!" She gyrated slowly on the mats between grunts, displaying her labour to all of the audience. "Uugh! Uugh!"

After a few minutes, the accompaniment began again. "Uugh! Uugh!" Softly, then louder. "Uugh! Uugh!" I looked around and I could hear them all now, even the bald provost, the anxious headmaster. "Uugh! Uugh!" All of them grunting in cadence. "Uugh! Uugh!" Her voice still dominating, sweat running down her face now, and her breasts. Her audience sweated with her, beads of sweat glistened on every face in that gymnasium. "Uugh! Uugh!" And now we could see the waters bursting out from between her legs. "Uugh! Uugh!" And now her vulva bulging, stretching. "Uugh! Uugh!"

She began to scream, the thin scream of a trapped rabbit. "Eeeeh!" The audience took up the scream, hardly breathing. "Eeeeh!" Her white face, her white body was gradually taking on a purple tinge, her eyes stared. "Eeeeh!" The audience screaming louder with her. "Eeeeh!" We all watched the widening vulva of the black-haired woman on the gymnasium floor, she gyrating still in spite of her pain. "Eeeeh! Eeeeh!" Letting us all see the dark circle that was forming between the brilliant thighs fringed with wet black hair. "Eeeeh! Eeeeh!" I noticed I was screaming too, we were both screaming along with her.

The woman stopped moving, stopped screaming. The creature inside her would wait no longer. The crowd watched without a sound as something slithered from inside her agony onto the mat. She too was silent now, as death. I remember we turned to each other anxiously.

What was it we all expected? I ask myself that, every now and then. A demon? A monster we were looking for? A thing each one of us had brought to that place and expected to appear before us now in the flesh? I can only testify to my own fear.

But, oh, the relief, the delight, when I saw that on the gymnasium floor lay a baby, a simple, human baby, still connected to its mother. I could have cheered with joy, as most of the children around us were cheering. We smiled at each other. We smiled, and all the audience in the gymnasium seemed to be smiling too, smiles of relief at the birth of that child.

The provost stepped forward, his chain of office glittering, his glasses sparkling in the overhead lights. He looked down at the woman. She was lying unmoving on the floor, only the rhythmic movement of her breasts showing she was not dead, in spite of the blood still oozing out of her. The little heap lay between her legs, coated in blood and mucous, no sound, its arms and legs fluttering from time to time. The provost, a pair of scissors in his hand, stooped and snipped. Then he carefully picked the baby up and held it high, turning around with it so that we could all see his trophy.

At first, silence. Then murmurs of pleasure, then shouts of "YES, YES, YES," from all round the gymnasium. I joined in, we both did, hugging each other, shaking hands with our neighbours. The baby, high in the provost's arms, steadied its head, and those eyes that had never seen opened wide and looked around the gymnasium, taking us all in.

The woman on the mats lay in her pool of blood, waiting for the afterbirth. She turned her head painfully to see what it was she had delivered. She looked up at the baby just at the very moment the baby looked down at her. On the woman's face was only weariness and pain. The baby's face became a purple wrinkle and it began to scream, and its screams could be heard above all the rejoicing in the gymnasium that night.

The hotel bar was busy after the first event. Customers shook our hands and bought us drinks. They were delighted that visitors, especially visitors like us, should have witnessed the event. It was a marvellous beginning to the festival.

"Should we, one last time?"
  "Why not?"

We could hardly wait to get away from the bar, and up the stairs to our room. We paid no attention to the damp, we threw our clothes off and fell into bed, holding each other the way we once had so long ago. We stroked each other, hugged each other, mounted each other, writhing in pleasure. And then we slept.

Hours later, I felt the chill and drew the blankets up, and we slept with arms around each other for the rest of the night.

The second night, the fog lingered still. We walked to the gymnasium with the others. For the most part they were farmers and coal-miners, with their families robust and red-cheeked, or pale and wiry. They were courteous as ever to us, but I thought I could detect more restraint than I had noticed the night before. We disagreed about that.

The gymnasium was filled by seven-thirty. Only some floodlights lit a wide strip of floor stretching between the emergency doors at each end. The provost, energetic as ever, and the headmaster, looking quite uncomfortable, walked together to the middle of the floor. They separated: the provost walked down the illuminated strip towards one set of doors, the headmaster to the other. There they turned and bowed to each other very formally. Then each pushed the doors open to the dark outside.

"Perhaps it isn't too late for us."
"Has anything changed?"

Fresh air wafted in, diluting the ingrown smell of liniment. All of us breathed gratefully and waited for the event to begin.

We didn't wait long. We heard a faint buzzing noise, distant, it might have been someone sawing down trees. The sawing noise became louder, getting nearer to the gymnasium. We looked at each other, wondering what it could be.

Then, from the open doors on our right, we noticed a black ooze spilling slowly onto the illuminated floor. The ooze was alive. It was a flood of insects spreading over the floor, its front edge straight as a ruler.

A sea with a voice. Not the buzzing we had heard a few minutes before and could still hear in the background, but a rustle, a hiss, a scuttling of papery limbs, scaly bellies on the varnished wood floor. We watched the whispering advance fearfully, alert for the tide to spill over our exposed feet.

But the insects never left the illuminated strip. The leaders were, so far as I could tell, ants and silver fish: minuscule creatures in great masses, followed by larger members of their species — speckled in colour, some of them — carrying their tiny pearls. They kept to tight formation though some of the ants would make brief forays towards the debris of popcorn, which they would portage back to the main armies without disrupting the march.

Cockroaches appeared, with bristling antennae and hairy legs we could plainly make out, millions of them, then slithering centipedes, and millipedes, some of them a foot long. We kept our feet tucked under our seats, ready to climb up on them at the slightest hint of disorder.

Yet, already, we were beginning to feel comfortable in spite of all the insects, and some of the audience were talking amongst themselves without any sense of fear. We had the feeling we were spectators at a parade, and that the insects were consciously showing off, aware of their role.

The PA system encouraged this notion by coughing suddenly to life, and a nasal voice began calling out the names of each species as it entered the gymnasium. I heard names I had never known. Bristletails,

cockchafers, buffalo beetles, harlequins, sacred
scarabs, stink bugs (I could see some of the children
holding their noses, giggling) dung beetles, kissing
bugs, stag beetles with their enormous antlers, and
walkingstick bugs looking as though they'd come
straight from some insect battlefield.

We could still hear the buzzing outside, getting
louder in spite of the hissing in front of us and the noise
of the audience. None of the insects had so far left the
hall. They would reach the other exit and begin march-
ing on the spot, so that after a while, much of the illuminated pathway was jammed up.

Now, a splintering sound filled the gymnasium. All
the crickets within a hundred miles began hopping
through the door in great chirruping masses. I could
not help thinking they were Mexican jumping beans,
leaping six feet in the air, or black flying fish skimming
over a wooden ocean.

The last stragglers amongst the crickets had just
made their entrance, and the entire illuminated strip
of floor was full, when the buzzing noise we had heard
all night exploded into the gymnasium. I put my hands
over my ears to block out the pain.

Flies. Pillars of flies, twisters, cumulo-nimbuses of
flies, dense fogs of flies of every kind, house-flies, black-
flies, midges, horse-flies, dragon-flies, mosquitoes,
obscuring the space above the crawling insects. They
filled the air like inky water poured into a huge aquar-
ium, so that the still leaping crickets would disappear
up into it and drop out moments later, inverted divers.
The light in the gymnasium was almost obliterated by

the living, buzzing wall of flies that cut us off from the human beings on the other side.

Only about a quarter of the air space remained. In the dim light, the children cowered against their parents. They felt, as we two did, the whining presence of these flies, how they could engulf us, smother us in horror, if they once went out of control. But like the masses of crawling insects on the floor beneath them, they stayed in control, hovering in place, as though they knew exactly why they were there, the entire building vibrating with their power.

The buzzing became so loud I thought my ears would burst, even with my hands covering them. We could not speak. No ordinary human voice could have penetrated that sound. So it was that we saw, rather than heard, the entry of the bees. Bees and wasps, colourful even in the dim light, their humming causing even more vibrations, bulkier in the air than the flies, their undercarriages dangling. Platoons of them flew on the flanks of the main body, scrutinizing the audience with their multiple eyes. Behind the swarm, the vibrations were deepest, as the ponderous bodies of a million queens filled the last space above the strip, and cut off the light, like the drawing of a huge brocade curtain.

In the darkness, we all sat still, waiting. In the confined space in front of us, countless billions of insects hovered and massed, under perfect control. We were all waiting.

Suddenly, the birds were amongst them. We did not at first know they were there, snapping and gobbling. Then light appeared in the middle of the gymnasium as the insects, on the floor and in the air, divided and surged towards the two entrances, climbing over each other in their terror. I don't know how many escaped, for they crashed into a wall that devoured them, an enemy with a million mouths.

The calm nasal sound of the PA system intruded itself into the bedlam, identifying the predators. I could hear the names, and eventually could see the killers as the lights brightened: swallows, evil-looking horned larks and screamers, frenetic thrashers, swifts, goatsuckers, nightjars and nutcrackers pecking furiously at the floor, thousands of sparrows of every sort, shrikes and razor-bills pouncing on the trapped crickets and bees. With their canny, greedy eyes, they were more frightening than all the monstrous-looking insects they gorged on.

In less than ten minutes it was over. The twittering of the predators stopped, as though on a signal, and they swooped out of the gymnasium. All that remained were a stunned audience and wastes of broken insect bodies, papery wings occasionally fluttering in the stark light.

For a time, no one spoke. The children were openly crying, leaning into the adults. Some people began to get to their feet and move towards the exits, carefully skirting past the heaps of bodies.

We followed the townspeople out into the cool night, no one talking and walked back to the hotel.

Some of the usual customers were in the hotel bar, drinking quietly, with none of the previous night's joviality. I would have liked to ask them about the event, listen to them compare it with previous years. But I kept silent. We both were too busy, nursing our private dreads.

"Perhaps we could still . . ."
  "Stop talking about it. Please stop."

In the damp bed, we lay as rigidly apart as if a sword had been set on its edge between us. For it was a damp bed that night. The sky was full of rain, and the bedroom was chilly. That night was our last chance to talk, perhaps to agree to try again. We didn't, and there is no more to be said.

The third and last night of the festival was a clear one for that region amongst the hills. The fog had disappeared somewhere. I could see stars and a gibbous moon. We knew we were a little late as we walked along the road to the school gymnasium. The provost and the little headmaster were waiting anxiously at the door, to the background strains of music on the PA system, looking anxiously up the street towards us. They greeted us warmly. The provost took us both by the arm and spoke:
  "You still want to go through with it?"
  We both nodded.
  The lights were already dimmed, and the audience was looking in our direction. The provost waved to them as he led us in. All was well.
  The middle of the floor was lit by spotlights. The provost stood under the lights and spoke:

"My townspeople and my dear children. Tonight is the final night of another successful festival, and we will all see a new and very exciting event. This event takes a lot of preparation and co-operation from a lot of people, and I'd like you to join me in a big hand for everyone concerned, and especially for our two honoured guests who have travelled many thousands of miles to be involved in this event for our pleasure tonight."

He paused for the applause, then went on to explain the rules of the event to the audience. I didn't listen very carefully, I knew them only too well. Before we had accepted his invitation so many months ago we had gone over the rules many times.

He finished his speech, and the audience applauded again, and hummed with anticipation while we went to our separate changing rooms, the provost himself taking charge of me. As I walked in front of the benches, people shouted, "Good luck," "Take care," and I could almost have believed them. Someone even called out, "God bless."

The preparations were simple enough. In the changing room, I took off my coat as the provost showed me the workings of the heavy wooden-handled, single-shot pistol, letting me see the bullet already in the breach. He reminded me that each of the six members of the squad would have the same kind of pistol, but that only one of them would be loaded.

"Do they know which of them has the loaded pistol?"

"No. They draw the pistols by lot — that's part of the event."

He asked me if I wanted to go out into the school-yard and take a few practice shots. I thanked him for his concern, but assured him that we were both excellent shots, otherwise we would never have accepted his invitation.

Through the door, we could hear the PA system blaring out dramatic music with drum rolls. The overture of the final event of the festival. There was loud applause, and I knew something was happening.

The provost opened the door a crack.

"Your friend and the rest of the squad are all ready now. Shall we?"

We walked slowly out into the gymnasium, the audience clapping. The squad was lined up in place, six of them. They were all about the same height and weight, all of them covered from head to toe in white cloaks with eye-holes cut out, and wearing white gloves and white shoes. I tried to spot the familiar shape, the stoop of the shoulders, the tilt of a head, the way the arms hung. I could not be sure.

Each of the six held a heavy wooden-handled pistol like my own.

I took my place on the mark ten yards away, facing the squad. Six shaded pairs of eyes measured me. I peered back at them, trying without success to find eyes I knew only too well.

The tension in the hall erodes my calm and my heart batters not just out of excitement, but because I know that you are one of the six facing me, that you may be the one with the deadly pistol. I take a deep breath.

The first figure raises its pistol slowly and takes aim at my head. The voice of the provost asks me the formal question:

"Do you wish to shoot?"

Surely they would not want to end the game so soon. I take my chance.

"No."

I see the finger begin to curl on the trigger, and I stand firm.

CLICK.

The hall fills with applause and the little provost nods, and smiles his congratulations to me.

After a moment, the crowd settles down again and I concentrate once more. The second member of the squad takes aim. I see the glint in the eyeholes, but not the colour, the greenness. Not the intention. Could it be your hand aiming the weapon that might mean my death? What are you thinking?

My own hand is sweating on the handle of my pistol.

"Do you wish to shoot?"

"No."

I watch with absolute clarity the gloved finger tighten on the trigger, perhaps the last thing I will ever see.

CLICK.

The right choice. The hall resounds with applause, shouts of approval. I breathe deeply.

Silence again, more sudden this time. I suppose the audience can't wait to see how the game works itself out. The squad stands unwavering, two of them now only spectators. The third member raises an arm and aims the pistol directly at my head.

I am breathing too quickly. That steady hand, those inscrutable eyes. Could this be the pistol with the bullet? Could this be you, after all we've been through together, ready to kill me with such resoluteness?

"Do you wish to shoot?"

I need time, but there is none.

"No."

CLICK.

The audience shouts with joy. I would like to breathe deeply, not this sweaty air. But the silence falls again. The fourth figure has already raised its arm, and the pistol points at my head. I must think, analyse, figure the odds. Which of the three remaining pistols will contain the bullet? My heart is thudding with excitement I have never known. I must forget about whose hand holds the weapon. I am certain now that you will not change your mind, give yourself away. I know that, like me, you will not hesitate to fire, and I love you for it.

"Do you wish to shoot?"

Instinct gives my answer.

"YES."

I raise my pistol, keeping my arm steady, and take aim. I squeeze gently, as I have so often done in practice. The pistol bucks, and the hooded figure lifts right off the floor, a brown hole appearing where the nose would have been, and the body falls backwards, the blood spurting, the pistol still snared in its hand.

The crash of the shot rings round and round and round. The stink of gunpowder overwhelms the gymnasium smells. Silence, no cheers, only the ringing in my ears. I have killed someone, but I feel nothing except that I have played the odds. I have made my choice, that part of the game is over. Now I will join all the others, a spectator. I hear my empty pistol drop to the floor.

The squad seems indifferent to the gap in its rank. The fifth figure raises its pistol.

Suddenly, I am drowning in feelings. Why, why did I fire so soon? I look towards the provost. I want to protest to him about the unfairness of the game. But I can tell nothing from his frowning face. He is too wrapped up in the game, like the crowd. I can feel their sympathies are against me. They all hope I have made a mistake, and that the bullet is in one of these last pistols. That they can enjoy another killing.

I look directly into the barrel of the pistol. My legs are weak. But I must show no fear, as we agreed. I wonder what you feel there in the squad watching me. I wonder if it is you holding the pistol. I wonder how it will feel to die.

I watch the finger tightening. I stop breathing.

CLICK.

Elation. This time, I am full of elation, alive and enjoying the game. But the audience is deadly silent, and I can't help wondering why. I have given them almost everything the game could give. We are down to the last member of the squad and my death may be seconds away. I want nothing but to get on with the game.

The pistol slowly rises in the hand of the sixth figure. There is an expertness about it that reminds me of you, when we used to practise for the festival. If only I could see the eyes. Nothing could make this moment more exciting than to know that you are the one about to fire the pistol. Please give me a signal of some kind.

The finger begins to squeeze the trigger. Will I be able to hear the blast, the first rags of sound, see the bullet winging its way towards my head, taste the metal, the shattered brain? My heart is beating wildly, I cry out.

"Is it you?"

CLICK.

Nothing has changed. Just the thud of my heartbeat, the sweaty smell of the gymnasium, the glaring lights overhead, the squad standing erect, the silence of the audience.

Vaguely I see the provost come forwards. He is not smiling. He congratulates me without enthusiasm, then murmurs that perhaps I should go now. The festival is over. The silence is disturbing, the lack of approval for my survival, the hostile faces amongst the audience, even the children's.

I drop the provost's hand and walk towards the squad, to the crumpled body on the floor, slightly on its side in a puddle of blood. The five figures still flank it, unmoving. I stoop and pull, clumsy-fingered, at the hood, tearing it away from the head. And see your hair. The hair that spills out of the hood, the fair hair, wet with blood, I have touched morning and evening all these years. The provost takes me by the arm.

I shake off his hand. The pistol. The pistol is still clutched in your gloved hand. I bend down and loosen your fingers. I slide open the breech.

The chamber of your pistol contains no bullet.

I remember leaving the village early next morning, one of those foggy mornings that are so common in the hills at that time of the year. The provost and the keeper of the hotel helped me downstairs to the taxi with my luggage. All the rest of the village was still asleep. The provost did not invite me back, as he had two years before.

We drove north, past the grey buildings on the edge of town, past the graveyard, the gravestones poking eyes in the fog. The taxi-driver was not a talkative man, but I could see how he would sneak a glance at me now and then in his rear mirror.

I did not sleep on the plane. That was something neither of us had ever been able to do.

And when I got back here, to the city, I drank a good deal. I took a long time to settle back into the humdrum life. I explained to our friends why we were no longer together, and I think, though they were shocked, they understood.

When I found out, after the last event, that all of the squad's pistols were empty, that I had the only loaded pistol, I looked at the provost and said, quite calmly, I think:

"You lied. You've made me commit murder."

He did not answer, he just looked at me. Then, in a very gentle voice, he told me that it was time to go.

Nowadays, I sleep rarely, but when I do, I sometimes dream that you are alive, and we are talking to each other. Talking, talking. Perhaps, all the long conversations we never had. And when I wake up, my eyes are wet, and I can never remember anything we said.

No Country for Old Men

It is a Christmas party. An old man conjures up for us the bitterness of an old war, his mind penetrating the years. He remembers the wisps of trees in the dawn haze of a dale of passion. He remembers dark, rain-filled craters, seducing the war-weary to death by drowning. He remembers the trenches joining together with intricate stitchery fabrics of opposing weft. He remembers the scattering of corpses in the half-light of no man's land, arms still protecting their dead faces. He remembers the emerging shapes of hillocks of shells, innocent-seeming as heaps of canned dog food. He remembers, his eyes hollow, the echoing snap of the fixing of bayonets at dawn: our soldiers, uniformed in grey mud, suck on a last cheap cigarette. They smell the heavy smell of tobacco wafting across from the other trenches, where German soldiers puff securely on huge carved pipes, weighty as Mausers.

"All dead now. All losers in the long run."

He says this without a smile. We listen intently.

"My own life is a miracle. Feel here. Feel the shrapnel? It floats around in my flesh like bits of broken eggshell in the white of an egg. Notice how I stoop to draw breath? Mustard gas, inhaled sixty years ago."

The old man speaks of one regret. We are all ears.

"Of those I killed, I remember clearly only one German soldier, a boy as young as myself. I was on sentry duty on Christmas day. I woke from a doze and found him leaning over me in his alien helmet. His hand was reaching into his kitbag. I stabbed upwards, as I had been taught, thrusting till I saw the blood appear on his lips. I pulled down. The blood drained along the bayonet's gutter neatly, as it should. As he fell, his kitbag spilled out a bottle of wine and a loaf of white bread. Too late, my comrades came running to tell me there was a Christmas truce amongst us, no war for the day. We hid the murdered soldier so that they would not stop bringing the wine and the bread."

That is the old man's regret. Now he means to tell us of a dream. We listen urgently.

"For the last seven nights I have dreamt of that murder. I see myself back in the trenches, the German soldier leaning over me. I know what I must do. I jab the bayonet up into his stomach, holding it till I see the blood at his lips. I pull down, noticing how neatly the blood drains along the bayonet's gutter. Then I step back from the body, and I am in my study. I walk to my desk and open the right-hand drawer. I carefully place the bloody bayonet on top of a sheaf of notepaper, close the drawer, and go back to bed. I have dreamt this for seven nights. On six of the mornings when I awoke, I went to the desk drawer to check, just in case. Only the blank paper confronted me. But this morning, Christmas morning, something was not the same. Even after I awoke, I could still feel the chill of the trenches in my bones, I could remember the weight of the bayonet in my hand. I arose, aware of the beat of my heart. The light of the first snowfall reflected into my study. I walked towards the desk: this time I had no doubt I would find in it the bayonet, on a sheet of blood-stained paper. I gripped the handle of the drawer firmly and wrenched it open. I found nothing. Just a sheaf of clean white paper as before. No miracle had happened. I was the same as other men. I could not cheat a nightmare, steal a part of it, smuggle it into the waking world. Was I not foolish to think that I would find in my desk the bayonet from my dream?"

He appeals to us, his face tired, his eyes pleading. We are ready to forgive anything. Then a grave young man I do not know stands up from amongst the group of listeners. He speaks quietly, his voice compelling. We make a circle round him.

"Last night I dreamt about a Christmas party. In the dream, one of the guests, an old man whose face I cannot remember, tells a group of people (I am one of them) how he murdered a German soldier on a Christmas day long ago. He says he is haunted by a nightmare in which he commits the murder over again, and that he has tried to end it by bringing the weapon out of the nightmare, without success. He begs for pity. The party finishes, and in my dream I follow him to his home. It is snowing. He enters his house. I watch over his shoulder as he bends over the desk in his study. He slides open the right-hand drawer. There, on a sheaf of stained paper, lies a black-handled bayonet. The old man reaches into the drawer and slowly raises the blade, still red with the blood of the victim, to his own red lips. After that I awoke."

Now his eyes are burning as he stares at the old man. The old man lowers his head before us all. He stands still, makes no appeal, for he knows there is no for-giveness in us.

A Train of Gardens
Part I: Ireneus Fludd

We wait beside the Seventh Car of the Train of Gardens. Even if Ireneus Fludd emerged, right now, many of us would not know him. We have never met him in person. Nor is it easy to picture him, for there are so many varying descriptions of him. He is one of those who can undermine words. He has been called — for he has had his share of criticisms — "lank," "a pygmy in physique," "a lump-sack," "a bone-bag," "mister macho," "listless as a lettuce." Otherwise reliable observers are of little help: they speak of "that inimitable voice," "that studied reticence," "that bulbous nose," "those aquiline features," "that fiery diadem of orange hair," "that reptilian poll," "that honest laugh," "that insinuating snigger." It is not easy to picture so motley a man ("Frenchified," they say, or "Hebraic," "Mongolian in feature," "your pint-of-Guinness Dublin looby"). Yet we persist in the hope of seeing him with our own eyes, here at the exit of the Train of Gardens.

"He hasn't come out yet?" we ask.

No answer. None is needed. The morning sky is brilliant, and some of the group have loitered here all night. Is this, then, what it has all come to? Is this the end of the discoverer of the secrets of Oluba? We cluster, his admirers, uneasy beside the Seventh Car of the Train of Gardens. We, remembering, are not willing, as yet, to surrender to grief.

oozed onto cloth of silk
We wait beside the Seventh Car of the Train of Gardens. Will Ireneus Fludd ever emerge? We, his admirers, may never know the secret of his youth, only the rumours, only the insinuations that have so readily been embraced by his enemies. I think of the claims of Alfredo Florentino, erudite son of an ecclesiastical brickmaker. Florentino avowed to a newspaper reporter that in the past he knew Fludd (Fludd acknowledged this only with reluctance). Florentino, hawking up brick-red phlegm in his brickyard in Venice, declared that Fludd once confided to him the great trauma of his early life: the memory of his alarming ride, slide, along the chute of the natal canyon. Florentino, a man who prided himself on exactness of recall, spat neatly, perhaps without malice, and recalled:

"He said he experienced a state, then a state, then a state: comfort, security, warmth. Then a state and another state: discomfort, pain. Then three things: a squeezing of the skull, a feeling of being sucked through the insides of a monster worm, then a short drop into noise and cold." To Florentino, Fludd

sounded Italian, rolling his r's, spitting out his t's with
Latin aggression. Florentino's own red spit dribbles
down his black beard.

(Fludd has always hinted darkly that he cultivated
the Italian mannerism for a time to allay suspicions,
conceal himself from his critics: all his life he has
known there would be certain unspecified forces
hostile to someone like him.)

Florentino said that Fludd even described his natal
bed:

"Five things he told me about that bed, that room: a
four-poster, he said that bed was, with blue curtains
around it. A *camera da letta,* he said that room was,
very beautiful, with windows, he said, looking onto a
garden full of lilies at one end. A maze, he said, a maze
of privets at the other." Florentino, coughing violently,
had accused Fludd to his face of being an aristocrat.
Fludd had sighed at the charge, regretting Florentino's
persistence. "The oak understands the axe," he liked
to say.

the frangipani mourns

Those Oluban findings should have astonished the
world. Those Oluban findings did nothing of the kind.
Instead, because of his unorthodox methods, his lack
of footnotes, they cost Fludd all intellectual respectabil-
ity. He did not mind. The Oluban phase came at a time
(he was then twenty-five) when he was dissatisfied
with received opinion and felt that he must personally
re-examine certain aspects of human behaviour. As
always, despite his lack of formal training, he pursued

his goals with the utmost rigour. The results were remarkable.

He chose as his operational base a remote South Pacific island called Oluba. To protect the island, Fludd says, from marauding anthropologists, he will not give its exact geographic location. He reveals only that it lies at the western extremity of the New Caledonia group. He flew to Queensland, Australia, in February. From there, he took a berth on a fishing schooner bound for the islands. It was the cyclone season, but nothing could dampen his excitement and his sense that a great spiritual adventure was under way.

The journey was rough (they say he mutters about "mutinies," "keel-hauling," "force tens," "great white sharks," "the cat-o'-nine-tails"), but eventually the ship thundered through the perilous entrance of a reef into a translucent lagoon, and he beheld the island of his hopes, Oluba. Steamy Oluba. "A teeming carbuncular eruption in a soupy ocean," according to Fludd, in a poetic moment. Oluba, clamorous with fertility and energy.

It was on this island that he encountered that Oluban hallucinogen, the ineffable *sarga*. (He learnt its secrets from a native girl, Watonobe; she it was, too, who introduced him to the bizarre sexual practices of the islanders.) On Oluba, all the males are expected to eat the *sarga*, which is a product of the hormone of the red sponge-fish peculiar to the island's reef.

The account that follows is a transcription of Fludd's unpublished manuscript, which, in spite of attacks upon its veracity by academics, has enjoyed a cult following for its description of the *sarga* customs and for its analysis of his sexual initiation on Oluba. He intends to revise his manuscript for publication and to answer scholarly criticisms, after the Train of Gardens project. Here it is as he left it.

Oluban male children eat *sarga* whilst they suck the mother's milk. They eat a quantity daily till they arrive at their sixteenth copra harvest. At that age, the young males prepare, for the first time, to join with the veteran devotees, and *ratinake* ("pay the price") for the *sarga*, to which they are completely addicted. The price is a very severe one. In exchange for continued access to the drug, they must sacrifice, annually, in advance, one of their limbs.

I am the only outsider ever to have observed the ceremony (this came of my friendship with Watonobe), and only on one occasion. It was at the end of March. For weeks there had been an aura of unhealthy excitement all over the island. Even the dogs were nervous, and not merely because of the cyclone season, humid and overcast.

On the evening when the ritual was to be performed, the drums began pulsing at six o'clock as the stormy sun sank into the rough sea. Bonfires lit up the central gathering place where all the islanders assembled. There was no sign of their habitual joyousness on their faces.

Suddenly the drums reached fever pitch and into the middle of the arena leapt a huge naked female figure wearing a vivid devil mask. Her body glistened with sweat as she danced, the coronas of her great breasts rolling wildly like extra eyes. This was the high priestess of the cult of the *sarga*. She lurched to a halt and the drumming ceased.

And now, into the firelight, the devotees walked, hobbled, or were carried by the young boys who were about to *ratinake* for the first time. I have never seen such a collection of maimed bodies: it was worse than any photograph showing the aftermath of trench warfare. Aside from the novices, who were still intact, even the younger devotees already lacked noses, or ears or eyes, or fingers, or toes. The older men were proportionately more mutilated: an arm, a leg or two might be gone.

Last came a small group of disciples, carrying on a litter an elderly man, who had managed to reach *Otusuna*, "The Thirty-One Years." For him the sacrifice had now become a deadly one. The name, "The Thirty-One Years," came from the traditional Oluban theory that a man has thirty-one expendable external parts (ten fingers, ten toes, two arms, two legs, two eyes, two ears, a nose, a tongue, a penis — which, with the testes, the Olubans regard as a unit). Few men survive the amputation of all thirty-one, retaining only the internal organs of their stumps of bodies.

The amputations of the younger men's limbs began on a slab of rock in the middle of that arena. Let me say only that the butchery was performed with great dexterity by the priestess and her assistants, who were soon smeared with blood. The sand around them was stained with blood. Blood congealed and dripped from that stone slab like candlewax from a great squat candle. The victims gave themselves willingly, many of them uttering no sound of pain, even when their wounds were cauterized in hot tar. They were cheered wildly by the Olubans according to the extent of their sacrifice. Special applause greeted the neophytes, whose families looked on with pride.

But a great hush came over them when the turns came, at last, of those who had little left to give, the ascetics who lived almost solely on *sarga* and water, who hummed constantly a tongueless monotone, and were in perpetual ecstasy. That huge priestess's knife might now be the instrument of their deaths.

Watonobe, clutching my arm tightly, whispered that among the *Thirty-Oners,* those who have retained their penises till last are revered by the women of Oluba and it is considered a great honour to be allowed to sleep with one of them. In such cases the disciples will lay the saintly devotee on top of the woman so honoured, and act as his missing limbs. They will join the two bodies in a sexual union and discreetly rock the man back and forth, back and forth, gently increasing the momentum till, by the quality of his humming, they sense that orgasm is imminent. A few moments later, after a signal from the woman, they will detach the *Thirty-Oner*, and carry him away looking, as Watonobe said, for all the world like a long-spouted teapot without a handle.

Young girls plead to be given to these terminal devotees for sexual initiation, and if they are lucky enough to conceive a child, it is treasured, and known as *erace* ("nearest to the gods"). Watonobe told me with pride that she herself was *erace*.

The elderly man I had seen earlier was the last to be brought to the altar. His name was Baratee. The islanders crushed forward to brush his body with their finger-tips as he was carried to the stone. Horribly maimed as he was, he had retained his penis, nor did he intend to part with it now. He had communicated to his disciples that he wished instead to forfeit his heart.

A great sigh arose from the assembly when they heard this. As Baratee was laid upon the altar, he hummed his cheerful monotone. He hummed on for a time, then, still humming, nodded his eyeless, earless, noseless head. The priestess plunged the knife into his chest. The humming stopped. In the profound silence, she excavated the heart, and raised it in the air, the blood dripping onto the body which still twitched nervously on the stone of sacrifice.

That was the end of the ritual. The Olubans now turned to feasting and dancing, rejoicing over the death of Baratee. His body was to be boiled and fragments of it distributed as relics amongst the islanders.

Scholars may be interested to note that not all devotees of the *sarga* persist in their dedication. Some have escaped its charms after losing only a few limbs. They are looked on as apostates, or feeble-minded.

"Look how they treat me," one of them told me, "I must help harvest the copra" (and act of self-pollution for a male in Oluba), " I am forbidden entry into the village, they will not allow me to play with the children. Only the most destitute of the prostitutes will entertain me. Didn't I give up enough? Look at my ears, look at these fingers."

Even lower in regard are the males who refused to sacrifice any limbs at all. They carry the scars of their wholeness with them, and not even the prostitutes will associate with them. They are violent men prone to suicide and bestiality.

That is how the first part of the manuscript ends. "Ah! the whiteness of the leper," Fludd would often comment to those of his disciples who read the segment, "the whiteness of the leper is the only true whiteness."

phalanxes of immortals
Fludd has allowed us to read his unpublished manuscript on the myth-making powers of the Olubans. The subject was clearly of great interest to him (it is a little

too iconoclastic for some of his critics). A brief summary shows its general directions.

To begin with, Fludd tries to impress Watonobe with the variety of gods in the world he has come from. He names their sacred names: Jupiter Fulgur, Orcus, Agdistes; Heindall and Frigg; Morrigan and Grobniu; Sarasvati and Avalokitesvera; Jagannath and Narsinh; Amen-Ra and Thoth; Ereshkigal and Upnapishtim; Amatsumar and Ninigino-Mikoto; Changs and Wangs innumerable.

She hears him out and laughs. She tells him something he can hardly conceive of: Oluba is an incubator of cosmogonies. Each Oluban family invents its own creation myth, vying with the others in originality, splendour, vulgarity. To convince him, Watonobe introduces Fludd into the longhouses at full moon, the myth-telling period.

He visits the Makibo family longhouse and hears their family myth told by Amra the loud, happy minstrel-aunt. Between sucks on her pipe, she sings of the self-indulgent deity, Butobo, who overeats then defecates and vomits into the void, forming the stars, the planets, the Milky Way. The ocean on which Oluba floats is Butobo's almighty urine, the island itself a marvellous turd on which his parasites, the Olubans, grow. Amra the minstrel supplies the sounds of Butobo's exertions so realistically that the audience is filled with wonder.

In his visits to the other longhouses, Fludd makes notes on countless creators. A creator who lives in two-syllable words. A creator who is suffering from the Oluban equivalent of a nervous breakdown. A creator who, like a coral snake, casts off his skin with each millenium, every skin becoming a new world. A creator whose sleep must never disturbed, for this world is a dream of his. A creator who has made the world so perfect he envies it and wishes to annihilate it. A creator who didn't really make this world, but came into possession of it through a potlatch with a demon, its real maker. A creator who created the world so that it might enjoy *sarga* forever. A creator who made life by accident through pronouncing the wrong spell, and who must be prevented from finding a counter-charm. A creator who is afraid to reveal himself to his creation because he cannot live up to its image of him. . . .

Watonobe's own family myth delights Fludd. She herself was conceived on the last night of the life of her father, Simpe (a legend on the island), a *"Thirty-Oner,"* who had died upon removal of his penis. He had composed the myth before losing his ability to communicate, and Fludd now hears it sung by Watonobe's mother, Panua.

This creator is named Rampa, the sexual power. He controls a vast ("a million times a million") harem of sex-goddesses, with whom he consorts infinitely, inventing a myriad love-techniques, some of which survive only on Oluba. Rampa is at the heart of all creation. When he observes an earthly man and woman make love, Rampa mates simultaneously with one of his goddesses. He then miraculously transplants the divinely fertilized egg into the womb of the earthly mother. He is thus truly the father of the human race, and is kept very busy.

The only rite he insists upon is the act of love itself, which gives him supreme joy. Watonobe's family is not remiss in its observation, as Fludd is soon to discover. In later years, he will repeat to his disciples with approval the pithy Oluban proverb, "many gods, few sins."

behold the waters

We wait beside the Seventh Car of the Train of Gardens. We stand here thinking now about the hands, the feet of Ireneus Fludd. His hands and feet occupy us, because of a version of the first eighteen years of his life that has been widely circulated. The source is a broadsheet by Fortescue and Perdonta de Medullin, brother and sister, bachelor and spinster, amateur ichthyologists, joint Elders of the Church of Reformed Morals, and renowned ascetics. The de Medullins, prolific authors of admonitory broadsheets and pamphlets on the ethical behaviour of fish, have loudly condemned Fludd as a liar, a pervert and a corrupter of fish. They claim to have known Fludd's parents (Fludd has denied the claim vigorously). In a broadsheet entitled *Leviathan in a Goldfishbowl*, the de Medullins take turns in proclaiming their version of Fludd's youth to the world. The first part is written by Fortescue, the cosmopolitan *par excellence*, who has been hounded out of every country in Europe and Asia, and incorporates a number of their linguistic peculiarities into what he calls his "universal voice of prophecy." He begins:

The person, "Ireneus Fludd," is a creature of the most unnatural. Not is this suggesting he is of entirely to blame. Consider to this background. His father, which the name of I am sworn to conceal (such is his depraved the conduct, one is understanding his desire at anonymity) was a professorial of Biology at the Sorbonne. His mother, a most moral weakling, became all pregnant, and feared the carry of her child, for it might in her inside have an explosion. Sparing to her, *M le Professeur* debagged the foetus at her womb and transferring did into a construction plastic womb.

Oh! sadly, sadly! The foetus insettled down to it, unfortunately if I may so say it for the world, to grow at quite a health. After the nine months having been so passed to the fulness, it was for born urgency.

But now, *M le Professeur* and the so moral weakling wife wanted the preference of being expecting the baby, not having one not actually. They much desired the need to keep him in the plastic womb the longer more awhile. Renovations of such plannings were needed. Enlarge the womb was done, a liquid thousand of liters pumped over, and glassy windows made this womb a plastic so to be like a tank of very fish.

At this point in the pamphlet, the hand of the sister, Perdonta, takes over:

You can imagine the warped pleasure of the parents when their spawn made his first tentative breast strokes into the annex of that artificial womb. Now they could watch the monster's daily growth. They saw his reddish-black bristles begin to sprout, the blue-green eyes exploring his watery world. The infamous parents pursued their abominable course to its end. They gradually introduced into the tank, to keep him company, instead of teddy-bears and toy cars, a variety of cold-blooded companions. They surrounded him with kissing gouramis, loach gobies, intemperate basses, a croaker or two, a disgusting goatfish, some porgies, some irresponsible black pomfrets and flagtails, a quota of halfmoons and moronic bonnetmouths, five sand stargazers, two three fin blennies and a graveldiver. Fitting company for such a child! They were all as corrupt in the end.

The baby, however, was curious about the creatures outside his tank, forever spying upon him, and soon began to recognize them. He would swim over to meet his parents accompanied by the other fish who accepted him, because of his strangeness, as their natural leader. The fiendish parents would call out, "Ireneus! Come, Ireneus!" and his lips would bubble intuitively the words, "da-da," "ma-ma."

They hired a Scottish nanny with the kind of debauched past that assured her co-operation to see to the needs of their son. She taught him to read, holding up the alphabet books to his inhuman eyes. The conniving witch would press her lips against the glass and shout words. He

would gurgle them back to her till the tank rever-
berated with their grotesque communications.

The remainder of Fortescue and Perdonta de Medullin's
tale is predictable: one day, many years later (Fludd was
now eighteen), a beautiful female student of *M le Professeur's,* a *Mlle* Madeleine de Rocheau, inadvertently
entered the tank-room and gazed at the lily-white
youth, still harnessed to his umbilical cord. Fludd swam
to the window of his tank, and gazed back at her in
astonishment. Till that moment, he had experienced
undefined longings only for a sleek amberjack, or an
aloof papagallo. Now, for the first time, he felt a
swelling in the area of his genitalia, in which the *mademoiselle* was showing an interest. Clutching himself,
he kick-stroked awkwardly to the opaque part of the
tank. The water seethed. A moment later, filaments of
a milky substance drifted like mermaid's ribbons before
the eyes of the curious *mademoiselle.*
   That night, Ireneus Fludd asked *M le Professeur* to
release him, to let him at last be born.
   A few hours afterwards, he who for eighteen years
had breathed only under water gulped down his first
shock of air. He who had touched only the cold scales
of his fish friends felt for the first time the warmth of
human contact. He who could swim as expertly as a
dolphin made his first terrifying efforts to walk upright.
He who had only gargled the soliloquies of Shake-
speare, the lyrics of Tennyson, spoke for the first time,
a burbling Scottish twang like his nanny's.
   He heard his own voice with amazement.

This is the de Medullins' version of the early years.
Some of Fludd's former friends say that he does have
webbed fingers and toes (he tries, they say, always to
keep them covered, insists on mittens, will not wear
sandals). They say he will gaze longingly at an ocean-
scape. They say he will visit only cities with aquaria,
and prefers to socialize only with friends who have fish-
bowls in their homes. They say when he approaches a
bowl, the fish congregate by him, and that he has often
spent whole evenings staring at them with dilated eyes,
making peculiar lippy noises.

Fludd, on the other hand, has only one word for the
de Medullins: "charlatans." Yet he will often say to his
disciples, "Consort not with the darkness of waters,"
and he will smile enigmatically:

sneaked into innocence
Watonobe, Watonobe. The name chimes all through
the Oluban papers of Ireneus Fludd, sometimes
doodled sensuously in the margins. She attached
herself to him, though as a rule Oluban women
scorned unmutilated males. Fludd's deviance was
overlooked, a foreigner's eccentricity. Many of us
have seen that remarkable though incomplete manuscript dealing with her sexual tutelage of Fludd.
Though professional anthropologists have (for their
own reasons) rejected the whole document as utterly
specious, he regarded this tract as of primary importance, and meant to give it his full attention when he
put his affairs in order. Some of the terms are still in
their original Oluban form:

Watonobe intended me to be her *unor* ("student") in the Oluban way. She was beautiful, her eyes were ageless. Like all Oluban beauties, she had great muscular thighs, which she constantly exercised by flexing and knee-bends. She had spent the years since her twelfth copra-harvest in perfecting the love methods of *ana pria* ("ways of loving"). She would refer to her many previous *unors* as a scholar acknowledges some authority. Her frankness disconcerted me at first, though I was aware she was simply displaying her credentials as a tutor. That first night's lesson was unforgettable, the moon over the lagoon, the breakers distant and soothing. The air was full of spice and flowers.

Watonobe began by coaxing me to the longhut to chat with her mother and the rest of her sisters. I felt a little awkward as she told them that I was to be her *unor.* They laughed knowingly, and said they'd learn all the details of the lesson from her in the morning. Her mother, Panua, still an exotic creature herself, more like an elder sister, massaged Watonobe's neck and shoulders with *santra*-oil, an absolute pre-requisite for love-making on Oluba.

Then Watonobe and I bade them good night, and walked hand in hand to the little hut dedicated to such *ana pria cuna* activities. Thus began a night, the first of many I spent on Oluba, which I shall never forget.

We entered the hut. Slowly, without any shyness, she unfastened her sarong and allowed it to

slip down to the rattan floor. Then she undid my
shirt, and peeled it slowly from me. Then my
trousers. As she undid the zip, I could feel her cool
fingers slide along my *umpum*.

Despite my efforts to remain calm and obser-
vant, I was becoming excited. She took my head in
her soft hands and gently pressed it to her scented
body, my face against her swelling *zumbas*. We lay
down together, she above me. And now she began
to kiss me, gradually moving her warm lips down
my body, until I felt their moistness brush my *bagu*.
Her fingers began the soft caress known as *iserime,* which ensures that passion does not come to
a head prematurely. And now, still fondling
umpum and *olbolu*, she lay beside me so that I
might admire her magnificent body.

As a courtesy to my teacher, and so that I
might learn more about these Oluban practices,
I took a deep breath and kissed her neck and
shoulders, adjusting my body so that she did not
need to interrupt her caresses. Soon I was
kissing her magnificent *zumbas,* noting all the
time the coloration and texture of the upright
atitas.

She also was beginning to breathe more quickly
and utter signs of contentment, as I intuitively continued the exploratory path with my tongue. Her
palpitating *ulavula* loomed before me, exuding
the most exotic odours and my tongue probed it
much to her delight.

Then suddenly, forgetting for a brief moment all

my scientific objectivity, I lunged at that incredibly well-developed *nimpaclic.*

Now she began to squirm as we both, she with her trembling, no-longer-cool fingers, I with my earnest tongue, continued our lesson.

I fully realize that a scholar might well object to all of this. He might complain that these practices are in no way particular to Oluba; they are the common-or-garden, stock-in-trade of lovers the world over. I acknowledge the validity of the point. Bear with me.

For now began my initiation into the unique carnal rites of Oluba. During one of my manoeuvres, Watonobe uttered a delirious squeal, and the door of the hut burst open. In came running her mother, the comely Panua, and her two sisters, Carama and Anata. They were all as beautiful as Watonobe, with their shining dark brown hair and delightful features. Imagine my curiosity when all three, laughing with joy, threw off their sarongs, and joined us on the rattan floor, grasping and fondling parts of my body in the most titillating way. I was totally immersed in *zumbas,* all fragrant with the most beautiful of odours, whilst my own *umpum* and *olbolu* were constantly and variously manipulated.

This was surely the most mystical of sensual experiences: I entered into an unparalleled divine unity with the four, all of whom devoted their energies to my compliant flesh.

Watonobe had no sooner coaxed my throbbing *umpum* into her *ulavula* than I felt a moist pressure behind me in the area of my *asana*. It was the gorgeous sister, Carama, whose tongue was delicately probing whilst her elegant fingers were dandling my *bagu*. As if this were not enough, that other delightful sister, Anata, stood over me, spread her legs, and descended upon my face from above, inviting me to insert my tongue into her own moist and odorous *ulavula*. This unlooked-for familial hospitality to a stranger touched my heart. All the while, the maternal Panua encouraged her daughters to do their duty, delicately adjusting limbs, wiping untimely spills, or excessive perspiration, with a sandal wood sponge.

My nerves were tingling with such pleasure, in spite of my efforts to maintain a scholarly perspective, that Panua would occasionally *rumubumu* me in a certain way, and by uncanny skill, prevent my too early *lodawe*.

Yet the moment surely could not be delayed much longer, for I was ready to discharge, regardless of her technical skills. Panua clapped her hands, and suddenly, outside the hut, a bevy of drums began to beat a pulsating, driving rhythm. "Now is the time for *meniveni*," Panua whispered, "at last! at last!"

A dozen other beautiful Oluban women dashed into the hut, and they too fell to the rattan floor. They began stimulating each other with great energy and laughter till the floor was moist with their activity, for they administered *rumubumu* and *iserime* to whichever body was nearest, including, especially, my own.

I had never witnessed such acts of selfless devotion; my heart was thudding to the drumbeat, though I made every effort to maintain my academic detachment. The most curious part of the entire evening was still to come, however. Now Panua took Watonobe by the hand and led her towards a horizontal bamboo pole suspended about five feet above the floor. She helped my athletic instructress to leap up to the bar, and hang there by the knees, her legs apart, her head downwards, her long raven hair trailing on the rattan mat. Watonobe was looking at me from her upside-down position, calling to me, extending her arms towards me. At first I was quite at a loss, then the realization of what I was expected to do dawned upon me. Panua and the others, smiling with pleasure and anticipation, led me to her. They gently turned me upside down too, and with great expertise, hoisted me into the air and slotted my *umpum* neatly into the open, glistening *ulavula* of my teacher. Then they let go of me. We hung there like a leftover clothes-peg on a line. At first I was mortally afraid of injuring myself, and clung desperately to Watonobe. She wrapped her arms around me with pleasure, and now I understood why these women had developed their quadraceps so highly. She was able to take the weight of both of us with ease, and began to make scissoring movements with her thighs. Never have I experienced such bliss. Watonobe was squealing with pleasure as we embraced upside down, like mating bats, or trapeze artists at a private orgy. Our audience looked on with smiling faces, then continued their own activities. Everywhere, I could see nothing but *atitas, ulavulas, zumbas* abounding, a frenzy of *rumubumu, iserime, meniveni, nimpaclic,* and *lodawe, lodawe, lodawe,* until I cried out, "Dear Heavens!"

Here the manuscript peters out. Fludd planned to complete it and render into appropriate English the rather obscure technical jargon after the Train of Gardens project.

We are aware of the importance of the Oluban period to Fludd. He saw in that remote island society glimmerings of a truth which he would express to his disciples in his most profound dictum: "The rule of the imagination over the senses is the only key to human happiness."

His Oluban researches have been rejected, of course, by professional academics. He came to feel that, by "originality," what they really mean is the invention of ingenious ways to support outmoded ideas. Fludd never lost confidence in his own vision, which he would embody ultimately in his ineffable Train of Gardens.

A Train of Gardens
Part II: The Machine

We wait beside this Train of Gardens glistening in the morning sun, the masterwork of Ireneus Fludd. The plan for it matured during one of his philanthropic periods. He had considered building a fleet of mobile swimming pools using cast-off oil-tanks, in which, on sultry days of summer, the city's ghetto-children might dip themselves.

He forsook this idea for the appeal of a grander scheme: a Train of Gardens. He would construct a travelling Botanical Gardens to bring the true splendours of nature into every city, town, village, hamlet of North America, South America, Europe, Asia. THE WORLD.

Yes, his ambition grew, and so did the conception: his Train of Gardens must be the great experience in the lives of all who entered. It must be that perfection of nature he had always desired. He would fit his Train with adjustable wheels to bring all the world within its reach: already he saw it teetering along narrow rails through the outback of Australia, skirting the white beaches of Fiji, the barren moors of the Aleutian

Islands. He saw his Train steaming along the volcanic ridges of the Tuamotu Archipelago and the Marquesas, flouting the mountain winds and glaciers of Tierra del Fuego and Greenland. He saw it chugging along the toy tracks of the sugar-cane fields of Trinidad, the bogey-rails of the coalfields of Central Scotland.

Fludd's plan was and is prodigious. Here stands the Train, a great steam-engine, at rest now, shackled to seven rebuilt freight cars with thick glass roofs. In each car, an episode of the Train of Gardens.

Three weeks ago on this day, a sunny morning, Ireneus Fludd entered the First Car, began his journey. He would be the first human being to travel through to the Seventh Car. It was an enterprise for which he had been preparing all his life.

The First Car
the north woods. Fludd immediately encounters the dark walls of green forest on all sides. He steps precariously on pine needles, their scent rising to him. The woods are silent, restful, no cry of a bird. Now he breaks into a clearing, now he sees a fragment of sky, an eagle, its prey dangling, sloping towards its eyrie. He comes upon tracks. He sniffs the air. He smells the stink of bear. He stiffens, on guard. Does he glimpse a malevolent face? Mad eyes assessing him from a thicket? She moves out from behind a huge pine tree, a black-haired woman of great beauty, in a green robe, innocent blue eyes surveying him. She smiles and slowly unbuttons the front of her robe, her golden

breasts welling out before him. She smiles. He begins
to speak. Each word, like a blow, beats her down. She
crouches, then swells, matted hair covers her face, her
body. Fangs protrude from her snout. She growls
deeply, reaches towards him with scything claws. He
stumbles from her, runs as fast as he can, runs, runs
endlessly. "In the body of the beast dwells pleasure,"
Fludd tells himself, as he runs.

The Second Car
the river. A torrent is sucked through the groins of a
ravine. Fludd embarks in a wooden canoe. The current
snatches him along. White foam, shredded by black
rocks, flies everywhere. Whirlpools pock the surface
entrapping the unwary. Fludd, exhilarated by the
speed and danger, holds on tightly to the spar of his
canoe. His arms ache, he is chilled to the bone. She
appears straddling a slick black rock in the middle of
a swollen section of the river. She is naked, her body,
her red hair, glistening in the spray. She is slowly
rubbing herself on the smooth finger of rock. She
opens her arms to welcome him to her. Her beauty
overcomes him. He smiles, and she disintegrates. That
beautiful body turns gelid and formless. That face is
disfigured by warts and wrinkles. Like a great toad she
slides into the water towards him. No path leads up
those walls fringed far above by bushes. Sometimes a
boulder plunges down, as though deliberately aimed,
almost striking the canoe. "Beware lest you drown in
the spirit," Fludd tells himself. He hears the plunging
of the beast in the water behind him.

The Third Car

the mountain. The only route lies through a high pass
of unearthly beauty. Cold numbs his body, avalanches
constantly threaten. The rock-face climb taxes even
Fludd's skill. Pitons and axes are the only help in that
cruel place. Ropes dangle ready in position, but he
knows they are not to be trusted, for he can see they
have been partly sawn through. He hears a crunching
in the snow just below him. She stands there, looking
up at him, more beautiful than ever, wearing a white
smock, flowers in her golden hair. In that frigid air,
she caresses her breasts through the flimsy dress,
slides her long fingers between her thighs, looking at
him. There is no resisting her smile. He stoops to help
her up, raises her cool white hand to his lips. The flesh
sears, and he looks into the insane eyes of a wolf,
burning eyes, the smell of putrid flesh in the air. He
tears himself away and climbs on, with urgency. Fierce
winds wrench at him on the ice face, threatening to
plunge him into the abyss. The ice cracks terrifyingly
around him. In the dark and the cold, he knows he
must bivouac in an ice cave and await the ferocious
dawn. He lies, shivering, waiting, hearing inhuman
howls from outside. "Ascend ye therefore to unknown
valleys," Fludd tells himself.

The Fourth Car

the ocean. It shimmers at the foot of the mountains.
The water sparkles so clear that Fludd can see fish
flicking around on the bottom. A fisherman's empty
sailboat waits on the white beach. On the distant

horizon squats the outline of a coast. He pushes the boat gently into the swell, raises the sail, lowers the centreboard, grasps the tiller, and bears away westwards. Now the sea changes its mood. The sky darkens, a whistling offshore wind and driving rain assail him. No hope remains of beating back to that haven in this flimsy craft. The wind turns to gale-force, batters the tiny hull, rogue waves threaten at any moment to breach or pitchpole the vessel. Off his port quarter a black sailboat rapidly approaches. She stands in the bow, clutching the foremast. Her robe is completely open, billowing like a cloud, and he sees that she is straddling a marlin spike upon which she gently moves up and down, up and down, swaying in the sea's swell, in all her beauty, there in the bows, singing a lilting song. Her red hair, her loose silken gown are flying in the wind. She smiles at him, sings "Come hither love to me." He luffs the sails and is about to step across into her boat when her song changes into inarticulate howls, and he sees she is swathed in torn bandages seeping pus, St Elmo's fire running up and down the scarecrow masts, illuminating the shape that was hers. He leaps back into his own craft and flies before the wind. He must steer with courage and hope. Any lapse in concentration will surely mean death by drowning. Darkness will ensnare him before he reaches that distant coast. He will be unable to see the reef that protects it, he will hear only the dull roar of the breakers. Behind him comes that ominous hull, ahead lies the coast. That coast is peopled by ruthless savages, and is called Wreck Coast; God help any sailor

driven upon it. "Trust only in the permanence of
sorrow," Fludd tells himself, as he runs before the gale.

The Fifth Car

the desert. A world of sand of many colours, parched
by sun, assails him. Fludd searches in vain for shade.
The plain teems with poisonous snakes, and, most
deadly, scorpions scuttling amongst rocks. Somewhere in the midst of the wilderness a muddied water-
hole surrounded by palm trees awaits him. The desert
is littered with skeletons; some of the skulls are
human. She rides towards him on an Arab stallion, the
sun gleaming on her burnished brown hair, her long
brown hair her only garment, her skin golden in the
fading sun. She is smiling, offering him a drink from a
leather bag. His heart is bursting with love. As she
swings her leg over to dismount, his heart soars at the
glimpse of her pink sex. He raises the leather bag to
his mouth and pours ashes into his greedy throat.
Choking, he looks into the empty sockets of a skull, a
skeleton clattering to the sand in front of him, a rat-
tlesnake rearing at him out of the bones. Fludd flees
once more, sensing all around him the wraiths of
savage Tuareg horsemen, waiting, waiting for the darkness. "Joy is the shadow of earthly pain," Fludd tells
himself, as he flees.

The Sixth Car

the jungle. Fludd must hack a path with his machete
through barriers of bamboo. Clouds of mosquitoes
blind him, killer-bees attack, army ants sting, blood-

suckers attach themselves lovingly to his limbs as he wades through the green scum of the swamps. A boa constrictor, like a great moving jigsaw puzzle, heaves on a branch above his sweating head. Death-masks hang from creepers. Shadows flit behind gross ferns, and he fears the prick of a blow-dart. Fetid streams block his progress, brimming with the razor-jaws of piranha fish. At dusk, the clamour of the jungle abruptly ceases, and ominous silences chill him. She appears just before dark, from behind the great lianas. Her hair is black, her naked body oiled and perfect. She smiles reassuringly, and lies on the jungle floor, opening her dark crotch to him. His love is boundless, he discards his clothing and lies down beside her. As darkness descends, he hears the inhuman laughter of the jungle, sees the twin fangs protrude from red lips as she moves her mouth towards his neck. Fludd does not recoil. He smiles, embraces her with great affection. For the first time he thinks of no words, tells himself absolutely nothing.

The Seventh Car

the car of rest for the traveller. A cottage with spruce sides stands on a meadow, green and misty, hills in the distance are luminous with snow. Streams criss-cross the parkland in the cool light. From the cottage, man-icured lawns run to the edge of the deep woods where fawns perform a quadrille. The walls of the main room of the cottage are blue. A large four-poster bed and an armchair take up the centre of the room. Blue curtains fringe the bed, the sheets are fresh and blue. A servant girl dressed in white will escort the traveller to the bath, where she will wash him tenderly, massage his weary body with odorous oils. She will dry him and help him into light pyjamas. She will bring to his bedside a tray of delicacies so that he may assuage his hunger. She will collect the tray, draw the curtains and leave him to his dreamless sleep.

The Seventh Car awaits Ireneus Fludd and we await him outside the door of the Seventh Car. It is now three weeks since he set out on his journey through the Train of Gardens. Rescue parties have searched for him with fatal results. Only one survivor, torn and terribly injured, fought his way back to the entrance of the First Car and staggered out, gibbering. But as yet, no one has given up hope. Many of the friends of Fludd assemble each morning outside the Train, daily bulletins are given. Watonobe (she is very beautiful and very sad) has arrived from Oluba, and awaits, as we all await, the triumphal return of Ireneus Fludd.

The Hobby

The wrinkles on his face were as complex as a railroad junction, a chain of mandalas converging on his eyes and mouth. Somewhere within them lay a secret not disclosed by the facts: sixty years working for the LMS (London-Midland-Scottish), a terminal "thank-you-very-much," a silver pocket-watch in remembrance. Began his travels then, always by train, and came to be in Southern Ontario for a time, took a room with a Kitchener man and his wife who'd only ever boarded a cat before, never had a human being winter over with them.

Like a cat, too, he nuzzled around their house on the first day, unselfconscious, sniffing into all the corners, a lithe old man looking for a particular place. And settled on the basement. The man and his wife agreed to install a bed there. The basement was his. He brought down his suitcase, later his wooden box of equipment. He told them that between journeys he liked to build his own railroad, an old man's hobby, an old man with railroads on the brain. Who hoarded words like nuts, occasionally squandering them in reminiscences. As on a morning of snow in January:

"There was a lot of snow that day. Still the plough should have been able to clear the lines. They nearly had to cancel the parade. That was a good fire in the waiting-room, but the station-master wouldn't let us enjoy it. 'Do this, do that.' Keeping the platforms clear for the spectators. We were just as glad when the trains arrived. They came right out of the snow. The Flying Scotsman, the Royal Scot, the Caerphilly Castle, the Lord Nelson, the Princess Elizabeth. You could see the names right on their sides. Those engineers ignored us as though we weren't even there waving and shouting at them. The noise made us forget the cold. The ground was trembling and people were laughing, even the station-master, and he never used to laugh. After they were all past he said, 'You'll not see anything like that again.' I said, 'Maybe not.'"

Always remembering the old days on the railroads. But talking was not his hobby, he had to get on with his work behind the locked basement door. Then he would emerge late in the day, grimy, nod over a snack, and off to bed. He always locked the basement door after him and made it plain they must on no account go down until he had finished his work, whenever that might be. For he had so much to do, laying the tracks, wiring the dynamos, installing complicated parallels, cycles, assembling the platforms, the station itself.

Yet by the end of January they suspected he was

nearly finished, for one night as they sat in the living-room overhead, they heard what sounded like a train pecking its way along the tracks. They smiled and went to the basement door. But the noise stopped and he did not answer their knock.

Next day he told them they must be patient, he would not abide prying into his work. Right now he was organizing a full timetable and was too busy to amuse sightseers. He had crews to dispatch, mail-loading to supervise, tracks to inspect, all the burdens of assembling an intricate operation.

They co-operated. Instead of setting a place for him at table, they would leave his dinner on a tray at the door of the basement. Often when they went to pick up the tray they would find the meal untouched and so they worried about his health too. When he did consent to come to table, it was usually by way of celebration, some difficult piece of machinery successfully installed. He would wash the grease from his face and hands, and sit cheerfully, quietly, his mind elsewhere planning the next move. Only on Sundays would he luxuriate in bed late, storing up strength for the Monday-morning onslaught. On one of those Sundays, he rose late and had lunch with them. Over coffee he looked at them directly and spoke:

"That boy wore me out. I tried to get him to help me build a railroad after I retired. I showed him how to put it together and how to fix it when it broke down. But the tunnel frightened him the way it gobbled things down like a snake. I told him you couldn't do without a tunnel. He said he was scared it would swallow him, and me too, if I didn't look out. He just wanted to sit upstairs in his room, all alone, like he always did. She was the one that found him in the bath, and she never recovered from that. I always feel bad when I think about it, for I loved them both, and I think they loved me."

They wondered what he meant by it all, but he looked desolated, and they could think of nothing to say.

Mostly at table he listened absently to their small talk now, every so often checking his LMS silver pocket-watch with furrowed brow. They sensed that he grudged the time away from his hobby. When they would gently try to interest him in a stroll along the neat, tree-lined Kitchener streets, or coax him to come with them in the car to inspect the lush Mennonite farmlands of Waterloo County, or see Niagara Falls, he would excuse himself, pointing out, as to irresponsible children, that there were schedules that had to be met. For their part, they accepted all his rebukes with remorse, perhaps pride. They were thankful for him, their lives were curiously purposeful as they had seldom been before.

And now a manic period began. He would start work in the basement at first light and they would hear him hammering urgently all day long and into the night. Whenever they saw him he was covered in grease, eyes red-rimmed, clothes dirty. His face had become so wrinkled it might have been a mask under which a stranger hid. They fretted over his neglect of himself, they did not want him to die on them from exhaustion. Yet their concern seemed to menace him, and he would mutter cagily that they should not worry, he was used to this, his railroad must be finished on time.

They did not have long to wait.

The next Sunday morning. Two A.M. They had gone to bed at midnight, he had stayed up late, working in the basement. A tremendous howl awakened them abruptly, the whole house vibrated with it. Oh my God, they thought as they rushed downstairs into a cloud of foul smoke that made them wheeze and cough, he's set the place on fire.

The basement door was locked from the inside. A terrifying grinding and screaming came from behind it. They stood helpless, then put their bodies resolutely to the door and splintered it open. They stumbled inside onto the landing at the top of the little staircase, and through the smoke they saw his work.

Under the dim ceiling lights, the basement was transformed. It was now a grimy old British railway station bustling with activity. On the platform beneath them a swarm of people they had never seen before, one of them carrying a baby in her arms, jostled onto a single passenger carriage attached to a huge, old-fashioned glistening black locomotive, a monster of hissing steam. A golden LMS was emblazoned on its side. Paralysed, they watched as officious-looking porters in dowdy uniforms with tin buttons began slamming the carriage doors behind the last passengers, and an amplified voice whined something about

a departure. Other travellers on the congested platform seemed to have recently disembarked and uncer-
tainly escorted trolley-loads of luggage pulled by brisk
porters towards various murky apertures. A guard
waved a red flag.

That was when they saw him. He was in the engineer's cabin, leaning his left elbow on the window
ledge, peering ahead of the train up into a vast tunnel.
The brakes exhaled numbingly. The wheels began
slowly to lumber towards the tunnel. With his right
arm they saw him reach expertly in front of him and
pull back and forth, back and forth. A shattering
double wail permeated the air. He glanced back in
their direction for a moment. He was all concentration, he was all contentment.

They did not know what moved them. Hand in hand
they rushed down the stairs in desperation, yanked
open the last door of the moving carriage and scram-
bled aboard. One of the porters slammed the door shut
behind them as the train entered the tunnel.

A sudden silence. The smell of stale cigarette smoke.
Before them stretched an aisle giving access to half a
dozen compartments. As they swayed along the aisle,
the passengers behind the glass paid no attention to
them: some were reading newspapers, some con-
versing with their neighbours, some staring idly out
of the windows into the darkness, the train advancing
further into the tunnel picking up speed. All the compartments were filled except for the very last, marked
"FIRST CLASS." The only occupant was a bushy-haired
man who loured up at them as they gazed in. Distantly

they heard the engine screech a muffled defiance of the darkness. They entered the compartment, slid the door shut and sat down opposite me. They told me how they came to be on that train. Then they asked me who I was, and we looked at each other with growing anxiety.

One Picture of Trotsky

"The women's cloaks were as black as the morning," she said.

I'm sure that's what she said. Then again, maybe I heard wrong. She's been mumbling a lot and I can't make out much of it. Something about morning. She doesn't sleep much, she just lies here, dozing, on and off. Something about the morning being black and cold.

Start with a morning, black and cold, make the sun quick to withdraw its probing finger from an opening in the low horizon. Let there be women, thirteen of them, in hooded cloaks, standing in a huddle on the cobble-stones in front of the prison. They might have been a death-fleet, their black sails flattened by the gale that howled across miles of ocean and harrowed the coastal plain.

It was almost six o'clock. Behind the prison's massive granite walls, a drum rolled deeply. Then a sharper drumming: hobnailed boots rattling against stone, the boots of the death squad leading out the prisoner.

He seemed very relaxed, sitting there, legs crossed, on the stool by his crib. The chaplain asked him if he'd like to say a prayer or two, but he declined, politely. He said he wished the prison breakfasts had always been as good. He had treated the guards with great courtesy all the night before, and when he turned in, around midnight, he told them not to be afraid to wake him during the night if they needed an extra hand at cards. Naturally, they did not disturb him. The warden's message came at ten minutes to six: no reprieve. He showed no sign of disappointment. When he heard, a few minutes later, the sound of the escort coming along the corridor, he rose and smoothed his clothes. He thanked the chaplain for his company during the past days, and was sorry he couldn't oblige him in the matter of prayer. He shook hands with the guards, squeezing the shoulder of each of them affectionately. They seemed embarrassed when he told them they should be proud of the way they'd done their unpleasant duty. The escort arrived at the cell door, and he greeted them cheerfully. He allowed the officer to manacle his hands, then marched away at the head of the escort with a confident stride.

The women strained their ears. The boots and the drum had fallen silent, even the wind no longer whined. The stitching of minutes was nearly done.

A shout of command, the crash of a trapdoor. It was over. Now the wind could begin its whining again.

The women outside crowded around the oak prison door with its metal studs. They were all attention as the locks rasped, the door creaked ajar. It was the hangman, wearing half a face, half a mask, holding a lantern. One of the women curtsied, and he held his lantern high, looking her over, looking them all over through his slits. He signalled them to come into the prison-yard, one by one.

The yard was empty. They could see no one but the hangman's masked assistant, all of the soldiers and officials having hurried inside out of the cold. The assistant stood in the middle of the yard beside the scaffold, a wooden skeleton of ribs and props, filtering the light of torches. No one else. Though there may have been onlookers. From hundreds of barred windows around the yard, was there a blur of faces?

But the attention of the women focused on the gallows, their eyes yearned towards it. From the cross-beam of new wood, a body swung on a rope, to and fro, swaying gently in the wind, alive with flickering torchlight. The head tilted at an impossible angle in its black cover.

The hangman's slit eyes looked around the women. "Which one?" he asked, his voice soft, high-pitched.

One of the women, taller than the others, stepped forwards. He reached a gloved hand out and slid her hood back to her shoulders. Her head was shaved, a young woman with jowels. She did not look him in the eyes.

By now, the hangman's assistant had lowered the rope so that the feet of the hanged man, like those of an idle puppet, lightly brushed the damp cobblestones under the scaffold. The women ducked through the framework and began to undress the dead man. They did not bother with his upper clothing, for his hands were still cuffed behind him. They pulled his rough canvas trousers down round his black boots. His lower body was exposed to them all.

They looked to the bald woman. She did not waste time. She lifted her skirts above her heavy thighs and tucked them in. She put her arms round the dead man's neck and heaved herself up, straddling him, wrapping her legs around his buttocks, agile as a mountain climber. The rope creaked with the double burden. She began to bob up and down on him, straining in that cold dawn in the light of the torches. The hangman looked on, as did his assistant, and the twelve cloaked women, and perhaps another hundred pairs of eyes at a hundred barred windows.

The bald woman pumped up and down more and more quickly, sighing, grunting, a pennant of saliva flying from her open mouth. Then she stiffened, and whimpered loudly for a moment. She sighed, her body relaxed, and she slid to her knees on the cobblestones, her arms still clinging to the dead man's legs, her face in his groin.

The hangman wasted no time. He took her by the arm and gently raised her up. His small hands began untying the strings that kept the black bag on the dead man's head. He pulled the sack away. In the light of the torches, they saw the face of the hanged man, his smooth skin, his black hair wet, even in that cold morning wind, with the sweat of dying. He would have been a handsome man, except for his bulging eyes, but for his tongue, swollen and purple, protruding from between his lips. But for his neck. The rope had squeezed his neck so tightly, because of the double weight, it was the width of a thumb.

The hangman gave an order in his soft voice, and herded the women to the prison gate. He pulled back the big iron latch, leaning his shoulder against the gate till it creaked open wide enough to release the women into the blustery wind of the morning.

She's a loner, an old Scottish woman. She still has an accent, though she came here a long time ago. She's well liked, but she isn't sociable. She won't go to parties or anything like that. She's not a talker, you can't get anything out of her about her past. She was tall and heavy when I first met her, before the illness. She's slim now, deadly slim, so she says.

I could get a good angle-shot of her now, with the light coming in over her left side, making interesting shadows on the pillow.

She's mumbling again, years and places. Maybe something to do with her anthology. I don't know.

That would be in the winter of the year 1879, say, in a city on the north-east coast of Scotland. Let the cloaked women be members of The Pillars of Absalom, a cult formed in honour of the biblical King David's son, Absalom, who was hanged from a tree without leaving any children behind him. The women of the cult told everybody who would listen that one day a virgin would bear a child to a hanged man and the child would continue the line of Absalom, and, indeed, of David.

These Pillars of Absalom made their pilgrimage from prison to prison, from hanging to hanging (it was an age of hangings), occasionally finding a sympathetic or corrupt executioner. Men who were hanged, the women believed, achieved great erections and could reach orgasm even after death.

The name of the dead man, that dark dawn, is unknown. But the virgin was a woman of some education, Jenny Morrison, who had joined the cult just a few months before. She became pregnant in due course as a result of her union with the corpse. No one can say whether she was the only Pillar of Absalom to conceive in this way. In November 1879, Jenny Morrison gave birth to twins, a boy and a girl.

At the time there was a rumour that the old midwife who saw the little boy and girl slide out of their mother's womb onto the gloomy bed thought they must be Siamese twins. Then she realized that in fact the babies were linked together in pre-natal incest, the boy's tiny erect penis jammed inside his sister's tiny vagina. According to the rumour, the midwife held them up by the ankles, and had to slap their tiny backsides over and over again before they separated with an unearthly howl.

That was the rumour. What is sure is that Jenny

Morrison died of complications a week after the birth, and that her parents, who did not mourn their daughter's death, agreed to raise the twins as their own.

So Jenny Morrison died too early to meet Leon Trotsky. In fact, she died a few days before he was born. If they ever had met, she would certainly have asked him if his real name, Lev Davidovitch, meant he was by any chance a true descendant of King David. And, depending on his answer, she might have adored him.

Every now and then she says, "Trotsky," when she's dozing. I asked her once, when she was lucid, what's this about Trotsky? Do you mean the Russian revolutionary? I didn't know you were interested in politics. She said, "It was a long time ago, a long time ago." I told her Trotsky was dead now, I read that he was assassinated in Mexico a few weeks ago, did she know? She said, "I know."

She's dozing again. Poor Abigail. Mumbling about light or night, I can't tell which. Poor Abigail.

Gaslight is needed now, gaslight struggling with night in those streets, or hissing down angrily from the dark areas where the gas mantles are broken. Let it be Saturday night, wet and foggy. Saturday night was the night of fog, always, in the city.

The man was middle-aged, drunk. He would lurch to his left or his right, then steady himself till he gained confidence, then reach out with his right leg, his antenna for testing the spongy mattress of pavement. If he'd listened, he'd have heard the quiet steps behind him. Perhaps he did listen, stop, look back a moment, think he saw something. But didn't care. No, this man whooped a little instead, danced a brief jig, lost his balance again, then staggered on, singing loudly, "Sheee's the bonnieee laaass from Baaallochmyyyyle. . . ."

He rolled on like this for a few more blocks, till his walk became a run, and he swung suddenly up a dark alley off the main street. By the back wall of a factory, he began fumbling at his fly, baring his teeth, shuffling in discomfort. His urine sprayed the wall noisily. He sighed, and began buttoning up again.

Did he not hear, at that moment, the soft voice that spoke his name? He should have turned around instead of beginning to hum good-naturedly, for then he might have avoided the thin blade that slid smoothly into his back, again and again, till he fell on his face in the puddle of his own water, thinking something inside of him had ruptured, thinking his body had betrayed him in some agonizing way, seeing only at last, from the corner of his dying eyes, a figure bent over him in a long coat, an arm stabbing, stabbing, stabbing, feeling, at the moment of death, the blood seep from a dozen cracks in his broken body.

Her doctor says to try to keep her cheerful. But that's not necessary when she's awake. And when she starts sobbing in her sleep you can't very well wake her up just to tell her to cheer up. Maybe it's the pain gets to her sometimes, so she's entitled to weep in her sleep. I wouldn't tell her about it though, or she'd ask me to take a picture. I know it. She'd love to see a picture of it.

A link between the stabbings is needed. All committed, say, in the same slum district. Otherwise, they appear quite random. Men, women, and even a young boy who was out of doors too late died by the knife in those dark streets. Fear filled that city, where to be born in the first place seemed like punishment enough.

It turned out that the murderer was a local priest, widely known as a stern man. His housemaid reported him to the police one spring morning. She had become afraid because she had noticed blood on his clothing all winter. He himself showed no surprise when two detectives came to visit him, and he was quite willing to talk. He said he had, for years, listened in his confessional box to all the seedy sins, the same sins, repeated again and again. He had tried in vain to heal the sinners with the holy words. But they didn't want to be healed, only to hear the words.

So he turned to punishment. He could see plainly that the Church's authorized penances were not severe enough. He felt called to be a divine avenger, a butcher knife in the hand of God.

He began his mission of killing. He did not care who his victims were: one blood sacrifice was quite as good as another when all were guilty. For example, the night he killed the twelve-year-old boy, he had actually been on watch outside the house of a woman who was a recurrent sexual sinner. She had decided not to sin that night, it seemed. So he made up his mind to kill instead the boy with the innocent face who approached him in the shadows and asked, with a knowing look, if he needed anything tonight. No, there was no scarcity of sinners.

His trial was a sensation. The judge had to have him restrained, for he kept interrupting the proceedings, talking aloud to himself, his eyes staring ahead:

"'I will destroy man whom I have created from the face of the earth . . . they shall all be put to death, being filled with all unrighteousness, fornication, wickedness, covetousness, maliciousness, full of envy, debate, deceit, malignity . . . Whisperers, backbiters, haters of God, despiteful, proud, boasters, inventors of evil things, disobedient to parents, covenant breakers, they which commit such things are worthy of death.'"

The officers of the court tried to silence him, but he began shouting, hysterical:

"I have done what he commanded: 'I shall slaughter them all like doves of the valleys each for his sin . . . let not your eye spare, neither have ye pity: old men, young men, virgins, children, women, kill and exterminate them all.'" Shouting in a huge voice, foam in the corners of his mouth, that he had done his duty.

Now he looked about him, realizing where he was, and he called down curses on the court, telling them they too were sinners, every one of them, and that they had no right whatever to sit in judgement on him, the messenger of God. That God hated not only sin, but sinners too, and that none of them would escape in the end.

"Heaven and earth shall pass away," he shouted, "but my words shall not pass away."

His own body crushed him to death. Three years later, that was, in a prison for the criminally insane. One morning he had a seizure in which the powerful muscles of his upper body, the pectoralis major and minor, the deltoideus, latissimus dorsi, teres major and trapezius combined and contracted with such force that they bent, and then snapped his bones in half, his sternum, clavicle, scapula, thoracic vertebrae and every rib in their reach. He roared in agony, and thrashed about, but the orderly on duty could only stand and watch the jagged edges of some of the broken bones burst out of the flesh, while, at the same time, inside his ruined chest, the ragged ends of the ribs punctured his lungs, so that blood spouted from his mouth and nostrils, a whale, sounding before plunging deep into an invisible sea.

The name of the priest was the Reverend Ebenezer Morrison (known as Ebby, when he was a boy), one of the Jenny Morrison twins. His body crushed him in the year 1910. He was thirty years old, the same age as Leon Trotsky. He had never heard of Trotsky, but if he had, he would certainly have condemned him as just another sinner, guilty as all the rest.

There she goes again, "Trotsky." As though he was an old friend. I wonder if she had friends anyway, if she ever was in love, back in the Old Country. Maybe that's what's going through her mind, lying in this bed. One of her old lovers.

She never used to say much about her life. The only things she ever talked to me about were her work, or sometimes, her anthology. And even at that, not very much. She learnt photography by herself. She's down to earth about it, no frills. Leave the thing alone, she'd say, it's the thing that makes the picture, not the photographer.

There she goes again. I think it's her own name she's saying now, over and over. Yes, that's it. Abigail, Abigail.

Abigail at last. Abigail Morrison in her hospital bed under a red blanket in a linoleum-floored private ward. Every morning she turns her face towards the window, waiting for the dawn, for the bitter lips of the horizon to spit the sun back into the world.

Yet she breathes more easily this morning, she does not at this moment feel (though this may be a bad sign) the disease creeping through her internal organs. She has noted how it infiltrates, digs in for a while, takes over the territory piece by piece. It has been hiding inside her all these years, waiting. She admires its patience, knows it will wait a little longer still, till she is ready to die.

Abigail Morrison remembers the past. Every night, every day when the nurses and doctors will leave her in peace, she remembers. Though by now she wonders whether it is indeed the past she remembers, or her most recent version of it.

She would swear to this: her family was cursed, she herself saved by a miracle. To be fathered by a corpse. To be the daughter of such a mother. To be the sister of a murderer, her brother. Ah! Ebby. Her playmate, long ago. The love in him cut down, till only the stubble, the harsh prickles were left. She cannot think about him any more, it frightens her so much.

Abigail looked like her mother, they said, tall and heavy. But she loved everything alive. She was in her early thirties when she met Daniel, in his worn suit, a frail man who played the violin, a man with kind blue eyes, and she went to live with him. She loved him so much for loving her, she could hardly bear to look in his blue eyes.

At his cottage on the outskirts of the city, Daniel gave her a gift of a box camera, and showed her how to look at things and take pictures of them. She began to see everything for the first time: a thistle in rain, a hare limping in a field, a wall stone-grey in the morning, the dark green of the potato fields. Everything was charged with beauty.

Daniel was the subject of her first photographs, sitting with his violin in light or shadow, his dog beside him, still suspicious of the newcomer with the clicking box. She took so many pictures of Daniel in his every mood that, after a while, he became quite unself-conscious. Even the dog, in time, would admit to the camera's click only by the slightest flick of an ear.

For brief periods Abigail knew she was beautiful. Some days they would not leave the house, but spend the whole day naked. They would love each other's bodies, fondling and manipulating, rubbing against each other. They loved to inarticulateness. For hours on end their only conversation would be:

"Abigail."

"Daniel."

Again and again.

Yet sometimes when he was lying on her, exhausted, she thought that together they were a kind of sarcophagus, she was the squat tomb underneath, he was the carved miniature of a dead man. Her earlier pictures only impressed on Abigail how he was fading. In them, he was more substantial, more real than he was now in the flesh.

Daniel caught pneumonia that first autumn (they had lived together for only three months), shivering on the cold bus back from giving one of his lessons, and began, without delay, to wheeze his life away. She put him to bed. She hugged him, naked, warming him with her own naked body. It had always worked before, but this time he could not stop dying. He only kept muttering that he had to finish learning the piece he'd been working on for the last few weeks. She knew he couldn't bear to die till he'd mastered it. He wanted the violin always on his bedside table, and he would reach for it and play feebly from time to time.

She took pictures of her dying Daniel: every moment he had left was a gift to her. One day, around noon, he came out of a shallow sleep, sat up and reached for the violin. With trembling fingers he began bowing, the sound grating on her ears. The dog was sitting up too, watching him with great concentration.

She wanted to take the violin away from Daniel as he
sat there shaking with fever, she wanted to stop him.
She knew he was hearing something else.

He stopped at last, looked at her intently, then
breathed:

"That's it."

He fell back on the pillow, the violin clanged to the
floor. The dog barked, a hoarse bark she had never
heard before.

She went to Daniel. She saw his eyes glazed now
beyond sickness.

"Abigail," he whispered, and died.

He was gone, and she was alone, a sad, heavy woman
in an empty cottage. He once told her that amongst
primitive men up the Amazon a father would pass on
one of his lice to his child. They would laugh over that.
She knew he would not have wanted his body to rot
in a coffin. She paid a fisherman to row her out to sea
with the ashes of Daniel and his violin. A mile out in
the firth, on an overcast day, she sprinkled them into
the green water and watched them slowly sink. She
liked now to think of the fish nosing at his remains.
And sometimes she liked to think of herself down
there with Daniel in that clear water, each of them
draped in tendrils of seaweed, making slow and rhythmic love.

So she had no one now. Her grandparents would not
even come to Daniel's funeral. She decided to make
her move. She sold the cottage which she could no
longer bear to live in, and booked her passage for

Canada. She took with her only one small carrier bag, and her camera.

She's weeping again. Her face is soaked in tears. I suppose I could take a picture of her now, but I don't have her determination.

When it comes to taking pictures, she's not a shy woman at all. Don't hesitate, she always tells me. As soon as it dawns on you, take a picture of it. Good pictures are all around you.

She likes everything to be in pictures. She doesn't have any faith in words.

Wartime, the spring of 1917. Let her board ship for Halifax, Nova Scotia via New York on a Cunarder. Let it be an adventureless voyage to New York, she, camera in hand wandering around the great throbbing machine, prowling the glassed-in decks trying to find the sea air. But, taking pictures of everything, for everything was alive and new, and she could still hardly believe she was on a ship in the middle of the Atlantic Ocean.

On the morning of March 26, in New York harbour — she was now thirty-seven years old — she transferred to the Norwegian ship *Christianafjord*, which was to call in at Halifax and disembark those bound for Canada, then continue on its way to Norway. At noon the ship cast off and ploughed along the sound, east past Cape Cod, and north along New England, its foggy shore lurking in the distance. Abigail spent as much of her time as possible on deck, taking pictures of the dim coastline, hoping to give body to the ghost.

The ship was quiet that voyage, for no one felt safe at sea in wartime, even on passenger ships. Abigail noticed that one family would come up on deck each day and stand silently by the railing, bundled up in worn-looking clothes against the brisk spring winds. A man, a woman, and two boys of around ten. They would stare west, too, at the land, trying to will it visible, or they would move to the starboard side to watch the passing of small icebergs on the ocean's horizon.

The man was thin, taller than average, with sharp eyes behind oyster-shell glasses. Often he'd glance towards Abigail as she walked past with her camera, as though he would like to speak to her. Or he'd turn and say something quietly to his family in a foreign language. But he'd always nod to her politely. She would say hello, then shrink away, thinking how she must look to them, a big, ugly woman.

Sometimes she'd hear him at night at the dining-room table. He was a different man then, arguing aggressively with some of the ship's officers who would come over and sit with him. His wife and children would eat up their desserts then leave for their cabin after much kissing and hugging.

One of the passengers at her table told Abigail that the man was Trotsky, the revolutionary.

After a smooth voyage, the ship arrived at Halifax harbour. It was the third of April, another grey morning, only some swooping gulls and a few passengers like herself ready to disembark. But the ship had hardly docked when half-a-dozen naval police-men came up the gangway. Minutes later, they were dragging Trotsky by the arms along the companion-way to the deck, and down the gangway. He was shouting, but she couldn't make out what he was saying. The few passengers on deck, and the crew, watched. His wife and the two little boys stood looking down from the rail, saying nothing, doing nothing.

He eventually gave up struggling with the police and walked down the last few feet of the gangway.

When he stepped onto the dock, he hesitated. He looked back up to the deck where his family stood. Then he shouted something to them in that alien lan-guage, and the boys smiled happily back to him and waved. His eyes swept over the rest of the watchers on deck and caught Abigail's. He stare at her. She raised her camera and centred him in the viewfinder, still staring up at her. Snap! Then he was gone in a knot of uniforms.

So Abigail had a picture of Trotsky. He had not intended to stay in Canada at all, he was just passing, on his way back to Russia. Instead, he had to resign himself to twenty-six days in a Nova Scotia prison camp. At that time, his name meant nothing whatever to Abigail Morrison, but afterwards she heard it often. Whenever anyone spoke of his atrocities, which were frequently recorded in the newspapers, she would always say, "No. Not Trotsky. I have a photograph of him and I don't believe a word of it." He was the second man she had ever photographed.

Her eyes are twitching. She's smiling up at me. Abigail, you go right on sleeping, I'll be here for ages yet. Her lips are moving but I can't make out what she's saying. Her eyes are closing again.

Poor Abigail. Her hair's falling out, and the skin around her face has all caved in. Slim, all right. She'd be a stern-looking woman if it wasn't for her eyes. I wonder how they'd show up in a picture, they're so grey. She says looking through a camera often enough affects your eyes. You never see things again the way you used to.

Make the picture of Trotsky twenty-three years before. Let photography become her profession. She will settle in Toronto, and buy a new camera with tripod and accessories. She made a living taking photographs of newborn babies right in their homes, or in hospitals.

In the teaching hospital, a pathologist who had watched her with curiosity wondered if she'd be willing to photograph some dissections he was performing.

He took her down to his lab and showed her his work, observing her reactions, while he described the cases, gauging her nerve.

On the broad marble tables in the lab, two subjects lay under the cold lights, one of them covered by a sheet. Abigail Morrison at first thought the uncovered subject was a statue moulded in black, pitted metal. But trickles of red ooze were leaking from some of the pits. The left arm was half-severed by a metal saw whose teeth were clogged with flesh.

It was the body of a worker at the steel-mill who had fallen, just the day before, through the safety barrier and into a vat of molten ore. His workmates had looked on as he swam a few desperate strokes, screaming. He actually touched the side of the vat with his hand before he died. They scooped him out with the ladle, and as soon as the air hit the body, the metal began to solidify. The thing that the ambulance brought to the hospital was not a man, more a grisly work of art.

Normally, they'd just have buried him. But the pathologist wanted to see the effects of such a trauma. He suspected that the metal suit had become an elaborate can containing a thick meat stew. The body had been refrigerated overnight to keep it solid.

Abigail listened with interest to the pathologist's explanation of the case. She noted how the fragments of the man's clothing that remained and his boots had become ferrous, how the eyes were now steel ball-bearings, the penis a steel rod. How the body was still in the posture of a swimmer.

She said she would like to take some trial pictures, using the existing lighting in the lab, with the addition of one or two portable lights of her own.

The pathologist noted this response, then took her to the other table, and pulled back the sheet.

On the table lay a female, about twenty years old, already partially dissected. While she was alive, she had been unable to bear the sight of printed words.

She claimed that the words rose from the page to attack her body like insects, or microbes, or, ultimately, like a plague.

During the early years of her life, her parents had humoured her, though they could see no marks on her body. They kept books and newspapers out of the house. And that seemed to work. But as she got older, there was no placating her. A newspaper in the pocket of a passer-by, an advert on the side of a trolley-car, would cause her to howl in pain.

Her parents took her to the best psychiatrists, but no one could talk her out of her disease.

In the last year of her life, nothing could stop the onslaught. She said she could see words everywhere in the air, flying at her from every library and bookseller's in the city, like mosquitoes, she said, scenting her out. She said they were now flying directly into her lungs, choking her. She could feel herself begin to rot on the inside.

The other morning, her parents found her dead.

Abigail could see no sores on the body, but a section of lung lying on the table was ripe with pustules.

She asked questions about incisions and amputations, and tested various angles for lighting to take the clearest pictures. The pathologist hired her.

After that, the police and the insurance companies asked regularly for her services. Hospitals employed her to photograph techniques used in the performance of tricky operations. Her pictures illustrated textbooks on anatomy and surgical procedures, *The*

Art of Dissection, say, or *Scalpel and Surgeon,* and *An Encyclopedia of Disease, Common and Uncommon.* Everyone relied upon her discretion, upon the strength of her stomach.

But it was only in the last few years she had the idea for a book of her own. She had begun her professional career taking photographs of the newly born. Now she wanted to take pictures of people near to death, and make an album of them — an anthology of the dying.

Her undertaking was not an easy one. The regular hospitals would not grant her free range. So she went to the mental institutions, the old age refuges, the doss-houses off Yonge Street, anywhere she was allowed entry with her camera. She took pictures of old people, tears of grief on tired cheeks, or faces twisted in bitterness. Or eyes dull, careless, relieved perhaps that it would soon be over. She took pictures of the young, frightened, protesting against the verdict. Some of the children were unmoved, good as dead already. She recorded them all without discrimination.

She had a nose for the moment of death, she could sense it. She felt at times she was the keeper of a vulture which sat on its tripod at the bedside with patient, ruthless eye. It was her own eye, too.

Yet the dying were not hostile to her. She paid attention to them, valued their unique dances with death. Many of them, rather than asking for the consolations of religion, would send for her at the end. Her camera was, for them, an angel in a black cowl, but no longer frightening.

"Take it now," some would whisper, their last gesture in life. "Take it now."

I've seen the anthology. It looks like an ordinary family album in a loose binder. The first picture's old, taken in the 1880s perhaps, with a soft lens on dry plate and a silver halide emulsion in gelatin. It's a picture of a thick-set young woman with jowels. Her hair's swept back in a bun. She's wearing a high-necked blouse with a brooch in the collar, and a long skirt. She's the image of Abigail.

The second picture looks as though it's from the twenties. The lighting's a mix of magnesium powder and potassium chlorate. The picture itself is of a sharp-featured clergyman with his hair slicked back. His lips are full, but his eyes are cold.

Now come the pictures of the dying. The first one must have been taken by a box camera a long time ago on celluloid film with silver bromide emulsion. The angle is the same as in most of the others, from the left side of the subject at a height of about five feet.

The picture shows a sick man who seems quite young, lying in an old brass bedstead, lighted by a window. On the table beside the bed, there's a violin and a bow. The man's left hand is stroking the head of a black dog that hasn't come out well, only the nose and eyes. The man looks really sick, but he's got a smile for the one who took the picture.

Hundreds of pictures of dying people follow. They've all been taken more recently. Technically, they're like all Abigail's work. The lighting is muted, even when she's used the old gas-discharge flash tubes. They're not fancy, just straightforward, well-taken pictures.

"All you have to do is put the frame around them," she used to tell me. "Works of art are right there under your nose."

I must admit, I found it harrowing to look at the pictures of all those dying people.

The final page of the anthology took me by surprise. There's another old picture, and it isn't of somebody dying. It's been taken with a box camera from the railing of a ship. On the dock, a crowd of stevedores in workmen's cloth caps is watching a group of men in military uniforms. They're all gathered round a man in a long black coat. He doesn't have a hat on. His face isn't well defined, the lens is too weak for that, and the man's face too far away. He's bearded, and I think he's wearing glasses, glinting in the light. Of all the people down on the dock, he's the only one looking up at the camera.

He went indoors out of the warm Mexican sun reluctantly, for he had been enjoying his garden. His visitor was not a man he trusted or liked. They went upstairs to his study, and he sat down and brought the manuscript out of the desk drawer. The visitor stood behind him, asking nervously for his opinion of it. He cleared his throat to reply. The ice-axe struck him in the back of the head. He screamed, a thin scream, but managed to get to his feet, pushing the chair aside. Everything was clear. He hugged his assailant to him, carrying both bodies to the floor. The scream had brought his wife and his bodyguards running upstairs to the study. When he saw them, he rose from the floor and staggered towards them, the axe still wedged in his skull. His wife whimpered, took him in her arms and gently lowered him to the floor. He knew that the substance dripping from his head onto the polished wood was a mixture of blood and brain.

Beside the picture on the final page of the anthology, there's a space for one last picture. Funny how, with just the outlines, it looks like the blueprint of a grave. It's where Abigail wants me to put her own last picture, unidentified, like all the others. She wants me to take it at the very last minute.

I made all the arrangements at her bedside. I rigged a flash camera with a magnifying lens on an intravenous pole. While I was doing it, she watched me like a scientist at the crucial stage of an experiment.

Let her compose an epilogue to her anthology. Let her have a voice.

"None of us are dead. These photographs have no past tenses, no adjectives or adverbs, no subjunctives. They ask and answer no questions, fight no revolutions. They destroy nothing, except time."

She's mumbling again. "Time," I thought she said. And that sounded like "revolution." I suppose she's thinking about Trotsky. She'll be as dead as he is soon enough. I try to stay at her bedside as long as I can, but she's afraid I'll leave, for a coffee, or for forty winks. She made me fix the camera up with a delayed action shutter. She says if I'm not here when she's ready to die, she'll just have to get out of bed, press the shutter, and that'll give her twelve seconds to get back in bed. She'll see the flash and hear the click. Then she'll die in peace. I'm to develop the film with care, the way she taught me, then fix it to the space on the final page of her titleless anthology. She says there's nothing to it.

Lusawort's Meditation

It is noon.

John Julius Lusawort's body is in the supine position. Abed. Yet the world continues to flaunt itself before his open eyes. Through the bedroom windows, for example, these things divert him: a church steeple threatening to puncture the scudding November clouds, a factory chimney spouting its tubers of black smoke, the tops of maple trees jigging erratically at the corner of the frame. Nearer hand, other prodigies thrust themselves forward: the chiaroscuro of rumpled sheets and blankets, the charcoal hair and heavy sprawl of the woman Fatima beside him, the hulks of chairs and dresser crowding the bed. Yes, the world bombards him. He is, as always, unwilling to resist. Nonetheless, Lusawort summons all his willpower, forces himself to think on the fate of da Costa, the bow-legged Azorean.

Da Costa was formerly Lusawort's friend. Da Costa the Azorean harpoon-master. On frosty winter evenings in Ontario he would recall for Lusawort those days of his youth in the ocean-fringed Azores, how the men of the Azores hunted, in their flimsy rowboats, the great whales. Through the bright air, the boats would creak away from the wooden dock, planks wet with dew, red-tiled, white-walled houses slipping aft, volcanic shores sheering off. The boats would slide across the azure water that met, somewhere, the azure sky, towards the distant gleam of the black blisters of whales.

Smoothly rowing, they would laugh over morning rolls and red wine, till gradually the blisters swelled into sea-monsters. Now there would be tension in the air. Da Costa would stand up in the bow, balancing himself against the motion, weighing the harpoon above his right shoulder, alert for the strike.

"Seem, I had a gift, Hohn Hulius," he confessed once, not boasting. (This "seem" that introduced his statements, like a hook for reeling in the words, Lusawort at first took to be a sign of da Costa's diffidence. It was, in fact, the Portuguese *sim* for "yes.")

"Seem, sometimes the whales knew my harpoon and dived deeply before I could get to them."

But whales from other reaches of the ocean, not recognizing da Costa would linger too long and he would impale them unerringly.

He remembered the time the big bull whale challenged his arm. Da Costa struck, but still it foamed in on them and smashed boat after boat. It tried to find da Costa in the crimson water, spurning the others, singling him out. But the harpoon had done its job, and at last the bull plunged away, howling.

Long, grizzled John Julius lies abed, immersed in memories of stumpy, bow-legged Captain Ahab da Costa.

Time passed, whales dwindled in number, stayed away from the islands. Da Costa made preparations to come to the New World for other work. He told Lusawort about his farewell party and how the whole island came, the men in their Sunday suits, dead drunk. Da Costa remembered best what was said by the priest who, alone perhaps, was sober.

"Seem, he told me not many men were best in the world at a thing. He told me I was best in the world with the harpoon. Seem, the whales avoid the islands because of me."

Da Costa laughed sadly as he remembered this. Lusawort could see that the memory of greatness had failed to console him.

Many such things he told Lusawort to while away winter evenings. But after a year working for the Ford Motor Company, da Costa seemed to lose interest in his memories. Now when he spoke it was about his fears. He remarked casually one day that objects were trying to penetrate his body. Everything he saw, for example, seemed to enter through his eyes and bite into his brain. He could not understand why this should be so, but he must protect himself. He kept his eyes lidded as much as he could and wore dark glasses to blunt the sharpness of the images:

"Seem, Hohn Hulius, the light harpoons my eyes."

Lusawort, sensing da Costa's anxiety, congratulated him on his circumspectness.

Soon da Costa was trying to defend himself against the torment of sound. He began to wear ear-plugs as well as his dark glasses:

"Seem, you must understand, Hohn Hulius," (this in the loud voice of the deaf), "the noise attacks me."

In reply, Lusawort roared his approval of this defensive measure.

Da Costa quit his job with the Ford Motor Company. Lusawort wondered how he would live, how he would eat. This turned out to be a minor problem, for even food began to offend da Costa. He could hardly bear to eat and drink and tried to convince Lusawort to abstain with him:

"Seem, Hohn Hulius, it is foolish to permit bad things to enter at the mouth."

He was never more content than when defecating or urinating the intruders out of himself.

Smells finished him off.

Lusawort remembers how da Costa, sitting now at a safe distance, in dark glassed, ears plugged, shouted this confession:

"Seem, the smells, Hohn Hulius! The smells are too hard for me!"

He would occasionally wear a gauze face-mask but found the intimate contact with his own breath intolerable. The smells were insidious. Of differing intensities and densities, they moved at ground level the way clouds do in the upper air. Da Costa would navigate amongst them in constant peril. Often, seemingly clear passages became exitless fjords.

John Julius Lusawort thinks of da Costa at bay, unable to escape the treachery of the smells that clung to his clothing, his hair, waiting for a chance to infiltrate the orifices of his body.

Da Costa's own last act of penetration, to the certain knowledge of Lusawort, was into the body of this same fleshy Fatima, stirring now luxuriously in the bed beside him. Lusawort, all affection, kneads her plump breast and she giggles in her sleep. Da Costa had bequeathed her to him (how could a friend refuse?), for he had come to loathe the sight, touch, taste, and — oh! — the smell of her:

"Seem, Hohn Hulius, she has the smell of island goat."

With impeccable logic, da Costa at last refused to allow the tainted air to enter his lungs. A week ago, in the quiet of Lusawort's room, he had held his breath till his heart stopped.

John Julius Lusawort meditates, therefore, upon his *late* friend, da Costa, the only man he has known, or is ever likely to know, who has been the best in the world at something. He wonders if da Costa was not, perhaps, too good to live. Unlike himself. For John Julius Lusawort considers he is not too good; hence, he eats too much, drinks too much, enjoys penetration. He sighs, without remorse, brushes his hip lightly against the succulent body of the adaptable Fatima. Ever receptive, he permits the sight of her brown flesh to assail his reverent eyes. He feels all his senses tingle. His meditation on death is over.

Anyhow in a Corner

IS IT TRUE THAT YOU ARE A LOVER OF *OBJETS D'ART?*
His basement apartment does not please the eye. It is littered with crumpled Donut House coffee cups, an assortment of empty liquor bottles, and hamburger boxes like beached oyster shells. There are old newspapers a foot deep on the floor. From time to time he will read one, a paragraph here and there — he has a mind only for fragments — the *Globe* with his coffee, the *Sun* at his daily squat. The others are utilitarian and free: sales-flyers together with virgin bundles of university *Gazettes*. They are adequate to insulate a poor man's coat, serviceable as dog-litter (his dog is asleep, bristling in dreams). The man is grey, not well preserved. He perches on a wooden chair at a wooden table lit by a bare ceiling-light. Pen and paper lie before him, but he is busy, thinking.

WHAT WOULD YOU DO IF YOU WON THE LOTTERY?
He thinks, if only someone, a patron, would supply his

needs, he would live like Sir Walter Scott, his idol, long dead. He would find a River Tweed. Cold. Perhaps with trout in it, and a chill northern ocean for its destination. He would require some hills, yes, for his Eildons and Cheviots. He would insist on ruins (absolutely essential), for he could not do without moonlight on Melrose Abbey, or the black ruins of Dryburgh under a lowering Border sky.

DO YOU EVER THINK OF MOVING TO A MORE DESIRABLE RESIDENCE?
This man abhors imitation. Yet he would not hesitate to imitate Sir Walter. There must be, somewhere, an architect capable of building him a replica of Abbotsford on the curve of that cold river. He has no doubts about the structure (*she would have laughed, she would have called it, properly, his castle*), no doubts at all. It must assert its symmetry amidst an anarchy of trees, what with its turrets, moats, battlements, serried chimneys, barred windows, barbicans, portcullises, machicolation, with its newels and its quoins, and its colonnades, and its pilasters, and its acroteria, and its almighty megaron. Its pantiles and its spires. It must be, and this is foremost, a magnificent dog-kennel. His three dogs (let there be three) will have the run of its resplendent galleries, will mark out their territories against its Louis Quatorze furniture, and its baroque columns.

OUTLINE YOUR IDEA OF THE GOOD LIFE FOR US PLEASE.
Your library-cum-study is all you ever dreamed of,

lined with worn, leather-bound volumes, the outer
wall of glass, French windows opening onto verdant
lawns and the aspen-lined river. You sit in a comfortable leather chair at a desk of carved oak, or
lower your weary limbs into the underbelly of a
massive couch. You warm your nether parts, when
necessary, at the cavern of a fireplace, for you will
have a fire blazing winter and summer. Your dogs
sprawl on the shag carpet, scratching themselves
luxuriously.

DO YOU LIKE THE IDEA OF A WRITER'S BEING SUP-
PORTED BY A PATRON?
Your patron's motives will, of course, be quite mercenary. As they should be. You will be acquired as
though you were a penny black, or a silver Victorian
spittoon. Or a likely-looking thoroughbred for the
stable at the downs. Or another crew-member for the
vast, ghostly, rarely used yacht. The patron will never
actually read any of your books. But occasionally he
will inquire if everything is all right, how things are
working out. He tells you it will improve the image of
his corporations to support the arts.

DESCRIBE YOURSELF IN A NUTSHELL TO OUR
READERS.
Occupation: kept writer. Age: septuagenarian. Height:
exiguous. Build: oblate. Weight: diurnal fluctuations.
Health: dyspnoeic. Education: catalectic. Hobby:
multibibe. Marital Status: . . . (*she died too young she
died too young she died too young she died*).

WOULD YOU SELECT A SHORT PASSAGE FROM YOUR WORK FOR THE BENEFIT OF THOSE OF OUR READERS WHO HAVEN'T TIME FOR READING?

When I was twenty-seven, ladies and gentlemen, I published privately a book that caused a stir. I introduced some new characters into an old plot, as follows:

The *Nellie*, a cruising yawl, swung at her anchor without a flutter of sails, and was at rest. The flood had made, the wind was nearly calm, and being bound down the river, the only thing for it was to come to and wait for the turn of the tide.

The sea reach of the Thames stretched before us like the beginning of an interminable waterway. Marlow sat cross-legged right aft, leaning against the mizzen mast. He had sunken cheeks, a yellow complexion, a straight back, an ascetic aspect, and, with his arms dropped, the palms of hands outwards, resembled an idol.

Two strangers had signed on for our crew on that memorable sail. Let us call them the Actors, the small and the large. All day they had been stricken with that malaise peculiar to the sea (though as yet we had not left the river) which terrifies even the brave; now they were able, at last, with the dropping of the mainsail, to ascend the murky companion-way out of that dim interior, and noisily to usurp the placid deck, where Marlow sat, about to ruminate upon one of his inconclusive experiences. His reproving glare did

nothing to silence the relieved babble of the
Actors, freed from their involuntary imprisonment, like twin Lazaruses risen again from the
womb of earth. Their names were Stan Laurel and
Ollie Hardy.

That was how it began.

DO YOU HAVE TO REPORT REGULARLY TO YOUR
PATRON OR WHAT?
You are, obviously, under some . . . obligations. Once
in a while, the patron, as is only human, likes to
display his collection. You receive your summons to
the city. Even after all these years, it still excites you.
(*How she would have loved these command performances.*) The patron's mansion, quite naturally,
dwarfs Abbotsford. The guests usually number five
hundred. On very special occasions, when you have,
say, just finished a novel, he also invites several international reviewers (it would be unthinkable to refuse
one of his invitations) to come a few days earlier and
read it over. He's a businessman, and likes to know
how his investment is doing. You are expected to
read selections for the assembled guests. You follow
Pablo Casals, precede Maria Callas. You are sand-
wiched between the principal dancers of the New
York Ballet and the touring exhibition of the Picasso
drawings. You must do your part. You are his writer.
He has freed you from all the pressures that drag
others down. He requires three copies of each of
your works from his publisher, then orders the plates

to be broken. You are not upset by this, not a bit. For you, it's the writing that counts. Getting it down on paper. Off your chest. What happens then is of no interest to you.

TELL US MORE ABOUT THIS ATTRACTION TO THE LONG DEAD SIR WALTER SCOTT.
I admire, ladies and gentlemen, Sir Walter, for many things, but mainly for his indifference to the fate of his writing. He would not admit — can you imagine? — that he was author of the Waverley novels. He would not discuss them with critics, or reviewers. He never read over galleys ("an old dog sniffing its own vomit"). He had done his part, the writer's part. He told the editors to do whatever they felt was necessary to make the things sell. He didn't care much about plots. He often forgot how a story began by the time he finished it. He wanted only to rush back to Abbotsford and his dogs.

THEY SAY YOU TAKE THE OCCASIONAL DRINK. ANY TRUTH TO IT?
You couldn't do without a manservant in a place like Abbotsford. A kind of valet. A retired boxer, let's say, with irreversibly deviated septum. To keep the autograph seekers and the media spies away. To replenish the glass. Yes, replenish the glass. To deliver you from the gins and oranges of outrageous fortune. To deliver you especially from white wine: androgynous filth for fairies. Scotch whisky is what you require. How much have you swigged of it in the last forty years?

$$26 \text{ ounces per diem}$$
$$\text{for } 365 \text{ days}$$
$$= 9490 \text{ ounces per annum}$$
$$\text{for } 40 \text{ years}$$
$$= 379600 \text{ ounces}$$

Every one of them the best. How would you survive otherwise when you have your bad dreams?

WHAT KIND OF THING ARE YOU WRITING THESE DAYS?
He is moved by his own words as he never was before. For months (or is it years now?) he has laboured over one paragraph. Every time he rereads it, rewrites it, it halts him in his tracks. There is no going beyond it.

> And I said to him, and he said to me, and I said to
> him, and he said to me, and I said and I said and
> I said, and he and he and he, and then and then
> and then, I said to him no and he said I agree and
> I said to him no and he said yes I agree, and I said
> said said, and he said said said, and then and then
> and then and then, and only then.

He has written innumerable combinations of it. Is it the long-awaited, long-feared summary of all he ever has written, ever will write? The diamond in the rubbish-heap? (*Would she have liked it?*)

DO YOU, LIKE EVERYONE ELSE, GET DOWN ON YOURSELF OCCASIONALLY?
At times he drinks more than usual, for on certain

days everything is pitch black. He could even begin
to envy the others their successes. It is a mood that
comes on him for no good reason, like a cold out of
season. Against his will, he lifts the cover, sees the
real thing. His life, like all the others, futile. Yet he
does not, any more, resist as he once did. Is he too
weak now, or too wise? These unwanted glimpses
may be the only authentic part of his life. They are,
at least, his own: his visions, unearned gifts, not to
be rejected. He has learnt, armed with a twenty-six-
ouncer, to accept their visitations. He has always
emerged from them in due course. It seems entirely
possible to him nevertheless, that one day he will
not emerge.

WHAT KIND OF READERS DO YOU HAVE IN MIND?
*(There was a time, ladies and gentlemen, when I
tried to please someone with my writing. But she's
dead now, she's dead. I have never cared much about
anyone else's opinion of my work. When I write,
though, I still think, "Now would she enjoy this part?"
or, "I'll leave this part in for her." That's what goes on
in my mind. I write for the dead. There it is: my ideal
audience is dead.)*

TELL US ABOUT YOUR MOST MEMORABLE
MOMENTS?
He sits at his desk, writing, perhaps rewriting. The
tip of his pen slithers across the yellow notepaper,
stutters, lashes out, poises itself for another wriggling advance. His sparse hair is lank and his bald-

spot glistens, a pink balloon contained by a lattice of
silver thread. Often his eyes become vacant, meditative, his writing slow and meditative. It is a habit of
his to call his dog to him from where it lies on its
bed of newspapers. Good-natured, it stretches, wags
a stump of tail, sidles over to him, tongue lolling,
positions its sleek head under his dangling hand. He
pets it, caresses the soft ears automatically. After a
few moments the hand stops its fondling and the
dog sinks to the floor, sighs, resumes its slumber.
The pen, with renewed vigour, weaves across the
yellow paper.

AND YOUR LEAST MEMORABLE?
Some evenings, he writes nothing, he stares at
nothing. Once in a while, he twitches. The dog's black
ears prick, but there is no summons. Dog and man
continue their comfortless meditations.

WHAT DO YOU MOST REGRET IN LIFE?
He is saddened by the knowledge that he will never
again be loved. His body has buckled, bottom-
heavy. There is no spring any more in his steps. He
still has all the parts, but they no longer work efficiently. The skin of his hands is flaky and blotched,
the strong hands inherited from generations of
working men, now tremulous, effete as a fairy's.
The once-blue eyes are now yellowed, lustreless as
fried eggs. He is a victim of dispepsia, lumbago,
and, hardest to accept, piles. He would be afraid
to sleep with a woman (if he got any offers) for fear

of what his body might and might not do: the farts, the burps, the incautious snores, the humiliation of impotence. (*Ah! but she could have told them how he once was. How each had adored the other's fine, firm body. He is too fond now of his solitude. He has neglected himself, in spite of all her warnings.*)

IS THAT AN OLD GIRLFRIEND YOU KEEP REFERRING TO OR WHAT?
(*Tell me did you ever see so fair a creature in your town before? Sweet lovely mild. I kiss her eyes goodly as sapphires shining bright. I kiss her ivory-white forehead. I kiss both her cheeks sun-reddened as apples. I kiss her lips tempting as cherries. I kiss her neck snowy as a marble tower. I kiss her breasts luscious as bowls of cream. I kiss her belly smooth as alabaster. Where now my lips are set my seal shall be. Lead me in my mine of precious stones. Lead me in. To enter in these bonds is to be free.*)

WHAT KIND OF MAN WOULD YOUR PATRON BE?
The fabulous patron. An unsentimental man, honestly acquisitive, worked his way up from the bottom, amputated his imagination, devoted himself to making money, assessed everything as a possible gainer, married in order to conclude a financial deal, bought works of art as investments, funded symphonies for tax purposes, sired two boys because he knew he'd need a business manager and an investment broker

he could trust, pensioned off his wife when she began to drink too much, has never been disappointed in the boys' selfish behaviour, hopes they will thrive just as he did. Without the encumbrance of an ethical code.

OUR READERS WOULD LOVE TO HEAR ABOUT YOUR FAVOURITE CLOTHES.
There are days when he shrinks from the squalor, the stink of dog's urine. At any moment he can expect the landlord's voice at the basement door, the demand for his unpaid rent. He must bestir himself. His preparations are epic:

undergarments Today he favours a rather informal style, long woollen underpants to combat the intemperate weather, his undervest a subtly matched off-white.
pants No difficulties here; he opts for the modishly torn dungarees rather than for his galligaskins, plus-fours, or toreador pants for more festive occasions.
shirt He hesitates a trifle over the pourpoint and the *gipon,* decides on a simple evening shirt, the left sleeve cunningly removed.
sweater Eschewing the cashmere and the cardigan, he chooses a crew-neck with well-ventilated bodice that allows tantalizing glimpses of the shirt and flesh beneath.
jacket Carefully he selects the delightfully *passé* Mao-jacket, rejecting the redingote, the swallowtail, and the unsuitably heavy Norfolk jacket.

overcoat Always a problem; this time, definitely, it must be the elegant raglan (discreetly lined with chic items of news reportage), not the pretentious Inverness cape, the burberry, or the serape.

hat Renowned for his headgear, he intuitively selects the French-Canadian-style *tocque* as vastly more practical than the *chateau bras,* the astrakhan, or the fedora.

socks and gloves The true sophisticate, he knows these must complement the entire ensemble; he ponders, sweating lightly, eventually decides upon thick woollen socks, gracefully ventilated at the extremities; so taken is he by this choice that he will wear a similar pair on his hands in lieu of gloves, no matter how tempting the suedes and the *mousquetaires.*

neckwear He will forego, on this occasion, the rabato, the ascot, the fichu, and plump for the tried-and-tested, charmingly unravelled, Montreal Expos comforter.

shoes Perspiration always affects this choice; what? brogans, chukka boots, perhaps? what about the hessians? the espadrilles today? the legendary *veldschoens*? the stogies? he decides ultimately upon a seasoned pair of air-freshened tennis-shoes, shrewdly perforated at the sides, insulated with well-chosen gobbets of newsprint.

Thus, dressed. Thus dressed, he sets out, with canine accompaniment, to face the world, beard the bureaucracy in its den, collect his old-age pension.

OUR READERS WOULD LOVE TO HEAR HOW THE
ÉLITE SPEND A NIGHT OUT.
You fill your glass for the trillionth time, is it? marvel
at the amber fluidity. You have just arrived outside the
patron's mansion in the black limousine. You alone are
the guest of honour at this great gathering, a fitting
climax to your career. (*If only she could have been
here.*) You can hear, through the car window, the
twenty-piece chamber orchestra playing a mathemat-
ical selection of Bach. They are all awaiting your
entrance. The chauffeur opens the door for you and
you climb out, stiff at first. You are, after all, not young
any more. A servant springs down from the front door
to take your arm, lead you in. Through the open
doorway, a drum-roll, the hubbub of excitement, the
faces peering towards you. The patron appears,
smiling possessively:

   "My dear chap," he murmurs.

   You finger your evening coat, your black tie. You
prepare to be exhibited. You take the podium, accept
the applause, shuffle your papers, continue:

   "I have long, ladies and gentlemen, admired Sir
Walter Scott . . ."

OUR READERS WOULD LOVE TO HEAR HOW THE
ÉLITE SPEND A NIGHT AT HOME.
Now he is suddenly hungry. The excitement,
perhaps. The anticipation. He ignores the attentive
listeners, laden banquet tables, bowls of caviare,
trays glittering with champagne. He pokes about
amongst the debris that litters the apartment floor

beside his chair, disturbs the dog, fishes out a
package of assorted biscuits. He picks out one for
himself, throws a broken piece to the anxious dog,
concentrates again upon the work at hand.

THANK YOU FOR THIS. AND THANK YOU.

A Long Day in the Town

From this far, the buildings were nothing to me but a heap of rubble shored against the base of the mountain. It was morning in the sun. Everywhere, white scraps of butterflies trembled a foot above the ground. I kept walking, and after a while I could make out a church steeple sticking up like a dagger from the prostrate town. I walked on, as I say, uphill, always uphill, into that town, looking for the hotel. I was almost there, in the midday heat, only an occasional wisp of cloud in the bald sky. I was feeling very weary from carrying the burden of my thirst.

Then I saw a woman on the road ahead trundling a cart along behind her. She was moving so slowly that soon I was close enough to see that on her cart a corpse lay sprawled on its back, unclothed, a great creamy slug under the empty blue.

The woman stopped and waited for me. Her daughter, she sobbed, it was her twelve-year-old daughter on the cart. The woman's long brown hair was roped with sweat as though she had just given birth. She was wearing a floral dress of wilted roses. She was a thin woman, her body dangling around her. All over the corpse of the dead girl, I could see large pustules, pitched battles of flies. A white headscarf clamped the child's jaw shut, a wooden cross jutted from her stiff fingers.

I recognized the plague, the worst of deaths. I said to the woman, "Plague."

But she shouted out, "No, no!" She sobbed that her daughter was always a good girl, always full of love, and she would never leave her. She wrenched the handles of the cart away and dragged it over the cobble-stones up towards the town.

I walked behind her, watching how, after every few dozen steps, she would lay down the handles and take a damp yellow rag from her pocket. She would shoo away the flies and tenderly begin to wipe the face of her daughter, cooing and smiling to her, alert for any sign of life.

As we entered the town, some of the townswomen, black headscarves over stocky bodies, came out to their doors to see her passing by. With soft voices, they crooned, "Ah well, she's dead now and you must bury her." They told her she would never wipe death away with a wet cloth.

But she kept shouting, "No, no!" She told them, sobbing, that she was a raped woman, raped from inside by sorrow. She said she was a woman dying of hunger, starving to death, for her daughter was her only food. But always they repeated to her, "Ah well, she's dead now and you must bury her."

By this point, we were near the town hotel, so I left these women to their sad dialogue whilst I booked a room. When I came out a few minutes later, the street was empty. There was a little park opposite, so I brought a mug of beer and sat on the park bench. A few gangling trees grew in that park, and grass brown with drought.

For an hour, nothing happened (I, on the bench, sipped my beer, transforming myself gradually into a human oasis; above, the sun journeyed on its way a thousand more miles; at my feet, a regiment of black ants on the dusty path dismembered a solitary cater-pillar), then a bearded man of about twenty-five sat down beside me, his head motionless, his eyes scan-ning back and forth like a search-light, resting on me for a moment at the end of each lateral swing. He wore a black dress suit, stained down the front, rotted with sweat at the armpits.

"You're not one of them," he said in a whisper, hardly moving his lips.

I showed no interest.

"No, you couldn't be, not this soon," and I could see that he had convinced himself of something, and felt secure.

Then he began to talk, determined to tell me what was on his mind.

He said he had good reason to trust no one. He and his two brothers and a sister had been raised on a poor scrub-farm. He was the youngest child, unwanted by his mother and despised by his father, who, he said, looked very like him. It still disgusted him, he said, this likeness. He could not help feeling his father in himself — his hands, his face, his nervous ticks.

When he turned twelve years old, the others made up their minds, as a family, to murder him (he had seen it coming). Yes, he assured me, they began their efforts to kill him at the age of twelve.

Their first attempt was clumsy but unambiguous. One morning, his brother, who had spoken to him only to insult him for as long as he could remember, began to encourage him to eat up his porridge. At the same time, they tried not to show too much interest, not to look at his plate. His parents and his sister loosed a smoke-screen of chit-chat through which, nonetheless, he could make out the glitter in their eyes.

He decided not to eat the porridge. Instead, he put the plate on the floor for the black-and-white farm collie. They all stopped talking and watched intently, his father, his mother, his brothers, his sister, as the dog, after eating, began to whimper and convulse, and in a few minutes fell on its side, dead.

No one made any comment.

After that first failed attempt to poison him, the family made an honest effort in those early days to arrange his murder in ways that might be mistaken, by others at least, for accidents. He remembered his brothers trying to force his head below water in the swimming hole. He managed to slither and squirm free for his life. He remembered his sister thrusting him one morning through the hayloft door as they were lowering bales to the trailer far below. He grabbed the chains of the pulley, swinging for a moment, like a hanged man, before shinning up to safety. He remembered other attempts: the pushes into the flailing arms of the thresher; into the knacker's bubbling cauldron; into the paddock of a rampant bull. Each time he escaped.

Yet he continued to live with them, intimate with his murderers, a scared boy, not knowing what else to do. He became used to their attempts on his life. He became skilled, like an animal, in avoiding his predators, taking their menace for granted, learning how to defend himself, always alert. He never knowingly let them get behind him. He relied on his hearing, smell, taste. He became quick and tough, so that after each murderous attempt, he was harder than ever to kill. Asleep, he was a watch-dog, pricked awake by the creak of a tree, the wind's rustle.

When he turned fourteen, they changed their tactics.

One day as he was working in the high-walled vegetable garden behind the house with his brothers and sister, he noticed, too late, his father and mother at the kitchen window, looking out with great interest.

Before he could move, one of his brothers leapt on him and wrestled him down onto the potato drills, kneeling on his arms. His sister ran over and straddled herself across his legs. Then the eldest brother, seventeen years old, who had never called him by his first name in all his life, put his thick hands around his neck and began to choke the breath out of him.

He did the only thing he could, he made a desperate kicking motion, landing his knee right in the fork of his sister's spindly legs (she was her mother's daughter), so that she screamed out in pain and crashed into the younger brother. He was able to wriggle out of their grasp and run to the corner of the garden, at bay, with a pitchfork in his hands. They all looked towards the window where his parents watched. His father stared for a while, then shook his head slowly. The elder brother reluctantly opened the garden gate and went away, followed by his brother and sister, she limping and sobbing, to go about their day's work. Nothing was said.

But he knew now he could not stay. That night he packed a potato sack with his few clothes, crept out into the darkness, and left his home forever.

That was only the beginning, twelve years ago. Since then, they had tracked him down, time after time, no matter where he went, determined to finish him off. By now, they had tried innumerable ways to kill him. As he had become an expert survivor, they had become skilled assassins. In a steamy Malaysian swamp, for instance, they had grazed his back with their parangs. In Patagonia, they had almost entangled his nimble feet with a set of leather bolas. In a midnight alleyway in Istanbul, they had dangerously wounded him in the shoulder with yataghans. In Madrid, twice in a single day, they had inflicted severe injuries on his naked flesh with a misericord and a bilbo. In the Scottish Highlands, they almost had him, partially pinning his coat sleeve to a wall with expertly thrown skean dhus. Once, in the veldt of southern Africa, they had barely missed him with a hail of deadly assegais. He, in turn, had beaten off their shillelagh-attack in Phoenix Park, Dublin.

In every corner of the globe they had ambushed him with Gatling guns or Thompson sub-machine-guns. In one hemisphere they had almost slipped a garotte around his scrawny neck. In another, they missed him, but eliminated five hundred innocents by means of a limpet-mine on a trans-ocean crossing. One night, in Borneo, he detected, just in time, a cunningly placed castrator mine they had hidden in the toilet bowl of his hotel room.

As for poisons, they had tried wolfsbane in his beer, banewort in his Ovaltine, aconite in his ham and eggs, bearded darnel in his bread pudding, corn cackle in his angel cake, death angel in his cornflakes. Still he had survived.

As he told me all this, he never stopped looking around the park, his right ear cocked for any sound, like a morning bird on a summer lawn.

"You're sure you're not one of them?" he asked again, flicking at me with his eyes.

He told me how he had once fallen in love with a prostitute. Night after night they had made love, becoming a marvellous machine. But one night, in the middle of the night, he woke by some instinct to see her reared above him with a pair of scissors in her hand, tears streaming down her face, about to stab him. He jumped clear, realizing with horror that the prostitute was his own sister. He himself had been a master at spotting her disguises, never so nearly failing until now.

So he had come here, to play for time, to decide on his next move. He had heard of this town by chance, he had heard that a life here was no life, and they might leave him alone at last. Yet he often wondered what he would do with himself, what he would do with his life, if they left him alone.

I waited till he was finished, then asked him if he had any idea why they had spent all those years trying to kill him. He looked at me, puzzled. Even, perhaps, with pity. I could see he thought I must be a madman, and that my question made no sense to him, no sense at all.

He rose to go, saying he'd been exposed here in the park long enough, looking me up and down, his bird-head twitching. Then he left, picking his way through the park as though it was a minefield.

The air was suddenly chilly. I looked up, and saw that the mountain had already lopped off part of the early afternoon sun. So I crossed the street again to the hotel, a dilapidated three-storey building. The outside was brick except for a few feet of stone at the bottom, like a pair of socks. A single turret above the entrance was a finger, stained from scooping decades of dust out of the air.

Inside, the furniture, distorted pieces of plastic passing for chairs and tables, was worn as though from overuse. Yet I was the only guest, and the room-clerk assured me the town had never been busy. Disembodied smells wandered the corridors, needing exorcism by fresh air.

In the evening I went down to the dark cellar that was the hotel bar, and tried, unsuccessfully, to chat with the bartender, a man whose hands quivered constantly and who spoke so rapidly he seemed to say everything in machine-gun bursts of sound. His tone of voice was friendly, though his face was nothing but a scar adorned with eyes and mouth. He served my drink, spilling much of it over the table.

Around eight o'clock, a woman of great beauty wearing an elegant summer dress came in and ordered a drink. She looked towards me, and came and sat beside me.

We talked for some time, a camouflage of noise, neither of us revealing our positions. Only one thing she made plain: she liked to spend time with strangers in the bar, and she liked nothing better than to spend the night with them in their beds.

When she had drunk enough, we left the bar and its tremulous keeper and groped our way through the smells up the dim flight of stairs. We plodded along the spongy corridor to the dark room allotted to me out of all the other rooms in the hotel.

I closed the door. She stood in the middle of the floor and began to undress without hurry, allowing her fashionable summer dress and her bra to fall carelessly on top of her sandals. She smiled at me, her body beautifully symmetrical, her skin brown, her breasts slightly drooping, mature and brown, her legs shapely, a space between them at her crotch. She wriggled out of her pants, exposing the pubic hair, shaved neatly to accommodate the slight swimsuit whose outline I could see bracketing her groin.

She took my hand and walked me towards the bed. She lay down and watched whilst I removed my own clothing, carefully folding each item and placing it on a chair in the exact order in which I would later put it back on. Then I lay down on the side of the bed nearest the black, fetal telephone.

I took her in my arms. That was when I noticed the first faint scar, as I was kissing her neck, the smell of her perfume in my nostrils. A very fine scar it was, running along the side of her jawbone all the way from her ear to the tip of her chin, and on past the tip, up to the other ear. There it connected with a faint scar running all along the scalp line of her hair. I looked at her face, and saw now, on the bridge of her nose, the very fine scars in the shape of a cross, an insignia.

She seemed unaware, so far, of my inspection and was becoming more active, fondling me. So I moved down her body, noticing now, like a fisherman glimps-ing trout in dark waters, the fine group of scars around the bases of her breasts and the smaller scars ringing the nipples that were now erect under my fingers. I traced, as I progressed down her body, the long fine scar that ran from the breast-bone, traversing a cross-hatching of delicate horizontal scars patterned on her stomach, deep into the pubic hair.

Between her legs, I saw two long dainty scars sweep-ing from the vulva along the inside of her thighs to her knees.

I turned her gently onto her stomach. With height-ened acuity, I immediately noted the scars that curved around her buttocks, shapely scimitars sweeping from the hips in towards the cleft of the anus. I saw too the long elegant scars that ran from her waist towards the shaven, perfumed armpits.

She had stopped her writhing, and was enduring my inspection. She turned over. I looked into her eyes, searching for her. Behind the fashionable mascara I could see the ancient sadness of those eyes. She sighed, and her left arm swept her long black hair onto the pillow behind two ears of almost identical shapes. Her right arm lay across her breasts as she spoke, selecting each word as though it were a scalpel:

"I am a patchwork woman. I was so ugly I had to put a wall round myself to keep others from seeing me. I was made beautiful by surgery. But the scars are judases. I used to think my heart would die, but it always lets me down.

"I came to this town in the end thinking that someone who chose to live in this place might be willing to love me. But they use me here like a rubber doll, a good invention, life-size, but not a woman."

After she had spoken, I rose from her, and began to dress myself carefully, smoothing each garment into place, checking myself constantly in the rusted mirror, gauging with my fingertips the soft texture of my cheeks, patting the stray hairs into place. I went out into the silence of the drab corridor, without looking back, and closed the door firmly.

When I returned a few hours later, the room was empty and I did not go looking for the woman.

The next morning was bright and sunny. A stale roll and a cup of tepid coffee in the hotel restaurant convinced me I was not hungry. I went outside, wading ankle-deep in butterflies to the park bench where I sat down in the soothing morning heat.

A man of middle height, not old, black curls, came and sat beside me on the bench. Lunar craters pitted his face.

When he saw that I was staring at him, he leaned over, his whole body rustling, and asked in a foreign accent if I would give him money for coffee. I could see that the rustling came from scraps of paper stuffed under his clothes, protruding at the neck and the placket of his shirt, stuccoing his sleeves and trouser-legs.

He apologized for "the inconvenient noise" of these papers under his clothes, saying he was a poet. When he was working on a poem, he said, he would write down on separate scraps of paper each of the words he intended to use, and tape them to various parts of his body. It was bad luck to reveal which parts of the body were more effective for certain words, and anyway, he was still at the exploration stage. He hoped I would forgive his reticence.

He only knew that, in a few days, he would feel the words were permeated by him, he by the words. They would possess each other intimately, he would *become* a poem with human organs.

I took him back to the hotel restaurant which had been given over now, in the morning heat, to a convention of bluebottles. He fought with them for the remnants of hardening bread, and drank down cup after cup of lukewarm coffee, holding the cup in both hands, till beads of sweat acknowledged the labour of eating and drinking.

He began to talk about his past. How, at university, he had come to idolize an outspoken group of writers and thinkers. How one of them, a poet, had told him, "A real poet is a terrorist, a knee-capper, a mixer of Molotov-cocktails, a man who NEVER writes a poem." How, in the excitement of it all, he had become a member of a cell of anarchists. How, in a basement room, he had chosen the straw that singled him out to blow up the police headquarters surrounded by high electrified fences, and battlements of sandbags. How, next day, he had walked softly up to the entrance of the headquarters with his hands above his head. How the guards had searched him thoroughly, he beseeching them not to handle him roughly. How he dared not flinch when they had probed his anus for a weapon. How they could not have guessed that he himself *was* the weapon.

He had been transformed into the weapon ten minutes before he had presented himself at the head-quarters. In a nearby apartment, his friends had poured, with the utmost care, through a long plastic tube down his throat and into his stomach, a litre of nitroglycerine. All that he had to do was to walk into the headquarters and bruise himself against any object, or tumble to the floor, or jump up and down, and a fifty-yards-wide chasm would be created around him.

But, there in the headquarters, he changed his mind. Everything changed when he suddenly realized, right there inside the target, that all he had ever wanted to be was a poet, all the time, an old-fashioned poet, a writer of poems. It was like meeting himself for the first time, saying "How do you do?" to himself at long last.

Yet there he was, the major actor in a nightmare-drama in which he no longer wished to say his lines. To tremble would mean obliteration. He was almost afraid to speak in case his epiglottis detonated him. So he signalled, ever so cautiously, to one of the policemen, and whispered the plot. The policeman saw his terror and knew he told the truth.

Within minutes (during which a huge hairy insect, nausea, began to creep over his stomach and intestines, during which he glimpsed, sadly, the beauty of a dozen fleeing faces, the last he would ever see, during which he felt the warmth of the sunbeams streaming through the windows above him, alive with atoms of light), the headquarters were empty.

Then he couldn't hold it in anymore. He vomited up the nitroglycerine, it erupted from him, spouted into the air, and curved to the floor in front of him with a great sloshing splash.

And nothing happened. No void, no annihilation, no negation of being. Only a sick boy, shuddering with nausea, wishing he were dead. Something had gone wrong, he realized. His terrorist friends should have remained poets: the nitro they had filled him with was contaminated, useless. He might just as well have

chugged down a litre of camel-piss for all the chance
it had of exploding.

So he betrayed them all. When, after many hours,
the police cautiously returned to the building, he
was determined to talk. He told every name, every
last one of them, and when he saw the disappointment of the police at how little he knew, he told
more, making up incidents, incriminating friends
and enemies alike, anyone who could testify to his
foolishness, anyone unfortunate enough to have
been in his past, wiping his life behind him clean,
like a slate, so that he would have no past to haunt
him. And all the while loving it, loving the lying,
loving the obligation to lie, feeling like a poet once
again.

Now, in the restaurant, he began eating once more,
a hungry poet, fatigued by his memories. As I left, he
was squabbling with the bluebottles over the relics of
breakfast.

That night, around midnight, I saw something that
frightened me, and I decided to leave that town as
soon as possible.

I had gone out for some fresh air, but a thick fog
obscured even the little park across from the hotel.
Further up the street, the haze of the street lamps
shone faintly, and I walked towards them.

Soon, I could hear shuffling sounds, and I could
make out something huge swaying down the street
under the lurid lights. Noises came from all along its
length, a monster of many mouths talking to itself.

From the shelter of a house door, I was relieved to see that it was only a mass of the townspeople slowly shambling along the street. Many of them were contorted into grotesque postures, supported by crutches, and canes, and all the iron paraphernalia of pain. The laboured breathing in the heavy fog was a chilling chorus. They advanced cautiously, as though the street was a quicksand, and they had to be careful to step only on the solid parts.

All at once, all of the faces turned to look in my direction. I could not be certain in that light, but I thought I recognized some of them: the hotel bartender, the mother of the plague victim, the man whose family sought his death, the woman with the scars, the traitor-poet, all of them looking towards me. The moaning became more highly pitched, the whole procession swayed towards where I stood. Many stretched their arms out towards me, but without menace, their eyes, their mouths, smiling, as though to welcome a friend.

I turned away and began to walk, as quickly as I could, back to the hotel, where I locked myself in my room, propping a chair against the door handle. All night I could hear the creaking of footsteps on the carpeted corridor, soft tapping on my door and even my window. I could hear unpleasant laughter. I heard it all, for I did not sleep.

Next morning, I left the town behind me for good. The sun was up early, an orange eye with cataracts in the eastern sky. From several miles away across the plain, I looked back, a last look at the town, a pile of rubble from here, heaped against the base of the mountain with its misty top. I made a clenched fist of my brain and kept walking, walking, up to my knees at times in a vast, shallow lagoon of butter-flies, till I could see ahead of me the green plain that stretched, far away, to another horizon.

Twins

People swarm from north and south, abandon the rituals of Saturday afternoon shopping expeditions and ball-game attendances, in favour of him. One thing: no children. He demands no admission fee, so he is entitled to say "No children." ("Say" won't do. Even that woman, his mother, the crutch on which he has limped his eighteen years, can never be sure of what he "says." He, therefore, writes. And has written, with his right hand, and with his left hand, "NO CHILDREN.") For children are always the enemy: they suspect something, frown at him, tire of his performances, spoil everything. (As for dogs, they are wary too when they see him out walking. They sheath their tails. They slink growling to the opposite side of the road.) But, ah! The adults! The benches of the old church hall sag under the weight of their veneration. His devotees. How they admire him, how they nod their approval of his enigmatic sermons. He bestows upon them tears perhaps of gratitude, howls perhaps of execration. Either way, his votaries (the tall man with the blue eyes sits among them) are content.

The name of the one they come to hear? Malachi. That, at least, is sure. He has a sickness (is there a name for it?). His sickness attracts them. He is the one who speaks with two voices, two different voices, at the same time. One of the voices trolls smoothly from the right side of his mouth. The other crackles from the left corner. How memorable, how remarkable, the sound of those two voices emanating from that one flexible mouth.

Is his affliction, then, a miracle? No matter, it certainly complicates his life. It might be easier to bear if the two voices would speak in turns. But whenever he wants to say something, both voices chime in, overlap, each using an exactly equal number of syllables. Without euphony. There is discord in the sounds, there is dissent in the things said. What allures is the eeriness of it. The right-side voice thanks the tall man with the blue eyes for a gift he has brought:

"Thanks a lot."

But the left-side voice remarks simultaneously:

"You're a fool."

(Or is it vice-versa? Often it is hard to tell.) The hearing is a difficult experience. Words sometimes twine together, like this —

```
"t          k          o
   h        n     s    l       t
     a             a
          r    e        o   o
     o  u           a  f       l
  y"
```

— braided like two snakes. Or a discrepancy in timing produces a long, alien word: "*thyaounksreaalfoolot.*" Or exact synchronization causes a triple grunt: "*th$_y$a$_{ou}$nks$_{re}$a$_a$l$_{fo}^{ot}_{ol}$.*" Leaving the hearer to rummage among fragments of words, palimpsests of phrases. Did he hear, "you're a lot," "thanks a fool," "yanks a lol," "thou're a foot?"

A disease of words. When Malachi was a child, nobody was willing to diagnose his problem. No father to turn to. His mother never revealed who fathered him in the bed of her clapboard house, imitation brick, a mile north of town. Malachi squirmed out of the womb, purple. Let loose his inhuman shrieks. It was presumed his brain was not right.

See him at the age of ten. A boy unable to cope with anything scholastic. No one understands his noises, the drooling, the maddening grunts. Then, lying on the floor on a Sunday morning in June, in his mother's presence, tiger stripes of sun through the shutters on his prone body, he who has never written a word, picks up two pencils, one in each hand, and writes two messages simultaneously on a sheet of paper. With his right hand, a neat firm line:

"Help me, Mother."

With his left hand a scrawl:

"Leave me alone."

She stares at the paper, squints at his mouth, understands at last.

The why of it? How can such a thing have happened to her son? She expounds her theory to the tall man. (He has blue eyes, fine lines web the corners.) Malachi, she says, is meant to be twins, but somehow the division has not occurred, and he has been born, two people condemned to one body. Reverse Siamese twins. When she speaks of her theory in Malachi's presence, his face seems to confirm it. The right side blooms smooth, and innocent boy's. The left side shimmers with defiance. His head becomes unsteady, wobbles like an erratic planet with orbiting satellite eyes.

The German pastor is the force behind the audiences. He has spoken at some length to the tall man with the unflinching blue eyes. The pastor suggests to the mother that it will be good for the boy's confidence to exhibit himself. Is the pastor concerned about therapy or theology? Is he convinced that ultimately one voice or the other will prevail in open combat? Is he enthusiastic because he himself marvels at the sight? (Understands something?) He never misses an audience, sits rapt, engrossed in the turmoil in the face, the voice, of Malachi.

A sudden change. In the middle of the eighteenth year, tranquillity. The harsh voice silent, the soft voice alone emerges from the twisted mouth, unencumbered. The left side of the mouth still curls, the left cheek still twitches, the left eye still glares. People still cringe ready for the snarl. But they wait in vain. And Malachi appears one morning wearing a black cloth patch over the left side of his face. A black triangle.

They ask him, "What has happened to your other voice?"

He seems surprised at the question, as though unaware of the years of struggle. Soon, no one asks him any more, everyone becomes used to his masked face. They admire it, a portentous half moon. Malachi is a kind-hearted boy. His long illness is forgotten.

Three years later, he dies. At the age of twenty-one, he is sucked into the spirals of the river on a dark night. The verdict at the inquest: death by accident. The pathologist does not fail to take note of Malachi's remarkable tongue, wide as two normal tongues, linked by a membrane of skin. It must have made breathing difficult in those final moments. Malachi's mother attends the inquest, too distraught to be called as a witness. Afterwards, in the car park, the tall man catches up to her. He is about her age. (He has blue eyes. Fine lines web the corners.) He is silent. The sun beats down, mid-July, a day that ridicules mourning. She is still a woman of some beauty.

"It would have happened long ago," she says, "but for a pact. Three years ago I made them agree to it. One voice was to be in command all day, then after dark the other would take over. They just shifted the patch. But the girl drove them against each other again. They were jealous over her. They couldn't share her any longer. They needed to fight it out. But there was only the one body to hurt."

She can no longer control herself. She sobs, and begs the man to leave her alone. A neighbour takes her by the arm to a waiting car. The man with blue eyes watches her go. He knows what must be done.

He drives to where the girl lives, a country motel, a run-down place, peeling green paint. She greets him solemnly, invites him up to her room. A lank-haired girl, not beautiful. He savours her quiet voice.

"He was a good friend to me," telling of Malachi. "I could trust him. On sunny days, we just sat by the river and talked. He said everything was under control. I was not to worry about his moods at night. I told him I liked him just as much at night when he switched the patch and changed his voice. At night, he would drink and drink, and make love. I told him how much I loved the feel of his tongue on my body. I suppose he didn't believe me."

She asks the man with the blue eyes to wait with her for a while. He stays, consoles her. It is dark when he leaves.

Ten years have passed. I am on an assignment to this country town. It is a pleasant summer's morning with, strangely, an arc of moon still visible in the bright sky like a single heelprint on glare ice. I am here to observe two children. They are twins, I am told. I am a little afraid of what I may find. I have a fear of children.

They don't look especially alike. One is fair, composed, the other dark and fidgety. They are ten years old. They speak in a babble no one has been able to understand. Aside from themselves, that is, for they seem to understand each other.

I am here with the other observers because of a curious development. The twins have discovered how to communicate with the world. When they wish to

be understood by others, we are told, they join hands
and speak in unison. The sounds blend together and
produce words that are intelligible.

The twins do not seem happy to meet our group of
linguists, philologists, semanticists, etymologists,
cynics, believers. Amongst us, the tall man with blue
eyes. Fine lines web the corners. He seems anxious.

At length the boys' mother, who has not changed
much over the years, asks them to speak to us. They
hesitate, resolve to please her. They join hands. The
two solo voices that, separately, are incomprehensible
to the audience, blend together in a curious duet:

"Please help us, Father," they cry.

This evokes great delight on the part of the other
observers. They demand more. But the two little boys
stand firm, hand-in-hand. They look directly at me.
They repeat, for me, their shy, angry chant:

"Please help us Father," they plead.

They are staring directly at the man with blue eyes.
He glances around fearfully, understands that the boys
are making their appeal only to him. He looks at me
in desperation. He can no longer refuse to acknowledge me. I, for my part, am ready to acknowledge him.
I try to control my terror. I extend my hand to him. I
find I am alone. Alone, for the first time, with my
children.

The Fugue

Where are the beginnings, the endings, and most important, the middles?

Cortazar

Knowing it well, the cedar-timbered house high on the river bank. That a man would be there at this time of day. That he would be alone in the house, its back-yard descending to the river in stages. His mind explored it for the thousandth time. On the top level, a lawn with a few apple trees still in blossom spread itself out from the walls of the house. Next, a thicket of uncultivated bush acted as a kind of natural barrier, penetrated by a rough path to the edge of the plateau. Finally, a wooden staircase of fifty rotted steps tottered down the steep embankment of weeds and brambles to an overgrown lane by the riverside. This was the lane on which he stood, invisible from the house, used mainly by dog-walkers and fishermen. Lovers too. Lovers. Anger began to seep through, he must breathe deeply, be calm. His fingers circled the hand-rail, and he began to climb the stairs with exaggerated caution, though no sound he made would reach the house. At the top he paused. Now, as ever, there was no turning back. He advanced with care through the belt of bush till he could see the well-trimmed lawn powdered with apple blossoms, and, dominating everything, the cedar walls of the house. The chill of the steel knife-blade tucked into his trouser-waist comforted him, slowed the pounding of his heart. He slid from the cover of one tree to the next until he was able to peer into the downstairs study with its long picture-window and adjacent sliding-door. Elation. There he sat, in the study, as expected, his head showing above the stuffed armchair, its back towards the window. Stealthily he worked his way closer to the house, making use of the intervening trees. The last few yards, he lunged forward, pressing his body against the section of wall between the window and the door. He tensed himself, held his breath. No noise from inside. He had not been seen. A quick squint showed the man still secure in his chair, the back of his greying head magnified from this close. Reading. On a heavy wooden side-table at his right hand stood a tumbler of what must be Scotch — he liked his Scotch — still nearly full. He was a man of habit, would read for an hour then take his nap. Another squint to check that all was well. From this far he could not make out the book, doubtless some cheap novel, the kind he loved, though he masqueraded as a scholar and a man of culture. Deceiving those who could know no better. Bitterness must not prevent him, especially now, from thinking clearly. Gently he tested the sliding door. It slid noiselessly on its well-oiled tracks, as he knew it would. On such a windless day, no draught would betray his intrusion. The man was preoccupied with his reading, quite unaware that someone was now in the room behind him, gliding silently towards his chair, holding a knife warm from the heat of his body, eyes glinting. All his attention was concentrated on the book before him.

Marvelling, for the thousandth time, at the delight reading gave him. To lose himself in a book, savouring the characters, the plot, the words. He often felt that for him fiction was a necessary escape from the unpleasant reality of his own personality. For though he admired the romantic qualities of fictional heroes such as the well-meaning detective in this book, he had no urge to emulate them. He preferred in his own life to get what he wanted by any means he could. He enjoyed these wishful fantasies of an ordered universe, but understood the world well enough to know their place in his own particular jungle. He wondered, with amusement, whether it was possible for a man to squander, quite vicariously in reading, all his human potential, and then to return to reality as he himself always did, calloused and even more cynical. It was ironic that people enthused over the great empathy and sensitivity he showed in his critical writings. They had certainly ensured his success in academic circles, most of all with women. Those cultured, naïve women fell for him, often aspiring female graduate students or the wives of colleagues. They presumed that

despite his hard shell a man of such understanding
could never abuse their love. She had begged him to
invite her here not two weeks ago — to discuss her
term paper. Well. They both knew what that meant.
No sooner had she had a drink than she was writhing
in his arms coaxing him up to the bedroom. All the
time adoring him with her eyes as though she had
found the Holy Grail and not the same man who'd
already had it off with her best friend last semester.
Surely she knew he desired nothing more than a bit
of variety. And variety she supplied, with her ardour
and her agility. But a nuisance. Insisting he treat her
as more than the obligatory spring-season lay. He'd
sent her packing back to her boyfriend a little sooner
than he'd meant to. He was not tolerant of such an
inability to separate natural cravings from romantic
delusions. Now take the hero of this novel: he was an
idealist, but that was exactly as it should be in fiction.
This policeman was committed to some principle of
justice, no matter how vaguely understood, and his
sense of duty forced him to offer the protection of the
law to everyone, even to those he despised. Here he
was now in the predictable climactic confrontation
scene of the novel, agonizing over his role, yet hero-
ically carrying on.

Urging the squad-car driver to get there as quickly
as possible. Though they were not far away, the heavy
traffic frustrated their efforts. Yet he had to forbid the
use of the siren for fear of precipitating the crime. He
could only hope they would not be too late, otherwise
he might have on his conscience a man's life, a man

not altogether guiltless. For the thousandth time he put this thought out of his mind. It was not his responsibility to judge final guilt or innocence, so why make a hard job unbearable? At last the car swung off the main road onto one of the quiet suburban streets near the river, then into the familiar heavily treed crescent, the lawns glistening with sprinklers, fruit trees remarkable in their spring bloom. He was thankful he could still savour such things, no matter what unpleasantness lay ahead. The car drew up in front of the house. It struck him how easy it would be for someone to approach from the rear unseen, and he leapt from the car and ran quickly round to the backyard. No one. He strode across the lawn, looking down the path towards the river. No sign of an intruder. Perhaps her fears were groundless, the delusions of a wronged woman. He turned towards the house and at once the open sliding-door assaulted his eyes. Now, through the picture-window, he saw everything. One of them sat in an armchair, his head slightly bowed, all his attention riveted on a book. Behind him stood the other, a knife raised ready to strike. Time suspended them all. Then the knife began its smooth arc. He hesitated for a particle of a second, raised the revolver and squeezed the trigger.

THE
PARADISE
MOTEL

A Novella

For Nancy Helfinger

What, should we get rid of our
ignorance, the very substance of
our lives, merely in order to
understand one another?

R.P. Blackmur

PROLOGUE

He is dozing, sitting in a wicker chair on a balcony of the Paradise Motel. The squat, clapboard building looks out across a beach onto the North Atlantic Ocean, a grey ocean on a grey day. The man is wearing a heavy tweed overcoat, gloves, and a scarf. When he opens his eyes, as he does from time to time, he can see for miles to where the grey water meets the slightly less grey sky. Today, he thinks, this ocean might easily be a huge handwritten manuscript covered as far as the eye can see with regular lines of neat, cursive writing. At the bottom, near the shore, the lines are clearer, and he keeps thinking it might be possible to make out what they say. Then, crash! they break up, on pale brown sand, on black rocks, on the pitted remains of an old concrete jetty. The words, whatever they are, dissolve into white foam on the beach.

The name of this man, that is to say, *my* name, is Ezra Stevenson. I play a minor part in what follows. The principal figures are the four Mackenzies, whose childhood was mysterious, perhaps horrific; what happened to them later is the major concern. A few other people are important, too: JP, retired newspaperman; the man called Pablo Renowsky, philosophic ex-boxer; Doctor Yerdeli, Director of the Institute for the Lost; Donald Cromarty, old friend and scholar, who helped me in the search for resolutions (comforting word in an uneasy universe); and one or two others.

Not forgetting, of course, my own grandfather, Daniel Stevenson. He's the one who told me about the Mackenzies. If he hadn't come home to die, after a disappearance of thirty years, I doubt whether I would ever have heard of them.

Maybe no one would. Most often, in the matter of individual lives, time, with implacable energy, wipes out those who would have been worth remembering, along with the rest of us. That, for me, is the sad lesson of history, as well as the great solace.

PART ONE

DANIEL

1

As I grew older, I began to look like Daniel Stevenson, my grandfather, who died when I was twelve. In the mirror, each day, I could see him in me. My eyes were green, like his. By the time I was fifteen, I had grown to his height and my face had thinned a lot, so that the resemblance was even stronger, as though his face had been hiding underneath mine all along, the kernel beneath the skin. Whenever someone else, an outsider, pointed out the likeness, my grandmother, Joanna, and my mother, Elizabeth, were not pleased. As for myself, I can't say I was thrilled either. For I had seen how the old man looked as he lay dead, and could never forget it; I knew that was how I would look some day, if I lived to his age, and died in a bed.

I only knew him for the length of one week, but during it, we talked and talked. I don't think, looking back, that it is strange I never asked him why he ran away from Muirton, thirty years before. Some children are too devious even to dream of asking such questions. He gave me hints, all along, without my needing to ask. He had a habit of not looking directly at me when he was about to say something very personal.

As, for example, when he said in his hoarse voice: "Ezra, it's a miracle I left this place, you know. It wasn't planned."

He seemed to consider that, for a while. Then he said: "Like a squall at sea on a calm day. It just happened."

Another time, he said this: "Muirton was too hard for me, or I was too soft for it. I don't know which."

And once, too: "The sky here used to remind me of a tunnel. I felt I could never stand up straight."

That was the kind of thing he might say when he wasn't telling stories about his travels. And he would use words like "ugliness," and "beauty," words none of the other men of Muirton ever used. He said he'd decided there must be beauty in life somewhere, and he was going looking for it.

The afternoon he told me the story of his journey to Patagonia, thirty years before, was one of those wet afternoons in Muirton, with heavy rain sluicing the slate roof and the sooty windows of the attic where he was lying. Perhaps the rain reminded him. Or perhaps the bone. He had been showing me some odds and ends from his trouser pockets: tin coins with holes in them, from Chinese tombs; a complicated knot in a hemp rope from Oluba (to untie it meant bad luck); some fragments of red Mayan pottery, a thousand years old (he said the red was human blood). As for the bone, it was a greyish colour, scrimshawed with a three-masted ship, sails bulging in a stiff artist's gale.

"That's how the *Mingulay* looked," he said.

I was sitting on the edge of his mattress, and could just make out, at eye-level, through the attic window, the rain-distorted outline of the hills of Muirton, worn down by history. Or even if I could not actually see them, I believed in them, I was sure of their reality. As he talked, I could smell his stale breath; but his beaky face was less yellow than usual. It was washed clear, for a while, by the flood of memories from that time, thirty years before, when he was strong, with the whole world in front of him.

2

He had signed on as a deck-hand on the *Mingulay*, the musical-sounding name of a small three-master. It was to carry a party of scientists and adventurers to Patagonia, the grim wasteland at the foot of South America. He knew nothing about the place then. Its name was only a satisfying-sounding foreign word in a school textbook. He did not know that the region was famed as a dinosaur graveyard. That, for decades, archaeologists had ripped open its surface to expose strange and massive relics.

Near the turn of the century, rumors began to spread, from the few natives left in the hinterland and from travellers hurrying through, that a live monster had been spotted trundling around the foothills, almost big enough to pass for a small foothill itself. Experts said it sounded like a mylodon, a primitive kind of giant sloth. Country after country began sending expeditions to Patagonia in the hope of being the first to capture a creature so slow to change that a million years of evolution had not been long enough.

In the end, of course, no one found any such monster. The sighting was a hoax or, just as likely, a dream, hatched by dreamers in a dream world.

So the expedition to which Daniel Stevenson was attached was no more successful than any of the others. But for him, the adventure was what counted. He had spent most of his life, till then, working in the Muirton mine. He had told lies to the leaders of the expedition so that they would sign him on as a deck-hand, and when they did, he could hardly believe his luck. Everything, from the start, was marvellous: the feel of a wooden hull under him, breathing and creaking and rolling; the salt-water smell; the secrets of the ship itself, a country with a strange language: "booms," "spars," "starboard," "port," "bow," "stern," "fore and aft," "gunwales," "fo'c'sle," "topgallants," "mizzens"; new words to be learnt every day. He was always the one most willing to climb the rigging to the swaying topmast and the open sky. He saw himself as a bird, no longer a blind mole condemned to endless, dark tunnels.

The voyage was a long one. At night, the sky seethed with fragments of light; but even on starless nights, the ship's wake created its own milky way. In the day, Daniel would spend hours at the bow, watching the ship drive forward into the winds. The harder they blew, the more determinedly the *Mingulay* advanced. He felt a great bond with her.

But when the ship was, at last, coasting down the final miles, how unpleasantly familiar Patagonia seemed to him, how the swirls of mist on the squat hills, the treeless swamps, reminded him of the country around Muirton.

As though a trick had been played upon him, and his escape tunnel ended up back in the prison-yard. He almost expected to see, around every headland, the great Ferris wheel of the Muirton mine elevator rotating with the earth, to smell the acrid smell of coal smoke, and to hear the siren hooting at his failure.

The *Mingulay* anchored a quarter of a mile offshore, and the crew worked all day ferrying provisions. The surf was a great hostile machine that crushed the arm of one sailor between the ship's hull and the tender, and never gave up trying to drown the others. But, at last, just before nightfall, the provisions and the men were ashore, except for a skeleton crew left to guard the empty ship. On the endless white beach, the expeditioners lit fires of driftwood, and the cook made a meal of bannocks and fish-stew.

3

Those evenings in Patagonia Daniel Stevenson never forgot. Gathered in a ring of light round the fire, their backs walling out the night, the men would sit with their mugs of rum, telling stories as though they were still in their hammocks in the fo'c'sle on the voyage south.

One story Daniel heard there, in Patagonia, thirty years

before, implanted itself in him with the solidity of the landscape of the place itself. The expedition had, by then, travelled inland for about a week, and set up camp on a plateau in the foothills. It was night, rainy and cool. The teller of the story was Zachary Mackenzie, the Engineer, whose job was to take care of the auxiliary engine of the *Mingulay*.

He was a youngish man, tall, his fair hair already thinning. He knew something about medicine. When Daniel Stevenson injured his hand in a ratchet early on the voyage south, Mackenzie washed and poulticed it daily. Often, Daniel knocked at his cabin door for treatment, to find the Engineer scribbling in yellow notebooks. He never seemed to mind interruptions by Daniel. Perhaps, he said, they got along so well because his own specialty was the innards of a ship, while Daniel had been intimate with the innards of the earth. This was as near as he ever came to humour.

Unless one other comment of his to Daniel was meant to be funny. They knew each other pretty well by that time, and had been talking about love, and women.

"I have never been in love," Zachary Mackenzie said. "Take my advice, Daniel, never put too much confidence in a man who has never been in love." He didn't laugh.

This Zachary Mackenzie, then, was the one who told the story long ago, in Patagonia, his light-blue eyes like steel reflecting the firelight.

4

Up in that damp attic, all those years later, Daniel Stevenson wanted me to know he had never told anyone else the story.

"Ezra, this is the first time," he said.

He paused, and said, "Never before, not once."

Then, after a while, he said again, slowly, "Ezra, yes. This is the first time."

Then he was silent, lifting a lid, peering into a box sealed thirty years before. His yellow-green eyes were burning. He remembered exactly what kind of night that was, who was sitting there (all dead men now, surely) around the fire in the Patagonian darkness.

I myself could hear the rain outside the attic slacking off a good deal. It was still telling its own story, but softer now, to the slate roof and the beaten, huddled hills beyond the dirty window.

5

The firelight was a brilliant incision in the great belly of the Patagonian night. Bats were wheeling around, in and

out, and rain was whispering softly to the blazing logs.
The hills had long ago disappeared.

The Engineer spoke up. He said he remembered
something that might interest them, something that had
really happened. He was a man from the islands who kept,
in his cabin, notebooks filled with jottings no one else was
allowed to see. His hands were familiar with bunker oil
and heavy steel piping, yet he had the elegant fingers of a
pianist or a surgeon, the milky blue eyes of a dreamer. He
rose from his squatting position with the others and took
the higher place on an upturned barrel. Then he spoke in
a soft, northern voice.

"When I was a young boy, a strange thing happened in
our town. A new doctor with a southern accent came up
to practise at our end of the island with his wife and four
children, two boys and two girls all under ten years old.
The doctor was thin with a head like a snake. His wife was
beautiful, with long, fair hair tied in a bun behind her
head, and always happy, always singing. That's all I
remember about her.

"After only a month, the thing happened. On a sunny
morning in September, this new doctor came to the
duty-desk of the police station looking very upset, to
report that his wife was missing. He said she'd gone for
her daily walk the day before and not come back. He had
looked everywhere, not wanting to make a fuss. But now
he was becoming very anxious.

"The police went to work. They made sure first of all
that she had not boarded the ferry for the mainland, and
then they organized a search for her. Many of the men

helped out. They searched everywhere, day and night, for two days, but they could find no sign of her.

"Life had to go on. The four children showed up at school the next day as usual. But they did not look well. They were all pale and washed out as though they had been crying. What was most noticeable was the way they walked. They all walked stiffly, as though they were old men.

"The island children hadn't known them long enough, and were shy about asking what was the matter, thinking it must have something to do with their mother's disappearance.

"But on their second day back at school, one of the little girls, who was about six years old then, turned very sick at her desk and fell over onto the floor with convulsions, holding her stomach and groaning.

"The old schoolmistress took her to the staff room and made her comfortable with blankets and a pillow. Then she phoned the girl's father, the doctor, to come right away.

"The little girl kept on groaning in agony, and the schoolmistress tried to coax her to show where the pain was. The little girl was not willing at first, only she was in pain, and saw the schoolmistress wanted to help. So she began to unbutton her dress.

"But a car drew up outside, and her father, the doctor, came rushing into the staff-room shouting, 'No! No!' and lifted her away in his arms. He then came back for the other three children, and took them all away in the car with him.

"The old schoolmistress had seen enough. She phoned the police station.

"Without any delay, the sergeant and his constable drove to the doctor's house on the cliffs overlooking the sea. They knocked and stood waiting for a few minutes till the doctor, looking nervous, came to the door. The sergeant said he'd like to see the children. The doctor at first said they were too sick to be disturbed, but the sergeant insisted, and the three of them went inside.

"All the children were lying in their beds in one large room on the ocean side of the house, and anyone could tell how sick they were. The sergeant knew what he had to do. He asked them to open up their clothing for him. They all did so, with groans and gasps of pain.

"He understood the reason for their suffering.

"The sergeant saw that each of those four children had a large incision in the centre of their abdomens, the sutures fresh, the wounds inflamed.

"Their father, the doctor, who had been standing watching all of this, was sobbing quietly. When the sergeant asked him why the children had been operated upon, he would say nothing.

"The sergeant called the local ambulance and took all four children to the hospital at the other end of the island.

"The resident surgeon there, a kind man, saw the sergeant's concern. He ordered the little girl who had been in the greatest pain to be taken into the operating theatre where he had been about to conduct a class in pathology for some nurses. The little girl was anaesthetized. The resident and the nurses could see how pus mixed with blood was oozing from the wound. No wonder she had been in agony.

"The resident then cut the sutures and lifted them away. He slid his fingers into the wound and groped around. He could feel a lump of some sort. With a pair of calipers, he managed to grip part of it. He carefully fished it out and held it up in the air.

"All of those assembled round that table saw something they would never forget. The resident had snared in the calipers a severed human hand, dripping blood and pus. He was holding it by its thumb, and they could all see, quite clearly, the gold wedding ring on its middle finger and the scarlet polish on the long fingernails."

The Engineer stopped for a moment to take a drink of rum from his tin mug. The night had turned chilly, and the members of the expedition crouched nearer to the fire's heat. He continued:

"That was how they found out that the new doctor had killed his wife. He had cut off parts of her and buried them inside the children. Each of the four children contained a hand, or a foot. Later the family pets, a Highland collie and a big ginger cat, were found lying in the house cellar, half alive. They too had abdominal incisions. The local veterinarian discovered the woman's eyes in the dog and her ears in the cat.

"The resident testified later that he hoped never to perform such a salvage operation again. He was sure that if the man had had enough children and pets, he'd have managed to conceal every part of her. As it was, a fisherman found the rest of her body under some rocks by the shore.

"The resident said the father's workmanship was a marvel, though. He had never seen such skill with the knife. The murderer himself was silent. He was later sentenced to death, though his children pleaded for his life. The islanders would never allow hangings on the island for fear of bad luck. They did not object, however, to his being hanged on the mainland. And he was."

The Engineer had finished. He was nodding his head slightly, as if to support the truth of what he had just said.

"I don't believe a word of it," said one of the crew, a fair-haired man from London. "It's a load of codswallop! As though a human body could be used as a repository of dead limbs!"

Many of the others sitting around the fire began to laugh too, with relief as much as anything, at the thought that it was all really a joke.

The Engineer slid slowly to his feet from the barrel. The rain was hissing down into the fire now even more noisily, as though the logs were debating the issue too. In and out of the firelight, bats were wheeling, one instant solid and tangible, the next annihilated by the night.

The Engineer stood for a minute, as though he was going to head off to his tent. But instead, he slowly unbuttoned his sou'wester, exposing his white shirt tucked into the black officer's pants. He pulled the front of his shirt out of his pants and held it up to his chin, baring his midriff. There, just above the waistline, the watchers could all see a long horizontal scar, a white corrugation about nine inches long dissecting his pale, northern skin.

The men were silent. The Engineer carefully tucked his shirt back into his trousers, pulled his sou'wester together, turned and walked away into the darkness.

—
6
—

Daniel Stevenson, my grandfather, had almost finished his story. In the dull light of the attic, his yellow-green eyes were growing old again, as the elapsed thirty years filled back in.

"The next day, I asked the Engineer what were the names of the children. He said they all had biblical names: his sisters were called Rachel and Esther, his brother, Amos. And himself, Zachary. He said he was glad I asked."

Daniel Stevenson was lying back as he told me this, his lips barely moving, so that his head might have been a skull, with an army of tiny, stale-smelling black ants crawling over his jaw-bone, their legs rustling out the sounds, "Rachel," "Esther," "Amos," "Zachary." He lay exhausted, as though something vital had been cut out of him. Throughout the entire story, his hoarse voice had been, at times, scarcely more than a whisper that

conspired with the swish of the rain on the grey slates of
the attic roof to make sure no one else in the world could
hear, but me, Ezra Stevenson.

7

As I said, I only knew Daniel Stevenson, my
grandfather, for a week. He had run away from Muirton,
our village high in the moors, thirty years before. On a
gloomy September morning, he had been walking along
the hawthorn-hedge-lined roadway to the mine, for the
early shift, with five other men. The time was just before
six-thirty in the morning. As they passed the red-brick
railway station, the weekly passenger train was about to
leave for the coast. Daniel Stevenson, who was not
dressed for travelling, quietly said goodbye to his
workmates, vaulted over the station's picket fence, and
hauled himself aboard the train, which was already
moving. He left behind him, in Muirton, a wife and a
young son.

Then, thirty years later, he came home.

Once again, it was September, but the weather was
cold and windy. In Muirton, winter was often hard to tell
from summer, for the temperature did not vary much up
in the moorland hills. But at a certain time in September,

the leaves of the few trees that grew there would cast off and tack wearily to their final berths.

In September, then, Daniel Stevenson came home. Really home, that is. He moved right into our house without anyone noticing he was back. He must have come in during the night, for doors were seldom locked in villages like Muirton, where burglary was much less common than those crimes locked doors only encouraged. Daniel Stevenson must have entered by the back door, slunk across the brown linoleum floor of the kitchen (he would have noticed the smell of floor-polish and cooking) to the brown-painted door of the attic stairway, then climbed the narrow, enclosed stairs that sneaked up along the side wall of the house to the attic, once a maid's quarters. And settled down.

How he even knew which house was ours is a mystery. His grown-up son, John Stevenson (my father: a man who never sang, who had never been known to join, even, in communal singing), had become the manager of the mine just three years before. Only then had we moved from the small row-house, among all the other miners' rows, into this big house, formerly the mine-owner's mansion, at the edge of the village.

How did the old man know we lived there now? Had he been spying on us for a while before he entered? Not very likely. In that village, a stranger would have been too obvious. And, anyway, how would he have known what his wife and son looked like after thirty years? Unless someone else was collaborating with him? Someone who never owned up, not even afterwards? Perhaps. These things cannot now be determined. What is sure is that one

night he must have come up into the kitchen through the
back door, put on his old carpet slippers (a point, surely,
worthy of note), and climbed up into that attic cautiously.
Caution was needed, for the stairs passed a part of the
wall of the main bedroom. The Stevenson house was a
house of light sleepers.

8
―――

The woman who was my grandmother, Joanna
Stevenson, was the first to notice he was back. She was of
middle size, with grey eyes, fine features (though her nose
wandered off slightly to her left), her hair held back by a
wooden clasp carved in the shape of entwined snakes. In
the centre of her long grey hair was a thick, black streak
that had not aged.

She was the one who saw that the worn felt slippers she
had preserved for thirty years had disappeared from the
boot-tray by the back door. She was the one who found
out that bread and cheese and apples and milk were
missing from the pantry. She knew this with certainty, for
it was her pantry, she was in charge of the kitchen.

She said nothing.

Once or twice during the early days of the return, my
mother, Elizabeth Stevenson, thought she heard a faint

creaking of boards in the attic. She was soft faced and plump, characteristics of many of the women in Muirton. But she was a fiery woman, orphaned as a child. So when she heard something up there, she urged John Stevenson to take a piece of wood, and go up and kill whatever creature was making the noise, for it might be a mouse or, even worse, a rat. She said, as she frequently did, how foolish it was not to kill those things that ought to be killed. She was in charge of keeping the house clean.

John Stevenson, my father, was a red-haired man (red hair was another common Muirton trait), heavy shouldered from mine work, a man who ordered other men about all day, but who was happy at home to submit to Elizabeth. Unless my grandmother, Joanna, contradicted her, as she did now. She said the noise wasn't mice or rats at this time of year, just the wind. Elizabeth looked at her and looked at her, a long time.

9

In those days, Joanna began to change her behaviour. She had always gone to bed early, even before me, and I was only ten at that time. But now, she would stay up after the rest of us, saying she wanted to do some reading (something I had never, in my ten years, seen her do) or knitting. Or just sit there by the night fire a little longer.

What she'd really do, after we had all said good-night and gone to our rooms and fallen asleep, was this: she'd take the old Golden Jubilee tin tray down from the sideboard and load it with buttered bread, and perhaps a piece of beef, a bottle of stout, and some rhubarb pie. She'd leave the tray on the deal table in the kitchen with a clean shirt and fresh woollen socks. Then she'd go up to bed.

In the night, Daniel Stevenson, the unacknowledged guest, would slip down, take the tray and the clothes, and creep back up to the attic.

Night after night, she prepared food and clothing for him in this way. Night after night, he came down the stairs to return the dirty things and pick up his provisions. She would get up first in the mornings, despite her late nights, to clear away the evidence.

So he knew, of course, that she knew he was back.

10

But one morning (I suppose he had been in the attic at least two weeks) when she got up, the tray and the clothing still lay untouched on the deal table. All day, she wondered what was wrong. That night, she set the provisions out for him again. She went to bed, but was hardly able to sleep for worrying. Was he lying up there, sick or dead? Had he, perhaps, finished whatever it was he had come home to do, and had left Muirton again, without her knowing? She could not bear that thought. She got up just before dawn, went down to the kitchen, and saw the fresh clothes and food still lying on the table. That was enough.

She went straight to the main bedroom, which she had never before entered, opened the door and walked in. My parents, John and Elizabeth Stevenson, had, of course, heard her, and were in the act of sitting up with the blankets half-around them, like creatures to whom a lumpy monster was giving birth.

What must have passed through their heads as that old woman told them what had been going on for two weeks in their house? How she wanted her son to go right up to the attic and see if Daniel was all right. How she was afraid he was dead, or that he'd gone away again.

John Stevenson, whatever he might have thought, heaved himself into the cold air of the bedroom and went down (a descent in order to ascend) to the brightly lit kitchen, opened the attic stairway door and, taking a broom-handle with him, just in case, began climbing the narrow staircase into the attic. His wife and his mother stayed in the kitchen.

11

When John Stevenson came down from the attic, hours later, he did not tell the women what it felt like to meet his father after all those years. He was not one to speak about his feelings. He tried, instead, to tell them what he had heard. It is difficult enough for any man to match his supply of words, most of them worn smooth and round, like stones in a river, with the erratic, jagged truths of experience. John Stevenson, a man of few words, could only give an outline of what Daniel Stevenson had told him about his thirty years' absence. Here is what he said.

Daniel, after he had run away, travelled from country to country working at any job a strong back qualified him for: bricklayer, longshoreman, sailor. Mainly sailor. A travelling life. The last ten years, however, he had spent living on the island of Oluba, in the South Pacific Ocean. The island had been a port of call when he worked on the copra schooners. He had a woman there, and a family of Stevensons, too.

A year ago, he found out he was dying, and for the first time in thirty years, he wanted to come home. He was not afraid of death, but he wanted to be near them all: his wife, his son, his daughter-in-law, if there was one, his grandchildren, if there were any (I, Ezra, was the only one). He wanted to die in the place where he was born, to exchange hibiscus for heather.

As for Oluba and his life there, the Olubans did not like the idea of a foreigner dying amongst them. They were fearful his spirit (they believed in such things) might never settle. He had always known he'd have to leave. He agreed with the Olubans that life was a journey, and it was right for a man to close out his travels in his own home port, in the place where he had begun them.

Now, up there in the attic, he would not hear of allowing a doctor near him. That was not, he said, why he came home. He assured John Stevenson he had seen men die, and knew how to die. His dying would give them no trouble.

"Syphilis, most likely," was Elizabeth's comment on it all.

Joanna Stevenson, who had listened with great attention to the life story of the old man, her husband, was silent. In her grey eyes and on her face were traces of what might have been a smile.

12

He stayed alive for another week. He said he did not wish to see anyone but his son, John. Joanna continued to prepare his food (Elizabeth would have nothing to do with him: "Wasn't I right? A rat in the attic?"). He wouldn't see any of his former workmates, either, though word was all round the village that he was back, and some of the old men would have liked to talk to him. According to John, Daniel Stevenson said he hadn't come back to talk to people, he wanted to remember them the way they had been. He wouldn't even look out of the windows in daylight in case Muirton had changed. He would only talk to his son, who took care of the old man's physical needs, helping him eat, change his shirt, support him to the grimy attic toilet, unused since the last maid lived there many years ago.

13

This is where I come into it.

At the beginning of that week, the last week of Daniel Stevenson's life, on a wet Monday afternoon, when rain obscured the hills and the smell of coal-smoke was in the air, he changed his mind about not talking to anyone and said he did want to talk to his grandson. (That's me, Ezra.) I don't know why I wasn't at school that day. Maybe I had pretended illness, I often did that. John Stevenson, my father, came down from the attic with the request. When Elizabeth heard it, she was against my going up. Joanna Stevenson, my grandmother, stayed silent, and I couldn't tell from her face what she thought.

I do remember being afraid of going up there. Not because I knew I would have to meet an old man who was not like the other old men of Muirton. No, the real reason was that even though I was only ten, or because I was only ten, I sensed that everything was about to become too complicated. Since the discovery of Daniel Stevenson's return, the atmosphere in the house had not been the same. In the past, we had never, as a family, talked much. We did the things families do, but we didn't talk about them. Now, with him upstairs in the attic, family conversation was even scarcer. My grandmother Joanna's body seemed to me to be inhabited by an unknown person who had grey eyes that were too bright, and whose lips were constantly rehearsing a faint, unfamiliar smile.

I agreed, nonetheless, to go up to the attic.

14

I glued my hand to the great, red-bristled hand of my father, and we climbed the steep stairs to the attic, a place I had been in only once and feared, because of the mottled light, the gritty floor, the cobwebs, the real vermin, the imaginary bats, the ghosts of ancient housemaids under shrouded furniture, the bent rolls of carpet, like broken cigarettes, the smell of decay, of sadness. I could not help feeling, as we climbed, that a gloomy monster was slowly devouring us. Its insides stank of urine and sour breath.

15

The old felt slippers are on the floor near the mattress where the old man lies, on his side, under the bare bulb. Weather and age have clawed the flesh around his yellow-green eyes that aim out from under a battlement of thick grey eyebrows. Half his body protrudes from the shell of blankets as he beckons feebly, a snail waving its antennae.

The boy uses his father's hip as a shield. Thinking this sick old man with the yellow skin, this man who smells so sick, is his grandfather. The face is a mask of fine wrinkles, hiding the man beneath. This old man looks like a painting in a book, symbolizing something.

As he raises himself on an elbow, the seamed yellow of his stomach shows through the placket of his shirt. The hands squeezed out by the white shirt-sleeves are yellow too, the fingers are still a miner's blunt fingers, but without the crescents of coal-dust.

The green-yellow, yellow-green eyes examine the boy. The remnants of the life that is retreating from his body have gathered in the circles of his eyes.

"So, Ezra. It's good to meet you."

Such an adult greeting to a ten-year-old boy. His voice is brittle by the time it reaches his lips. The accent is almost foreign, that of a man who has for too many years eaten strange foods.

16

In that final week of his life, I spent hour after hour listening to him talking, talking. In his brittle, urgent voice, he spoke about things he had done and places he had been since he had left Muirton thirty years before. He'd visited the most remote parts of the world, and he loved to tell me about them ("Did you ever hear of Oluba?" he'd begin; or "Did you ever hear of the River Merape?"; or "Did you ever hear of Cape Horn?"). He'd seen animals and men of every description, and he'd faced danger and death.

Always, when I came downstairs after these sessions, Joanna, my grandmother, would be waiting. I would tell her all the old man had said, and she would listen with great attention, asking me for details (especially when he told me about the women he'd encountered on his journeys, his eyes shining with pleasure as he talked.) I would try to memorize the important words and transmit them to her. She would listen with that look in her grey eyes, that movement of the lips that never quite became a smile. He knew I told her everything, and when next I went to visit him, he would ask me if she had made any comment on his adventures.

In all those long conversations, he never wanted to know anything else about her. How strange that seems to me now. But no more strange than that a boy of ten could have enjoyed so much the role of go-between, observer.

17

It was on one of those afternoons that he told me about his journey to Patagonia, and the story of Zachary Mackenzie and his sisters and brother. I remember, afterwards, going downstairs. Joanna was waiting for me in the kitchen. I could smell the freshly made tea, as usual.

"Well?"

She waited for me to talk. But I said I didn't feel like tea
or talk, I wanted to go outside. I put on my coat, trying
not to look at her, and went outside into the cold air. And
even though I told her nothing, I felt I had lied to her for
the first time in my life, and I was sure she knew it. I don't
know why I didn't, but I didn't tell her the story that day,
or any other day, no matter how she looked at me from
then on.

18

The last Sunday morning was a dreary one, rain and fog
mixed. We ate breakfast silently, and when I had finished
John Stevenson told me to run up to the attic, and see how
the old man was, for he hadn't been too well earlier.

As I entered the attic, a little breathless, Daniel
Stevenson didn't turn his head to greet me. I went over to
the mattress and looked down at him. His face was as
grim as the morning. He lay flat, staring at the peaked
attic ceiling. The yellow-green eyes were very yellow,
and no longer shining.

He took a noisy, shallow breath, and whispered: "Ezra.
Get your grandmother."

I ran back down the narrow stairs into the kitchen

where the three of them were sitting finishing off their bacon and eggs. The fire was blazing. Their faces, even John Stevenson's now, even Elizabeth's, all of them were like strangers' as they turned to look at me. Perhaps I knew what was going to happen, perhaps not. That day was so long ago, and so many things to understand. But I was excited by the strangeness of their faces.

"He wants you," I said to my grandmother, Joanna Stevenson.

Did I hope, even then, that she would go rushing up to him? I like to think so. She smiled at me, not that trace of smile I had seen her lips nurture for many days, but the fully developed version of it, an unpleasant smile.

The three of them sat there, without moving. So I said, again, just to make sure: "He wants you."

It was John, my father, who spoke.

"Ezra, you go outside and play till dinner-time."

I was about to protest. What about the rain? What about the old man up there? Instead, I went slowly to the back door, and took my raincoat from its hook. I kept glancing to the right, towards the open door to the attic stairway, listening for any sound. Was that his voice, a very weak voice calling her name? Or my name? Didn't he understand yet? I looked back to the table where the three of them sat, watching me.

They must have seen, at that moment, the last flicker of boyhood in that boy of ten's eyes, the painful recognition that the world could no longer be, never really had been, his own invention.

19

I stepped outside, pulling the back door closed behind me quickly, so that I would hear no more, and I walked away up towards the hills.

The air smelt cold and hard after the warmth inside. I made my way from the house, from the village, across narrow fields and fat, opaque streams, till the land began to rise much more steeply. The rain was pouring now, on my bare head. I climbed and climbed, leaning hard into the hill, the wet bracken soaking me to the waist. At times the gusts of wind were slabs of stone.

After about two hours, I stopped and looked back for the first time. I was perhaps a thousand feet above the village. Muirton huddled in a crack of valley, the smoke belching from a thousand chimneys. The buildings lay like broken letters of an alphabet, the remnants of their message half obliterated by the rain. All around, the noose of blunt hills seemed tighter than usual, and I could see no way out, except far to the west, where they dipped a little towards the coastal plain.

Something came over me then. I may have wept, but my face was already wet from the pouring rain, so that no one in the universe could have known for sure if I was crying. And if I cried, the tears must have been saved up for many years, and it was a long time before I began to make my way down to the village.

20

When I returned to the house, it was almost dark. Elizabeth, my mother, was in the kitchen slicing onions for dinner. She said Joanna and John Stevenson were up in the attic, and that she herself would join them in a while. I asked if I should go up, and she said: "Yes, for a minute."

In the attic, the two of them were standing by the mattress, holding hands. The old slippers still lay on the floor. My grandmother, Joanna Stevenson, turned to me as I came in and told me what I already knew.

"He's dead."

She spoke again, smiling that way: "He died up here, alone."

I tried to keep all expression out of my face. He was stretched out on the mattress, looking the way he always did, except for the dead eyes.

We heard the heavy creak of the stairs. Elizabeth, my mother. She came into the attic, slightly out of breath, and went straight to grandmother Joanna Stevenson. For the first time in my life I saw her embrace Joanna, her plump right hand stroking the back of my grandmother's head, her fingers touching the wooden fastener with the entwined snakes that held the grey hair and the black streak neatly apart. She kissed her cheek. Only then did she glance down at the dead man.

"So that was him," she said.

We were all looking down at the corpse of the old man, and I couldn't get it out of my head that the four of us, Joanna Stevenson, Elizabeth Stevenson, John Stevenson, and myself, Ezra Stevenson, even though we were on our feet and breathing, were no more alive than he was. It was an awful feeling. But I was young enough, then, to be certain that it would go away.

"Come down now, Ezra," said Elizabeth Stevenson, my mother.

Then she took me firmly by the hand and led me downstairs, and I remember that my hand was moist, but hers was dry as sand.

21

Nothing more needs to be said about my grandfather, Daniel Stevenson. He served his purpose. Whatever kind of man he was, he brought the Mackenzie story out of Patagonia, handed it on to me in Muirton, and died.

And that was that.

As for Muirton itself, it died too, not long after the old man's death (Elizabeth Stevenson, my mother, saw a direct link between the one thing and the other, a cause and effect).

Early on a July morning, forty Muirton miners, men and boys, were in the cage, descending the mine-shaft to the coal-face, when the cable snapped. The cage plunged, uncontrolled, one thousand metres down the shaft. When it struck bottom, twenty-seven of the miners died outright, and thirteen were maimed. That maiming was the cause of an unwanted, fleeting celebrity for Muirton: it became known as the village of the one-legged men.

Every single one of those who survived the disaster lost a leg. The miners had followed the safety procedures they'd practised since their apprenticeships: when they saw that the cage was plummeting out of control, they reached up and grasped the leather straps attached to the struts of the ceiling for just such a situation, then each of them lifted one of his legs off the floor. As the cage slammed into the bottom of the mine-shaft, the straps snapped, the legs that supported their body-weight were smashed to a pulp, but their lives were saved.

For years after, people from the capital used to take their Sunday drives to Muirton in the hope of spotting one of the survivors. What would have been regarded as a tragedy, had it happened to only one man, was transformed into a farce because of the number of the survivors and the bizarre nature of the injury.

But the people of Muirton fooled the sightseers. While the injured men became adept at disguising their limps, many of the uninjured villagers, men and women, cultivated an exaggerated hobbling walk. Almost all of the children of Muirton learnt to limp expertly. Who knows what the visitors made of it all?

The disaster caused the permanent closing of the mine,

which had not been very profitable. A few years later, the village itself was deserted. Even the one-legged men went their separate ways to other mining towns, where their uniqueness enabled them to find some dignity, if not anonymity, once more.

And what about the other Stevensons? They're all dead now. Joanna died a year after Daniel, having no reason to wait any more. John Stevenson, my father, was kept on as superintendent of the derelict mine property, to check the gas levels and monitor ground shifts in those endless dark excisions of the earth's core. He and my mother, Elizabeth, lived out the remainder of their lives in Muirton, the ghost town, and died in due course, in the old run-down house.

As for me, Ezra Stevenson (I had noticed, even as a boy, the curious fact that my name, E-Z-R-A, was an acronym for the names of those four Mackenzies: E-sther, Z-achary, R-achel, A-mos), though my own story is of little importance, I may as well dispose of it here, in the interest of neatness. I went through the educational grind, without distinction (no matter how many books I read, wisdom eluded me), and eventually graduated after a university career memorable only for friendships with one or two fine women, and with Donald Cromarty. He was a student of the more obscure regions of sixteenth-century history. And he was a careful, honest man. He *will* have a conclusive role in all of this, later, at the Paradise Motel.

A couple of years after graduation, I set out, like thousands of others, for the New World. I stayed for a while. I thought it might be possible to live contented here, and so I stayed longer. I have lived half my life here now. I travel a lot, I meet people. And I have a good friend, Helen.

22

Did I say nothing more needed to be said about my grandfather, Daniel Stevenson? I take that back, for a moment, just to tell one last thing.

I heard about it on the day of his funeral. (I would have preferred to avoid talking about funerals. But so much of this happened so long ago, and so many people are dead. The past often seems like one of those cornfields in the autumn, when the stalks are left standing, to wither.)

The day was an unpleasant one. Muirton could be relied on for good funeral weather. The rain was even heavier than usual. The church, with its panoply of spiky gravestones, was a fortress against joy. On that day, its blunt forefinger of a steeple warned the heavens against any such unwanted frivolity as a glimpse of sun. Hardly anyone attended the service, for it was a weekday, and most of the men were at work in the mine.

After the damp silence of the church, the graveyard was noisy with the splat of rain on umbrellas, on the muddy ground, and on the heavy wooden coffin. John

Stevenson and I, four local men who helped carry the coffin, two grave-diggers, and the clergyman were the only witnesses. After the ornate coffin was lowered into the fresh-smelling earth, I threw in a piece of mud. The clunk of it against the darkly varnished wood was satisfying.

My father and I, chilled and hungry, walked back to the big house after the burial. The two women were in the kitchen, waiting. As we warmed ourselves by the fire, I asked my grandmother, Joanna, the question that was foremost in my mind: would she give me the contents of Grandfather Daniel Stevenson's pockets, especially the scrimshawed ship? Smiling faintly, she shook her head. She'd burnt everything, she said, everything of his was gone up in smoke.

John Stevenson, to change the subject, told the two of them how the clergyman had said a few words at the graveside to the effect that it was good for a grandchild to have known his own grandfather, even if only for a week. How we should be thankful that, in the end, the prodigal had come home after his long journey.

Elizabeth couldn't restrain herself.

"Long journey? What long journey? Rubbish!" she said.

She'd heard another version of Daniel Stevenson's life several times in the past few days. Even that very morning, while we were at the funeral, when she'd gone to shop for groceries, the storekeeper told her the rumour was all round the village. That Daniel Stevenson *didn't* go very far the morning he'd run away, thirty years ago. What he really did was this: he stayed on the train till it

came to one of those little mining towns, Lannock, only
thirty miles away to the south. Lannock was a replica of
Muirton, as were most of those small mining towns in the
hills. They all had their heaps of slag, their coal smoke,
and rain. Daniel got off the train at Lannock, found a
room to rent, and within a week, started work in the mine
there. He had worked there, all those years, living on his
own, till he became ill and returned to Muirton.

"Long journey! He didn't go anywhere!" Elizabeth
said.

John Stevenson grunted. It was always hard to know
what he really thought, he was such a quiet man. My
grandmother, Joanna, looked as though she'd heard the
story from Elizabeth already, and anyway, was no longer
interested; just that faint smile whenever anyone
mentioned Daniel Stevenson.

I didn't say a thing, because at my age, what could I
say? At that time, for me, the barrier between truth and a
convincing story was so fragile that I could penetrate it
with ease, from either side. I did not see the need, in the
interest of coherence in the world, for the segregation of
the two.

23

That funeral was many years ago. I was remembering it
and the events that led up to it, on a recent summer

morning, on the balcony of my third-floor apartment. Helen was carrying out the coffee-pot to pour another cup, stepping carefully (I always pretended not to notice) to avoid the flowers on the living-room carpet. Just then, as she refilled my cup, I was remembering that boy Ezra, still inside me somewhere, but overgrown by this middle-aged, grey-haired Ezra; the one who lived in an expensive apartment overlooking the lake in the park, in a country where breakfast on the balcony in summer was possible; the one who could take a trip, at a whim, to the east coast and the Paradise Motel; the one who lived with a woman of satisfying beauty and wit, a wisp of whose fair hair had been in his mouth that morning when he awoke. To whom he occasionally liked to tell, as a variety of love-making, bits and pieces of his early life, so remote it might have been someone else's.

On that warm summer morning, as the smell of cut grass from the park drifted in with the scent of the coffee, I began telling Helen, now sitting opposite me, about Daniel Stevenson, and how he passed Zachary Macken-zie's story on to me. I told her that I had always regarded it as my personal inheritance from the old man, and how, when I was about sixteen and going through a poetic phase, I sometimes thought of the story in a romantic way, as some force inside Daniel Stevenson that had kept him alive all those years. He had begun to die so soon after passing it on to me.

I said that as I grew older I wondered if the story wasn't more of a poison he had swallowed, a rotting thing within him that brought him, at last, to his grave. Maybe he had got rid of it too late. I believed then, and still do, that even a thing made of words can grow inside the body, like gallstones which will one day make their necessary and painful exit.

I told Helen that I came to consider the story, years later, as nothing more than a story told to an impressionable boy, who eventually grew up to be too sophisticated to take it literally. It was nothing but the baggage of dreams. And yet I had kept it to myself.

Till now. Now, I wanted Helen to hear it. I wondered what she would think, for she was very astute. Like her father, a man who could make fishing lures, flies that were so genuine the fish did not notice the tiny hooks under their perfect wings. I wanted to tell her Zachary Mackenzie's story as I had heard it from my grandfather, so that it would affect her the way it had affected me when I was a boy.

But words seem to have the quality of magnets that, in time, become so smothered in pins, and scraps of this and that, they have no force left. As I spoke, the old words were no longer spare and correct, the way they had once seemed to me. I could hardly stop myself from smiling, as I told her about the burial of the limbs inside the children, and about the scar on Zachary Mackenzie's belly. The whole thing sounded so improbable, I even told Helen that, in retrospect, the rumour was probably true that Daniel Stevenson hadn't travelled at all, that he hadn't escaped, only wished it all, a pathetic old man.

Helen smiled while I told her this, but her blue eyes, behind their peculiar, convex lower lids, were not smiling.

And when she saw I was finished, she asked: "What happened to them all?"

"What do you mean?"

"The three children. Rachel, Amos, and Esther. Or Zachary, after your grandfather met him? Did he ever say what happened to any of them?"

"No. You think Daniel did go to Patagonia? You think the Mackenzies actually existed? Do you really?"

"Well, I don't know. Maybe."

She looked at me, or perhaps through me.

"But maybe it's better not to know. Maybe it's better just to forget the whole thing."

24

That afternoon, more for the fun of it than anything else, a silly thing to do, really, I wrote a letter to my old scholarly friend, Donald Cromarty, who was now Professor Donald Cromarty. It was a long letter. I told him everything: about Muirton, and Daniel Stevenson, and the *Mingulay*, and the expedition to Patagonia, and the Mackenzies. I asked him (I knew he wouldn't mind; this was exactly the kind of thing he loved to do) if there was any way he could find out, at his leisure, whether there was any substance to the story. I asked him to do it for Helen's sake (though I did not tell Helen I was writing to him). I assured him I, personally, thought it was all nonsense. But I said I'd be grateful to him, nonetheless.

And that night, as Helen and I lay in bed, looking out through the picture window at the stars arranging themselves into wild beasts, she said that my reluctance about telling the Patagonian story till now was more revealing than anything else she'd ever discovered about me.

I think she may have been right. Odd isn't it? How you know it within yourself that what you *don't* say is so important. How almost everything you *do* say is just camouflage, or perhaps armour, or perhaps the bandage over the wound.

PART TWO

Amos

At the age of eight Amos Mackenzie was consigned to "The Abbey," a home for waifs and strays (boys only), in the south of England. The institute was operated by the priests of the Holy Order of Correction. For five years he was the victim of a debilitating stutter, which caused him to drag himself from one consonant to the next, like a climber scaling a difficult rock-face. On the day of his thirteenth birthday, the stutter disappeared. By then, he had grown into a lean, ugly boy.

Botany was the only academic subject in which he expressed interest. In class, he often shocked his priest-instructors with his comparisons, suggesting once, for example, that the undersurfaces of certain leaves were "as soft as the inside of a girl's thigh." He said this without guile, so the teacher did not dare reprimand him. The boy had an intensity about him that disconcerted all prospective bullies.

At the beginning of his fourteenth year, he left the orphanage and found a job in the Botanical Gardens. He secretly believed that human society was little different from a collection of plants distinguished by sex, skin, smell, and colour, and flourishing in a variety of climates; and that if only a method could be worked out for determining which were the flowers, which the weeds, the blights of war and disease would be eliminated. The human practice of burying the dead was, for him, a wasteful perversion of the idea of planting seeds. Dead humans, he felt, ought either to be burnt, the way any good gardener burns off the residues at the end of the growing season; or they ought to be heaped into containers and allowed to turn into a mulch, for fertilizing new plants in the spring of the year. His daily exercise in those days was to walk round the park near his lodgings, and admire the "natural families" there. By which he meant the pairs of adult trees with their seedlings around them.

In the years after he left the orphanage, he met his brothers and the rest of his family only once. As he grew older, his youthful ugliness remained; that, together with a voice harsher than a winter wind, imparted a crudeness to what he said, no matter how elegant his language. He was never known to smile or make jokes. He never formed an attachment to any woman, but carried in his pocket a collection of female seeds which he would fondle gently from time to time.

Then, around the age of forty-five, he developed quite suddenly a passion for anthropology and archaeology. It was the idea of probing the roots of human culture and of unearthing lost artefacts that exhilarated him. His unprepossessing face became almost beautiful as he imagined how it must feel to take a machete (he liked the idea of a machete) to the brittle shell of appearances, and liberate raw truth with one blow.

He had found his vocation.

Notebook, A. McGaw

1

That year, early in August, I said my goodbyes to Helen and went down to the South Pacific to visit the Institute for the Lost, a research establishment situated on an island thirty miles offshore in the Coral Sea. The quickest way to get there was by plane from the mainland. We flew out over the coastline, and, from five thousand feet, I saw the island, a crescent-shaped scar on the smooth belly of the ocean. Our seaplane swooped down and landed on the lagoon.

Around the Institute itself, lawns of tough tropical grass were engaged in futile battles with the invading sand, while palm trees tried to hold their ground against the persistent, sour-smelling trade wind. The Institute consisted of two large L-shaped buildings, with some flimsy bungalows at the tops of the L's, all of them bracketing a blue-tiled swimming pool that looked as though it was never used. It was a tiny inland sea of dead leaves and live lizards.

A small woman, quite stooped, came down the steps of the main building into the sun (it was always summer there) to meet me. I recognized her from photographs: Doctor Yerdeli, the Director. From close up, I could see how lined her cheeks were and how, when she spoke, her mouth had a foreign twist. Her white hair was very white, and her lab coat was spotless, but the stethoscope that dangled like a divining rod round her neck and over her chest had metal ends with scabs of rust. As she welcomed me, she gesticulated with her left hand, as though she was conducting a piece of music, slow music, for she was a deliberate speaker. Whenever her sleeve fell back during one of these gestures, I could not help noticing the series of numbers tatooed in blue ink just above her wrist.

In spite of her formality, in spite of her stoop, she seemed pleased to see me. I had requested an interview with her some months before, for I had thought she might be able to help me with a biography I was researching at that time (the life of a well-known, now dead philanthropist who had spent years in that region). In her reply, she had said that she could be of no help, but that I might find her own work here interesting.

So here I was, and here she stood. At times, as she spoke in her slow way, she would squint her eyes upward, into her skull, reminding me of someone reciting a speech learnt by heart or else translating words written in another language on some mental pad. This quirk caused an emptiness between her words. As we were going inside for a tour of the main building, she said:

"We have so many visitors. But sometimes they can be utterly . . . delightful." I had feared she was searching for a less flattering word. She said, too, that publicity was always good for the Institute and brought interesting cases, as well as wealthy visitors from all round the world.

"I'm afraid I don't fit either category," I said.

"Your certainty is . . . admirable," she said, in her hesitant way. Then laughed a surprisingly quick, light laugh.

In the corridor of that first building, a brisk-looking man wearing the same white coat and rusty stethoscope as Doctor Yerdeli was walking in our direction. The man, whose eyes seemed to me particularly alert, must have presumed that, since I was with the Director, I was a medical man, for he greeted us both in a formal manner as "Doctor." I was about to correct him, to let him know I was no doctor. But Doctor Yerdeli took my arm and urged me on along the corridor. When we were out of his hearing range, she told me that it was just as well to let him believe whatever he liked, for the man was here for treatment and might become disoriented by any challenges. Playing roles was often the prescription for certain cases, so playing at being a doctor might well be an important part of his treatment.

"And of my treatment too, of course," she said. And laughed in that quick way.

2

As we walked along, she opened doors here and there, and showed me some of the Institute's offices, its comfortable lounges, its cafeteria, the research lab with its whiff of ether, the insulated counselling rooms. The Institute, she told me, specialized in the treatment of amnesia. She welcomed three basic types of students (the word "patient" was anathema to her). The first were those who were delivered to her in a chronic amnesiac state caused by some accident; their original identities were irrecoverable. The second were those who could no longer bear themselves and who, in spite of years of therapy, insisted on having substitute identities; some of these students had even, by a deliberate act of the will, erased their memories. The third were made up of a variety of students, not necessarily amnesiacs, who for any reason excited Doctor Yerdeli's curiosity; they were known as "The Director's Specials," and she worked personally with them.

The Institute could only deal with up to ten students at a time, though dozens applied for admission each month. Aside from her work with her "Specials," Doctor Yerdeli's main occupation, and that of her colleagues (whom I saw briefly, from time to time), was to invent new lives and pasts for her students.

I interrupted her: "Do any of them ever reject the

new lives you make up for them?"

She did not answer this immediately, so I rephrased my question:

"You spoke of those who come to you knowingly for substitute identities. Are the lives you make up for them always more satisfying than the ones they rejected before?"

She assured me she was not avoiding giving an answer. It was just that she wanted to think first. Smiling a little, she said she could speak for all of her colleagues in saying that their profession was totally satisfying. Indeed it was an art rather than a science. Simply put, she had to create for each student in her care a story with a main persona (a favourite term of hers), a stock of subsidiary figures, all of them developed enough to be credible, and a vast array of appropriate facts. Then she had to coach her student to *be*, convincingly, the new persona, no matter how long it might take.

I was about to interrupt again, but she held up a hand. She was working her way round to answering my question.

Granted, she said, as with any artist, sometimes a sketch would turn out badly, a character might have to be excised, no matter how painful that might be to the creator. But the method itself was sound. Years ago, after a few such disappointments, she had thought it better to use already created characters from novels as personae for her students. That had been a failure. Literary characters seemed to violate credibility in some way that made them useless, even dangerous. Such classical creations as Becky

Sharp, or Horatio Hornblower, or Molly Bloom, or
Agent 007 (she had used them all at one time or another)
turned out to be flimsy verbal scaffoldings that collapsed
in the sweat and stress of life, when the actual people
around them no longer adhered to a pre-determined plot.
She wished that some of the literary critics who lauded
these fictional characters had been able to see how poorly
they fared in real life!

Another danger of this method was that, in spite of all
her warnings, the students to whom characters from
literature were allocated would secretly read the novels in
which their prototypes appeared, and try to emulate
them. The results were predictable and disastrous. She
had resolved to write a paper on the hazards of the
practice, she said, smiling again.

"These matters are so . . . complex."

I understood that this was all of the answer she
intended to give to my question, so I left it at that.

——
3

In the course of this preliminary stroll around the
Institute, I was surprised at how often Doctor Yerdeli
returned to the question of her image. At times, she said
she thought of herself as a plastic surgeon of the mind,

cutting away residual rot, and reshaping what was left. But she much preferred the view of herself as an artist. Yes, she said, she was more a sculptor of the psyche than anything else.

One thing I could see plainly: in spite of her frail appearance, she was enthusiastic about her work, and seemed to be a kind woman. Her students either needed or wanted a new persona, and all she asked from them in return was that they present her with what she liked to call a *tabula rasa*, a blank slate on which she would delineate her attempted masterpieces.

At one point, I remember asking her:

"Have you or any of your colleagues ever invented characters that exceed you? That are, say, wiser than you yourselves are?"

Again, I thought for a moment she was going to ignore my question. But eventually, in that deliberate manner, as though she was reading from an already prepared script, she said:

"My colleagues are too . . . intelligent to do such a thing." She laughed her quick laugh.

4

Doctor Yerdeli was sure I would like to meet one or two of her students. She took me outside to where one of them, a tall, middle-aged woman with faded dress and faded brown hair, sat on a lawn-chair, frowning into the morass that was the swimming pool.

The woman glanced up nervously at us, then went back to her scrutiny of lizards and leaves. Doctor Yerdeli put a hand comfortingly on her shoulder and began to tell me about her; or perhaps I should say, deliver a prepared lecture to me; she seemed to have lost her hesitations.

"This is Maria. Authorities in the south sent her to us. She suffered a total loss of memory after being knocked down by a car. She was carrying no identification, except for a bracelet with the name 'Maria' on it. No amount of advertising could find anyone who knew her. She wasted two years in a hospital down there before they sent her here."

Maria seemed to be paying no attention to us as Doctor Yerdeli spoke. I presumed the students were quite accustomed to such demonstrations. Indeed, I wondered if this public narration was for my benefit or for Maria's, or whether Doctor Yerdeli was simply enjoying an opportunity to display her art, smiling as she talked.

Maria, it seems, settled into the Institute, and showed herself to be co-operative and intelligent. Doctor Yerdeli immediately began to invent a new persona for her. She decided, after studying Maria for a while, to give her a cautious character: she would make Maria a spinster schoolteacher from any one of a thousand little outback towns where everybody knows everybody else. She would make her a specialist in history, a soprano in the church choir (why not?), a well-adjusted woman content with small-town life. Just to give her existence some tinge of pathos and adventure (I could see Doctor Yerdeli relished this part of her creation), Maria would have a secret memory of a sexual interlude in her early twenties and a back-street abortion.

Doctor Yerdeli invented hundreds of such details, spending countless hours elaborating on them, drilling Maria in them daily. Until Maria herself became persuaded of the possibilities and entered into the spirit of the persona, manufacturing details on her own, filling in the gaps. She was beginning to make it her own invention, she was on her way to believing that this was, indeed, her life.

Then, just when she was settling into her new persona, starting to feel whole again, a peculiar thing happened. One morning, she came rushing into Doctor Yerdeli's office, babbling excitedly: she remembered everything! She remembered who she really was! During the night, her own, original memory had come back to her!

Doctor Yerdeli calmed her, made her sit down and talk.

Maria repeated that it had all come back to her. She really had been a schoolteacher from a small town in the bush. She congratulated Doctor Yerdeli on her perceptiveness. She remembered the name of the town she lived in, it was called Kikiburee. She did indeed have a degree, but in geography, not history; and though she was in the church choir at Kikiburee, St Martin's Church, she was actually a contralto.

As Maria talked, Doctor Yerdeli was sure she was simply embellishing some of the details of her new persona to her own taste. She was convinced Maria was displaying the symptoms of a supremely successful case: one in which a student has actually *become* her new persona, without reservation, no longer playing a part.

Yet Maria seemed well aware of the resemblances and differences between Doctor Yerdeli's creation and the real life she claimed she now remembered. She kept pointing them out. And she told Doctor Yerdeli the biggest difference of all. She had a husband! Back there, in Kikiburee, a husband whom she loved was waiting for her in their old house! Above all else, she wanted to get back home and see him again. She pleaded with Doctor Yerdeli to let her go immediately.

Doctor Yerdeli settled her down again. Could Maria remember the car accident? Yes, she said. For the first time, she had a clear memory of crossing a street in the city, a violent blow, then emptiness. Now, everything from the past had a name again, she could remember all the faces and names, even the smells, all the details of a fully lived life. And her husband! her husband! She was overwhelmed with excitement.

After hours of questioning, Doctor Yerdeli conceded. She felt a little sad at the useless expenditure of effort on what she had hoped might turn into one of her true masterpieces. But she had no doubt she would be able to adapt it for some future student. At the Institute for the Lost, no exercise of the imagination was ever wasted.

She decided to accompany Maria back to her home, to gently reintroduce her to her background. She would not warn anyone in Kikiburee in advance; it would be invaluable for research purposes to note the spontaneous reactions to Maria's return by all those who had known

her previously. She had been three years at the Institute
for the Lost by then.

5

They flew together to the city, rented a car, and drove
two hundred miles west into the bush, to Kikiburee.

As they drew nearer the little town, Maria couldn't
stop talking. She pointed out hills and creeks and peculiar
clusters of gum trees, she forecast land formations and
bends in the road, as only a native could. When they came
to the little bush town with its board sidewalks and its
wide verandas along the main street, she recognized some
of the people they passed. And look! there was the little
wooden gothic church of St. Martin's! And behind it, the
school she had taught in! And just there, further along,
the grocery store she used to visit every day!

Doctor Yerdeli parked the car and they got out.

Maria rushed over to two women coming out of the
store. She held out her arms.

"Judy! Heather! It's me!"

The two women did not respond to her familiarity.
Being country people, they smiled politely, but in the way
they would to a stranger. Doctor Yerdeli encouraged
them. Didn't they remember Maria, who had lived in

Kikiburee till five years ago? Perhaps she had changed a little.

They said, puzzled, no, they didn't remember her. How could they, they had never seen her before.

Maria insisted. Of course they had. Didn't she know their first names, the streets they lived on, didn't they remember growing up with her, how they had played games together, how she had often visited their homes?

One of the women was looking a little frightened by now, and the other was becoming angry that this person, who, she said, was an absolute stranger, should know so much about them.

Maria wanted to argue, but Doctor Yerdeli gently coaxed her away. She said they should go now to where Maria remembered her house had been. They walked along a shady sidestreet. And there it stood, exactly as she had described it, a small wooden house with a veranda round all four walls, a flaking turret, and gum trees overhanging.

Doctor Yerdeli knocked at the screen door. A middle-aged man with a wisp of hair and a pleasant smile pushed the door ajar and asked if he could help. He didn't give Maria a second glance.

"John!" she said.

The man looked at her.

Just then, from inside the house, a pale, dark-haired woman in an apron came to stand shyly beside him at the door, wondering who the visitors were.

"John! It's me!" Maria said again. "I'm Maria!"

"Do I know you?" he asked.

Doctor Yerdeli saw how perplexed the man was and explained that Maria had been in an accident some years ago. She had the notion that he was her husband and that this was her house.

Maria wouldn't be kept out of it. She said it was not a notion. John and she had been married twenty years. She could tell them anything they wanted to know about him: didn't he have a long scar on his belly that she had touched, herself, many times? Didn't he have a web-toe on his right foot, like his father before him? And what about the house? She knew the location of all the rooms, everything that was in them, the smell of the attic. Even the pictures on the walls: who did they think had bought them? Need she go on? What was wrong with everybody?

Doctor Yerdeli could see the couple was astonished at all of this. But the woman, timid as she was, spoke up. She asked how Maria could possibly be John's wife, for she herself had married him twenty-five years ago, when she was only eighteen.

Maria was the bewildered one now. The man obviously did not know her, and this woman did not seem the kind to tell a lie.

Now a dog appeared, a black and white collie, running to them from somewhere, wagging its tail at the visitors.

Maria became excited again.

"Robbie!" she said. "Come here, Robbie!"

The dog stopped in its tracks, cowering away from her outstretched hand. It growled fiercely, baring its fangs, coat standing on end, paws trembling. The man soothed the animal. He said Robbie was indeed the dog's name, and he had always been a friendly dog. They had never seen him act like this.

Maria began to cry now, helplessly. Doctor Yerdeli took her by the arm and walked her away from the house along the shady street to the car. They drove out of Kikiburee without looking back.

6

Maria was still staring into the fetid water of the pool at the Institute for the Lost. Doctor Yerdeli patted her shoulder again.

"It's a very interesting case, and we're working on it together now," she said to me. She looked down, brightly, at her student: "Aren't we, Maria?"

Maria, looking more faded than ever in the bright sun, her long face straining, as though she was trying to remember something, at last glanced up at her and smiled back, half-heartedly.

As we walked away, Doctor Yerdeli talked about the case. Years of research at the Institute had convinced her that many individuals wake up each morning of their adult lives having forgotten who they are. Most of them put on a brave face and carry on, playing whatever role seems to be expected of them: husband, waitress, bank manager, teacher, bus driver. They become skilled at gauging their situation. Without panic, they adapt themselves. This was a daily, common occurrence.

"A man like you must have . . . experienced it," she said.

I could not tell whether this was a question or a statement.

Doctor Yerdeli wondered if what had happened to Maria in Kikiburee might not be a variation of the problem. Might not an entire community suffer this kind of memory lapse? Was it not conceivable that Maria had indeed once lived in Kikiburee, but that all of the townspeople there had adjusted their memories to exclude her, the way we exclude certain unpleasant smells? Indeed, Doctor Yerdeli speculated, people like Maria might have a certain lack, a metaphysical deficiency, possibly, that induced this type of amnesia on the part of others. Perhaps instances of the phenomenon were widespread yet went completely unnoticed, because of our tendency to trust the collective memory rather than the individual's. Was it not possible that not only communities, but even countries, even whole civilizations might be subject to the phenomenon?

As she presented these possibilities, she was gesticulating as usual, so that I could not help noticing those little blue numbers tatooed above her wrist. She said she would be addressing an international congress on her theory soon, and was in the process of setting up some models for testing.

I considered asking her this question: "Wouldn't it

be better, in the case of someone like Maria, just to let her go out into the world on her own and start a new life from scratch, without stocking her mind with inventions?"

But I didn't ask. I was certain she would have some confident, expert reply, such as: "No, that would be very unwise. Nothing is more dangerous to civilization than those who lack memories."

And then what could I have said?

7

Looking at me shrewdly, she asked if I would like to meet her most fascinating student, one of her "Director's Pets." I said I would be only too happy.

We crossed to the building on the ocean side, and climbed the breezy stairway to the second floor. She took me to one of the rooms that looked eastward, out onto the tops of palm trees. We could hear, vaguely, the sound of breakers beyond the lagoon. She knocked and opened the door.

"Good day, Harry," she said in a cheerful voice. And we went in.

He was sitting upright in his pyjamas in a chair: a thin, bearded man, with dark hair and dark-rimmed, fright-

ened eyes that were constantly scanning the room. There
was a smell, perhaps of stale sweat, that even the open
window did not dispel. The man paid no direct attention
to us, but occasionally moved his head slightly to look
past us and round us, as though, at times, we were
blocking his view.

This was Harry, she said, formerly a successful lawyer,
with a wife and two children. Some time ago, in bed one
night, he heard noises coming from somewhere in his
house. He got up to see what was going on, thinking it
must be the children. But they were both fast asleep. His
wife told him she couldn't hear any noise at all. He asked
her to listen. Was she sure, if she listened very carefully,
she couldn't hear a sound? Like someone shouting, but
muffled, so that the words were incomprehensible? She
told him no, he must be imagining things. So he lay there
for hours, straining his ears, till he fell asleep out of sheer
exhaustion.

This went on for weeks. Harry was losing a lot of sleep,
nothing more serious than that. During the day,
everything was normal.

Then, one morning, when he was at his desk in the city,
wearily going over some documents, he heard the distant
shouting again. That was the first time he had ever heard
it outside his own home, or in the light of day. He checked
with his secretary. No, she could hear nothing. What
about his partner, his old friend? No, nothing at all. They
told him not to worry, perhaps he was under stress.

And he didn't worry too much. Until he began seeing
something. Just a glimpse, but something, both in his
own house and at the office. If he looked up suddenly,

he'd catch a glimpse of it, just for a second, almost like an after-vision left by a light switched off. He thought it was a man. In fact, he was sure it was a man, but it was hard to say, he couldn't catch sight of it for long enough. Though it was often nearby, sitting on the spare chair at the dinner-table, or in the passenger seat of the car, or standing by his desk. Disappearing before Harry could get a clear view of it.

He, by now, had learnt from his past experience. He told his wife and his children, just once, what he had seen. And asked them, just once, if they had spotted a stranger prowling around the house, outside. Or inside.

As he feared, they had not. He didn't mention the subject again. In fact, when his wife asked him, later, if he was still seeing things, he laughed. Clogged sinuses, he said, the problem must be his clogged sinuses.

But as the weeks went by, she noticed, they all noticed, that often, as Harry was doing some routine thing, eating his meals, or reading legal documents, or speaking on the telephone, or even in the middle of small-talk with one of them, he would suddenly become alert, straining his ears. Or he would turn his head sharply and look past them, his eyes wide with alarm. Yet, if they asked him what was wrong, he would say everything was just fine.

Within another month, he was completely useless. He spent all his time, day and night, listening to the distant shouting, trying to get a good look at something no one else could see. More and more, now, his eyes were filled with fear.

He recovered immediately they took him away to the coast for a week's holiday. He was his old self again, making love to his wife for the first time in months, playing with the children the way he used to in the old days. Till one afternoon while he was at the beach helping them build a sandcastle, whatever it was caught up with him. He sat for the rest of the week, in the hotel, without saying a word, engrossed in his private torment.

They took him home again on a Monday. That day, he spoke for the last time, just as darkness was falling, the time he feared most. He spoke to his wife with the studied effort of a man tearing himself away from some dreadful preoccupation. But he spoke clearly, and struggled to repeat himself, to make sure she understood. No one, he said, should worry about him. He would fight to the end, he would protect them, he would not let them down.

She wept and asked him what he meant. But he could not speak again.

From that day, almost a year before, all his attention was focused on that other voice, that invisible companion he seemed so fearful of.

Six months ago, desperate, all other treatments having failed, his wife brought him to the Institute for the Lost. At their first meeting, Doctor Yerdeli, on an impulse, put her stethoscope to the top of Harry's head. From inside, she heard quite plainly a sound. Like a distant voice roaring. She decided immediately to take him on as one of her "Specials."

Doctor Yerdeli, at that point, offered me her stethoscope, so that I myself might listen. She said Harry would not mind at all.

I declined.

The case fascinated her. She and one of her assistants

were making tapes of the sound in Harry's head, amplified through the stethoscope. A computer was in the process of analysing them. She hoped for the results any day now.

Had I noticed, she asked, how Harry's eyes roved constantly as though he was tracking the movements of something else in the room, some third guest that we couldn't see? And how terrified he seemed to be? Well, some weeks ago, she had called in a specialist to construct an optometric device to measure the refractions in Harry's eyes. The data gathered so far had been fed into a computer. They hoped to be able to make a composite figure, on the screen, of what Harry was looking at. After a few more sessions, the specialist expected he would have a very good idea of what it was. So far, even from the incomplete data, all he could say was that the body on the screen seemed human, but not necessarily the head.

8

As we left that room, with its inbred smell and the man, Harry, sitting there, absorbed in his fearsome, private world, I must admit to a certain sense of relief. Walking along the corridor, I asked Doctor Yerdeli:

"Why did you take him in?"

"You can't be careful enough in matters such as this," she replied, looking at me in her shrewd way.

I thought about that.

"And if you were to discover what the voice is saying, and what the thing looks like, what then?" For I could sense that she felt that no one in all the world was better equipped than she was to deal with Harry's problem.

"You, of course, think it would be ... better just to leave it alone, trapped inside him?" she said.

And when I said yes, I did think so, she only shook her head, and shook it again and again. She smiled at me, a cheerful smile.

"Ah, it's so rarely I meet ... optimists," she said.

And would discuss the case no further.

9

The day had not been a dull one for me, so I accepted her invitation to have dinner at her bungalow, instead of flying back to the mainland at five o'clock as I had intended.

After a good meal, we sat on wicker chairs on the veranda, smelling the sea and the coffee, watching the reef aerate the incoming waves. The palm trees were curtsying to a pleasant easterly that kept the mosquitoes down. The sudden tropical night fell as Doctor Yerdeli was telling me about her youth in Europe, her training, her condemnation and imprisonment, her escape. And her return.

"I went back there, years after the war was over. It was very foolish of me. I was hoping for the impossible. I found . . . nothing. There was nothing left."

She lingered over the nothings.

"I hoped most of all that my dog, Rex, would be waiting for me. Isn't that strange? But of course, even if they did not kill him, he would have died of old age, long before."

She sipped her coffee.

"For a long time after that, I used to ask myself, does it really matter? Either way, there is no . . . constancy. I had to learn again to believe in constancy."

Women in her profession were rare, and she had trouble getting a job. She found one in this part of the world, in a little jungle hospital, where she spent her time trying to understand the forms of madness peculiar to those who live their lives in jungles.

In the dim light of the veranda, I sensed suddenly that she was looking at me very intently. The way I had seen her look at her students. And for the first time, I wondered if she had any ulterior motive for asking me to stay for dinner.

She said she thought I might want to hear about a case she had encountered in those early days. A man who was not a native. He was a very elderly European who had undergone a trauma up in the highlands, amongst the head-hunters.

"He would have been a . . . marvellous student for the Institute, if it had existed then. If we could have saved him."

She was watching me. She enunciated her words emphatically.

"His name was Amos Mackenzie."

The name alerted me immediately. Mainly because it was not long since I had told the Patagonian story to Helen. And because, only a few weeks ago, I had asked Donald Cromarty to investigate the story. On the other hand, I knew the world was full of Mackenzies.

But I was curious, so I asked, "Amos Mackenzie?"

"Yes, that's right. He was an old man. He came, I remember, from your part of the world. Have you heard of him?"

Suddenly, I felt the need to be careful.

"There are so many Mackenzies from my part of the world. Did you talk to him?"

The veranda light was not strong, but I could see she was still watching for my reaction. Whatever she saw, she decided not to ask me any more questions.

"He did the talking, mainly. About his experience up in the high jungle. It must have been a . . . difficult journey for a man of his age."

She sipped at her coffee, studying again her mental notepad, finding the words to fit. And I myself relaxed, thinking that it was very improbable, to say the least, the old man could have been one of those Patagonian Mackenzies. I just sipped my own coffee, and listened.

She said that when Amos Mackenzie was brought to the hospital, the resident, after doing what he could, was very relieved to be able to ask for her, to see if she could help. Mackenzie had been carried in by some hunters who'd come across him in the jungle, in a terrible condition.

She remembered how he looked, lying there in a bed in the little tin-roofed hospital. He was a tall man (she could assess a man's height, even lying down), emaciated, his skin like bark, at least seventy years old, though it was hard to tell, for he was one of those who look as though they've always been old.

She had no trouble getting him to talk and that was good. He was an articulate man with a reedy voice and seemed happy to have an audience. He said he'd been on an archaeological expedition to one of those remote areas between the maps (he used that phrase), on the banks of the Merape . . .

10

. . . on the banks of the Merape, I sweated, along with my colleagues, to uncover several small pyramids, just fifty feet high, overgrown for centuries by jungle. Dangerous brown snakes lived in their geometrical corridors. In that region, we kept finding great egg-shaped rocks hewn out of some kind of limestone. They were as high as lanu trees, but they were hard to see from any distance because of the thick jungle. We thought at first they were just peculiar earthmounds till we noticed how the bottoms were indented behind the loose curtain of vines. The brown snakes lived there too.

These things we had all seen the likes of before, but in other parts of the world. Never here, in this country. We had no theories to account for them.

The weather was awful. In the late afternoons, just when the heat was at its worst and the humidity most oppressive, the rain would start and would pour down hour after hour till dark. The trees gave us no protection, for their leaves, high above, just stored the drops long enough to allow them to accumulate greater weight. We would keep on digging, nevertheless, though we were attacked by the innumerable mosquitoes and stinging flies the rain seemed to encourage.

On our last day at that site, about dusk, we found a stone hand. We had seen the overgrown mound, and thought it was probably the same as the others, though more misshapen. But as we hacked at the vegetation with machetes, careful to avoid snakes, we saw the huge stubby fingers protruding through their glove of vines. They seemed to be clutching at the air, the gesture of a giant drowning in quicksand. We were all astonished to find such an object here, so far from any known civilization.

But it was not just a hand. With twenty-foot long prods, we thrust down into the soil around it, and could feel, down there, the outlines of an arm, a shoulder, a head. We speculated that the entire figure must be seventy feet tall, and must have been interred upright in this pit, only the hand left above ground. We felt apprehensive. But we were all too rational, too engrossed in our work.

The morning after, the sky was still overcast, the jungle silent as ever. We launched the boats on the brown river and pushed on further upstream.

They attacked us about six miles upstream, where the Merape waters were dark brown and narrow, and where the jungle rose high on either side, like unending bookcases full of the same books. We were near to the east bank and had no sign of their presence. Then, the air was full of spears, and arrows, and howls from the bank. We tried to paddle away, but dark arms burst out of the water under our boats and seized the gunwales. Some of them had been hiding in the water, breathing through reeds, waiting.

Then, I was in the water too, lashing out at the mad faces and the hands that were grasping, pulling me under. I breathed deep and dived. I could see nothing, except perhaps the outline of one of those evil figures clutching at me. I kicked at it, and kept swimming.

Fear made me endure. When I surfaced, I was fifty yards downstream. I could see, back there, the water thrashing as though fish were being gathered in a net, and I could hear screams. I plunged under again, and when I came up, I did not look back, but kept swimming with the current, choosing the river dangers rather than the treacherous shore.

How long I stayed in the river, or how far I went, I do not know. But in time, I could hear again the monotonous shrieking of jungle birds, a sound I had not heard for so long, and knew I had better begin to work my way towards the bank, the west bank. It was by then completely shaded, so sunset must have been near. I swam towards some mud-flats where I thought I might be able to rest for the night. I thought no further ahead than sleep. I was fearless from exhaustion. I crawled out of the Merape onto the wet bank and, in spite of the stench of the mud, fell asleep immediately.

When I woke, a chaos of devil faces hovered over me, and I knew with certainty that before long I would die painfully. The Ishtulum had found me. I recognized them by their tribal paint and war-hats as the most savage of all the tribes along the Merape. A group of them stood round me, prodding with their spear-hurlers at my white skin, a diseased whiteness to their dark eyes. They bound my hands, and dragged me back to their village. Before them lay a long ritual cleansing of the pollution of their territory and the ritual elimination of the polluter, me. Like many a traveller who falls into the hands of the Ishtulum, I wished that they had killed me with their spears.

For the next three weeks, I was kept closely guarded in the centre of their village, tethered at the ankles to a lanu tree. Yet I cannot say I was lonely. For a tribe so ferocious, the Ishtulum are garrulous, they love to talk, and made no effort to hide their secrets from a stranger sentenced to death.

Their shaman, for example, has an eye in the back of his head. I saw this eye many times, whenever the shaman, in his cloak of feathers and painted face, would turn his back on me and would strain this painful and bloodshot organ to look me over. One of my guards told me that the wives of the shaman select a child of four or five years old to be his successor. Over a period of about ten years, they gradually coax the child's left eye from its socket, millimetre by millimetre, stretching the eye ligaments till the ball of the eye nestles behind the left ear. It lies there, wrapped in a constantly oiled banana skin which is attached to his head by a cord.

Though the sight in the shaman's rear eye is not acute, it is powerful in other ways and is the eye members of the tribe fear most. They say it looks into the house of the dead. They say it can paralyse the enemies of the Ishtulum. Its wavering, disembodied gaze centred on me all too often.

I learnt too that for the Ishtulum, certain animals are extensions of human beings, almost extra limbs. Like many of the better-known tribes in that region of the Merape, they keep tiny monkeys in their hair to devour fleas and lice. But they go further. At puberty, each boy must swallow a small blue lizard about eight inches long, which will live inside his stomach for the period of one moon. The boy has to lie as still as possible for fear of causing the death of the lizard. He may drink only water, and may defecate only with great care. The Ishtulum believe that if the lizard dies while in his stomach, the boy's own spirit will die within minutes. My guards told me they had all seen such deaths.

From my lanu tree, I had a good view of the ceremony at which these lizards are withdrawn. I had been a captive for just a few days at the time. One day, when the sun was

at its height, eight boys were carried on stretchers from
their huts by family members and placed in a circle. The
shaman appeared, still dressed in his coat of feathers, but
with his face painted vividly for the occasion to look like a
reptile. His rear eye was tucked away, the ligaments
trailing along the side of his head and disappearing into
the empty eye-cavern. He danced and chanted for a while,
then began the ceremonial withdrawal of the lizards. He
took a long, thin piece of twine and tied on a little yellow
fruit fly, the lizard's favourite food. Humming a noisy
prayer, he fed the twine down the throat of the first boy,
who lay still and tense.

The shaman paused, then began gently to pull on the
twine, like a fisherman, while the boy started to repeat
over and over his family name. The tribe watched in
absolute silence. In a moment, we could see the head of
the lizard at the boy's mouth. The shaman plucked it out
quickly and gave it to one of his assistants who carefully
placed it in a wicker basket.

I was filled with admiration for the shaman's skill. Any
clumsiness by him might result in the lizard's refusal of
the fly, meaning death for the boy. This day, all was going
well. The lizards were successfully and quickly coaxed
out of seven boys undergoing the rite. The boys lay there,
weak, relieved that the ordeal was over, and the members
of the tribe began to relax.

But the shaman was having trouble with the eighth
boy. His lizard was not responding in spite of numerous
jiggings of the twine. The boy kept repeating his family
name, trying not to sob. The shaman eventually attached
a fresh fly to the twine. Still no response. I could see on

the faces of the Ishtulum their fear that the lizard inside
the boy was dead.

But the shaman would not admit defeat. He stood up
and, with a dramatic gesture, uncovered his rear eye. He
glared through it at the boy for many minutes. Then he
tucked the eye back in the banana skin, and bent over the
trembling body. He inserted the twine again, waited for a
while, and began to tug gently. The boy continued
repeating his family name over and over like an
incantation, till very gradually, the sound changed to a
gurgle, as the shaman withdrew from the throat a lizard
that looked none too healthy. Even under all that paint,
we could see the jubilation on the shaman's ghastly face.
If he had not succeeded on the third try, that would have
been that, and the boy would have died soon after. The
Ishtulum roared their joy. I think they marvelled at the
shaman's skill, but even more at the boy for withstanding
direct exposure to that grotesque eye. Only the
imminence of death could have given him the courage.

That gastric experience at puberty prepares the
Ishtulum males for another intimate relationship, entered
into not long after, between a warrior and a small rodent,
a type of coatimundi.

I had noticed that if my guard was an unmarried man,
he would have one of these creatures attached by a small
gold ring to the tip of his penis. The coatimundi would
feed on the semen of its owner. Whenever the guard
masturbated (the Ishtulum are prodigious masturbators,
and guards would no sooner appear for duty than they
would begin this exercise, quite conscientiously), his
coatimundi would clean up the spill. It seems, also,

though I did not witness this myself, that when an unmarried warrior makes love to one of the women, his coatimundi, clinging to his erect penis, enters the vagina of the woman first and gobbles up all the seminal fluids. I could not help admiring this very practical way of ensuring that no children are born out of wedlock, or before the proper potlatch has been arranged.

When a marriage ceremony is performed, the shaman again plays an important role. He formally snips off the rodent's ring, thus permitting fruitful union. As in the case of those lizards at puberty, it is very bad luck if a man's coatimundi dies before the official snipping. The Ishtulum take it to mean either that the semen of its owner is sour, or that it is not strong enough to keep his animal alive. The man may not marry within the tribe.

They call marriage the linking. No sooner has the man been freed from his coatimundi than he is linked to his bride in such a way that infidelity would be very difficult. The shaman is again the central figure. Before the assembled tribe, he sews together the flap of skin between the thumb and the forefinger of the man's left hand and the woman's right hand. He uses a thin needle made of fishbone and a twine made of gut. The stitching only takes a few minutes, and, since they are Ishtulum, the couple shows no sign of pain as he joins their flesh. For the first six months of their marriage they are obliged to do everything together. He is with her as she cooks, eats, gardens, urinates, defecates, menstruates. She, in turn, goes with him through the hazards of the hunt, the weekly palm-beer-drinking orgies, and, if she is unlucky enough, the inter-tribal wars.

After six months, when the woman is advanced in pregnancy, the shaman carefully separates the couple's hands, leaving only a wedding scar. She goes off to join the other women in preparation for her childbirth.

I wondered at first why some of the older members of the tribe still had their hands linked. I found out that these were the childless couples, their hands sewn together for life. Everyone treats them with great kindness, though nothing can make up for the tragedy of their barrenness.

But there was no kindness to spare for me, at least not as I then understood the word. And I expected none. After three weeks, with the whole tribe present, the guards took me from my tether at the lanu tree and spreadeagled me on a low wooden frame to which the shaman tied me with ritual knots. His incantations became louder. The final purification process had begun.

With a sliver of razor-bamboo, he began making little incisions over much of the front of my body. When he was satisfied that he had made enough of them, he wiped the sliver carefully, gave it to his assistant, and moved on to the next process. With the fingertips of his left hand, he spread the cuts open slightly, and with his right hand forced in small quantities of dirt which mixed with the blood. Then, he began to stuff into the incisions a variety of seedlings of jungle plants and trees, chanting while he worked.

I remained conscious during this painful process. He performed all of the intricate operations with his back to me, relying upon his uncovered rear eye. When he bent over me, he smelt like a jungle animal. The assembled tribe, exerting their collective power in these purifications, also kept their backs to the ceremony. The only Ishtulum eye that watched me was that bloodshot eye in the back of the shaman's head. I am certain I saw in it compassion at my pain and despair.

For a whole week I was left lying there on that frame in the middle of the village. But now the members of the tribe were permitted to look at me from a distance. Every few hours, the shaman himself would come and sprinkle a bad-smelling mixture on the plants that protruded from me, and force a few spoonfuls of it into my mouth.

At first the plants drooped feebly, and he had a worried look. But after two days, they seemed to spring to life, as all jungle plants do, and began to grow in the cuts. I think they drew nourishment from the pus in my sores. Eventually, I could sense a tickling sensation inside of me as the tiny roots groped around for places to attach themselves. I could feel my body being turned into a garden.

At the end of that week, on a fine morning, the whole tribe assembled again. Six of the strongest warriors, chanting rhythmically, lifted me on my frame. They carried me in procession to the river bank, a half-mile north of the village, to the place where they had found me. My little plants were gently weaving in the morning breeze as though the Ishtulum were moving a rack at a plant nursery.

Beside the river, on the dry mud just above high water, a shallow grave had already been dug into which they lowered me, still on my frame. The shaman, chanting to the river, covered my body softly with the fertile soil, leaving only my little plants and my face exposed.

I understood. I was to grow into the soil in the very place I had contaminated, returning myself to nature all cleansed and blessed, amending the pollution I had caused.

Before they left, each member of the tribe, mumbling prayers, came and looked down at me with, I thought, forgiveness, and even affection. Then they were gone and I was alone.

I lay there for three entire days and nights, watching and feeling my plants grow tall and strong. I was contented that they were so healthy I could feel their longing to rejoin the jungle soil beneath my body. Sometimes I would try to speak to them, encourage them, but my words became a trembling of branches, a sighing of leaves. Insects were beginning to build their nests in my plants, and once a small bird with a worm in its mouth landed on my favourite tree, the dwarf suma growing from the middle of my chest. The bird stared down into my eyes for a while, quite unafraid.

On the third day, I could feel my entire body begin to take root in the river soil under and around me. I could even feel the fingers of my own hand growing down, down. It was what I had been waiting for, or, should I say, what *we* had been waiting for. I knew then that nothing remained but to think no more, just allow myself to grow into that fertile earth, accept what was no longer pain but an intensity of pleasure no living human being had ever before enjoyed. My whole body had become part of a universal, endless orgasm.

Then I woke here, in this hospital. Some hunters, it seems, had found me staked out, still alive. They had hacked away the foliage from me (my poor children!), and brought me here. The surgeons gather round me in a ring for tortuous hours each day, cutting the roots out of me, leaving my body burning. When I am alone at last, I lie here looking out of the window and watch, only a few hundred yards away, my jungle, my love, waiting for me patiently, no matter what they do, welcoming me in the end.

11

"There was not a mark on him," said Doctor Yerdeli. "But whatever his disease was, it was too . . . virulent to be cured by any words I know. I could do nothing. He lived a few days longer, and then he died, cradling his stomach. We buried him at the edge of the jungle."

"Did he have any scars at all? Was there a scar of any kind on his abdomen?"

She looked at me with those shrewd eyes.

"I never saw one. Why do you ask?"

I gave no reason, and I asked no more questions. She was the kind of woman I didn't wish to confide in. Though I was certain, by now, that she had no other ulterior motive for inviting me for dinner than to talk to me and look me over. I think she regarded everybody as a potential student, and something about me must have made her hopeful.

I sat silently, allowing myself to wonder if this Amos Mackenzie really was a member of the Patagonian Mackenzies. Wouldn't that be remarkable? The past, in an odd way, seems to depend so much upon the future: everything would be different, somehow, if it were to turn out that those Mackenzies my grandfather had told me about really did exist.

Doctor Yerdeli was still watching me closely, so I tried to close my face to her as though it was a hand and she was a reader of palms. I was sure she had the art to decipher a whole life history in a face.

I made a fuss about looking at my watch and being surprised at how late it was. I said good-night and goodbye, and retreated to the safety of the guest-house.

I never saw her again. I flew out of the island early the next morning. As the plane circled before heading south-west to the city, the ocean beneath was misty and flat, and the island was like a blot on a huge grey page on which nothing had yet been written, or everything had been erased.

12

Answers depend upon questioners. A passenger on the plane home asked me about my trip, and I chatted about blue skies and seas, beaches and reefs, palm trees and trade winds.

To tell Helen such things would be to tell her nothing at all. On the night I arrived home, we made love with great tenderness: I was so happy to be home again, and to be loved. Then I told her about Doctor Yerdeli and the Institute for the Lost, about the neglected swimming pool, about Maria and Kikiburee, about Harry's invisible torment. And finally, I told her about Amos Mackenzie and the Ishtulum.

She was as surprised at that part of it as I had been.

Her head lay on my chest, and I was stroking her fair hair, breathing in her scent, soothing her smooth shoulder and back. We could see night clouds through the big window, imagining them to be various creatures and shapes, not content to let them be what they were.

I said, thinking of Amos Mackenzie:

"If he really was one of those Mackenzies, you could almost believe there was some pattern behind it all."

"Perhaps," she said.

"When Doctor Yerdeli started talking about him, I felt strange, as though I had stepped back into something important in my own past."

She kissed me gently, as I continued in this philosophic mood.

"Perhaps I was remembering how my life was when I was a boy. What it was like to hope. Maybe it was the memory of once being full of hopes that made me feel so strange."

Helen was silent for a long time. I thought perhaps I had made her sad. But when she spoke, it was about Amos Mackenzie. She said it was futile of him to have believed his life could be transformed into trees and plants. When all that was left of him was a story, in words. When words are, in a way, our only lasting blossoms.

I liked the idea that words were blossoms. How sometimes, somebody gathers the most pleasing of them and preserves them. I told Helen so. This was the kind of conversation we used to have, and used to enjoy so much. And, as always, at a certain point, she began laughing, and snuggled in, and before we knew it we were again involved in a form of grafting peculiar to men and women.

Afterwards, I promised myself (I still had not told Helen) I'd write to Donald Cromarty once more and let him know that I'd heard about the life and death of one Amos Mackenzie, who might have been a member of the Patagonian Mackenzies. Perhaps the information would be of some value to him in his research into my grandfather's story. I did not then realize how he would use all these things, at the Paradise Motel. I turned on my side, inhaling the sweet scent of Helen, and went to sleep, and slept that night as well as I have ever slept.

PART THREE

RACHEL

Rachel Mackenzie and her older sister, Esther, spent several years in the Border country, at St Fiona's Home for Waifs and Strays (for girls only), run by the Sisters of the Holy Order of Correction. From the start, Rachel was a very withdrawn child, which was a good thing in an institution where catatonia passed easily for obedience and docility. When she was fourteen, she was already beautiful, slim, and delicate.

She took to sitting for hours each day in the darkened boiler-room of the orphanage. She told Esther, her sister, that she did this because she could feel herself splitting into pieces, evaporating in the daylight. The darkness left her intact.

As she grew more beautiful, she spoke less frequently and used simpler words. But her sister and the other orphans found it was ever harder to understand what she meant. Her beauty was so jarring in that arid place that everyone was relieved when it was time for her to depart.

She went to the capital, where she found a series of jobs till she had earned enough to enrol in night classes to learn typing. She had many lovers in this period. They were permitted to enter her body, but never her mind.

She met the rest of her family only once after leaving the orphanage. She sailed for North

America in the year of her twenty-fifth birthday, on the *Mauritius*. She stayed in her cabin with her portholes covered on all but the dullest days. On land again, she travelled by train into the interior of the continent in a private compartment with the blinds drawn. On arrival at her destination, at night, she was relieved to find the quality of the darkness had not diminished, but if anything, improved with the distance travelled.

Notebook, A. McGaw

1

Two, or perhaps three months later, on a day when Helen had gone up to the city, I drove down to the country house of JP. He was a very old man (at least eighty), very elegant, with slick silver hair. In fact, it would not be going too far to say he exuded a kind of silveriness: silver skin, silver voice, a slight silver smile. I wanted to talk to him about a woman photographer, long dead herself, who had specialized in taking pictures of those who were dying. She had occasionally worked for JP when he owned a large newspaper in the city. But he remembered nothing about her. Anyway, he was an old man who was more interested in talking about his own experiences.

We sat at either end of a couch in a room that smelt faintly of aftershave, and was furnished with comfortable modern furniture and machinery: in one corner, a stereo and a shelf of records; on a table beside us, a crouching ivory-coloured telephone. It never rang while I was there. From time to time as he talked, I could see horse-drawn buggies, all black, easing their way along the road at the end of his driveway. They were of a kind used by a religious sect that still farmed this area. Watching them from this side of JP's window was like watching a movie with a period setting. I said, for the sake of conversation, that it must feel strange to live in close proximity to such an anachronism. He breathed for a moment. The idea, he said, did not excite him any more or less than did the notion that the solid continents we inhabit are slowly drifting, or that we are spinning helplessly, all our lives, around the sun.

I gave up my efforts at small talk. He had more to say, however, on the subject. He said he was, perhaps, a man nothing could surprise any more. He had heard others suggest that in old age, everything ought to be a surprise, even waking up in the morning; perhaps as a defence against such a barrage of surprises, some men develop surprise-proof exteriors that are easily mistaken for complacence. Even by the individuals themselves.

2

"Then again," he said, "perhaps I lost my innocence too early."

When he was a boy, he said, in another country, living on his father's farm, it was customary to go out in the autumn, hunting rabbits. Some of the men would use a combination of guns and demonic little ferrets. They would set their trained ferrets loose in the warrens to panic the rabbits out onto the guns.

But JP's father would allow neither guns nor ferrets on his property. He preferred to trap the rabbits. His method was to set snares, tiny gallows with wooden uprights and wire nooses, in the well-trodden rabbit paths. The snares would be left overnight, and next day he and JP would collect the catch.

JP, as a boy, half-enjoyed the trapping, though he was half-sorry for the rabbits. He thought it a gesture of kindness in his father to use snares: at least the rabbits had some hope of avoiding them. He told his father so. He laughed and patted JP on the head (he was then about twelve). JP's mother was the one who insisted on the snares, he said, and not out of any sense of fair play to the rabbits. On the contrary, she believed there was no treat like a rabbit caught overnight in a snare; the flesh turned so tender it was a delight. She said it had something to do with the duration of the rabbit's suffering. Guns killed them too quickly.

JP's tongue was a small silver blade flicking along his

lips, slitting his face open from the inside to let the words slide out.

"If duration of suffering had the same effect on human beings, what tasty morsels we would make," he said. I was not certain whether he was referring to the two of us, sitting side by side on his pleasant couch in that modern room, or to the world in general. I felt a little uncomfortable at the knowing look he gave me with those silvery eyes.

Suffering was one thing, he said. But what about death? He had seen his fill of deaths. Bloody deaths, as much as any man. Especially during the period when he was a war correspondent. That was long ago. But there were other deaths, the more remarkable in peacetime. He had retained what might be considered sentimental recollections of two of them, both violent: one of a man, the other of a woman.

The first happened when he was a cub reporter down here in one of the big country-towns. It was a clear case of suicide. Yet, a man would have hanged for it if he had not stopped to buy a cigar.

"Let me show you something," JP said, getting to his feet a little stiffly (the silver had entered his joints). He went to a cabinet beside his writing table. He riffled through a drawer, then came back to the sofa, holding a sheet of paper that was yellow with age. A brief message was typed on it in an old fashioned type-face:

> I am afraid for my life. Jack Miller
> has threatened to kill me if I don't
> pay him back his money. Don't let him
> get away with it. For God's sake.

The note was signed, in pen and ink, in a small, neat hand
— "Gerald Lundt." Lundt, said JP, was the one who
killed himself. Jack Miller was the man who might have
hanged.

The note had been acquired by JP when the inquest
into Lundt's death was over and the case closed. The
police let him keep it, for a half-dozen similar notes had
turned up. Lundt had sent them all over the place, to his
doctor, his lawyer, his co-workers, to arrive in the mail on
the day after his death.

"Each note said the same thing: that Lundt was afraid
Miller would kill him." JP leaned back, his silvery eyes
half-shut. "In those days, if Miller had done it, he'd have
been hanged by a villager from Basden just five miles
south of here."

I knew he would tell me now about Basden, though I
would have preferred to hear about Lundt. I wondered if,
in his mind, things were connected, if there were no
digressions. Or perhaps directness was too unsophisti-
cated, too blunt for a man like him. Or perhaps the path
through his memory was criss-crossed by so many
half-forgotten intersections and dead ends he could no
longer walk with complete certainty to his destination. At
any rate, he was leaning back on the couch, flexing the
long silvery fingers of his right hand so that they rustled,
the way dry bone would rustle inside loose skin.

3

Basden, he said, was a small village of fieldstone houses, nearby. All the public executioners in the last hundred years had been members of one family, the Morrisons, and had lived in the village for several generations. JP himself once interviewed two of the Morrison brothers during the peak years of the hanging era. He had been apprehensive about meeting them, but the brothers, slimly built with flaming red hair, were quite normal and cheerful. The village took great pride in them, and had named the children's playground with its swings and maypole after them.

The brothers were certainly conscientious about their work. They practised for three hours a day on a fully equipped gallows in their basement (they took JP down to see it, and allowed him to try out the lever; the crash of the trapdoor echoed in his ears for days after), and kept themselves in shape by jogging and weight-lifting. They showed JP an illuminated family Bible with a list, inside the cover, of four generations of family members who had been executioners on two continents.

These Morrison brothers wanted JP to know they were "platform men": whenever they were hired, their sole responsibility was to make sure the gallows were mechanically flawless, and to perform the hanging expertly. They would never consent to clearing up underneath the platform afterwards. Victims of hangings tended to lose control of their bowels as they dropped. To say nothing of the fact that in the case of a hanged woman, the uterus would almost invariably keep on falling after the body itself had jerked to a stop at the bottom of the rope. Certain work, the Morrisons felt, was better left to house-cleaners.

Years after the first interview, and not long after capital punishment had since been abolished, JP met these same Morrison men again. They were as cheerful as ever, operating their own market-garden stall in the town, specializing in tomatoes. JP asked them what they thought of the abolition. The younger brother (they were both old by then) said he really did not mind, he still had his wonderful memories. But the elder mourned the passing of their profession. It wasn't as if killing had stopped since abolition, he said. The only difference was that nowadays almost every killing was performed by a bungler. He himself, he said, would rather be hanged by an expert than mutilated by an amateur with a sawn-off shotgun, up some back alley.

JP was smiling at the memory. "I have a copy of my interview in my files," he said, "if you'd like to read it." At times, his skin reminded me of a snake's when it is near shedding. I wondered if he had a true colour, or just another layer of silver underneath.

4

"Of course, in the Lundt case," he said, "there was no hanging. But there might have been."

Lundt, he remembered as being middle-aged, bald, not handsome (JP had actually known him by sight), a clerk in the Roads Department at City Hall, an avid reader of detective novels, an unmarried man who avoided people as much as possible. Jack Miller, Lundt's supervisor, on the other hand, was not at all shy. He had ambitions to rise in the public service, he was a ladies' man, a hunter, a gambler. He had little to do with his staff, especially the male staff, and least of all with the most retiring of them, Lundt.

The night Lundt stole a pistol, a black Beretta, from Miller's collection of guns (it was the first criminal act of his life) was the night of the annual Christmas party for the Roads Department, held in Miller's own house. While all the other guests were being sociable, Lundt went prowling. In the basement, in a dark corner, he came across a glass-doored cabinet containing Miller's guns. The Beretta glistened lethally at him.

The sight of that pistol transformed Lundt. Lying there on its shelf, clean and conclusive, it told him everything. He wrapped the pistol and some bullets in his chequered handkerchief and slipped them into his pocket. He was a thief. He was prepared to be worse.

"Lundt," said JP, "had merely joined the human race.

My father, when I was young, often said to me: look around you my boy; look at the world, with its thousands upon thousands of years of wars, plagues, famines, murders, public and private brutalities, injustices, parricides, genocides: one would have to be a cynic not to believe there was some great plan behind it all."

JP smiled. I thought of a crocodile with its jaw slightly parted. He blinked once or twice.

5

For two weeks following the theft of the Beretta, JP said, Lundt was happier than he had ever been. His work at the office and his obsessive reading of detective stories had always seemed so unrelated: parallel roads leading to different towns. Now, miraculously, the roads met. He knew that this was the moment he had been training for all his life. During his lunch breaks at the office, when no one was around to disturb him, he prepared the trap. First, he typed letters to himself, mimicking the crude style and bad spelling of Miller, then forged his supervisor's large, easily imitable hand. The letters contained threatening statements by Miller, demanding repayment of a gambling debt.

Lundt was careful to spread the dates of the supposed correspondence over a few months. The eventual killing must not seem an impulsive act. He placed these letters around various drawers of his desk, so that they would be found in an investigation. He knew there would be an investigation. Then he typed his "replies," in which he begged Miller for time to pay off his debts. He tore up the originals of the "replies," but kept carbon copies prominently in his filing cabinet.

His next step was to confide, or pretend to confide, in some people at the office. He let it be known that for years he had been gambling heavily, the passion of a lonely man, and was now in some kind of trouble. Later that week, he visited his doctor and asked for sleeping pills to help him through a bout of depression. He allowed his doctor to prise out of him the fact that his depression was caused by gambling debts. Lundt then paid a call on his lawyer to ask what would be the best thing for a man to do, if he was threatened. The lawyer suspected that Lundt himself was the man in question.

To conclude this stage of his plan, Lundt went to the police station and made inquiries about the kind of protection they could offer a man afraid for his life. He was so jittery the policeman who spoke to him had no doubt he was talking about himself.

On the day he had chosen for the killing, a slushy January day, Lundt did not go to work. Around noon, he phoned Miller himself. This was the key moment. In his most timid voice, he asked Miller to come to the City Hall, to Lundt's own office, at exactly eight o'clock that night. He said, whispering into the phone, that he had

found information on a land scandal that would ruin
Miller's only opponent in the next council election.

Lundt understood his man well. Jack Miller could not
resist the bait. He said he'd be there at eight. He did not
even wonder why Lundt would want to do him a favour.
He was the kind of man who expected favours, who was
too cocky even to suspect that he was hated.

"Miller," JP said, "was a man with little imagination.
Lundt was a man with too much."

He crossed his legs over tightly and leaned against the
arm of the couch as though he was being squeezed into
the corner by his memories. I could see above his elegant
shoes and thin socks, a silvery, hairless shin. He settled
himself, and talked, not about Miller or Lundt, but about
imagination.

6

Years ago (he was still a reporter), he knew a man who
was the epitome of the true man of action, a war hero.
This man could be persuaded, with difficulty, for he was
modest, to tell about his time as a soldier, before he
inhaled mustard gas in the trenches on a winter dawn. He
remembered everything: the grey mud of no-man's land,
the stumps of trees, the rats, the aching guts, the fear, the

obscene litter of the dead. JP had heard this man talk and
had seen old soldiers weep silently as they listened.

One night, on his way home from an assignment, JP
went into a pub in another town, and saw the same man at
a corner table, surrounded by a group of intent listeners.
JP bought a glass of beer and joined them. He was looking
forward to hearing about those nightmare battlefields
again. But this time the man was not talking about trench
warfare. He was telling how a ship, the *Vaunted*, with a
crew of six hundred, was torpedoed one night in winter.
He said that he himself was one of those who had
survived the blast and staggered half-clothed out of a
sudden furnace onto the tilted deck. They could feel the
ship being sucked down as they leaped into the numbing
sea. With a few shipmates, he managed to climb onto a
wooden raft, and spent three days on it, with one man
after the other dying of cold and despair.

At that point, the man noticed JP standing listening.
He paused, then carried on. He said that, in the end, only
two of them were rescued from the raft, in such bad
condition they were never able to return to sea. Their war
was over.

JP finished his drink and left. He found out, later, that
because of a bad heart, the man had been excluded from
service in the war. But he could tell his imaginary
experiences so well, he was more convincing than those
who had actually been there.

"He was a liar," said JP, "and yet the real men of action
did not betray him."

He was silent for a long time, watching me closely. I
knew I must respond in some way. So I tried to smile, by

making the skin tighten around my jaws and my eyes. He seemed satisfied with my effort, and returned to the story of Lundt.

7

The office is lit only by his desk light. The door is slightly ajar. He sits upright, the black pistol on his desk, waiting. Two minutes to eight. He hears the squeal of hinges at the far end of the corridor, the thud of a door, the snap of leather soles on the tiled floor. He picks up the phone and dials. He breathes into it:

"Police? My name's Lundt. A man's outside my office with a gun. At City Hall. Please come, right now."

He puts down the receiver. The footsteps in the corridor stop outside the door. His heart does not pound as much as he had feared. His hands do not shake. He knows he will have the strength. He desires nothing more in life now than to see the face of the man who will die.

He picks up the pistol with his handkerchief and presses the end of the cool barrel against his ear. He hears the tap on the door. He takes one last, deep breath:

"Come in!"

The door swings further ajar.

"Is everything okay, Mr. Lundt? You're here late to- . . ."

The wrong voice precedes the wrong face. It is Tomson, the janitor, who stands at the door, shocked.

He looks back at him. Just for a moment. Then he squeezes the trigger.

8

"Did I mention," said JP, "that as my father grew older, he was always trying to show me that the world made sense, pointing out patterns, anything that would indicate order. He was afraid I might grow up to be a cynic. I couldn't understand his fear. Some men do not need to search for order, they are overwhelmed by it, everywhere they turn. They feel as though they're in a prison where each moment of the day is planned, every action overseen. They hunger for the smallest particles of chaos, for things that do not fit. But everything always fits, in the end."

He said this in a light tone, but I thought I detected a touch of self-pity that made the silvery voice squeak slightly, in need of oil. After a moment, he went on with the story of Lundt.

"*The Post* sent me over to City Hall about nine o'clock

that night. It was snowing heavily. The building was in a commotion. The police let me upstairs to take a look so that I could make an accurate report. The force of the shot had knocked Lundt's body over against the wall. The gun was lying near him, and a handkerchief. There was blood on the walls and the floor. I had to go right back outside for some air. I was very young then." It was hard to believe JP had ever been young.

Two police officers, he discovered, had answered Lundt's emergency call and arrived at City Hall just after eight, at the same time as Jack Miller, all three of them like latecomers to a party. They all heard the shot, and ran up to Lundt's office. Tomson the janitor was standing at the door.

The police immediately arrested him, presuming he was the killer, the one Lundt had phoned about. Tomson said he was no killer, he was just doing his usual evening rounds and had noticed Lundt's office light. He opened the door and saw the poor man with a pistol at his head, and watched him shoot himself.

As for Miller, he said he had come in answer to Lundt's telephone call earlier. He would have been a few minutes sooner, but he'd walked across to the tobacco shop to buy a cigar.

Tomson was released next morning. By then, the letters about the debt had been found in Lundt's office, and several people had received those other, ominous notes.

It was all very strange. The police interrogated Miller again. He insisted he knew Lundt only as an employee, he certainly hadn't lent him any money, and he'd neither written any letters to him, nor received any, for that matter. As for the Beretta with his prints all over it, he had no idea how Lundt came to have it. The police were puzzled. Miller's own lawyer assured him that if he'd arrived at City Hall a little earlier that night, he might well be facing hanging, so much incriminating evidence pointed to him.

So far as the police were concerned, the matter was closed. Lundt was dead, a clear-cut case of suicide. The coroner speculated that Lundt had most likely intended to kill Miller and plead self-defence. When he saw Tomson, not Miller at the door, he knew his scheme had failed. He had set too many elements in motion, what with the theft of the Beretta, the letters, the final phone call to the police. He could not face the consequences, and shot himself.

9

"But," said JP, "why did he want to kill Miller in the first place? That was what interested me. Lundt was such an unlikely would-be murderer. I talked to Miller about it once or twice, but he was no help. By the end of the week, he'd put Lundt out of his mind. All he cared about was his election chances."

It took JP nothing more than a conversation with Lundt's landlady, an elderly widow, to discover that he hated Miller. Lundt had often spoken to her about his supervisor's success with women. He became especially bitter when Miller seduced one young woman in particular, a new secretary at City Hall. Lundt secretly adored her. So when Miller, after a few weeks, cast her aside in his usual way, it was the last straw. Lundt told his landlady, several times, he'd gladly die to see justice done.

JP rearranged his limbs on the couch. From time to time as he talked, he would pat his silver hair in place, an unconscious vanity. I wondered if he himself had once been a ladies' man.

"I think the coroner was only half-right about Lundt's reason for killing himself," JP said.

In JP's view, Lundt was afraid, most of all, that everyone would know he was nothing but a romantic misfit.

"To avenge someone implies great intimacy," said JP. "Lundt had gone to such lengths for the sake of a woman who would probably have loathed him, if she had ever noticed him. He realized the futility of his gesture in that final moment, and chose death."

10

JP was motionless, watching me from behind a faint odour of shaving lotion. All at once, I realized he was waiting for me to say something. So for the first time since he began his story, I spoke.

"But according to Tomson, Lundt already had the pistol at his own head when he pushed the door open. How did he expect to shoot Miller after he'd shot himself?"

JP, smiling his sick lizard smile, congratulated me on asking the right question. As for the right answer, he could only speculate. Lundt, he said, was a moral man, a man with a conscience, quite incapable of killing anyone else. His landlady had told JP this several times, and insisted Lundt wouldn't hurt a fly.

"But he didn't mind if the state killed Miller," said JP.

He was certain that Lundt's plan was to commit a reverse murder-suicide: from the start, he had always intended to shoot himself with Miller's Beretta, having arranged for the police to arrive immediately afterwards and catch Miller on the scene. Miller's lawyer was right, there was so much evidence against him he would surely have hanged. What judge would even have suspected that a man could be foolish enough to kill himself as a means of bringing about someone else's execution?

Nor did Lundt regard his proposed killing of himself, anyway, as suicide: he was too moral for that.

"He believed," said JP, "that he was simply executing himself, in advance, for his indirect murder of Miller. He was so certain his plan was foolproof and that Miller would hang. Then Tomson, the janitor, opened the door, and that was what turned his death into suicide."

JP's mouth opened a little wider, and I saw his fine silvery teeth for the first time. He said, "A month later, Miller won the election."

11

The lizard cackled, then was silent, then spoke quite soberly:

"Lundt was a man to whom women were too important. I myself once had the same weakness, at a certain time of my life."

I could see he was now confiding in me; that, after testing me with the story of Lundt, he was about to tell me something more personal.

When he was an adolescent, he said, he used to browse through the telephone directory and touch the names of women. That was the forerunner of the time, in his twenties, when he spent most of his energy in the pursuit of flesh-and-blood women. He was a man of many faces then, not out of hypocrisy, but because he didn't yet know for sure what kind of man he wanted to be.

I listened to him attentively now. Perhaps I sensed that something of peculiar interest to me might lie somewhere in his memory.

12

He said that during that period of his life (his late twenties) he began to live according to a theory he happened to have constructed for himself. It went like this: a truly well-balanced life will inevitably undergo abrupt alterations or deflections to counterbalance its moments of relative constancy. If life became too pleasing, the wise man would positively court his quota of pain; if his life became too secure, he would deliberately expose himself to danger.

Accordingly, JP would from time to time drive cars that were too fast for him; or he would climb cliff-faces too steep for a man like himself, who frequently stumbled on staircases; he would shoot rapids (he told no one he could not swim); and when, in the course of time, he became a war correspondent, he would expose himself needlessly to hostile bullets.

As for women. Once, at that time, he wooed a woman who was different from any other he had known. She frightened him a little, a woman who loved the night.

He licked his silver lips. This was what he wanted to tell me about.

The war was over, he said, his assignment in Europe ended. He was working for a newspaper in the city, settling down, when one of his friends happened to mention that a woman of some beauty had joined the evening typing pool. JP, ever on the look-out, took an article to the typists' office that night. He saw the woman. She really was beautiful. He fell in love with her and made up his mind to have her.

That was the beginning of a strange affair. Sometimes she would respond to him with passion and energy, sometimes she would treat him with contempt. He could never entirely trust her, but he wanted her. He asked her to marry him, something he had never done before.

JP rose again stiffly from the sofa and poured us each a goblet of wine, a silver goblet. As he handed it to me, he said, casually:

"She was from your part of the world. Some island. Her name was Rachel Mackenzie."

I did not give myself away as I had at the Institute for the Lost. I stayed calm. I thought, Mackenzie is such a common name. Rachel is such a common name. I did not interrupt him. I did not ask him to proceed. I knew he would. If he expected me to say something, I disappointed him. He sipped the wine through silver lips, for a while, then put the goblet back down on the table, and began to remember his last meeting with the woman on a warm night in August . . .

13

. . . on a warm night in August, she decided to kill Rachel Mackenzie, for she could take no more. They had managed to get along together passably well for years; indeed, at times, she thought she could almost have loved Rachel.

But the end was inevitable, hope was as good as over when Rachel met this man, and decided after a few weeks to encourage him. Nothing would make her understand how foolish it was to bring another man into their lives, even as a diversion. The idea was intolerable. Rachel wept and tried to conciliate her, as she always did. But this time her pleading wouldn't work. This was the last straw, she would take no more.

He, whenever he came to the apartment, looked uncomfortable. He was so attracted to Rachel, nonetheless, that he kept coming back, no matter how awkward she made things.

She knew she herself was beautiful, just as beautiful in her own way as Rachel. But she was not the type men liked, no matter how much she forced herself to smile at them, no matter how hard she tried to camouflage her eyes.

Rachel, as on other occasions when she had a man, would be impatient with her.

"Just leave me alone. Why do you spend all your time watching me?"

"Do I?"

Rachel would occasionally plead with her, tears in her eyes: "Please, tell me why. At least talk to me. I am the one who is not good with words."

"Oh? Is that so?" she would invariably reply.

And listen to her sobbing.

On the night of the killing, the house smelt musty from the sun all day, and the sky outside was thundery. Rachel and the man had gone out for dinner, to celebrate something, any excuse to get out of the house, away from her, to be alone together. When they came home, Rachel, looking marvellous in her low-cut green dress, greeted her with that false smile she would put on when she was determined to have her way.

But she herself looked right back at her, not saying what she was thinking: Rachel, I loathe you, you've gone too far.

She watched, disgusted, as Rachel took him by the hand, neither of them paying any more attention to her, and led him into the bedroom. She pushed him back on the bed and lay on top of him, the two of them fully clothed, and kissed him, slipping her tongue into his mouth, running her hands over his body. She unbuttoned his shirt, pulled it from under him, and dropped it on the floor. She began kissing his neck, his white shoulders, nuzzling the sprinkle of reddish hairs on his white, sweaty chest.

They ignored her, though she was standing watching as she always did. She had seen Rachel operate so often before, she could forecast what she would do. She would run her tongue along his chest, sipping at his tiny, man's nipples. She would undo his belt, as he breathed faster and faster. She would kneel, and pull his pants and his underpants slowly down over his knees, till they were shackles around his ankles. Then, slowly, looking at him looking at her adoringly, she would lie beside him and fondle him, and she would take him into her mouth till he was bursting with excitement.

He was hardly able to contain himself, begging for her, and she stood and began to undress herself, deliberately, letting him admire her.

Then Rachel turned to her, still watching.

"Do you want to?" she asked, sneering. "Why don't you go ahead?" The old routine.

Rachel knew her only too well, that in spite of herself, she was roused, that she did, indeed, want him.

So she herself lay down on the bed, spreading herself to receive him. He hesitated at the sight of her, but then he climbed on top of her, his body slippery with sweat, and thrust at her for a few minutes with his eyes tight shut and, with a shudder, released himself into her. Smelling his sweat, she squirmed under him, milking every drop of him, leaving nothing for Rachel.

She decided, at that very moment, that she would kill the bitch before the night was over.

After a while, he arose, looking a little embarrassed, and dressed hurriedly. He kissed Rachel goodbye, saying he would phone her tomorrow. And left.

She herself went to the bathroom to sponge away his sweat and his semen. She preened herself in the mirror, stretched her arms luxuriously, aware Rachel was looking. She combed back her hair, noticed how blue her eyes were, bluer than ever tonight.

Then she slid open the right-hand drawer. She could see the tip of the knife protruding. She made no attempt to disguise her action even though Rachel was now watching her intently. Her fingers caressed the point, brushed along the blade till they felt the handle of the bread knife that had lain there so long for just such a night as this. She was aware of the beating of her heart.

She raised the knife in the air, looking directly at Rachel. Those eyes did not flinch. She had expected to see terror in them. Why was she not pleading, instead of watching her raised hand, long fingered, the nails scarlet, a gold ring on the middle finger?

And now Rachel began taunting her, laughing at her, come on, do it, do it, why don't you do it?

Till she herself could stand it no more. Inflamed with anger, shouting her contempt, she hacked once with the knife at the white, naked throat, ripping apart the soft carotid artery.

As she herself lay on the cool, white-tiled floor, the blood bubbling out of her throat and her mouth, relief filled all of her being. She had heard Rachel's cry of fear as the knife struck. She had glimpsed, as she fell, the bread knife at her neck, the spout of blood. For the first time in too many years, her own world was singular and full of light. At long last, she really was herself, alone, and at peace.

14

Jp came to her apartment the next night, a little anxiously, for his telephone calls had not been answered. He had warned her about the dangers of living alone, and she had laughed.

He opened the apartment door with his duplicate key.

Rachel's body was fastened to the white-tiled bathroom floor by a stalagmite of blood, and there were splashes of blood on the mirror and the counter. The knife was in her hand, and he had no doubt it was suicide. He looked around the apartment before calling the police. In the perfumed drawer of her desk he found sheets of paper with circular shapes on them. At first glance, he thought they were tremulous drawings of mad eyes. Or they might have been whirlpools or coils of rope. But then he saw that the marks were, in fact, thin spirals of her tiny handwriting. On some of them, she had begun her writing in the centre of the page and continued in concentric form till she reached the edges. Conversely, on

some of the others, she had starting writing at the edge
and gradually narrowed the spiral till she reached the
centre. Some were clockwise, some anti-clockwise. On all
of the sheets, the same words were written, either from
the edges in, or from the centres out, "weperisheacha-
loneweperisheachaloneweperish . . ."

15

Later, said JP, the police found some notebooks of hers.
They too were full of her spirals. Except on one page,
where she had written that, for years, she'd had sex with
men in order to become pregnant. She'd aborted the
foetuses and preserved them in jars of formaldehyde. Of
course, no such jars were found.

Both JP and the police considered the idea to be
nothing but the fantasy of a poor, demented woman.
Aside from certain moments (often, JP admitted, the
most intimate of moments) when her eyes would become
distant, she was a quiet, beautiful woman. He saw no need
to tell the police that it was because he was a little afraid of
her that he had pursued her in the first place.

I sat watching and listening as JP leaned his head back
on the sofa, and put his silvery hand to his mouth to cover
a yawn, a snake's yawn.

"I was surprised I did not feel very sad at her death," he said. "Like Lundt's, it seemed to me more of a tidying up of loose ends than the annihilation of a life."

He talked on like this for some time, the old man, JP. He looked very old, I could see he had grown tired. The scent of his shaving lotion (a fine, silvery scent) was stronger now in proportion as his energy weakened. The time was right for a question.

"Did she have some kind of abdominal scar?" I asked.

He looked at me, curious. But he was too worn out by his memories, as I had hoped, to inquire about the reason for my interest.

"Not that I ever noticed."

One more thing I needed to ask.

"Have you ever heard of Doctor Yerdeli, the Director of the Institute for the Lost?"

I was watching very carefully. But he might have been on his guard now, too. Certainly, that reptile face did not betray him in any way.

"No."

I had to be satisfied with that. He was not a man who would tolerate inquisitions. So I convinced myself that he had not told me about the death of Rachel Mackenzie to elicit some reaction from me, or make me commit myself. He seemed much too self-interested for that, and too tired now to care. Though perhaps if I had been a woman, he would not have allowed his tiredness to show. He might even have shown some interest in me, and asked about my own life.

As I left, he wound his elegant, thin legs together and

lay back on the couch. The tubular collar of his silk polo-neck sweater swallowed his scrawny neck and part of his chin. Lying down like that, there was no hiding the thinness of the hair on his oval head. It made me think of a tarnished silver egg disappearing into the throat of a misshapen snake.

16

I was glad to be alone in my car, driving back to the city. I had plenty of time to wonder if, in a world of so many people, I had actually chanced on another of those four Patagonian Mackenzies. I thought, it's too much of a coincidence, too uncalled for. I had seen no conniving gleam in the silver eye of JP when he spoke about Rachel, no hint that he and Doctor Yerdeli were conspiring; but when you stumble on too many coincidences, or on unexpected coincidences, or on coincidences you have no right to expect, it is natural to look for some sort of a joke, or for a joker. In the end, I concluded that if Rachel Mackenzie *was* a member of the Patagonian Mackenzies, I had found out about her by an incomprehensible stroke of chance. I wasn't sure I should be too happy about that.

17

That night, in a small restaurant near my apartment, as Helen and I were drinking brandy after dinner, I asked her about her day and told her about mine. I had saved it till then, organizing the details in my mind all the way home in the car and through the earlier part of the evening. I sniffed the brandy for a while, then I told her about JP and about Gerald Lundt's attempted crime. I told her about JP's affair with a woman called Rachel Mackenzie (I noticed with satisfaction Helen's surprise at the name), her delusions, and her death. I became a little poetic, from the brandy or from talking too much.

"JP told me all this down there in his country house. Through his long front window I could see soft hills, green fields, and blue sky. From time to time, one of those black horse-drawn carriages would go pecking along. There was a symmetry between them and JP's recollections that made me shudder."

Helen reacted to everything I told her just the way I had hoped: with curiosity, surprise, sadness. She had roller-coasted through these states, just as I had.

I remembered something else JP had said. A question really. He had wondered if he himself, by falling in love with Rachel Mackenzie, must take partial responsibility for her death. He wondered if love violates certain people: they have to reveal too much about themselves, they feel so full of holes and weaknesses, they can't live any more.

I told Helen I had not been able to think of anything to say in response. She looked at me and pressed my arm:

"Ezra, I think he's right, in a way. But there's no avoiding it. The more people love each other, the more they violate each other. They sweat and wrestle and howl and penetrate each other, and want to know all about each other. No privacy is permitted. They give each other the third degree. So he's right. But if lovers don't violate each other, love dies."

I laughed and said I'd like to test her theory: at least, the sweating, wrestling, howling, penetrating part of it. Just to see if I agreed. So we left the restaurant, and went home to bed, and tested it. And afterwards, before we fell asleep, I told her, yes, the theory was a good one.

18

Later that week, I wrote to Donald Cromarty. In my letter, I told him I had now come across another Mackenzie, named Rachel, and gave him the details. As I was writing, I realized I had still not told Helen that I had enlisted his help. I think I kept it to myself because I knew, instinctively, she would have disapproved. And perhaps if I had been less willing to confide in him, I would never have had to face him, in the end, at the Paradise Motel.

In my letter, I told him everything. I made it clear I was no surer this Rachel could be a member of the Patagonian Mackenzies than the Amos Mackenzie I had written him about earlier. Then I asked what progress he was making with his inquiries into my grandfather Daniel Stevenson's story. I let him know I was aware of the obstacles before him: the destruction of archives in the war; the depopulation of many of the islands; the discretion, almost amounting to deceit, of news reporting in that era.

I encouraged him, flattered him, thanked him. I hoped he would let me know what he had found when I returned from my next journey. For I was already preparing to go south.

PART FOUR

Esther

Esther Mackenzie was sent, at the same time as her younger sister, Rachel, to St Fiona's orphanage, near the Border. She was, by thirteen, a heavily built girl with black hair who had never seen herself naked. The day the first blood stained her underwear, she felt immediate sorrow for all the other girls, and ceased to believe in God (though she kept that a secret from the Sisters of the Holy Order of Correction).

She was an excellent mimic, but she displayed this gift to no one. She would go down to a little hollow in the fields near the orphanage and contort her body to simulate the mannerisms of others, particularly of Sister Marie Jerome, a small French nun with rickets, who was in charge of discipline. But she stopped going there after finding, one day, at the bottom of the hollow, a little image made of mud. It had bent legs, and was draped in a black cloth. The image had been pierced with sharp twigs. From then on, Esther Mackenzie stopped her mimicry, and trained herself to take all emotion out of her voice, so that everything she said was as inflectionless as the written word.

The other orphans sought her friendship because of her plain appearance, and would have liked her more if she had confided in them. But she preferred the company of the animals at the orphanage farm, because they asked her no questions.

By the time she finally left the orphanage, the thought of dying in that cold, Border country appalled her. She worked as a waitress for some months, then, in the last year of the war, spent a year with the Red Cross. She often watched surgery, marvelling at the body's capacity to endure bullets and scalpels. She had few sexual experiences, nor did she desire them much, though she had vivid sexual dreams. Her thick body, her monotonous voice disguised her mind. One morning she failed to appear at the hospital. She had taken passage on a ship bound south-west, for the tropics. She met her family only once, after leaving the orphanage.

Notebook, A. McGaw

1

Helen, out of a sense of obligation, had to go on a trip north for a couple of months to visit her family, so I, at a loose end, went south. A friend had suggested the idea. He had travelled in the region a few years before, in the course of exploring one of his cases (he was a policeman), and thought I would find the experience interesting.

So, a week later, I was in the tropical south. I took a room in a hotel in Xtecal, a village where the jungle meets the sea, about a hundred miles south of the main provincial city. Each mile, I found out, was a year's journey back in time. As for the village, it was shrinking. Not long ago, it had been a town; before that, a city. But this withering away seemed to concern no one who lived there. Perhaps the villagers shared the spirit of the ancient peoples who had settled that country, and who had built nothing to last. It was said that their greatest edifices were made to endure only the length of the builders' lives. At the end of that time, builders and buildings were buried, and new structures rose on top of them.

To trace the original, overgrown streets and the ruins of much of Xtecal would have challenged a cryptographer's skill. In the part that was still inhabited, clans of rats and domestic pigs disputed the right of way with the human population. Only a few hundred people persisted in living here, witnessing daily the powers of nature's bailiff, the jungle, as it reclaimed its rightful property.

The Plazacar Hotel, in which I took a room, was a relic of Xtecal's more recent glory days. It was a palace gone to seed, smelling of decay, with a wide, grass-roofed patio in need of repair. The owners lived far away, in the provincial capital, but they kept the hotel open. I suppose they felt that just as Xtecal had mysteriously declined, so it might as mysteriously resurrect and achieve its former glory.

The supreme attraction of the Plazacar, according to
the desk-clerk, was its portable beach bar, thirty feet of
polished mahogany that was carried each day onto the
hotel's private beach. The bar was set up in the middle of
the beach. If it had been of regular height, it would have
blocked the view of sunbathers, but it was only a foot or
two tall, and lay on the sand like a long coffin. The
bartender, too, and the waiter were each no more than
three feet tall.

This waiter, Gilberto, when I got to know him, told me
that for generations his family had produced a tiny waiter
to serve at the Plazacar. He himself, to carry on the
tradition, had married the shortest girl in Xtecal. But she
was four feet tall, and, unfortunately, their son had taken
after the mother. I used to meet Gilberto in the street
from time to time, with his son, who was then seven years
old and already a head taller than his father. The boy had
a birthmark in the shape of a perfect triangle of jet-black
skin around his right eye.

Every night, if the rain stayed away, dinner was served
on the hotel patio. Two local men, who accompanied
themselves on worn guitars, would entertain the diners
with sad ballads. The tenor, a very ugly man, had a long,
wart-covered nose and an angelic voice. He always stood
well away from the light. Gilberto told me that sensitive
guests, in former years, had complained of the presence of
that nose when they were eating. The sight of it, I must
confess, did have a damping effect on the appetite.

2

During my stay in Xtecal, I followed a routine: I would spend much of each day reading, sipping the local rum. Then, about four in the afternoon, I would defy the sun and go for long walks down the beach. Sometimes, in fact, I walked so far, darkness would creep up behind me, and the thick jungle would wedge me towards the sea. On those days, I would have to hurry back at a trot towards the distant lights of my sanctuary, Xtecal.

Those were my usual habits. But one morning, after a surprise storm had howled all night, I went on my walk early. The shore was a chaos of beer bottles, broken palm fronds, detergent containers, putrid fish, and pieces of styrofoam wrapped in seaweed.

I was passing the last huts at the edge of the village, when I saw a man coming along the beach towards me, not in a straight line but weaving, his head down, as though he was hypnotized by the litter on the beach. But nearer, I saw he was drunk, that he was not a native, and that he had seen me.

I would have avoided him, but there was no place to go except into the jungle or the water. So I tried not to see him, to make my face a blank wall to him. But he was not to be put off, and as he came nearer, he greeted me in fisherman's Spanish: "*Buena dia*!" And I could not ignore him.

He was a man in his late sixties, perhaps, with a long, wiry body, and a bush of thick grey hair. A labyrinth of old scars and age wrinkles bracketed his eyes. The half-empty bottle of rum in his left hand oiled his walk.

He stood in my path, now, swaying, but his blue eyes were steadier than mine. He held out his bottle, a sociable gesture. I refused it as politely as I could. The edges of his words had been smoothed by the rum. But he seemed good-humoured and harmless, and after a few minutes, I was glad to stand and talk to him, or listen to him talk.

$$3$$

That was my first meeting with Pablo Renowsky. Nothing could have been more accidental, I would say. I had travelled south on a whim. I had come by pure chance to this village of Xtecal, a name chosen arbitrarily from a tourist guidebook. I had met him because there had been an unseasonable storm, and because that morning, the only morning in my whole stay, I walked early rather than late.

His name was really Paul, but the villagers called him Pablo or Pablito. They enjoyed treating him as the drunken gringo, and he did not seem to mind. I never did see him really drunk; his speech was slurred, but not only by rum as I had first thought. Boxing was the main cause. He had been a professional boxer for twenty years. In addition to the neanderthal scar tissue above his eyes, a pink cauliflower had sprouted in place of his left ear. But when he spoke, it was as though the door to a ruined mansion swung open, and revealed elegant furniture and curious paintings. For Pablo Renowsky was an intellectual boxer. He was, with his inquisitive, discreet attitude, a scholar: a scholar with a deviated septum which he often wiped with his thumb as he talked.

His ramshackle hut on the beach, where I spent several afternoons after our first meeting, was full of books, all of them well read by him. Many of them now served mainly as homes for families of ants, and scorpions, and tarantulas. Still, out of a feeling of gratitude towards his books, he kept them till they rotted or were eaten.

He talked quite a lot about his past, but never romantically, never boasting about his boxing days (he had been a jabber, not a big puncher). His life story was not, he felt, unusual: he once had strict farmer-parents; he resolved to run away from home; he lived on the streets; he discovered he had a talent for boxing, and could make a living at it; he served an apprenticeship, during which he was punched around too many times, till he learnt what he could do and what he couldn't. He had entered a world he had never known existed, whose inhabitants regarded gonorrhoea and head colds as equally minor, and who settled trivial quarrels in back alleys, wordlessly, with knives.

Pablo told me about his boxing life with its rituals of disrobing, the use of oils and massage; the embraces and fondlings in the ring; the bruises, the explosive releases; the climaxes in unconsciousness, or even in death.

He spoke, too, of the women he had known, many of them tough camp followers. But one or two were good women, the best. He showed me a faded photograph of the woman he had married. I could not decipher her features. She had died, not long after the wedding, he said sadly.

In the course of his travels, he read and read. Sometimes his trainer would rebuke him for reading as he lay in the liniment-smelling dressing-room just before a fight, when he should have been concentrating on the battle to come. But Pablo felt his reading and his boxing complemented each other. Nothing was more effective, he assured me, for establishing the relationship between essence and existence than the pain a straight left to the nose could give.

As he grew older, his wily legs let him down, and he began to lose easy fights. So he made up his mind to come down here and live out the rest of his life. He had saved enough money to survive comfortably in this place, and though it was no Eden, he felt better than when he was a target by profession. He bought this hut on the beach and settled down, thinking he might write about his experiences. But in that, he had never succeeded.

Was it possible, he wondered, his blue eyes fixing mine, that all the words in his brain had been pounded out of shape by too many punches, so he could no longer make them fit his life? Or (he looked at me hopefully), did I know if it was the case with words, that they never did fit anyway? But if that were so, how would anyone understand for sure what anyone else was saying?

He had tried learning Spanish, thinking that perhaps a fresh language was what he needed. But the foreign words made him feel stiff, constrained, like a jungle animal that must from now on travel only by maps.

Some years ago, he said, while he was asleep, he had *dreamt* an entire novel: dreamt that he had sweated it out of himself for months, or maybe years; then had polished it; that it was published; that it was admired by some readers, reviled by others. He dreamt all this in just a few minutes one night. Perhaps, he said, having experienced so vividly in a dream everything a writer goes through, his need to write an actual book had been satisfied? Perhaps that was why he preferred now to read, and to remember?

4

In his hut, as he sat drinking his rum, he would at times switch to his metaphysical concerns, some of which were disconcerting. For example, he might say:

"I wonder why it is that parents don't murder their children?" He could not understand why a mother, especially, did not hate the child who sucked her dry. Surely a mother's restraint was one of the great miracles.

Another time, he told me how, whenever he went to a zoo, the sight of visitors laughing derisively at the monkeys always made him sad. It was tempting to say the people were really laughing at themselves, because the monkeys were the next nearest things to human beings and, therefore, fit only to be laughed at. But Pablo wondered if they weren't, rather, laughing at innocence. He didn't go to zoos any more.

"When you know what innocence is," he said, "you know that you yourself are no longer innocent. Isn't that so?"

I could see he was anxious about my opinion on this, so I said that the problem was certainly worth thinking about.

During those afternoons in his hut, he talked mainly about the old days in Xtecal, when he first arrived. Then, newcomers always noticed, right in the middle of the town square, next to the bandstand, the bullet-pocked wall with its white-painted lines on the ground: the official execution area. A town where the symbols of law and order were so prominent was bound to prosper. And it had. But that was long ago. Xtecal had declined, reminding him of many broken-down boxers he had known, seedy but still worthy of respect for their pasts.

In this way, Pablo Renowsky would speculate, ask his questions, and reminisce. Of all the conversations I had with him, however, I remember best the story of his visit to one of the most notable places in the old Xtepal, a bar called La Cueva, now completely returned to the jungle. Pablo thumbed his nose more vigorously than usual as he thought back to the times he went there. It was, he said, one place he could never forget.

5

I wasn't the only gringo who lived here back then. There were a few others, mainly on the run for smuggling arms or drugs. I became friendly with one of them, and one night he came to my hut. Pablo, he said, it's about time you saw the real culture here.

So I went out with him.

We didn't have to go very far, just a half-mile walk through the town, towards the jungle. The jungle's grown back in now, like a scab over a wound. But at that time, the town was a big place, and it was eerie to walk through it at night. There were no street lamps. The main street was full of the shapes of people, hundreds of them, and you could hear voices from all the shops and cafés and houses. The insides of the buildings were lit by candles or hurricane lamps. It was easy to imagine that this was the way it must have been, for hundreds of years, and the voices must have sounded the same then, in the dark.

We came to the edge of the jungle and walked for a while along a gloomy path with big trees on all sides. There was no moon. It was after nine o'clock, and you could hear the jungle animals crashing and rustling in the bushes. I was always afraid, at that time, of standing on a snake. But never mind snakes, there were always plenty of mosquitoes biting at your ankles, even though the townspeople used to burn bushes to keep them down. I don't know what was worse, the mosquitoes or the smell of that smoke.

Up ahead, I could see lights, and hear guitars. There was a big grass-roofed building. When we reached it, I could read the sign outside. It said La Cueva. A woman of about fifty was standing at the bamboo gate, greeting everyone who went in. She was a gringo, too, I could see that right away. She was heavily built, but in a balanced kind of a way: I mean, the weight hadn't sunk into the bottom half of her yet. Her eyes were brown and her skin was brown, but she was a gringo, all right. She was speaking in Spanish, but as we came out of the dark, she saw my friend, and she switched to English. She knew him from before. He introduced us: Pablo, this is the Senora, she owns the place.

That was the first time I met her, but I met her often after that. I liked her, and I liked her husband, Delio, when I met him later. I don't know what kind of life she had before ending up in this town, owning a place like La Cueva. You didn't ask that kind of thing in those days.

But there was a look in her eyes I often saw in old boxers that made me feel she'd seen a lot. Delio was a professional carnival performer. They'd met in some other little jungle town, twenty years before, and hit it off. He was younger than the Senora, maybe ten years younger. Her voice was very monotonous, as though she'd had an operation on it: she played on one note all the time. They were two of the most contented people you could ever meet, a rare thing.

But on the first night, all I saw was a solidly built gringo woman who was the owner of this seedy bar at the edge of the jungle.

The inside of La Cueva was full of cigarette smoke and the smell of kerosene lamps and sweat. The main floor had a bar and about fifty tables with people at them. There was a wooden guard-rail along one side, where the ground fell away to a deep grotto, and a rickety wooden stair led down there. From the guard-rail, I could see tables down in the grotto too, and behind them an illuminated stage against a background of rock. On the main floor, where we were, a dozen half-naked women were looking after about sixty or seventy male customers. Some of the women were pretty, but most of them had sagging breasts, or big bellies, or no teeth. The men they were serving drinks to weren't much to look at, either. They seemed to have pot-bellies or no backsides. But they were drunk, that was for sure. There was some kind of gallery above the bar. You could see a row of bamboo cubicles with ragged curtains on them. Some of the women would take men up there, by a side-stair.

My friend had brought me here for the floor show, so

we found two seats by the guard-rail round the crater.
The show was held on the stage down there. The tables in
that pit were packed with drunks. We didn't have long to
wait.

The show began with a mad-looking Indian woman
coming out on the stage from behind some boulders,
carrying a bag over her shoulder. When she put the bag
down in the spotlight, we could see that it wasn't a bag at
all, it was a live baby, with no head. And no arms or legs.
It had a mouth and eyes set into a little mound where its
neck should have been. The woman began to feed it milk
and husks, and we could hear the slurping noise, and see
the little eyes rolling. The woman didn't do anything else,
just feed her baby. Most of the audience wasn't paying
any attention. As my friend said, you could see this kind
of thing in the streets any day, you didn't have to come to
La Cueva.

The next act was a repeat, but it was by popular
demand. The spectators were interested this time. A
nervous-looking old man came on stage, walking with a
limp, holding a cloth round his body. He dropped the
cloth, and everybody laughed. He had no trousers on, and
the cloth had hidden a scrotum that was as big as an
elephant's. It was hanging down to his knees, like a
watermelon, with a little stub of a penis at the top. The
audience were laughing and shouting to him, and the old
man stood there, quite happy.

My friend had heard about this case. The old man had
developed a hernia years ago, and couldn't afford to have
it fixed. His intestine had slipped down into his scrotum,
more and more, till the bag was full and weighed nearly

thirty pounds. He had earned enough money now to have it fixed, and in fact the doctor had warned him it might burst any day. But the old man said if he had it fixed now, they wouldn't want to see him on stage any more, so he wouldn't hear of it.

After the old man, the rest of the acts were the kind of sex acts you could see in a lot of taverns at that time: snakes crawling in and out of vaginas; men and women having sex with dogs and mules; a crazy thin man with a penis like a long twig, poking it into the eye hole of a one-eyed woman; a fat man, standing on a stool, trying to make love to a Brahmin cow. The cow didn't seem to mind, but all at once, it lifted its tail and emptied its bowels all over his legs. The audience thought that was funny, even if the fat man didn't.

That was a typical kind of mid-week show at La Cueva. But you wouldn't dream of comparing it with one of Delio's performances. No, not in any way.

6

Delio and the Senora owned the first car ever seen down here. She told me how they got it. They had to have it brought in by boat, for there wasn't a single passable road outside the limits of Xtecal. Even the town roads were

awful. They were meant mainly for walking or for mules.
The car was big and well sprung. I don't know how they
managed to keep it running, what with the heat and the
rot. The only driving they did was up and down the main
street, once a day. That was their only affectation, though
they were rich, for Xtecal.

For twenty years, Delio had been one of the
best-known carnival performers in this whole state. The
first time I saw his act, I knew that what I went through in
the ring was nothing at all. He was an *agujado*: once a
month, for twenty years, he had made a living by having
his body pierced with skewers. Not just through the flesh:
amateurs could do that. The really famous *agujados* had
the skewers run right through their bodies from front to
back or from side to side.

That was how Delio met the senora. He needed a new
assistant to insert the skewers, and she volunteered for the
job. The assistants were called *agujereadores*, and were
just as important as the *agujados*. Take the Senora: if she
was no good, if she made a single mistake, she could kill
him. She had to slide those skewers (*agujas*, they called
them) into his body with dead aim, so that they missed the
vital organs. Often she had only fractions of an inch to
work with. She needed a cool head, a steady hand, and
marvellous accuracy. She must have learnt somewhere
about the internal structure of a man's body. She had to
make sure the skewers went in and came out by pre-set
paths, without any deviation. The experts used to say an
agujado's body was his private minefield. There was only
one safe path through it, and only his personal
agujereador knew the way.

Delio was not the only *agujado* in the world. Every major carnival had one. But what made his act better known than all the others was this: he'd made it into a competition. Over the years, he'd gradually increased the number of skewers that went into his body. Every year, he'd go for a new personal record, and announce in advance that he was going to try. Big audiences, a lot of them down from the city, came to these major performances, and there was a lot of gambling on the outcome. People used to bet on how many skewers he'd be able to accept; or whether he'd set a new record; or whether he'd die before reaching his previous mark; or whether his *agujereador*, the Senora, would make a fatal slip and kill him.

Most *agujados* could take ten or at most fifteen skewers. Some of the best of them had even challenged Delio, but given up or died in the attempt to compete with him. He was so successful, some people who didn't like him spread rumours that he'd bribed the *agujereadores* of his rivals or arranged to have their *agujas* poisoned. But no one really believed the rumours. Delio was the greatest of them all, and proved it every time he performed. For Delio, ten skewers was just a warm-up. His record was twenty-five. And he had promised he would go higher before he retired.

There was a lot of gambling at these performances, but it was always kept discreet. That was part of the business, and both Delio and the Senora knew it went on. They knew their audiences were only human.

After a performance, the Senora would become Delio's nurse for a while, watching over him and tending his

wounds so that they wouldn't fester, especially in the
rainy season when everything rotted. Between monthly
performances, he was wrapped in bandages most of the
time, and there was always pus flowing from somewhere
in his body.

I saw his final performance. He had announced a
month before that he was going for his last record:
twenty-six skewers, and then he'd retire for good. So, on
that night, La Cueva was packed. My friend and I could
hardly find a place to stand. The mayor was there, and the
whole police department, and the lawyer-cum-dentist-
cum-doctor, and the priest (he had to sit on his own, in the
shadows: the church didn't approve of *agujados*). There
had been the usual debate about which angles were the
best for spectators: most preferred a side view, to see the
entry and exit of the skewers; others like to look over the
agujereador's shoulder, to watch the placement. Others
felt it was only important to see the exit of the skewers;
they said that you could only judge how good an
agujereador was if you could see how accurately the
points came through.

7

A hush descends as the small man with deep brown
eyes walks onto the stage, wearing a brief loincloth.

She follows him, solid and serene. She straps him to the *estaca*, a post set up on the stage especially for the purpose. He stands sideways to the audience. The bindings are tight, so that he will remain steady during the performance. His slight body is marked by the stigmata of twenty years.

The woman, dressed in black, asks him if he is ready to receive the first skewer. He nods his head. She turns to the table that stands beside the *estaca*. A white cloth is laden with two-foot-long bone-handled skewers that glint in the light. She chooses one, turns and surveys the man's body the way a painter assesses a canvas. She places the point of the skewer at a scar just below his ribs, then thrusts smoothly till the skewer emerges through a corresponding scar in his back. La Cueva is silent enough for devotees to hear the swish of the skewer as it passes through the *agujado*'s body.

The man smiles. All is well. The woman continues with her task, sliding one skewer after another through the well-travelled passageways in his pale body. He begins to resemble a living statue of the patron of the *agujados*, Saint Sebastian.

After the insertion of the tenth skewer, the woman pauses to allow the customary applause.

The skewering begins again: fifteen, twenty. Another pause, another round of applause.

The tension is high. Twenty-one skewers. Twenty-two. Twenty-three. Twenty-four. The woman's aim is unerring, the man's flesh swallows the steel, blood drools from the tiny mouths in his belly and his back. He looks strong, he exults in his mastery of the skewers.

She slides the twenty-fifth skewer into him, equalling his old record. A roar of applause fills La Cueva. Now the woman looks at him, this tree of flesh that sprouts branches of steel.

She formally asks, as an *agujereador* must, if he will accept one more skewer. He, as the *agujado* must, formally asks her if she thinks his body will bear it. The woman looks to the audience for a moment, as though hoping they will tell her to stop. But this too is a formality. It is for this final skewer they have come to La Cueva.

She picks up the twenty-sixth skewer. She holds it delicately, her solid body steady as a rock in the grotto. She has dreamt this thrust a thousand times. The skewer will enter the man's body just below the bag of the stomach, it will slide swiftly through the space above the intestinal coil, and will exit on the left side of the fifteenth vertebra of the spine.

The woman places the point against the unbroken skin. She concentrates, like an archer willing a bull's eye. The man braces his body, closes his eyes. She thrusts. She sees the brief indentation in the flesh, she feels, without seeing, the swift passage, the point emerge unresisting, the tiny volcano of split flesh in his back, the trickle of blood.

The man is motionless. Then, slowly, he opens his eyes, and smiles at the woman. She smiles back. The audience roars its approval, a roar that crashes all round the grotto, all round the jungle outside.

But the man's head jerks suddenly back, his body convulses like a snake's. His eyes roll upwards, his head sags to his chest.

The woman snatches skewers out of the limp body, dropping them, glinting, to the ground. Spectators help her unfasten the straps. They lay the body on the stage floor like a withered parchment, and contemplate its bloody message.

8

During the uproar, my friend said to me, Pablo, it's too late for a doctor now. He was right. The lawyer-dentist-doctor was one of the first down onto the stage. He was there partly for that kind of emergency. But Delio was dead. There wasn't a breath left in him. He was lying in the grotto of La Cueva, in front of five hundred people, dead.

It was a sad business, though a lot of hard-headed gamblers made a profit out of his death. They say *agujados* always push their luck too far, in the end, and the gamblers are bound to win eventually. But even they were sorry. My friend said, Pablo, it's too bad: the fear we all eat every day tastes a little more bitter after a man like Delio dies.

As for the Senora, she wasn't the kind of woman it's easy to console. You always felt that she knew more about life and death than most of us ever would, so what could you say to her? For myself, I said nothing and hoped she understood.

9

Pablo Renowsky had gone this far in his recollections, and I still hadn't made the connection. Perhaps I was too carried away. Even the fact that he had said more than once that the Senora was a gringo hadn't made much of an impression: gringo women were no rarer here at that time than gringo men. No, it took his next words: "She had an accent like yours."

Immediately, I advanced from ignorance to shocked understanding. I could have predicted what he would tell me next. But I played out my part.

"What do you mean?"

"The Senora. She had an accent like yours."

It was a ritual now, a performance.

"Oh, really? What was her name? Do you remember it?"

"It wasn't Spanish. Delio used to call her 'Esther.' She told me her last name too. Mac-something or other, I can't remember."

"Not Mackenzie? Esther Mackenzie?"

"Mackenzie! That was it. Esther Mackenzie. How did you know? Have you heard about her before?"

I had been watching him carefully, looking for the slightest false move. But that rocky face, those blue eyes were so innocent. I had not thought of Pablo as the kind of man who would make up stories. I had him figured as one who only speculated or remembered. So I was feeling a little like a boxer who has walked into the Sunday punch of an opponent with no reputation for having a Sunday punch. The best I could do was to hide from him how dazed I was at hearing that name again. I had no doubt, this time, that the Esther Mackenzie he was talking about was one of the Patagonian family. And, I believed now, so must the Amos Mackenzie and the Rachel Mackenzie I had come across. How incredible it all was. And why was it happening? To have found out, in such peculiar circumstances, about the others. To have found out about her in this place, from this man.

I tried, successfully I think, to keep my mask in place as he told me about the funeral of Delio, and what Esther Mackenzie did, the next morning when she awoke . . .

10

. . . when she awoke, it was after six in the morning. She thought, the parakeets are making enough of a racket to waken the dead. The dead. And here she was, in bed alone. She remembered yesterday's funeral in the heat: the clusters of distressed faces; the cemetery's sterile, red earth and its crop of gravestones; the coffin's elegance deceiving no one, not the mourners, certainly not the ants, which were already crawling around it, sensing the rotting thing within.

Without opening her eyes, she slid her feet to the floor. She did not want to see the other pillow, nor the toes of the well-worn sandals protruding still from under the bedside chair, nor the other paraphernalia of a man's life. She did not want to see the dresser, with his photo, his thin arm around her. She did not want to remember his name. But her mind screamed: "Delio! Delio! Delio!"

She began her daily rites: the sacrament of washing her body; the sacrament of inhaling the scent of the soap; the sacrament of towelling off; the sacrament of buttoning her black skirt; the sacrament of tucking her white blouse into the waist; the sacrament of slipping her feet into her slippers; the sacrament of combing her long hair and pinning it up; the sacrament of making up her eyes, her lips; the sacrament of examining her face in the mirror; the sacrament of tucking in a last stray hair; the sacrament of assessing Esther, dressed for travelling.

She went downstairs, feeling the cool, smooth wood of the bannister run through her hand. She walked along the cool hallway feeling the smooth tiles under her shoes, coolness to coolness. She put her fingers round the front-door handle, smooth and cool to her touch. She opened the door and stepped out onto the veranda, feeling the warmth already in the morning air, the warmth that always preceded another long, hot day. The world was striped with long shadows. Except for her, in the shade of the veranda, except for all those things in shadow, except for the sun, which casts shadows but has none.

The street was quiet. The fishermen had long ago walked down to the shore, and sailed out into the moving waters for the morning catch. She wished them luck, as always. In a half-hour, the wind would begin stirring. She picked up the thick hemp rope, neatly coiled by the rattan couch on the veranda. She carried the rope down the three wooden steps into the yard, the coarse fibre prickling her soft palm.

The car was parked, in its usual place, its front fender almost touching an old palm tree. The tree, its long fronds brown with age, was taller than the house. It had played the part of the old servant who has learnt to cower before unpredictable masters, the wind and the sun.

"How perfect," she thought.

Then she laid the rope on the ground beside the car, and opened the driver's door, releasing the smell of old leather and motor-oil, and she slid onto the seat, cool against her thighs this early. The keys, already in the ignition, swung slightly from the weight of her body. She

made sure the automatic gear was in place before turning
the key. The engine growled, then barked, a caged dog
excited at the prospect of an unexpected run.

She waited till it was idling smoothly before stepping
down onto the driveway again. She dragged one end of
the hemp rope towards the old tree. She wound it round
and round the comfortable trunk, three times, then
knotted it tightly. She took the other end back to the car
and fed it through the small steel-framed triangular
window in the driver's door. Then she slid into the
driver's seat again and slammed the door shut. She pulled
most of the slack rope into the car. Through the metal
eyelet at the end of the rope, she made a loop big enough
for a head.

She sat back and breathed for a moment. Then she
lifted the noose and slipped it over her head, being careful
not to disturb her hair or the collar of her blouse. She
breathed again, deeply, put both hands on the steering
wheel, and concentrated on her journey. She felt nothing
now, no fear, only emptiness. She was thankful for the
gift of emptiness. She revved the engine a few times,
rhythmically, to be certain it would not stall.

She was ready.

She watched, for the last time, her right hand, as
though it were someone else's. The strong brown fingers
gripped the gear knob and shifted it into reverse. The sun
was filtering through the palm fronds, and the car hood
was flickering like fire. One last, easy breath. Then her
foot lifted from the brake and stamped the accelerator to
the floor. The car lurched backwards, and by the time it
crashed to a halt against the white plaster wall of a house

across the street, the thick hemp rope was slack again: but
in the course of that brief journey, it had bent the old
palm tree more than any hurricane had ever done, before
pulling her head right through that little triangular
window, ripping it from her body. So that when the
neighbours came staggering out to see what had caused
the almighty crash, they saw, on the roadway, a length of
loose rope attached to a red lump the size of a coconut,
trailing a dark mane; and in the car, they saw a stump of
body still pumping blood-fountains against the wind-
shield that, from where they stood, reflected back the
glory of the morning sun.

11
―

At times, Pablo Renowsky's face had the sculpted
appearance of a crude bronze bust. But, as he told me
about the death of Esther Mackenzie, his scars did not
succeed in undermining his words. He was sniffing more
than usual, brushing his broken nose with his thumb, a
boxer's habit. I noticed his blue eyes were moist, and that
was unusual for him. He seemed off guard, so I asked him
what I had been biding my time to ask.
    "Did you ever hear of a scar on the Senora's
abdomen?"

His blue eyes cleared instantly, and I saw the surprise in them: now I had revealed a move he had not expected from me.

"A scar? I don't know. Nobody would've known except Delio."

But he did not pursue me directly, he just circled, waiting to see what else I had to show. And I was watching him, too, but I was also thinking about the curious ways in which I had found out about the fates of each of these Mackenzies, about their deaths: Amos, raving in some bush hospital; Rachel, defying her image in a mirror; and Esther, taking that short, deadly trip.

Pablo began probing, testing me with some rumours he had heard, long ago, about the Senora. Someone, he said, had told him she had been a hooker, at some point. There was another story that she had been a drug-smuggler's woman who shot her man during a quarrel. Pablo had heard these things.

He was watching for my reaction. I confined myself to saying that nothing would surprise me. But the truth was, the inner sponge that absorbs surprises was, in my case, already saturated.

He spoke about the fact that every *agujado* knows he'll some day, almost certainly, die at the hands of his *agujereador*. Yet love between the two was not uncommon. Pablo wondered if that was consoling, to know your lover's hand will also be your killer's.

I looked at him, wondering how serious he was. I tried to read those blue eyes; but now he was the one who was giving nothing away.

$$\overline{12}$$

My last afternoon, before flying north again, I went down to visit Pablo in his hut by the shore. He was lying in his hammock, reading one of his mildewed books. We drank a glass of rum together. I thanked him for all his kindness to me, and especially for telling me about La Cueva and Delio and the Senora. I don't think I would have minded if he had asked me outright the reason for my question about her. But he would never do such a thing. He was much too discreet.

I cannot deny, too, that in spite of my caution (I had given nothing away) and in spite of my confidence that it was only by coincidence that I had found out about these three Mackenzies, yet in a corner of my mind, I was still afraid that Pablo Renowsky, and Doctor Yerdeli, and old JP might be part of some conspiracy that was too frightening to confront sanely.

But all along, Pablo had done the talking. He never once asked about me, about my life. I had presumed at first that this was a defence mechanism learnt in his boxing days. As though we were all opponents in some imaginary ring, where neither sympathy, nor hatred, nor even indifference should be permitted to hamper the outcome.

But, it occurs to me now, he may have been doing just the opposite. Exposing himself completely. Offering me everything he was, so that I would not be afraid to offer a little of myself in return. If that was so, I didn't take the opportunity. Some souls, it seems, will not take chances.

13

But I did open myself to Helen. She and I were ecstatic at being together again. During the weeks we had been apart, she said, she had not exactly enjoyed the sedate menus of family life, the bland stew of unvoiced covenants and assumed hypocrisies. So we threw ourselves together, savouring in each other the sauces we had missed. She stretched towards the warm bowl of southern passion; I, on the other hand, reached for the more northerly dish of endurance and affection. Somewhere half-way through that metaphysical banquet, our appetites sated, we moved on to a shared dessert.

We were lying in bed. It was a cool night, mid-November, and through the big window, we could see that all the stars had been erased by clouds. She had been shocked to hear about Esther. She, too, had no doubt Esther and the other two must have been the Patagonian Mackenzies. We talked about that, for a while, then in general terms about my trip, about Xtepal, about the

ancient civilization that had first settled that area, and the
retreat of the town to jungle once more. We were having
one of our best conversations. Helen was full of her very
finest opinions.

"Cultures that are most perfect, are also nearest
to disaster. They can't go anywhere but downhill.
That's why great nations have the greatest lapses into
corruption."

"Would you apply that to individuals, too?" I asked,
for the sake of debate. "Would you say that a human
being who is nearest perfection is on the brink of
corruption, too?"

She smiled: "Of course not. And anyway, the only
perfection human beings ever achieve is perfect aware-
ness of their imperfections."

She was an unpredictable debater.

"You mentioned," she said, "that in the old days down
there, they used to bury all their buildings every fifty
years. I wonder if that should apply to other things. Your
Patagonian story, for example. What if it had been better
left buried, and not disinterred and dragged into the
present?"

"Helen, you're full of ideas tonight."

"Yes. And another thing. As you were telling me
Pablo's story, I was thinking, words are the real *agujas*.
They penetrate, like skewers, and they can kill."

We were having fun. But though the earlier metaphysical dinner had satisfied my metaphysical appetite, my
body was still hungry.

"Helen," I said, "speaking of penetration. Many things
penetrate. I have something here, for example, that

penetrates. It's a sort of *aguja* too, and you can pierce yourself with it, if you wish."

I placed her hand on my penis. We then proceded to act out our own private carnival in bed, both taking turns as *agujereadores*, a procedure that seemed, in the end, quite equitable.

Afterwards, I almost mentioned to her that I intended to write to Donald Cromarty again, but I was certain the idea would ruin her sleep. Instead, I proposed that we pay one of our visits to the Paradise Motel. We would travel out to the coast, book in at our usual room, do all the things we loved doing.

Helen said she could think of nothing nicer. A few minutes later she was asleep. I lay there, feeling drowsier and drowsier. I resolved that I would write Donald Cromarty and let him know how I had found out about a certain Esther Mackenzie. I would tell him that both Helen and I were now quite sure that she and the other two Mackenzies I had written him about earlier were the sisters and brother of Zachary Mackenzie. I would ask how his own inquiries were progressing.

I did not realize then, though no one should have understood better, that a letter was no longer necessary. I still did not see what should have been obvious to me, that I was running out of time, and that soon everything would be resolved. Soon, and completely.

PART FIVE

Zachary

Zachary Mackenzie spent several years in "The Abbey" at the same time as his younger brother, Amos. The elder Mackenzie was shy but fearless. On the night of his thirteenth birthday, for example, on a dare, he climbed a high wall into the village cemetery. Inside, he jumped into a freshly dug grave and retrieved a marked handkerchief left there that afternoon. Another time, he invited a few of the boys to come with him to the orphanage chapel. He hauled himself up onto the altar and, while they watched, undid his fly and urinated over the tabernacle. That act of sacrilege frightened all of the boys.

He came to feel, around the age of fifteen, that the real Zachary Mackenzie was only a shadow of the image he had created of himself. The priests of the Holy Order of Correction were convinced that he was guilty of vanity, for he was often found looking at himself in mirrors. He did not tell them that the configuration of his long, bony nose, the milky blue irises of his narrow eyes, the regular mouth and chin in his slender face gave away nothing, not even to himself.

When it was time to leave the orphanage, he enrolled as an apprentice engineer at a merchant seamen's training school, the SS *Desolation*. In his second year, he was caught naked in bed with the Commodore's motherless daughter, Matilda, sixteen years old. She told her father that in six weeks, the period of her relationship with Zachary Mackenzie, she had learnt more than her father would ever know about what men and women could do to each other. She said that sometimes Zachary could be the most kind and considerate friend she had ever had, and that was what first won her over; sometimes he was an uncontrollable lecher and demanded her body over and over again, till she was too raw to take any more; sometimes he was a stern moralist, preaching at her, repent, repent; sometimes he was a sadist and tied her to the bed, lashed her with his belt, and bit her nipples, and raped her; sometimes he cringed and wept before her, and begged her soak him in her urine and rub her feces in his hair; sometimes he was a stranger and refused to acknowledge her, denying he had ever been intimate with her. They had both been virgins at the beginning of that summer.

Zachary Mackenzie, expelled from SS *Desolation*, found a berth as an engineer with a small shipping line. He was efficient with the crew, but in the officer's mess, his fellow officers did not know what to think of him. His words were often a camouflage he used to obscure his meaning. This opaqueness irritated some but was oddly comforting to others. On voyages, he was an avid reader, a journal-keeper. He met the rest of his family only once, after leaving the orphanage.

Notebook, A. McGaw

1

Around midnight the following night, I was in such a deep sleep that Helen had to wake me to answer the phone in the study next door to our bedroom. I was in the middle of a confusing dream in which I was at a party with some friends, but none of them seemed to know who I was, and when I tried to talk to them, to ask what was the matter, I could not hear my own voice.

I stumbled into the study to answer the phone, still half in that dream. Vaguely I noticed that the night was dark, and it must have been raining, for I could hear the occasional hiss of a passing car on the road outside. I picked up the phone.

"Hello?" What a relief. I could hear myself. The dream was over.

"Ezra, sorry to disturb you. This is Donald Cromarty speaking."

The soft Highland voice. I should have been surprised, but I was not, so I had to make myself sound surprised.

"Cromarty! How are you?"

For a while, we bartered long-distance courtesies, till he got round to telling me why he had phoned.

"It's about the four Mackenzies."

As though it could have been about anything else. I waited politely for him to go on.

"I've found a man with information on the eldest one, Zachary. I can't get him to tell me anything, but he's genuine. He knew the names of all four. He said Isabel Jaggard told him to get in touch with me. You won't know her, but she was prominent here at one time. That's all he'd tell me. He said he'd talk to both of us together, or not at all. So it's up to you. Can you get away?"

$$\overline{2}$$

The plane circled over the airport at nine in the morning. We had been travelling for hours, at thirty thousand feet, through an endless desert of detergent suds. But as the plane descended, it was suddenly at the underbelly of a dark monster that suckled, from its gloomy udders, the blunt, green hills of the land below. We landed unobtrusively and skulked along the runway to our refuge near the comforting lights of the terminal.

Enter, at last, Donald Cromarty!

He was waiting at Arrivals. He was an easy man to spot. Tall, stooped, his face a pitted battlefield from a childhood war with smallpox. His hair, I noticed, now lay in wisps across his head, and that suited him. His whole body, in fact, had at last caught up with a mind that had matured long before. The cautious smile, the soft voice remained the same. I told him it was good to see him after all these years. We greeted each other, and, if I had not noticed a hardness in his green eyes that was new to me, I might actually have felt comforted, I might even have felt at home.

3

We drove east towards the capital in his old Mercedes, passing through the dirty towns of the industrial wasteland. The highway was excellent, an expensive chain looping together a score of coal-cinders. We talked, and the journey passed quickly.

Cromarty told me how he had set out, so many months ago, to make inquiries about the Mackenzies. I had guessed right about the dead ends he had run into: archives incinerated in wartime bombing raids; the depopulation of the western islands, so that witnesses were impossible to find; the problem of pinpointing which one of several islands suited the needs of my grandfather Daniel Stevenson's story.

But what most frustrated Cromarty was the lack of any written reference to the alleged crime. He found it hard to accept that the press had ever been *that* discreet. He had checked out Mackenzies of every sort. He had speculated, on the basis of what I'd told him, that Zachary, with his notebooks and his liking for story-telling, might even have turned in the end to writing as a career. Cromarty had inquired into the lives of at least five hundred writing Mackenzies, in vain.

The break came when he decided to use, for his own ends, the very medium that had thwarted him. He placed a notice in *The Northern News*. His message was clear enough: he wanted to find out about a domestic crime somewhere in the islands about the turn of the century; the name of the family involved was Mackenzie; the father was a doctor, and the four children were called Amos, Rachel, Esther, and Zachary.

The next day, a man telephoned and asked exactly why Cromarty was interested. Cromarty told him about me. The man said his friend Isabel Jaggard had encouraged him to help, but that he was afraid of legal liability, so he needed absolute confidentiality. Cromarty knew who Isabel Jaggard was, gave the assurances, and arranged the meeting to which we were now on our way.

I, in turn, told Cromarty about my trip south, my discovery of Esther Mackenzie, and my certainty that she and Amos and Rachel were the Patagonian Mackenzies.

Cromarty shook his head when I had finished. He'd never come across such a set of events, he said, with so many strange interlinkings and coincidences.

Cromarty was certainly not the type to balk at the strange. He was the historian who had found proof of the existence, several centuries ago, of a group of hitherto unknown hermit monks who had lived out their perverse sanctity (they mutilated their bodies as part of their spiritual journey) on the islands off the west coast. That piece of scholarly detective work had gained him international prestige.

So when he said he was troubled, I felt uncomfortable, as though I needed to justify myself. I kept quiet, but I was afraid he doubted the truth of what I'd told him, from the start. It ran through my head that perhaps he didn't even believe I'd heard the story from Daniel Stevenson. I hoped that now he had uncovered someone else who knew about Zachary Mackenzie, he might be convinced I had not been making things up.

As though he could read my mind, Cromarty insisted that he intended to unravel the Mackenzie mystery, "no matter where it may lead." He said this several times, glancing at me. I kept my misgivings, and my reasons for them, to myself.

After about an hour, we arrived earlier than we had expected, in the capital. I booked into a small hotel off Duchess Street, and told him I'd like to stretch out for a few hours. I was tired after the rigours of a sleepless night-flight. Cromarty said he would be happy to pass away the hours before our meeting browsing in the various bookstores around the city.

4

I rested well, and, round six o'clock, Cromarty and I hurried down to the meeting place, a bar just a few blocks away. We hurried, for it was the middle of November, pitch dark, and a chill wind from the nearby Firth was funnelling its familiar, squally rain, into the city. Austerity in all things, it howled.

We were happy to get inside the doors of The Last Minstrel. Through a haze of cigarette and pipe smoke, I looked around. It was a respectable bar, one wall bristling with dusty claymores and targes on a tartan cloth whose veins seemed to have been bled, long ago, by a handful of rusty skean-dhus. On another wall, a dozen brown portraits looked out at us. They might have been the ancestors of the handful of gloomy customers (none of them women) who sat at plastic tables along the walls.

But the place was warm, at least. Cromarty and I went to one of the corner tables and began to thaw our chilled bones with lukewarm whisky. We had just settled down, when the door opened, allowing the cold air a vindictive foray. The cause of the draught was the entry of a very elderly man and woman. He was wearing a tweed coat, and the woman was dressed in black. She was white haired and white faced, and wore sun-glasses. The man was reddish and stocky for his age. He looked around, saw us looking at him, and, taking a firm grip on the old woman's elbow, as though he had done it often before, led her towards our table.

"Professor?" he said.

Cromarty rose, and the man spoke again, in a throaty voice.

"My name is Gib Douglas, I talked to you on the phone. This is Isabel Jaggard."

Cromarty introduced me. The old woman, Isabel Jaggard, said nothing, did not extend her hand to us, nor did she see our hands. She was blind. Gib Douglas helped her into a chair, in that familiar way, and we all sat down. Cromarty and I felt a little awkward at her silence. But she continued to say nothing. She just sat, gathering herself, slightly out of breath. Her white face was pinched from the cold night air. I couldn't help noticing her lips, how red they were, red as a healthy child's, at odds with the rest of her old woman's face. The rain had pimpled her dark glasses: naturally, she did not wipe them.

Gib Douglas went to the bar for drinks, then sat beside me. He looked like a man of action gone to seed, yet somehow too jumpy for an ex-soldier or an ex-policeman. He was clearly not happy about being with us. He drank a whisky down with hands that had a molten appearance to them. They guided Isabel Jaggard's hand to the glass of port she had asked for, and she picked it up and sipped at it slowly. He lit a cigarette for himself as she began to talk in a deep contralto voice, with only a slight tremor of age in it.

She wanted to ask me some questions. Who was I exactly? Why did I have such an interest in the Mackenzie family? What would I do with the information if I got it?

What did I already know about Zachary Mackenzie? Or think I knew?

This brief litany of questions flowed from a mouth that did not match the wilting face. I was so entranced by her mouth that I hardly noticed when it was no longer moving. Till she took off her dark galsses and laid them clumsily on the table. Her eyes were white, bulging, the dead irises staring outwards towards her left and right sides, like a rabbit's eyes.

I briefly told her everything I thought she should know, about how as a boy I had heard the story of the Mackenzies first from my grandfather, Daniel Stevenson; and how, as I grew up, I came to presume it was nothing but a story. Till I met Doctor Yerdeli at the Institute for the Lost, and she mentioned the name Amos Mackenzie, and told me about his fate. And that made me wonder, and I decided to enlist the help of Cromarty.

Cromarty had heard all this before, but he was listening and was watching me just the same. Gib Douglas just went on looking nervous, drinking and smoking, building himself up for something unpleasant. I do not know what Isabel Jaggard thought of my story. Her white face and blind eyes no longer served as a means of expression. But her head was cocked to one side while I talked, which I guessed was a sign she was interested.

I told her about my more recent discoveries of two other Mackenzies, Rachel and Esther, who certainly had the right names and might be from the same family. And I told her how they died. Once or twice, when I paused, she would shake her head.

"Is that so? Is that so?"

When I had said everything I had to say, Isabel Jaggard pursed those lips that looked sometimes to me like twin bloodsuckers wriggling in the middle of a dead face. She spoke again.

"Professor Cromarty's work is well known. Even though I can't read any more, I am read to, daily. Isn't that so, Gib?"

The question slid sensually through her lips.

"When I heard," she said, "that the professor was making inquiries about the Mackenzie family, I thought maybe it was time to clear the air, before all those who knew were dead."

So she advised Gib Douglas to respond to the advertisement, and found out that I was at the root of it. She aimed the words in my direction:

"I knew you had to be here when the truth was told," she said. I felt uncomfortable, for Cromarty was watching me. But she continued:

"I've never talked about any of this before, except to Gib. I persuaded him it wouldn't be a bad thing to put the facts in the hands of people who wouldn't exploit them for the wrong reasons."

I had no idea what the wrong reasons might be, or the right ones, for that matter. But I asked her, please, to proceed.

"Years ago," she said, "I was a publisher in this city. During the lifetime when I could still see."

That blank face was incapable of showing bitterness.

"I still think of myself as looking the way I looked then. My hair was brown, and my eyes were green. Gib

occasionally tells me how I look now, don't you Gib?
That's one advantage of blindness. You can't see yourself
getting old. You can't see somebody else's disgust."

Her lips were juicily red as she said that. Gib Douglas
glanced at her, but I could not tell what he was
thinking.

"Someone in my family has been in the publishing
business somewhere since the sixteenth century. I tried to
keep the tradition going. I inherited some money, and
started a small publishing house here. I knew it would
never make me rich. Money down the drain, that's what
they said. It's true, any publisher will tell you that."

I noticed her voice was a little less deep, a little lighter
when she spoke about those early days, about the time
when she wasn't long out of university and was trying to
get the business started, hunting everywhere for good
manuscripts to publish. She remembered the morning a
man came through her office door on High Street. He was
a tall, thin-faced man of about fifty, and he had a brown
envelope with him, containing his manuscript. He told
her he'd been writing on and off for twenty years, ever
since he retired from the sea, that he'd been a ship's
engineer for years. He'd had no luck having anything
published.

He said his name was Zachary Mackenzie.

"I told him I was willing to take a look at his
manuscript, but I wouldn't make any promises. I said I'd
be in touch with him. And he left."

Cromarty and I sat in that cheerless bar and waited
while the hands of Gib Douglas closed Isabel Jaggard's
fingers, caressingly, round her glass of port. Cromarty

watched silently, and I wondered what he was thinking. Here was solid, eye-witness (she could see then) proof that at least one Mackenzie, Zachary, had existed. Perhaps still did. Cromarty did not look at me.

Isabel Jaggard was in no rush. She was composing the order of events, this being her first telling of the story. Her rabbit eyes seemed to assess her flanks and find nothing to worry about. She breathed deeply and went on to tell us how she took Zachary Mackenzie's manuscript home with her that night and read it over.

5

She saw immediately it was no best-seller. The novel, entitled *The Cells*, was a brief, turgid account of life in a penal colony. The language was archaic and the characters quite unbelievable: a man, for instance, who had planted a forest of artificial trees; a witch who had vomited up all kinds of things, including books and pistols; a mayoress who had encouraged her citizens to exchange their identities with each other, whenever they felt the need, till they forgot who they orginally were; a prison warden who was no less eccentric than the prisoners.

Even if the novel had some merit, Isabel Jaggard was

well aware that the times were not right for it. The Great Depression was not long past. But more important, the nationalist movement was in full swing. People were in the mood for books that encouraged optimism and patriotism, not for obscure fantasies such as *The Cells*.

Yet there was something Isabel Jaggard liked about the book, she was not sure why. So, even though her fledgling business sense winced at her recklessness, something she liked to think of as the mature, aesthetic part of her goaded her on to publish it.

Even in those early days, she always made a principle of getting to know her authors intimately. Accordingly, she met Zachary Mackenzie several times on the understanding that the manuscript was not to be mentioned. It was only after a while, when she knew him better and was satisfied with his potential, that she arranged to meet him at her office and told him her official decision to publish his novel. The man was elated. She tried to warn him against great expectations. She said:

"Zachary, in all honesty, this is hardly a novel. It's really just a group of short stories loosely tied together."

She was surprised at how quick he was to defend himself. He said: "That's what life is, anyway: a handful of short stories pretending to be a novel."

When she asked him for a few more facts about his background for publicity, he became very reluctant to talk. In spite of how often she had met him, how well she knew him, he had not been willing to tell much about his earlier life. All she was able to get out of him was that there had been a tragedy in his family, and that he and his sisters and brother were sent to orphanages, and that he had ended up as an engineer on various merchant ships.

Then he had looked at her with his milky blue eyes and made a special plea. He had said he would take it as a great favour if she would abstain from using any of the vague information he had given her. Because he did not want his book published under his own name. His own name was one he preferred to forget. He would like to use the pseudonym, "Archie McGaw".

At the time, Isabel Jaggard was surprised, and thought the name a little peculiar. But she could see no real objection, so long as he would continue to publish under the name of Archie McGaw. He promised he would.

In the next few years she published three of his novels, *The Cells*, *Captain Jack*, and *The Feast*, none of them very successful. But the nationalists had taken notice of Archie McGaw. They picked on him, time and time again, denouncing his books for being irrelevant, and gloomy.

Isabel Jaggard advised him to do what others in his shoes had done, and pay no attention. She told him these kinds of political movements depended upon order and conformity. That they were the antithesis of life and art. But he wouldn't keep quiet. That stubborness was a side of him she had noticed whenever she tried to make editorial changes to his books. So, with the nationalists, he did the worst possible thing. He wrote letters to all the newspapers and to the major literary magazine,

The Homeland, pleading for tolerance and fairness. That just seemed to stir up even more hostility towards him. The editor of *The Homeland*, a man named Angus Cameron, never missed a chance after that to make unkind remarks about Archie McGaw.

But a most extraordinary thing happened. His most recent novel, *The Feast*, and then his previous two started to sell, really sell. Isabel Jaggard couldn't keep up with the demand. Every bookstore in the area was requesting fresh supplies, daily, of anything by Archie McGaw. His books had been gathering dust in her warehouse, so she was delighted to see them go. By the end of one single week, they were all gone, and she began making plans for second printings. It looked as though the career of Archie McGaw was at last taking off.

6

Now Isabel Jaggard turned to Gib Douglas, who was sitting there, looking more nervous than ever, in spite of all the whisky. Her deep voice took on a wheedling tone. She told him she knew it was hard for him, but he should tell his story now and get it over with. He went to get himself another drink first.

Donald Cromarty at last spoke. "Now I know why I couldn't find a reference to any Zachary Mackenzie in the library holdings. I should have thought of the possibility of a pseudonym."

I myself took advantage of the delay to ask her some questions.

"Did Zachary ever mention his trip to Patagonia?"

"I don't remember, he may have. He had been in so many places."

"Did he ever say anything explicitly about his family or the murder of his mother?"

"No."

Gib Douglas came back to the table with his drink.

"Maybe we should let Gib tell what he knows," Isabel Jaggard said. "And while he's talking, I'll try and think of anything else that might be of interest to you.

Gib Douglas rumbled, drank the whisky down, and inhaled deeply from his cigarette. He looked at Isabel Jaggard, then at the backs of his hands, and he was ready. He began to speak in his throaty voice.

7

"I was a student, back then, and I joined the nationalists. We talked a lot, that was all, and painted slogans on the walls of the railway stations. But it was more exciting than sitting at lectures."

Gib Douglas laughed the nervous laugh of a man who's on his way to telling something that won't be very funny. His hand, the one holding the cigarette, was trembling, and he noticed and wished that it wouldn't. Isabel Jaggard was listening to him with her head tilted. Her red lips were slightly apart.

"We were told to kidnap Archie McGaw (that was the only name I knew him by). As a kind of practical joke. I'd never even read any of his books. Angus Cameron was in charge of our group, and he hated McGaw's guts. That was good enough for us. I volunteered to help with the kidnapping, for the fun of it.

"We drove over to McGaw's place around midnight on a July night. He lived up one of the closes in the Old Town. There was nobody around at that time of night, but we were scared."

The telling of his story changed Gib Douglas. He himself was only a word in it, but he wanted the story to be a good setting for that word. He had been nervous and uncertain a few minutes ago. Now he was engrossed in his narrative, manipulating it, trying to make it effective and memorable, glancing at Isabel Jaggard, his real audience, anxious to satisfy her.

"We sneaked up the close stairs and pried open McGaw's door. It was only a one-room flat, and he was lying there on the bed. We just went over and grabbed him. I saw right away he was wide awake, but he didn't try to get away or shout for help. He just lay there, terrified, looking up at us. He was alone in bed . . ."

8

... he was alone in bed, as he had been for years now. He was afraid, but not very much, when the two men wearing wool masks bent over him. But he thought it would be wiser to look terrified, so he did. He could tell from their movements they were young. He would have liked to put his housecoat on over his pyjamas when he realized they were going to take him away, but they tied his hands behind him with a piece of electrical wire. He would have liked to ask them why they wanted him. But the square of sticking plaster they had stretched over his mouth stopped his lips from moving and made his words a groan.

One of the masks, a stockily built young man, spoke in a throaty whisper.

"Shut up! Or I'll shut you up."

They shuffled him downstairs, his legs not quite awake yet, his bare feet tender on the cold paving, and pushed him into the back of a car. It was an old, black car with torn leather seats. It lurched forward and began to chew up, with uneven gulps, the deserted cobble-stone streets of the city, then it drank down smoothly the black-tops of the country roads to the south.

He was only a little afraid, so he was able to consider everything quite calmly. He knew they must be nationalists. Did they really think anyone would pay money for his release? He couldn't believe they were that misguided. Perhaps the recent, unexpected popularity of his books had made him worth kidnapping, for some symbolic reason. Because he was only slightly afraid, he allowed himself to think: what an irony, what an unintended compliment, if, after all the abuse they'd lumped on him, he was now successful enough for them to want to kidnap him!

About twenty miles south of the city, whenever the moon broke through the high clouds, he could make out, through the car window, stunted hills that protruded from the landscape like the burial mounds of mountains. They were the kinds of hills he liked to set his novels among. This was the country, and because he was only a little afraid, he felt more and more at home. The car slowed, swerved onto a dirt road that wasn't much more than a scar on a hillside, and jolted along for a mile or two. It stopped beside a fieldstone dike with an opening in it. Silence.

The shapes of a dozen other parked cars lurked nearby. The stockier of his two kidnappers opened the back door.

"Get out!"

He stumbled out, feeling his age, his bare feet revolting at every prickle and stone. The man prodded him through the opening in the dike, along a winding sheep-path in a field, and up a rise. The air was clear and fresh. He could smell heather and smoke. The moorlands for miles around were playing hide-and-seek with the moon.

For the first time since the two men entered his apartment an hour ago, the thought crossed his mind that perhaps something very unpleasant was going to happen to him. Not that he was any more afraid. Just curious. As he would have been about one of his stories when he had just begun writing it and had no idea what would happen next.

He could see down in the valley, about a hundred yards away, a blazing bonfire and several dozen people milling about. The stocky man began shouting to them, straining his throat.

"Hey! We've got him! We've got him."

The distant faces, dark faces turned towards them descending.

The two men jostled him down to where the group stood silent and still, watching. The fire, like a beacon misplaced in a valley, was huge, the logs on it crackling loudly, the only noise in that cool night. The group were all wearing woollen masks and sometimes the whites of their eyes would catch the fire-light. The stocky man gave him a last push, causing him to sprawl over a mound just a few yards from the fire.

He caught a glimpse of the mound as he fell, just before the acute corners and the ruler-sharp edges confirmed, on his flesh, what he had glimpsed. It was a mound of books. The flat surfaces of some of them supported him comfortingly for a moment, but others made him slide, the harder he tried to stand up to balance himself, his hands still tied behind his back. Then the entire hillock of books opened and half-swallowed him.

His bare toes touched the ground. He got up on his knees and slithered out of the mound, like a creature it had given birth to. On his feet now, he recognized, whenever the flickering light would allow his eyes to focus, that some of the books were his own. He could make out the spines of his latest, *The Feast*. He could see some copies of *Captain Jack* and *The Cells*.

Truth crept up on him in a gentle way at first. Before gathering speed and slamming right into him, making him sob. *All* of the books in that mound were his: *he Fe, ast, in Ja, ell, The C, tain, ack, ie Mc, s Arc, ells Ar, ck Arc, east Ar, Gaw, ack, McGa, ack, ack*. Bits and pieces of his name, his titles, inverted or at awkward angles, but all his. He was full of dread. Where had they all come from, so many? Sick at heart, he understood.

"Yes, they're all yours," said a voice louder than the crackling fire, from the other side of the mound. In spite of the mask, he knew the thin voice of Angus Cameron, the editor of *The Homeland*.

"We bought up every copy. We ordered them from every bookstore in the city. It took us a couple of weeks to get them all. How does it feel to be so popular?"

In the fire's heat, he shivered and looked across the heap of his collected works, not a very large heap. He did not want to hear any more. But Cameron came round to his side of the mound. Through the holes in the mask, he could see those familiar, contemptuous eyes.

"Surely you didn't think anybody in their right mind would want to read this trash? Especially the last one."

He prodded a copy of *The Feast* with his boot, the way a man prods something repulsive, a turd.

"This one was even worse than the others. We had to

spend a lot of money buying them all up, but it was worth it, to save anybody else from having to read them."

The other masks were laughing at him, taunting. He had nothing to say, absolutely nothing. But he heard a noise coming from his sealed mouth, in spite of himself, the sound of all of his words, trapped together, making a single moan.

"We thought you'd like to see how much we value your books," said Cameron.

He signalled to the others (some of whom, from their clothes, their voices, were women). They began picking up armfuls of books from the mound and tossing them into the bonfire.

He watched all this, as though in a dream the books flapping their covers uselessly like crippled birds, exploding in the fire, sending up flares into the night air, in vain, for there was no one to rescue them. He watched the burning of his books, just tarted-up firewood, after all. The waves of heat billowed towards him, the acrid smoke blew back in his face, stinging his eyes and nose. The fire crackled and the stokers laboured. Till all the fuel was gone, and they stood enjoying the blaze.

As he ran forward, he saw for a moment another fire long ago, amongst hills just like these, a ring of men gathered around it, all dead men now, nothing of them remaining any more. He ran and jumped with all his strength into the heat and the noise, pumping his knees, running up the hill of fire, feeling nothing, till suddenly the flames were scalpels slicing at his white bare feet, and his legs, and his white belly, and his face, and most horrifying of all, his hands still tied behind him. But he did not scream as his own words devoured him cannibalizing their maker, devouring themselves too, though some of them rose again, not phoenixes, just wisps of ashy paper, floating off, disintegrating in the darkness, and in the night air.

9

Gib Douglas rested his head in his molten hands for a moment, and breathed deeply. But he was not finished.

Archie McGaw, he said, jumping into the fire, carried with him the youth of most of those who watched him. They stood paralysed. Gib Douglas and his partner tried to go in after McGaw, but those thousands of books burnt so fiercely, they could not penetrate the borders of the fire. So they raked at the blaze with long pieces of lumber, hoping somehow to snare his body. But it was no use. They could only watch him in there among his books, burning. Above the crackle of the fire, they could hear his body sizzling, they could see the flames shoot upwards, feasting on his melting flesh. Gib Douglas, in desperation, reached in and gripped one of the legs, but to the horror of everyone, the foot tore off at the ankle when he pulled.

By the time they did get Archie McGaw out, he was nothing but a charred carcass, with the ends of some bones protruding. They left him out there on the moors, beside the remains of the fire, and drove home, silent (Angus Cameron had not said a word since McGaw jumped into the fire). A few days later, a shepherd saw his collie sniffing at the blackened lump beside the ashes, and called the police.

The body was never identified. The investigation was not very thorough, perhaps because the police quickly found out that the sons and daughters of some very influential people were involved. In the end, the coroner said that the death was most likely a suicide, though the fire seemed extravagant, and there were signs a number of people had stood by. The newspapers said little about the affair, for that was a time when much more momentous events were happening throughout Europe. So Archie McGaw's death passed unnoticed as his literary career.

But, Gib Douglas said, nothing was ever the same after that. He and some of his friends were finished with the nationalists, or any other party for that matter. He spent a week in hospital with badly burnt hands. But even thirty years had not healed the real wound. Angus Cameron, in time, recovered his nerve and tried to coax Gib and the others to rejoin the movement. A tender heart, he said, is a luxury no true patriot can afford.

10

Gib Douglas was done with his story. He had never before told anyone except Isabel Jaggard what he knew about the death of Archie McGaw. He had tried for years not even to think about it. He drank down another quick whisky. He looked towards Isabel Jaggard. Could they go now?

No. First, she wanted us to know that it wasn't till a month after the burning, when she tried to get in touch with Zachary Mackenzie, that she realized he was missing. It had crossed her mind the burnt body on the moors might be his, but she kept her suspicions to herself.

"Everybody knew the nationalists had something to do with it. So I let it go. At that time, you didn't know who you could trust. I never heard the truth till Gib told me. By then, who cared about Zachary Mackenzie or Angus Cameron or the body on the moors?"

I wanted Gib Douglas to tell me something.

"Do you know whether he had a scar on his abdomen?"

He looked at me for a moment, then turned his eyes towards Isabel Jaggard. She could not see what we could see, the bitterness in his face.

"I'm not the one you should ask," he said.

Isabel Jaggard's impenetrable eyes rolled. Gib Douglas

stood up, buttoned his coat, and moved round to help her out of her chair.

But when she felt his hand on her arm, she told him to wait a minute. She said something had just come back to her. She had thought of it earlier, when I told them my grandfather Daniel Stevenson's story. And just now, when I asked Gib Douglas about the scar, she thought of it again. On the day she told Zachary Mackenzie she wanted to publish his first book, when he asked if he could use the name Archie McGaw instead, she had asked him why he didn't want to use his own name. He said, as far as he was concerned, his real name, Zachary Mackenzie, would be like a scar on the belly of his book.

"That was exactly what he said: 'a scar on its belly.' " Her eyes were bulging more than usual and her lips were wet with the phrase.

"At the time, I said to him, what a strange notion. He said it might seem strange to me, but there were other people who wouldn't think it was so strange." Gib Douglas helped her to her feet, and they moved towards the door. As they were leaving The Last Minstrel, just an old couple again, she called out that I should visit her next morning, and she would pass on to me whatever relics of Zachary Mackenzie were left in her files. She was certain she had at least a photograph.

11

Gib Douglas pushed the door open, letting them out and a scouring draught in. The brown portraits looked down their disapproval of Cromarty and me for staying on for a last drink. Cromarty had been so quiet, I felt I must talk.

"What a horrible fate," I said.

"Whose?" he asked. Taking me by surprise.

"Well, Zachary Mackenzie's."

"Quite."

He was silent. So for want of anything better to say, I asked: "Do you think Isabel Jaggard and Zachary Mackenzie were lovers? The way Gib Douglas looked at her, when I asked about the scar."

Cromarty, half-quizzical, inspected my face.

"What difference does it make?"

I was going to ask what exactly he meant by that. In fact, I was going to ask him what was going on in his head, his whole attitude was so strange. And perhaps I would have. But he had made up his mind now to talk, or at least to ask some questions, and he began asking them.

"Let me get this straight. You say that Zachary Mackenzie met your grandfather, Daniel Stevenson, years ago in Patagonia?"

"Yes."

"And he told your grandfather the story of a murder

and its effects on four children, one of them being himself?"

"Yes."

"And your grandfather, in turn, told the story to you?"

I agreed.

"And it looks now as though all four Mackenzie children died violent or abnormal deaths?"

"Yes, I suppose it does."

"And you found out about all of these deaths in the course of just the past few months?"

Again, I agreed.

He stopped, as if running my answers over in his head. His eyes, I felt, were not friendly, and I was nervous under their scrutiny. He said:

"I'm sure you would agree with me that certain things are puzzling. Principally the fact that in spite of all we've found out about the four children, it hasn't been possible to find any evidence whatever of the original crime?"

I agreed. What else could I do?

"Finally, you would concur that in the case of all four children, no one has been able to attest to the presence of scars on their abdomens?"

I could hardly disagree with that. In fact, I might have asked him, haven't I been the one who put the question in all four cases? But I was busy steeling myself for his next logical question.

To my relief, he did not ask it. The interrogation was over.

Still, I had not much liked being subjected to his

cross-examination, so I asked him if he was implying something by it.

"No, I am implying nothing," he said. His voice was calm, and he was choosing his words carefully. He said there was really no need to imply anything any more. The truth was almost apparent to him, and would be to me, too, if I were to examine the facts carefully.

"The truth will out," he said.

I told him, without hesitation, that I had no idea what he meant. He said that was a pity, and he stood up. It was time for him to go, for he had to drive back west.

We went outside into the rain, but that was better than sitting under those scowling portraits on the wall of The Last Minstrel. We walked in the downpour to where his old Mercedes was parked, in a lane near my hotel.

We shook hands, He said he'd enjoyed my visit and the meeting with Isabel Jaggard and Gib Douglas. I tried my best to read his face in the street lights. But the rain was filling in his pock-marks, giving him the smooth face of a stranger. I promised I'd write him when I got back home, if I found anything of interest in Isabel Jaggard's files. As he slid into the car, he said one last thing.

"I think everything will be settled quite soon."

His familiar face, now that he was out of the rain, had reappeared. He smiled, and nodded, pulled the car door shut, and drove away. As his car receded along the street, my peace of mind returned from its hiding place.

PART SIX

THE PARADISE MOTEL

1

The next morning, I got up early, breakfasted, then walked under a low, grey sky to Isabel Jaggard's house, one of those respectable old terrace houses with exteriors modest enough not to stir up too much envy. Gib Douglas opened the door. He had the sour look of a man with a hangover confronting the dog that bit him. He led me into a sombre, mahogany-panelled parlour where Isabel Jaggard, in her dark glasses, was sitting on a couch in front of a fire. The yellow brocade curtains were drawn back, and so was the neck of her housecoat, enough to give a glimpse of a thin pair of breasts. She patted the couch for me to sit beside her. I noticed, as I sat down, a faint odour, neither pleasant nor unpleasant, coming from her.

She said Gib had searched around amongst the boxes in the attic and had found, as she knew he would, the old Archie McGaw file. The cardboard file-folder lay on a small rectangular table beside the couch. I had noticed the table when I came in, because its shape and the brass handles that adorned it gave it the appearance of a child's coffin. She told me to take a look inside the folder, and I did. It contained two large, unsealed manila envelopes. I opened the thinner of the two, and slid out an enlarged photograph, a little brown on the edges (it must have been half a century old) but very professional looking.

"Is that the picture?" she asked.

"Yes."

2

Two young men flank two young women standing on a
Persian rug in front of a blank white wall. The wall might
be in a studio, or a restaurant, or a theatre. On the left of
the picture, the one who seems slightly the elder of the
two men stands wearing a high-collared uniform. He is
tall and thin-faced, with a drooping moustache. His
eyelids are narrow, his eyes barely visible. His bent right
arm ends abruptly at a white shirt-cuff by the jacket
pocket. On the other side of the picture, the younger man
stands. He is wearing a dress-suit, a bow tie, and spats. He
too is thin-faced, but with large, sad eyes and unruly hair.
His left hand rests on the stem of a rubber-plant beside
him. In spite of their formal pose, the two men are
deliberately not looking at the camera. Next to the
younger man, not touching him (there is a space between
each of the four), stands the younger woman. She is
fair-haired and slight. She wears a long coat with a fur
trim at the collar. She is watching, fascinated, something
not in the picture. The other woman, beside her, is the
only one watching the camera. She is solidly built, with a
square face and dark hair. She wears a dark suit, and a fur
stole fastened by a long, ornamental pin. The four might
be friends posing successfully as strangers, or strangers
posing unsuccessfully as friends.

3

Isabel Jaggard groped for my leg, bending far enough in my direction to reveal those thin breasts even more. The smell she gave off was slightly musky. She hoped the photograph was helpful, and was so sorry she couldn't give me copies of Mackenzie's novels. Gib Douglas had not been able to find any, though she was sure she had them in a box somewhere. She cocked her head, and I saw him enter the room from another door. He did not say anything, but came over and stood by the fire, examining his hands. Isabel Jaggard, kneading my thigh, said that if I looked hard enough, one or two of the novels might still be found in used-book stores.

The other envelope, she said, contained a manuscript Zachary Mackenzie had given her just a week before his disappearance. I was welcome to it. It wasn't a completed work, just some journal notes Zachary Mackenzie said he'd made when he was at sea.

I accepted the two envelopes with thanks. She was feeling around for my hand, so I clasped hers. How warm it was, how moist, despite the wrinkled skin. Her lips were red and wet. Because of the way she had twisted herself, her robe had opened at her thighs, and I could see wiry legs and a wisp of steel-grey pubic hair. The dark plastic of her glasses threw back twin distorted reflections of myself. They also reflected two Gib Douglases watching. I quickly withdrew my hand from hers, stood up, said goodbye, and went to the door. I noticed, in the hallway, a large framed black and white photograph of a striking woman with fine features, noticeable eyes, and slightly pouted lips. Of course. Isabel Jaggard, as she must once have looked.

When that heavy wooden door closed softly behind me, I stopped on the top step to turn up my collar, for it was very cold, as though there might even be snow. That was when, I could swear, I heard singing coming from inside the house. I may have been wrong, for a car was going past at that moment. But if Gib Douglas and Isabel Jaggard were capable of singing, I think that is how they would have sounded: a contralto and a throaty bass in a sinister duet. I strained my ears to hear the sound again. Nothing. I took a deep breath of the cold air, then with the envelopes under my arm, I started down the tunnel of grey light that was the street.

4

It never did snow that day. I spent much of the time walking, shopping for a gift for Helen (I found one in a little antique shop, a sixteenth-century anthology of poems, entitled, simply, *Poemes*, with an inscription in fading ink on the inside cover: "I am not I: pity the tale of me"). I climbed the hill to the squat castle and looked out from the ramparts down at the huddled city. The clouds, the trees, the chimney smoke made visible the stinging wind from the Firth.

I must have walked for hours that afternoon. By eight o'clock, I was feeling hungry, for I had not eaten since breakfast. I found a pub, a cheerful-looking one (no sad portraits on the walls), and ate a pub dinner: a pint of beer, a meat pie brimming with peas, and chips. I felt good.

But by the time I got back to the hotel, around ten o'clock, my stomach was a little queasy. Perhaps jet-lag was the cause, or walking too long on an empty stomach, or eating too quickly. I went to bed right away, and tried to force myself to sleep. But the longer I lay there, the worse I felt: a pain was developing that made me feel too sick even to take a sip of water.

Around two in the morning, the pain was very bad. I probed around my stomach lightly with my fingertips in the area of the appendix. Nothing. But, just below the navel, my fingers brushed against something. I switched on the lamp. Yes, there it was. A protrusion, an angular sort of protrusion right in the middle of my belly, a place where no angles should exist, straining against the flesh. My god. I tried not to panic. But as I looked, I could swear I saw the thing move.

Sick with fear, I phoned the front desk and told the receptionist I needed help.

By the time the hotel porter admitted two ambulance attendants into my room, I had already vomited a mixture of meat pie and blood onto the linoleum floor. The ambulance men loaded me, slightly feverish but still aware of everything, onto a stretcher and wheeled me along the spongy carpeted corridor into the elevator with its aura of dead cigarettes; then through the door of the hotel, into the chill.

The ride in the ambulance must have been only a few minutes, but it was an eternity of pain and fear. I was certain I could feel the thing moving around in my belly, making itself intimate with the raw inside of my body.

As they lifted me out of the ambulance and wheeled me into Emergency, each jolt forced a scream out of me. My belly was about to explode. I could see a haze of white and green shapes, I could feel fingers touching me, I could hear soothing voices and questions I could not answer, for fear my words would turn into vomit. Once or twice, I heard a deep male voice.

"We'll need consent."

And the same voice again, later, deeper still.

"If we don't go ahead, he'll die on us."

Then I was gliding along endless white corridors, with a white figure on either side of me, holding my hands, or holding me down, I could not be sure which.

5

He is lying on a cool table, an aureole of light above him. He tries to focus his eyes, and sees green figures and white figures gathered around him. One of them pricks his arm with a giant needle, all the time murmuring: "Breathe easily, just breathe easily, and let yourself go."

And he wants, desperately, to go, but he cannot. Part of him lies inside a soft cloud, part of him remains outside of it, awake, alert.

The voice murmurs to the others.

"You can proceed now."

He wants to shout: "No, not yet. Please, not yet. I'm still awake."

But his lips are paralysed, his limbs are dead, so he can make no movement or noise.

They are in a circle around him, gazing down on him as the scalpel slices through his flesh and his muscles. He feels the cold air of the room rush into the gash that has been opened in him, he feels it pour into him like water into a sinking ship. His blood, loving the knife, surges through his veins towards the opening, dragging the pain behind it. The light above him is wheeling round like a sun gone mad. Green figures, white figures, lights, words, the whole universe is wheeling around in the gravitation of his agony.

Then it stops wheeling, abruptly. He hears a deeper voice.

"What in the name of god is this?"

He struggles again to focus his eyes on a green shape crouched over him. He feels a tugging in the cavity in his body, he feels something sliding out, dragging against the raw organs. Through his bleary, slitted eyes, he sees the figure in green holding something up, displaying it in the still whiteness of the room.

He desperately blinks his eyes to see what those gathered around the table see. The figure in green is holding up, in a pair of calipers, a roll of parchment, dripping blood and pus. The hands that begin carefully to unfurl the parchment are dripping blood and pus too. The deep voice begins reading.

"They were sitting round the fire in the Patagonian darkness, telling stories, as they had done every night all through the voyage south . . ."

The deep voice reads on for a while. Then another voice, a woman's contralto voice, takes up the reading. And after a while, another voice, a soft male northern voice, reads, then another voice, voice after voice, throaty or slurred, sometimes silvery, sometimes with a foreign accent, in all ranges and tones, till the last voice, the deep voice again.

". . . The resident had snared in the calipers a severed human hand, dripping blood and pus. He was holding it by its thumb, and they could all see, quite clearly, the gold wedding ring on its middle finger and the scarlet polish on the long fingernails."

There is a long silence around the table. He struggles

with his paralysis. He tries desperately to say something, to let them know the truth. But he cannot move, he is a prisoner, bound by his own sinews and ligaments. The deep voice speaks again, pronouncing, as he had feared, his sentence.

"This is a monster. Let us put the parchment back inside him, and leave them together to rot."

All the figures assembled round that table nod their solemn assent. No one speaks up for him, asks for mercy. He would weep for his own loneliness, for the world's hatred of him. But he has no tears. He sees with what grim energy they bend over him, to finish their task. He tries again to focus his eyes. That hand reaching into him, is it scarred with burn marks? That face looking down at him, does it wear dark glasses, are those lips coloured a violent red? He makes one final effort to summon all his strength. He must explain to them, they must understand. At last, the word that will tell them everything explodes from him.

"NOOOOO!"

6

My own shout woke me up, the echoes of it still vibrating around the room. I was in a cold sweat, my heart trying to tear a hole in my chest. I was embarrassed, thinking I must have wakened the whole hotel. Yet, I could have laughed at the absurdity of my nightmare.

I did what I should have done before going to bed. I switched on the lamp and got out of bed, onto the cold linoleum floor, regretting my lack of pyjamas (I did take a glance at my belly, just to reassure myself. No, no angular protrusions, no scars). I tiptoed across the room to the upright mahogany coffin that passed as a wardrobe. I swung open the door, and saw the tops of the manila envelopes peeping out of the slit of pocket.

I took the thicker envelope back to bed, and sat with a blanket wrapped around my shoulders. The envelope smelt of the dust of the accumulated years. I pulled out the manuscript, only ten pages or so, fastened together with an old-fashioned wire paper-clip. The paper was of poor quality and a little faded. The title page read:

Notebook, A. McGaw

I turned to the opening page and began to read.

I don't know what I expected, really. Some kind of revelation, perhaps, a key to the mystery of Zachary and all the other Mackenzies. And at first glance, I thought I might have found what I had been looking for. The notes were about the Mackenzies. But a brief glance through them showed they would be of little help. They made no mention of the murder, or its effects on the children. The fact is, they were more like preliminary notes for fictional characters than coherent descriptions of real people. I tried to read the four sketches again, but I couldn't, this time, get past even the first lines: "At the age of eight Amos Mackenzie was consigned to 'The Abbey,' a home for waifs and strays ..." My eyes wouldn't stay open. The prose of Zachary Mackenzie was a splendid antidote to insomnia.

I laid the pages on the bedside table, switched off the lamp, snuggled back into the rough womb of hotel blankets. I yawned the requisite number of yawns and, this time, so far as I remember, slept my usual, preferred, dreamless sleep.

7

Home again, and Helen was happy with her gift, especially with the inscription at the front. She would quote it over and over again: "I am not I: pity the tale of me." She showed me, too, what I had not noticed, on the title page of the book: *Printed by Rbt Jaggarde, and are to be soulde at the sign of The Boar, London 1599.* Just such coincidences as this always delighted us.

When we made love that first night back in my apartment, I realized that it was her solidity that I loved so much. To touch her hard nipples, to press the tight coils of her pubic hair, to slide slowly into her, to smell her body was to school myself in the reality of substance. We spoke then our own, intimate language, used a vocabulary that required the intertwining of our tongues.

We lay back, looking out through the picture window at the clear night sky, speculating, as we often did, upon what shapes would appear if we were to connect the star-dots. Could that be the Big Dipper in the north-east? Helen thought it was. I saw only an ornate letter P. Despite our disagreements, we always took comfort in our ignorance, for the sky through this window was *our* sky, no matter how mysterious.

One thing puzzled me. Unlike the previous occasions, Helen had shown hardly any interest in my meeting with Isabel Jaggard and the story of the death of Zachary Mackenzie. I had tried, several times, to give her more details, to expound my theories on Archie McGaw. But she seemed to want to avoid the subject. When I told her about Cromarty's view that he expected soon to resolve the case of the Mackenzie family, she did not show any surprise that I had never told her he was involved. She looked at me as though she had been only half-listening or didn't wish to hear what I was saying. Till she looked at me and said:

"So it won't be long till we all know where we are."

I loved her too much to ask her what she meant. But that night, I decided the time was right for our trip to the Paradise Motel.

8

The Paradise Motel. We always thought of it as our refuge. The building itself was not imposing, a white clapboard structure on the rugged east coast. The owner, a small withdrawn man, trusted us. The maid, a jovial woman, never interrupted us. We invariably took the same room, a plain, white room, with a little balcony looking out to the ocean. Now, in the off-season (we regarded the off-season as our season), when the motel was deserted, all we asked was that our room be warm and clean. We did not need the restaurant. When we wanted to eat, we would drive north into the town, a few miles away. That was the way we preferred it, using the motel as our base.

Winter was well on its way, and we knew it might snow any day. It was a good time for walking along the beach, smelling the cold, salt air, or climbing among the treeless hills of the coast, so like the hills of other places. On the beach, we would often find pieces of flotsam clothed in seaweed so thick we could not tell what was inside. I would slash it open with my knife to reveal the true identities.

On our third morning there, as we were putting on our coats to go for a walk, the phone rang.

"Ezra, sorry to disturb you. This is Donald Cromarty speaking. May I come and see you, right away?"

This time, I was surprised, to say the least, but polite. I asked him where he was calling from. He said he was only half an hour away, down the coast. He didn't want to talk on the phone. What else could I do? I told him, by all means, to come to the hotel as soon as he could.

I could hardly believe he was so near. I had taken comfort in the thought that he, above all, was thousands of miles away. I had told no one else we were at the Paradise Motel. We never told anyone about our visits here. So how could he have tracked me down?

I had no doubt why he wanted to see me. The final resolution. He wanted to present it to me, personally. I tried to take comfort in what one part of my mind was telling me again and again: don't worry, how will he be able to tell the truth and save himself? Surely his desire to survive will keep him quiet?

Helen slipped on her coat to go walking on the beach. She felt it would be better to leave Cromarty and me alone. As she went to the door, I put the sad question to her.

"Did you tell him we were coming to the Paradise Motel?"

And she came to me and kissed me so softly I hardly felt her lips.

"I am not I: pity the tale of me," she said. Or, at least, I think that is what she said, for she spoke so quietly I was not sure of her words. Then she was gone.

9

So Cromarty found me sitting in my room alone, sipping a glass of whisky. Our handshake was only to establish the distance between us. Despite the fact he had come from the sea-air, outside, he brought no odour with him. His face seemed younger to me than when we had last met. That made no difference, for his purpose was old, and deadly. He sat down, unasked.

"Well. It's all over. I can tell you the facts quite simply, now that my inquiries are complete. They are as follows. No expedition ship named the *Mingulay* carried a party to Patagonia, at the turn of the century or any other time. No doctor named Mackenzie murdered his wife. No children named Mackenzie, the offspring of such a doctor, were sent to orphanages. No Holy Order of Correction, as the so-called Archie McGaw names it in his so-called *Notebook*, ever existed."

I might have objected strongly. I might have challenged his version of the facts. I might have suggested that it was surely a little naïve on the part of a scholar such as himself to place such faith in the simple matter of names. I might have asked him how he could possibly know what was in the *Notebook*, when I had not yet sent it to him. But what would have been the use?

"No record exists of a Doctor Yerdeli, or of an Institute for the Lost. Extensive checking has shown that no one with the initials JP was ever the owner of a large newspaper in this country. It has been established that no Pablo Renowsky, ex-boxer or other, ever lived in the town of Xtecal. No such town exists."

I might have said never mind all that. That kind of thing anybody may challenge. But what about Isabel Jaggard? You heard her yourself. Have you no faith even in your own eyes and ears? But common sense is wasted on a man determined to destroy himself.

"No Daniel Stevenson ever worked at a mine in Muirton. Muirton itself does not exist. As for you, Ezra Stevenson, your name is not registered at the university at which you say we were old friends. There are no records anywhere of the people you have called Daniel Stevenson, John and Elizabeth Stevenson, Joanna Stevenson, Isabel Jaggard, Gib Douglas, Angus Cameron, Amos Mackenzie, Rachel Mackenzie, Esther Mackenzie, and Zachary Mackenzie. Absolutely no records. In addition, your reports are a mishmash of anachronisms and impossibilities."

I might have given him one last chance. I might have pleaded outright: But, Cromarty. You yourself were there in The Last Minstrel. You heard, with your own ears, about Zachary Mackenzie, and how he became Archie McGaw, and burned. You were there. I was there.

"No. Whoever you are, I have never met you before in all my life."

I suppose I might still have gone on, looking innocent, denying everything, placing the burden of proof on him.

But I did not. He was the kind of man who was not only

willing to accept the logical consequences of his pedantic notion of truth, but who would insist upon them as his right. And I had known that about him, from the very start. He was waiting for me to ask the question he had been goading me to ask all along, the question that would prove him right.

I had my truth, too, to uphold. So I asked what I had to ask.

"What about you, then, Cromarty? If none of those others exist, if none of those things happened, where does that leave you, my friend?"

Because, all at once, I was sick of the whole thing, weary of keeping company with such demanding, ungrateful people, all of them depending upon me for their lives and their deaths, absorbing me limb by limb, making me feel so insubstantial, I hardly knew if I existed, myself, any more.

10

After Cromarty was gone, I felt like a man ready to begin recovering from a long illness. If only I could have talked to Helen: I needed to tell her how everything ended. If I could have done that, I would have felt better. But I knew she would never come back from her walk. So what was there to do but fill up my glass, and perhaps weep a little (if a man responsible for so much suffering may weep) at the frailty of love.

11

He is dozing, sitting in a wicker chair on a balcony on the Paradise Motel. The squat, clapboard building looks out across a beach onto the North Atlantic Ocean, a grey ocean on a grey day. The man is wearing a heavy tweed overcoat, gloves, and a scarf. When he opens his eyes, as he does from time to time, he can see for miles to where the grey water meets the slightly less grey sky. Today, he thinks, this ocean might easily be a huge handwritten manuscript covered as far as the eye can see with regular lines of neat, cursive writing. At the bottom, near the shore, the lines are clearer, and he keeps thinking it might be possible to make out what they say. Then, crash! they break up, on pale brown sand, on black rocks, on the pitted remains of an old concrete jetty. The words, whatever they were, dissolve into white foam on the beach.